THE BLADE OF RYL

A CORELLE OF DUR NOVEL

HAYLEY PRICE

A catalogue record for this book is available from the National Library of Australia.

National Library of Australia Cataloguing-in-Publication entry

Author: Hayley Price

Title: **The Blade Of Ryl**

ISBN: 978-0-9756238-9-3 (Print)

ISBN: 978-1-7637998-1-3 (ePub)

ISBN: 978-1-7637998-0-6 (PDF eBook)

❀ Created with Vellum

This book is dedicated to everyone who has ever battled alcohol abuse.
I understand your struggles. As this book was published, I was sixty-eight years old and still haunted by my inability to be the boss in my relationship with alcohol. Solutions exist, and I hope you find yours.

At times this book will change point-of-view. Please note each new scene does not necessarily follow the same timeline as the last.

A note for my American readers. This book is written in UK/Australian English. Many of the words will be spelled differently from what you're used to - realised, colour, centre etc.

In addition, we do not share your fondness for the letter 'Z.' I realise you may find this difficult and offer my humble apologies. We make up for this by using a plethora of "L's where you would make do with one. Marvellous.

All the writing and artwork in this book was created by a real person. No AI was used at any time.

ALSO BY HAYLEY PRICE

The Vermilion Saga

The Vermilion Ribbon

The Vermilion Cross

The Vermilion Triangle

To read the Corelle Of Dur series does not require you to have read The Vermilion Saga, but if you have not, you will not understand some small details of things that have happened prior to this series. None of the material you will not be familiar with is central to the events that take place in the Corelle Of Dur series.

N
NORTHERN OCEAN
MALKARTAS
ZHANGHAR
RYL
DELCAN
YERRSUN
DUR CITY
ORT
DUR
VJORT
STEINLUND
TARGISTVI
TORRIC
ALCMOUTH
EASTPORT
JUUSTEIN
KARNSTEIN
TANASTTRA
TORR SEA
LEBKLST
ARKKYD
YANTOGI
PORT UIRGILE
JAISELNIA
VYRRMOD
CORKANNAE
KUIRBEK
QANTI
QAQRUE
THE TORR SEA REGION

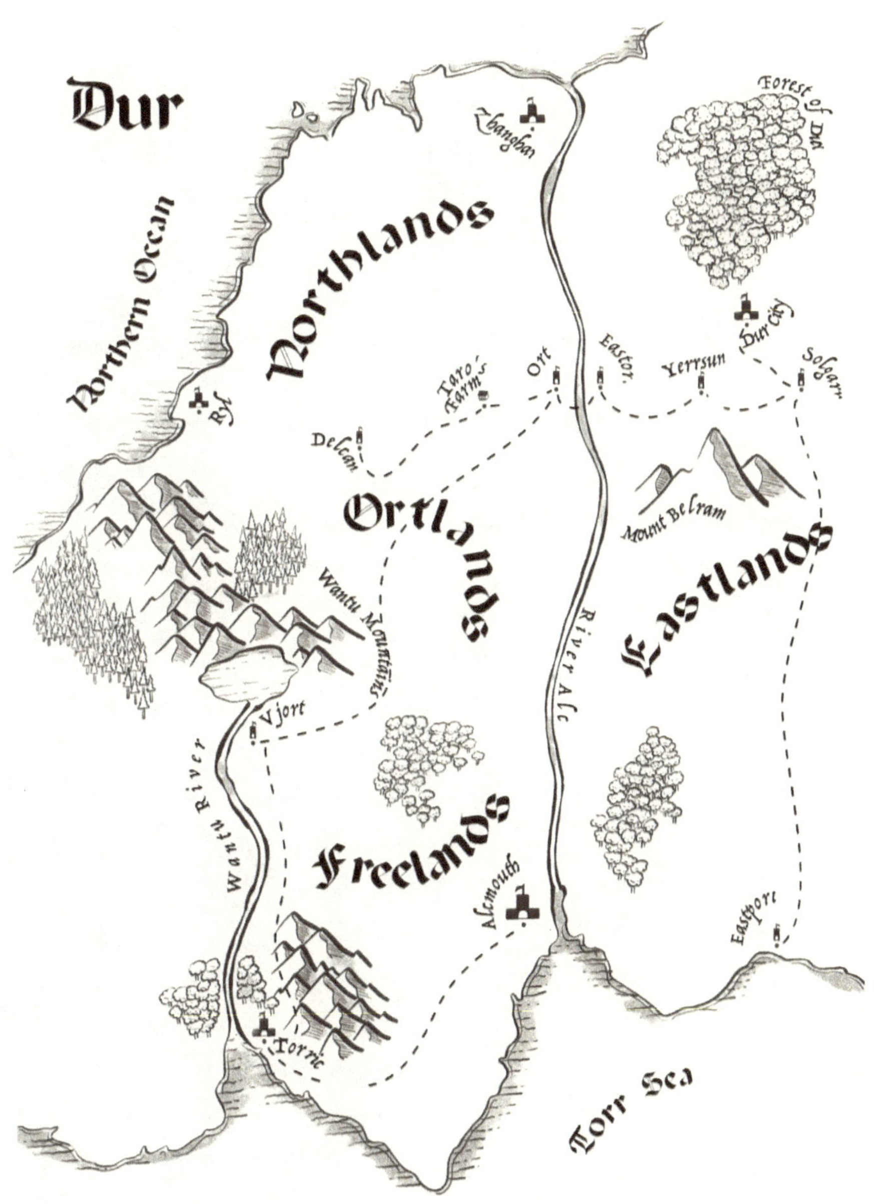

Dur
Northern Ocean
Northlands
Zbangban
Forest of Dur
Durr City
Solgarr
Taro's Farm
Ort
Eastor
Yerrsun
Delean
Ortlands
Mount Belram
Eastlands
Wantu Mountains
River Alc
Vjort
Wantu River
Freelands
Alcmouth
Eastport
Torre
Torr Sea

CHAPTER 1
CORELLE

The sails cracked and billowed in the wind as the two-masted ship ploughed northward up the River Alc. Its wooden hull carved a hole in the water and left it behind for the stern to close and repair, a wide white line left on the river's surface behind itself, as a snail leaves a trail on the ground. Seabirds wheeled and swooped in its wake in search of food drawn to the water's surface by the turbulent passage of the ship.

A solitary figure sat at the bow, its knees drawn up to its chest, its chin on those knees. Dressed in linen trousers and a tunic, the figure wrapped its arms around itself against the chill of an early winter wind that smelled of the rain it preceded. Long brown hair streamed backward in the wind, a darker reflection of the line left in the water by the ship. On the deck, a handful of mariners bustled about their work as the skyline of a town grew ever larger ahead of the vessel beneath the grey clouds of the late morning.

None of the mariners spoke to the lonely figure, a woman, short, with cold, empty green eyes beneath eyebrows that matched the brown of her hair. In truth, some had tried to talk to her on the four-day voyage north from Alcmouth, the capital city of the land of Dur. They found her cheerless, distant, and uncommunicative, content to sit at the bow in isolation and brood on whatever thoughts occupied her mind. Conversation with her proved so difficult and unrewarding, the mariners had abandoned any attempt at it after little more than a day. They had learned her name, Corelle, and precious little else.

Any journey into the abyss of Corelle's mind would be a test few would have the strength to endure, for death ran rampant in that mind. Myriad dead, nameless faces would swirl around them in that desolate, tortured place. Most Durfolk could not count high enough to reckon all the faces that would pass them by. They were legion, but the observant would notice two faces that came and went often, like a favourite melody a person will hum many times each day.

The faces belonged to two attractive women, one with blonde curls around her face, the other with black hair. Accusations and reproach gleamed in the blue eyes of each of them, their deaths brought about by the woman at the bow of the ship. The visitor to the mind of this woman could not begin to grasp the weight of guilt and self-loathing the two dead faces laid upon her. The mariners might think Corelle's exterior rocky, but inside itself, that rock bore scars and gouges that threatened its integrity, its survival.

The blonde woman, Arella, had died at Corelle's hands. They had both belonged to a secretive organisation, the Guild, created to assassinate anybody who stood in the way of its founder, Styrrach. When Styrrach betrayed Corelle to the Portreeve—the magistrate of each of the cities of Dur—Arella had sacrificed her own life to enable Corelle's escape. Styrrach himself had killed the dark-haired woman, Deineike. He had paid for that death with his life, vengeance extracted by Corelle, but his death brought her no joy. Her beloved Deineike had gone to the Pyre, and everything Corelle had ever yearned to be had burned along with Deineike's body. The Pyre left Corelle an empty husk, two feet that walked forward of their own accord until the day they would at last bring Corelle to her own ruin and free her from the twisted, tangled thoughts that rived her mind.

Until that day came, Corelle functioned each day as best she could. She sailed north now at the request of Dur's new Bailiff, Raolos. He had asked her to take letters to the town of Ort. The letters summoned his family south to Alcmouth, where he had been appointed Bailiff after Corelle's endeavours against Styrrach unmasked corruption in the corridors of power of the land. Corelle had agreed to deliver the letters, but she had refused to undertake Raolos's second request.

It would be a rare thing in Dur for a man to accept two women who lay together. Far rarer that a man would ask a woman to take his own wife as her lover, to spirit her away to a land to the south of Dur, yet Raolos had asked Corelle to do so. Pettra, Raolos's wife, had been Corelle's lover after the death of Deineike, although Corelle had tried to resist Pettra's advances. Distraught, grief-stricken, she had lost control of her senses and succumbed to Pettra's insistent demands.

Corelle had refused Raolos's request to take Pettra with her into exile, her punishment for the terrible crimes she had committed both in the Guild and since. She agreed to carry the letters north for Raolos while he occupied himself with the apprehension of any who had been part of Styrrach's organisation. Her mind too full of guilt for the dreadful things she had done, Corelle could not bear to take on the burden of Pettra, who professed to love her and refused to accept it for the infatuation it must surely be.

So it turned on the voyage north. Corelle pondered all the evil she had become since she had joined the Guild and shed tears for the innocents whose blood had been spilled through association with her. Like most Durfolk, she could not count high enough to reckon all the faces, but she could count to two, and Deineike and Arella were the two she counted most often, and the two she wept for without end.

CHAPTER 2
CORELLE

Corelle walked down the ramp and stopped on the dockside. As ever, she felt disorientation and unease as her legs adjusted to a surface that did not roll and pitch beneath her feet, and she gazed around at the now familiar Ort skyline as she waited for the sensation to pass. The heavy pack slung over her shoulder held coin taken from Styrrach's hoard in Alcmouth.

Raolos had funded her voyage north because of the letters she carried for him, and her first and simplest task in Ort would be to hand those letters to Ibie, Raolos's most senior assistant. With that task accomplished, she would need to deal with Pettra, and that matter vexed her. Pettra would doubtless be both delighted and relieved to see Corelle alive, and Corelle thought Raolos's wife would wish to leave Ort with her as soon as she could pack up her vast collection of clothing. Although Raolos had urged Corelle to take his wife with her wherever she went, Corelle had refused to agree to his request.

The dilemma of Pettra had occupied Corelle's thoughts throughout the voyage north. Despite Pettra's attractive, sensual body, Corelle's discomfort with the violent treatment Raolos's wife yearned for during sex further complicated an already complex issue. A life that had become violent beyond the worst imagination of Durfolk should have prepared Corelle for anything, but she could not mete out the violence Pettra craved. The thought of it raised gooseflesh on her arms, and she shivered from more than the chill winter air.

Corelle sighed in resignation. She should not have agreed to deliver the letters, should have slipped away from Alcmouth and headed south. The damage done, she chewed at her lower lip and cursed herself. *"You could have avoided the unpleasantness. Weakness brought you here."* Such thoughts would not accomplish the tasks she had agreed to perform for Raolos, and she would not break her word to the new Bailiff. She headed for Raolos's tally house, at the southern end of the docks.

The tally house's large front doors stood open as workers bustled in and out. It appeared a recent delivery had been unloaded from one of the ships moored at the docks. Resolute, Corelle entered the tally house and headed for the offices in the rear of the building.

A man whom Corelle had seen in the tally house before looked up from the chits piled on his desk and spoke. "Good morning."

"And to you. I seek Ibie, on official business from Raolos."

The man nodded. "He has stepped out, but I expect him to return within the hour. Can I be of any assistance?"

"My thanks, but I have letters from Raolos, and I must deliver them to Ibie in person. I will return within the hour. If he returns before then, please ask him to wait for me here. There is important news, and he must hear it from me before it comes to his ears from others. Tell him my name is Jorinda." Ibie would be less likely to remember her true name, since she had travelled as Jorinda when she met him.

"Jorinda." The man's face lit up with recognition. "I know your name. I will pass your message to Ibie if I see him before you return. Will Raolos return to Ort soon?"

Corelle hesitated. She did not wish for this man to know of the events that had turned in Alcmouth before Ibie, but she did not want to lie. "I do not wish to seem rude, but I would prefer to speak to Ibie first if you do not mind."

The man smiled. "I understand. Ibie oversees the tally house, and he must be first to learn any news. Good day to you."

"And to you." Corelle returned to the fresh air of the docks and sat on the same bench she had once sat on with Deineike as they considered a journey across the River Alc and onward to Dur City, where their friends, Wilash and Klordia, had fled as they tried to escape Styrrach. On that day, Corelle and Deineike had watched the little rowboat battle the waves on its journey from Eastort, and when Deineike had decided she could not face the journey across the river in the little boat, they had ridden off toward Delcan instead of Dur City. They had paused their journey at the farm of Taro, who had died in his sleep under the effects of a potion Corelle had given him. At the farm, guilt had prompted Corelle to return to Ort rather than continue to Delcan. From that point, fate had robbed her of Deineike and resulted in the death of Styrrach and many of his associates. Corelle would cast herself into the river to unwrite those fates if she could. Her head in her hands, she cried her misery for any who passed to hear.

She missed Deineike more than life itself. In search of redemption, she had confessed her crimes to the Duke but had not been sentenced to death as she believed she would. It would be some time yet before she learned whether anything existed afterward, and if it did, whether she would see Deineike and Arella again there.

The hustle and bustle of the busy dock passed her by as though she did not exist, and light rainfall began. The wet season had arrived, but so far this year's rains had not been as heavy as previous years. Visions of Deineike filled Corelle's mind, dark hair that framed her face after they had made love, her powerful, muscular body with the small sensitive breasts, but above all, her laughter, and her smile. Corelle's heart had broken as Deineike had died on the bed before her, a hand against Corelle's cheek as Deineike had left her alone and bereft.

In search of justice for Deineike's murdered mother, Corelle had killed an innocent mariner in Torric by mistake. The death of the man Deineike believed at the time to be the murderer, though it brought her a sense of vengeance she had pursued for most of her life, had not appeased her grief, and so it proved for Corelle. Styrrach's life had been spilled from his body, but it had brought no relief from the agony and grief that consumed Corelle over Deineike's death. Within days of Deineike's Pyre, Corelle had betrayed her memory when she lay with Pettra. Klordia had called Corelle a monster, and she had the right of it. Deineike and her memory had been shamed by Corelle's selfish desires and animal instincts.

Corelle lost track of how long she sat in the rain and brooded over Deineike. The rain intensified and saturated her, so she decided to head back to the tally house in the hope Ibie had returned. He had, and he directed the storage of some crates at the rear of the tally house. Although he looked up as she approached, he did not smile.

She spoke as she approached him. "Ibie."

"You are drenched. Where have you been?"

"I took in the sights." Corelle loosed a small laugh at her own jest.

"I did not believe you would return from Alcmouth. When will Raolos return? What turned with the Duke?"

"I have many things to tell you, and letters you must read. We will need privacy while we speak."

He raised his eyebrows. "Come to my office." He closed the door behind them and gestured to a chair.

Corelle shook her head. "There is much to explain, but I will be brief. We met with the Duke, and I told him my tale. He read all the letters I retrieved from Styrrach's pack." She sighed. "The Duke is a puppet, in essence. A figurehead, nothing more, powerless to act on all I laid before him. Only the Portreeves or the Bailiff may dispense justice, it turns."

Ibie shook his head and clenched his fists. "You travelled there for naught? No justice is served?"

"Not quite." Corelle felt anxious to comfort him before he became enraged. "The Duke can remove the Bailiff from office, it turns, and he did so. Glailam is no longer the Bailiff, and he and his corruption have disappeared."

He nodded and muttered. "That, at the least, is something. Who then is the new Bailiff?"

In answer, she opened her pack and took out the letters from Raolos. He raised his eyebrows again as he saw the Bailiff's seal on the letters. He tore them open and read them. He whispered as he read, "By the Five Cities." Once he had finished, he looked up at her. "You are banished?" She nodded. "You have done wrong, and some of the wrongs you have done can never be forgiven, but you have also done great things. You have saved Raolos's life and brought an end to this evil nest of killers at great risk to yourself. Banishment is a harsh punishment. I am sorry."

"My thanks." Corelle gave a resigned shrug. "Many would think the alternative more severe, although I craved it."

Ibie said nothing about the dark reference to Corelle's death. "There is much to attend to." He had become businesslike again. "I must assist Pettra and Raopul as they prepare to sail to Alcmouth."

For now, she allowed the idea that Pettra would travel south with Ibie to live on. Although Corelle would not take Raolos's wife south with her, it seemed unlikely Pettra would travel to Alcmouth to resume her unhappy life with her husband. That, however, would be a matter for Ibie to deal with. "I have a letter for Pettra, and I am sworn to deliver it to her. After that is done, I will head south on the first ship to anywhere. I will leave the arrangements in your hands. In truth, you will perform those tasks better than me."

He stared at her as sceptical lines creased his brow. "Your dalliance with Pettra is ended?"

She sighed. "You and I both know she is obsessed with me, and I cannot speak for her. I do not intend to take her with me, but only time will tell how that news will be received. I will go to the house now and hope to leave Ort before dark."

"I will wait here for a time." He sounded thoughtful. "I do not wish to become embroiled in that havoc. After the midday, I will go to the house and aid with the arrangements as best I can."

"My thanks. Farewell Ibie. You are a good man. I wish you well in Alcmouth. Raolos needs you, and I know you will be invaluable to him. I urge you not to delay. If any justice is to be served to the remnants of Styrrach's scheme, swift action is needed, before word can come to those whom Raolos seeks."

He nodded. "I will leave tomorrow if it can be arranged. I must take Raopul, at the least. He is young and will have need of his father at such an uncertain time."

Little else remained to say, so Corelle turned to leave. As she reached the outer doors, Ibie called her name, and she turned to gaze at him as he stood in the doorway of his office.

"Good fortune." He nodded at her, then returned to his office.

The steady rain soaked through her cloak as Corelle walked up the hill to Raolos's house. Painful memories of the times she and Deineike had walked the streets of Ort brought tears to Corelle's eyes again. Around the midday, she stood at last at the gates to Raolos's house. It loomed before her, large and grand, as she gazed on it for what might be the last time. She heaved a reluctant sigh and walked up the carriage path to knock on the door. Her cloak had proved inadequate protection from the elements; the rain had soaked her, and she shivered as she waited.

A servant opened the door and recognised Corelle at once. "Good day madam. Come in, and we will bring cloths for you to dry yourself. I will bring you to the parlour once we have attended to your comfort."

"My thanks." The servant bustled off, but two others soon appeared and handed cloths to her. One of the servants scurried away with Corelle's wet cloak. Corelle used the cloths to dry herself as well as she could, and, satisfied she would no longer drip water everywhere and damage Raolos's expensive carpets, she handed the wet cloths back to the servant who remained. The woman took them away, and the servant who had answered the door reappeared, led her into the parlour, and invited her to sit. They must not have told Pettra Corelle had arrived. Had they done so, it seemed certain the older woman would have rushed into the hallway and smothered her with unwanted affection.

Corelle gazed around at the expensive ornaments, art, and furniture in the parlour. Somewhere deeper in the house, she heard a scream, and rapid footsteps grew louder as somebody drew closer. She sighed in discomfort as Pettra ran into the parlour, arms extended. Her fingers clenched and unclenched in a familiar gesture.

Before Corelle could stand, Pettra threw herself onto her lap and wrapped her arms around her. She planted kisses on every part of Corelle's face. "You live. I knew you would. You return for me. How I have missed you."

Efforts to prise Pettra's arms from Corelle's body proved futile. Like vines that tangle a person in their embrace, Pettra seemed to have more arms than Corelle could fight off. She gave up. "I have a letter from Raolos…" Pettra kissed her and stifled her explanation. When Corelle could pull away from the kiss, she tried again. "Raolos is the Bailiff in Alcmouth."

Pettra stiffened and stared at her. "Bailiff? How?" The news distracted her from the overt display of affection for a moment.

Corelle gave a brief explanation of the events in the Ducal High-home. Pettra's eyes grew wider with surprise, and she raised her hand to her mouth when Corelle revealed the Duke had banished her.

"Banished? It cannot be. Raolos must overturn this decision. It is too harsh. You are a hero of Dur. Your name should be… You should be the Bailiff, not that man." Her face flushed, and her fists clenched.

"He is a good man and will be a fine Bailiff. I am content. When I travelled there, I expected—no, I hoped to die. The punishment is less severe than it could have been." Corelle watched anger and resentment grow in Pettra's hazel eyes.

"Where will you go?" Pettra's tone became guarded.

"Wherever the ship I board carries me."

"I see." Pettra's eyes watered, and she tried to blink away her tears, then mumbled, "Hard decisions must be made."

"No decisions need be made." Corelle strove to keep emotion from her voice. "I care not where I end up, so I need choose no destination. You and Raopul must be ready to depart with Ibie tomor—"

Pettra did not allow Corelle to finish the sentence. "I will not go to Alcmouth. I will ready Raopul for the voyage, and I will come with you." Pettra smiled. "A simple decision."

With a sigh of misery, Corelle stared into Pettra's hazel eyes. "Pettra, you cannot come with me. You must go to Raolos."

Pettra's face twisted with scorn. "I will not go to him. He and I are a song that has ended. I will not play his game any longer. He must find another trophy to dangle on his arm at Bailiff's balls, or whatever events he attends."

"Then what will you do?"

"I will come with you. We will have an adventure." Pettra's

hands clapped together in excitement, and Corelle's despondency grew. Little more than a year ago, Corelle and Deineike had ridden south on a journey some might have seen as an adventure. A terrible price had been paid for that trip. "When will we leave?"

"Pettra." Corelle could scarce contain her sadness. "You cannot come with me. Your place is with your husband and son."

"He is not my…" Pettra seemed to check herself before she blurted out words Raopul might hear. "I will not go. I will come with you."

Dismayed, Corelle could only shake her head. Even as Pettra insisted she would travel with her, Corelle wished to avoid that outcome at all costs. "I will not take you. I do not want you to travel with me."

Pettra wiped at her eyes with the back of a hand. "You do not mean those words. You jest."

"That I do not. I will travel alone. I will not take you."

Pettra stared at her, and tears streamed down her face. "I love you." The words whispered from her, miserable.

"That you do not. You are infatuated. You will find another and soon forget me."

Pettra looked up at the ceiling. "Why does everybody seek to tell me what I think and feel? I love you, whether you will believe it or not. I will not let you leave alone. I will follow you. I will dog your footsteps more even than that vile man, Styrrach."

Corelle let out a long, heavy breath. "Go to Raolos. Put right all the wrongs between the two of you, I beg you." Pettra did not reply, but her eyes burned into Corelle's. "I have a letter for you from him. It is in my pack."

Pettra tossed her perfect, coiffed hair. "Cast it into the fire. I will not read it."

"I cannot do that." Raolos had brought both the letters for Ibie and the letter for Pettra to Corelle's room himself, the morning after he had been appointed Bailiff, along with a pouch of coin. He had begged her to deliver the letter to Pettra in person and take his wife with her when she left Dur to begin her banishment. His insistence had worn Corelle down until she relented and agreed to deliver the letter, but she made no promise she would take Pettra with her. "I am sworn to deliver it to you."

"Then fetch the cursed thing." Pettra stood and extended an impatient hand as she spat the words out.

Corelle pulled her pack toward her and took out the letter. The rain had made it wet, but she hoped it would still be legible. Pettra snatched it from her and, without a glance at it, turned and cast it into the flames that crackled in the fireplace. Corelle rolled her eyes and sighed. "You did not read it."

"What did it say?"

"I do not know. It bore Raolos's seal."

"I will pack for the voyage and tell Raopul he must sail to Alcmouth." Pettra tapped a foot on the floor, her lips drawn into a tight grimace.

"Ibie will soon come for you and Raopul. He will travel with you."

"He will travel with Raopul. I will travel with you."

Corelle leaned forward, her elbows on her knees, and her head in her hands. What made this woman so stubborn? "I will not take you." She sighed, and her thoughts flashed back to the time a similar conversation had played out between her and Arella in Ryl. Corelle had been the stubborn one that day, as stubborn as Deineike or Pettra. Arella had put up little resistance, and fates had been written that would prey on Corelle for the rest of her lifetime.

Corelle said nothing more, embroiled in her misery until Pettra broke the silence. "I cannot live without you. I will not live without you."

Corelle shot a glance up at her. "What do you mean by that?"

"If I cannot live with you, I will not live without you. I will throw myself into the Alc."

"Pettra, do not say such things, even in jest."

"It is no jest. I will do it." Pettra folded her arms across her breasts in defiance.

Corelle lowered her head and dug her nails into her scalp. For some time, she had resisted the urge to dig at herself, but she found herself unable to control her fingers in this moment. Pettra pulled at her arms and wrenched one away from Corelle's head.

Pettra softened her voice. "Do not hurt yourself, I beg you. My heart breaks when you do this." After a moment's hesitation, she pulled Corelle's arm forward and moved closer. "Take me with you. I cannot face another day without you. I love you."

"I do not love you. I cannot love you."

"I do not ask it. I only ask you to take me with you. I will go with you, or I will go wherever I travel to afterward."

"That is unfair." Corelle's anger flared at the injustice of Pettra's words.

"That it is." Pettra paused, then continued. "I will make you happy Jorinda. You are owed happiness."

Corelle snorted. "That I am not. And I do not call myself Jorinda any longer."

"You may call yourself what you wish. I will call you Jorinda. I have already told you this."

Corelle could see no solution that would suffice. If she left without Pettra, then the life of yet another woman who had professed love for her might be lost, and another dagger of guilt would drive itself deep into her heart. If she took Pettra, she would betray another vow, for she had decided to leave the older woman behind. No future could be guaranteed for Pettra. Corelle now had coin, but it must be nothing compared to the wealth Pettra would have been used to with Raolos. Danger might still await. Corelle could not be sure none would seek her wherever she went, that a dagger might not slide between her ribs one night. Styrrach's scheme had made many men wealthy, and she had destroyed it and killed their colleagues in the process.

The additional guilt of Pettra's death would be impossible to bear. No doubt Pettra had bluffed, but as she stared it in the face, Corelle lacked the courage to call that bluff. "If I take you, will you promise you will no longer urge me to hurt you?"

Pettra drew in a long breath. "I will try. Will that suffice?"

"Why do you crave this violence? Do you punish yourself for something in your past?"

"I may do. I have done things…" She hesitated. "It excites me. It has always excited me. Even with…" She fell silent.

Pettra had been about to say Raolos's name. He had told Corelle he had succumbed to his wife's urges and had struck her when they had sex. With a resigned shake of her head, Corelle said, "Please do not ask it of me." Pettra had seemed close to another revelation, but Corelle could not delve into any more of the nuances of Pettra.

"I will try. I swear it."

Corelle sighed and wrapped her arms around Pettra, who ran her fingers through Corelle's brown hair. "Run then. Pack light. I wish to leave today."

"You will wait here for me?"

Corelle sighed again. "I will wait."

Pettra pulled away and moved to the door, where she paused. "I will bring the dress I had made with your coin."

"Do you have any trousers?"

"I might have some."

"Please wear them. Ships are no place for fancy dresses." Pettra blew her an exaggerated kiss, skipped out of sight, and left Corelle alone with her misery.

CHAPTER 3
CORELLE

Corelle sat alone in the parlour and shook her head. How low had she fallen? She could not keep any vow, it seemed. Promises were scraps of parch in the wind, blown far away as soon as they fell from her. She had sat at the bow of the ship for four days and told herself over and over she would not take Pettra south with her. Within an hour of her arrival at the house, she had gone back on all she had promised herself. It would be easy to say she had changed her mind, that Pettra's threat to end her own life had persuaded her, that her conscience could never be salved if the woman killed herself, miserable and alone. In truth, she had offered little resistance. When it came to the heart of it, Corelle feared to be alone, and if Pettra kept her word, did not demand to be struck and hurt as they lay together, her irrepressible spirit might provide some respite from Corelle's brokenness.

She hoped they could leave before Ibie arrived, certain his recrimination would be palpable, and she wished to avoid it if possible. "Pack light" for Pettra doubtless involved trunks that would require a cart to move them, and by the time it had been summoned, Ibie would arrive at the house

Half of an hour later, Pettra returned. "I have sent a servant for a carriage. The rain is heavy." She wore dark trousers and a plain white tunic.

Corelle could not repress a surprised smile. "Those clothes are not what I expected from you."

"They are comfortable. I sometimes wear them at home when my moon cycle is upon me, and I feel less than glamorous."

"You look glamorous to me." Corelle's tastes ran to simpler things than Pettra's.

The rose blush of embarrassment coloured Pettra's cheeks. "I am glad. I have limited myself to one trunk. It pains me to leave some of my clothes. I am sure you can be persuaded to make me some finery once we are settled." Her eyes sparkled, her excitement almost childlike.

Corelle laughed, amused by Pettra's continued desire to wear Corelle's making. "Do you have a cloak?"

"That I do. Many. But I will bring only one." Pettra smiled. "This will be fun."

"Have you sailed on a ship before?"

"That I have. I have been to Zhanghar and Alcmouth."

"Does it trouble your stomach?"

"I had not noticed it. Does it trouble yours?"

"That it does not." They would see how Pettra coped with the swell once they left the river and headed across the sea. Corelle could not be sure her own stomach would tolerate it, far out to sea and away from any land. This would be the first time she had sailed other than on the river or close to the coast, and she did not doubt the swell would be greater far away from any shore.

Pettra knelt at Corelle's feet with her chin on her arms, which rested on Corelle's thighs. Her face radiated adoration as she gazed at Corelle, who shook her head. A faint smile on her lips, Pettra whispered, "What is wrong?"

"You are a child, nothing more."

Pettra did not seem offended by the words. "That I am. Raolos told me all the time. I am a happy child who is about to leave on an adventure with the woman she loves." She sighed in contentment.

"Ibie will arrive soon, I think. He will come to arrange transport for the staff and Raopul. How soon will the carriage be here?"

"Not long, my guess. Shall I check?"

"Please." Now Corelle's resolve to leave Pettra behind had evaporated, she did not want to meet Ibie at the house. Pettra scurried off, left Corelle with her thoughts and self-hatred. She had decided to take Pettra with her and had compounded her betrayal of Deineike. She sighed, glanced at the fire, and wondered what Raolos had scribed to Pettra. It had been impetuous of Pettra to burn the letter before she read it. It might have contained some vital information about how he saw the future for them both. Corelle doubted there would be any lengthy future for her and Pettra, although the older woman seemed to hold a different view.

Pettra called from the hallway. "It is here. The carriage, I mean." Corelle picked up her pack and wandered out to join her. A servant held Corelle's cloak, which still dripped water onto the floor. Pettra had wrapped herself in a red woollen cloak. It looked expensive and warm and would be sure to resist the rain better than Corelle's own, some cast-off thing she had collected from some long-forgotten time. A large trunk stood nearby as a servant pulled the door open. Two men stood next to the carriage, and one of them held a door open.

Pettra ran through the rain and clambered into the cabin through the open door. Jorinda pulled her cloak about her and joined Pettra. The men picked up the trunk and took it out of Corelle's sight, then walked past the window again, and the carriage rocked as they climbed into the driver's box. It jolted, lurched forward, and Pettra placed a hand on Corelle's thigh.

"Where do you imagine we will travel?"

"I know not." Corelle forced an exasperated breath between taut lips. "I cannot come back to Dur, on pain of death. When you tire of this adventure and long for powder and ballgowns, I cannot return with you."

"Is that all you think of me, that these trifles interest me?" Pettra seemed put out.

The words had been ill-chosen and hurtful. "That I do not. I apologise. I think you will tire of life in a strange land, away from all we find normal, nothing more. We will not even understand anything people say to us."

"If it suffices for you, it will suffice for me."

"I have no choice. I would not choose this path otherwise."

Pettra sat in silence for a while. "It will suffice for me."

They passed Ibie. He rode his horse toward the house, his head bowed against the rain. They had avoided him, to Corelle's relief. He did not glance at the carriage, and Corelle realised she might never see him again. The thought saddened her, but nothing could be done to change all that had turned.

As they drew closer to the docks, Pettra laid a hand on Corelle's knee. "I have something for you. I collected it from Raolos's desk before we left."

Pettra handed her a thin item wrapped in cloth. When Corelle unwrapped it, she saw the dagger Wilash had dropped during the fight against the Guild in Raolos's office, the twin of her own dagger. "Raolos kept this?"

"He told me he collected it after the horrors of the fight in his office, when you saved him. I do not know what he intended for it, but it is not his. It belongs to you more than him. You are Wilash's friend, and you should have it."

"My thanks." Corelle muttered the reply as she placed the dagger into her pack. Whether she would ever see Wilash to return it to him, she could not guess, and he might not wish it returned. He had used it to kill a Guild member in Raolos's office, and it had sickened him. The dagger might bring him unhappy memories best left buried deep in his mind.

The carriage stopped once they had reached the docks. Corelle moved to open the door, but one of the men had climbed down and pulled it open. "Please." He smiled, and she climbed out to scan the ships at the dockside. Two of the three-masted ships the southerners preferred sat at the dock, and Corelle would need to board each ship and ask where they would sail once they left Ort.

"Wait here while I determine where these ships sail. I will return for you." Pettra nodded her agreement, and Corelle walked to the ramp of the first ship. She asked a mariner for the master, but the man did not seem to understand the language of Dur. She guessed the master would be on the aft deck, near the wheel, so she skipped up the stairs. A man in a long coat stood by the wheel. "Are you the master?"

"Not I. I bring." The man's dark skin and remarkable, chiselled features marked him as a southerner. He spoke the Dur language, however, and Corelle wondered how easy it would be to learn a new language wherever she ended up.

"You seek me?" A man's voice came from behind her, and when she turned, she saw a tall, dark man in an officer's coat. He wore a flat cap with some sigil on it, three vertical stripes. She guessed the sigil indicated the master of a ship.

"I seek passage south. Where are you bound?"

"We leave for Vyrrmod on the next tide."

Corelle had never heard of Vyrrmod and did not know whether it might be a city or a land, but she did not wish the master to know that. "That is ideal. I seek one cabin for two passengers if you have one suitable."

He paused. "We do not carry passengers south unless they are part of the business of those who own the ship."

Corelle turned to gaze out into the river. Should she push for passage, or try the other ship? After a few moments, she spoke again. "What business brought you to Ort?"

"Trade." He did not elaborate.

"With Raolos, or Ibie?"

He tilted his head at her words. "You know Raolos?"

"I work for him." That had not been true, but she felt it might not hurt if she stretched the truth. "He has now become the Bailiff of Dur."

He nodded. "I had not heard this. Respect is due."

His words rang a bell. The merchant who carried the message to Styrrach had used it, part of the strange customs and speech of his land. She searched for his name in her memory. "Do you know Rakulaj?"

"He is an important merchant in our land, and the owner of this vessel. You know this name?"

"We have exchanged names."

He nodded and pursed his lips. "Respect is due. Will you honour me with your name?"

"My name is Corelle." She could not recall the exact format of the exchange of names when she had met Rakulaj.

"Corelle of Dur?" He sounded surprised.

"That I am."

"Then you are an honoured guest aboard my ship at any time, for respect is due. You are known to us all. You brought about a change in our trade with Dur. It now works with greater fairness, and this change has removed the pall of fear that lay over the arrangement with Raolos's predecessor. Contar, my name." He favoured her with a slight bow.

Corelle felt the warmth rise to her cheeks. "I played only a small part in it." Ibie had worked hard to bring about the changed trade conditions, she reasoned, while she had done little more than kill Styrrach.

"Rakulaj tells a different story." He laughed. "Do you need assistance with luggage? I will send my crew to your aid if you do."

"That we do. We have one trunk. My thanks."

He called out to two mariners who worked nearby and spoke to them in their own language, and they nodded and replied with words she could not understand. He turned to her again. "We will prepare a cabin for you and your companion."

She pulled a pouch from her trouser pocket. "Please let me know the cost and I will settle with you now."

"For Corelle of Dur, there is no charge. You will be our guest, and it will be our honour to have you aboard. Respect is due."

"I cannot ask this of you." It horrified her to think she might not pay for the voyage.

"But you do not ask it. It is given with joy, for respect is due." He smiled.

"My thanks. Respect is due." He laughed and nodded.

Grateful, she turned and led the two mariners to the carriage. As they walked back to the ship, Corelle gave Pettra an explanation of the conversation with the master. The two mariners carried the trunk between them. It looked heavy, and Corelle shook her head. "I said 'light.'" She pointed to the trunk.

Pettra turned to look at the mariners as they struggled with the trunk. "I have left ten times as many clothes behind. Do you wish me to wander this strange land naked?"

Corelle laughed. "You would be popular, at the least."

Pettra smiled at her and laid a hand on her arm. "That I would."

CHAPTER 4
KRAGE

Krage stared at the man before him in disbelief, certain he had misheard. "Styrrach is dead? You are sure of this?"

"That I am. He has been slain by Corelle, as has his Senior Aide. I fled as soon as I heard. Alcmouth is no longer safe for any from the Guild."

"Porl is dead also?"

The man's forehead wrinkled. "I do not know this name. The man Corelle killed, Gill, had been appointed after Styrrach killed Balgow and—"

Krage held up a hand to stop the man and turned away. He did not wish the man to see his reaction to the news. In truth, he felt many emotions, not the least of them confusion. Why had Styrrach killed Balgow, the former Guildmeister of Alcmouth? Why had he then named this Gill as Senior Aide rather than Porl, who had served him in Zhanghar for many years? Most of all, he felt anger that Corelle continued to be a thorn in their thumbs, not least because Styrrach had promised she would be dead, shrouded and removed from the scene in Zhanghar, leaving Krage free…

These thoughts could not change what had turned. The jade had fled long ago and killed Arella as she did so. Despite Styrrach's best endeavours, she had evaded capture and wreaked havoc on their operations at every turn. Krage's anger at Styrrach, who had not succeeded in his attempts to kill her, also ate at him. He had another reason to be fearful, for with Styrrach dead, she might come for him, more so if she had learned about the attempt to shroud her. Even worse, the Guild would doubtless crumble without Styrrach. Glailam would lose his nerve. Styrrach had described the Bailiff as spineless, and Krage felt sure the man would flee before he could be hanged. Whoever the Duke appointed to replace him would not be beneficial to them unless one of the friendly Portreeves could be manoeuvred into the role. It seemed more likely Raolos would find some way to cast the death of Styrrach in his favour and worm his way into the Bailiff's role. That would be catastrophic, since he and Corelle worked together, hand in glove.

Disastrous. There could be no other way to see this news. How had Styrrach been so careless he had allowed her to get close enough to kill him? Krage had left Ryl to take temporary control of Zhanghar with great reluctance, and he had intended to persuade Styrrach to allow him to run both Guilds from Ryl, his home town, rather than Zhanghar. The issue had become moot, thanks to Corelle.

He composed himself and turned to the Alcmouth member before him. "My thanks for this ill news, which is not the fault of its bearer. What will you do now?"

"I thought I might serve you here. Doubtless it will take some time to re-establish operations in Alcmouth, but I am certain you will come up with some plan."

Krage smiled at the man. "Of course. You are welcome here." *"Stay here and die if you wish,"* he thought. *"I will not."*

The man returned the smile and left the small office. Krage had no desire to remain in Zhanghar now, nor Ryl. He would send letters to Priu in Ryl and Sisnop in Torric, the other two cities where the Guild might still be operational. Priu had been left in temporary charge in Ryl when Styrrach had called Krage to Zhanghar. They would meet up at Estway. It made perfect sense. The Guild had owned the farm in the Eastlands for years, a safe haven for the leaders if something ever turned awry. Krage could not imagine Styrrach ever anticipated events might turn as awry as they now had. They would meet up at Estway nonetheless and plan their next move. He imagined they would flee Dur, which would become unsafe for them if Raolos did become the next Bailiff.

Once he had scribed the letters, he summoned Mauvlin, the man who had acted as Senior Aide since Krage had arrived. He told Mauvlin to return to him with the three best men in the Guild as soon as the letters were in the hands of trusted couriers. Four bodyguards should be enough, Krage thought—five horses that could each bear a portion of the coin he would take with him. He could not now access his own coin in Ryl, but he knew where Styrrach hid some of his chests, and the Guildmeister would have far more than Krage, after all else. It would be a sum sufficient to ensure he could live a life of luxury far to the south, if that was the fate written for him.

"Curse you, Corelle," he thought. "*And curse you Styrrach, for you allowed her to get the better of you. Curse you both.*"

CHAPTER 5
CORELLE

The voyage south to Vyrrmod proved the longest journey Corelle had ever taken. The two women watched from the deck as Alcmouth slipped by, but the ship did not put in for provisions. They had been accommodated in a small but comfortable cabin at the rear of the ship. It had two bunks and a small table with two chairs. Mariners brought fresh water into the cabin each day, along with a bowl of fruit. The master urged them to eat plenty of fruit as they travelled south and said they risked illness if they did not eat enough fruit over an extended period. Although their voyage would take only two sevendays, he told them eating fruit aboard any ship made good sense, and they complied every day.

They ate with the master and his two officers three times between Ort and Alcmouth. The officers spoke the language of Dur a little, but none had the proficiency of the master, who spoke almost flawless Dur. The men amused and fascinated Corelle and Pettra with many tales of a life spent at sea. When the officers pressed them for tales of their lives, Corelle became cautious. She feared to reveal all the details of her life lest she be cast into the water, but Pettra regaled them with tales of the high life she had lived. The men soon ate from her hand as they became captivated by her charm and the mystique of all the important people she professed to know in Dur.

They also ate in the common room at times, and the mariners were respectful and as friendly as possible, given the language difficulties. They attempted to learn the language of Vyrrmod as they spoke to the crew. Pettra proved more skilled than Corelle and grasped the unusual words with greater ease. Within a few days, she elicited laughter from the crew she spoke to. Corelle could not discern if they laughed at her jests or her mangled attempts at their language, but they appeared to understand Pettra far better than they did Corelle.

Pettra demanded satisfaction from Corelle every night and often through the day as well, but true to her word, she did not ask for the violence she had sought in Ort. Lovemaking with her fulfilled Corelle, and more so now the older woman did not beg to be hurt whenever they lay together.

Corelle's nightmares had not been left in Dur, and Pettra consoled and comforted her whenever she sprang awake, fearful and soaked in sweat. Styrrach, Taro, Deineike, and Arella appeared in a constant series of ever more horrific dreams that left her drained.

Sure enough, as they travelled further south and lost all sight of land, the seas turned heavier, and the ship rose and fell with the immense waves as it ploughed through the tumultuous water. To Corelle's relief, her stomach coped well with the heavier swells. Pettra felt nauseous at times but fetched up only once, as rain lashed the ship, and the wind howled around them in a violent storm. The hideous weather meant they could not go onto the deck, and Pettra lay mournful in her bunk until her stomach could cope no more. She fetched up on the floor of their cabin, and Corelle went in search of a pail and some water to wipe up the mess. The weather tossed the ship about and dashed Corelle to the floor several times. It crossed her mind they might die; the ship might fall apart under such a fearful onslaught, but by the next morning the storm had passed, and the ship remained intact.

Contar visited them in their cabin to check they had survived the storm without mishap. When he heard Pettra had been unwell, he said the storm had been one of the heaviest he had encountered in many years at sea.

They dined with the master and the officers again on the last night of their voyage. They continued their attempts to learn more of the language of Vyrrmod, and Contar told them they should arrive in port around the midday the next day. They would arrive in a city called Arkkyd, the most important trade city in the land. Although he had been circumspect to this point, Contar asked them why they travelled to Vyrrmod.

Pettra lacked Corelle's caution. "We have run away together." Pettra laughed, and Contar needed to translate the concept to the other two officers. None of them appeared shocked, but it concerned Corelle that Pettra had blurted out such a controversial reason for their voyage. She considered a correction to the story but feared too much protest might worsen her embarrassment.

Contar, his explanations done, turned again to Pettra. "Why do you need to run away?"

Pettra again showed a distinct lack of discretion. "Dur is unfriendly toward women whose friendships cross certain societal bounds." Corelle squirmed in discomfort and wished the older woman would be less honest.

"That is strange. In Vyrrmod, we do not care about such things, unless respect is not due. You will encounter no problems here, Corelle of Dur."

Grateful for his assurance, Corelle smiled at him. "My thanks." Pettra laid a hand on hers. Corelle shook it off as she raised a fork to her mouth and hoped the awkward gesture had not been noticed.

Contar continued the conversation. "Where will you live?"

Corelle preferred to reveal as little as possible. "We may settle in Arkkyd, if it appeals, and if we can afford to buy a small property."

Contar's sad sigh matched his regretful expression. "Alas, while we encourage visitors from other shores, our laws do not permit those who are not citizens of Vyrrmod to own property. You can find many pleasant houses you may rent, of course."

The news disquieted Corelle. It would add a constant expense that might prove a heavy drain on her coin. They would try Vyrrmod on for size, but it might be preferable to sail to a different land where she could purchase a house and have more certainty of her future. She doubted Pettra would remain with her once the blush wore off the romance and their escapade. If Pettra did return to Dur, Corelle could not return with her, so ownership of her own house would be a more efficient use of her coin.

The next day, the ship docked in Arkkyd in warm sunshine beneath a cloudless sky. Alcmouth did not match Arkkyd's size, and the city spread before them away from the docks and rose up several hills in the distance. Many of the buildings were made from a pale brick, topped by bright red roofs. All the dock workers who scurried about below them had dark skin, and the Vyrrmod language carried up to them as they stood on the deck and gazed out over the city. Contar had given them some directions and instructions on how they might find a home to rent and had scribed some information on a piece of parch to make the process easier for them. He also arranged for two of his crew to carry Pettra's trunk off the ship and help them find a carriage to take them to the location he had told them about. He came to wish them good fortune as the ship tied up, and the dock workers below prepared to push the ramp up to the deck.

Pettra took his hand in her fingers. "Our thanks for your hospitality, and your help. Respect is due."

He laughed. "You will fare well in Vyrrmod, I think. Our land is honoured to have Corelle of Dur and her delightful wife visit us."

The reference to Pettra as her wife took Corelle by surprise, but she could find no appropriate words to say. Pettra gave a coy smile, blushed, and looked pleased at the appellation. At length, Corelle blurted out the only reply she could think of. "Respect is due."

"Respect is due." Contar nodded and left them to disembark.

They followed two mariners who carried Pettra's trunk down the ramp between them. The men lowered it to the dock as soon as they had moved clear of the activity around the ramp. One of them wandered away and returned a short while later. Corelle thought he told them he had found them a carriage that would arrive soon.

Pettra bowed to the man, who returned the bow, then whispered to Corelle. "He says a cart is on the way."

"You have adapted to your new home already, I see." Corelle laughed, but she also exchanged bows with the mariner. When a cart appeared and came to a halt before them, the mariners loaded the trunk aboard and helped them up into the seats. The men spoke to the driver, but Corelle could not understand any of the conversation. The cart moved off, and they gazed around in wonder at the unfamiliar sights.

As the cart rattled along streets filled with houses and shops, Pettra spoke in a soft voice, no doubt to avoid the driver overhearing. "Did you understand what the mariners said to the driver?"

"That I did not."

"I only understood part of it. I think they told him we are honoured guests. They said something about a home and gave him the address Contar scribed for us."

"We could become the Duke here." Corelle laughed at her own jest. "They seem fond of us."

"We would not be the Duke. That is for men. We would be the Duchesses."

"Are you certain?" Corelle had always thought "Duke" had been a job title, such as Portreeve or Bailiff. She would not have guessed it could be different for men and women.

"You did not know this?" It seemed Corelle had swapped one knowledgeable tease for another—Deineike had often teased her about the words she had not known. It would be worse with Pettra, she realised with horror, who would be more accustomed to the nuances of high society than Deineike had been. Life might become even more miserable.

"That I did not. I do not wish to be a Duchesses in any event."

"Duchess. One Duchess, two Duchesses."

Corelle shook her head in defeat. How could she learn the language of Vyrrmod when she struggled with her own language?

The cart lurched to a halt and the driver spoke to them, although Corelle did not understand his words. He pointed at a nearby building, and Pettra translated his words. "This is where we can rent a house."

"I see. How will we pay him? We have only Dur coin."

Pettra leaned close and whispered. "Give me a regal." She placed the coin on the seat next to the driver and said something to him in his own language. He laughed and picked up the regal. To Corelle's surprise, he bit it, then laughed again and leaped from the cart. What he did with the regal, Corelle did not see, but he pulled their trunk from the cart and helped them down.

Between them, Corelle and Pettra dragged the trunk to the door of the building as the cart drove off. Curiosity got the better of Corelle. "What did you say to him?"

"I think I said we only have Dur coin. Who knows?" Pettra laughed, a hand to her mouth as though embarrassed to laugh out loud in public.

"This is more difficult than I expected."

"It will be fun. Now, go and find us a home while I stay here with the trunk."

Corelle muttered as she entered the building with Pettra's laughter in her ears. "Nobody could steal it unless they had the strength of ten men." A woman looked up from behind a desk and flashed her a smile. Corelle had forgotten the parch Cantor had scribed, and she spun on her heels and returned to Pettra, who held it out toward her with a wicked grin on her face.

Once the woman had read the parch, she spoke to Corelle, but Corelle did not understand. "I do not speak your language well."

"I talk little Dur. You like to house?"

"That we do. We need a house."

"Have nice home of near. You see?"

"I am sorry, I do not quite understand." Corelle's misery grew as the conversation blundered along. It both embarrassed and shamed her that she could speak so little of the Vyrrmod language while the woman spoke passable Dur.

"Nice house near. You and I see?" The woman's smile did not fade as she tried again. Her jet black hair formed a large ball around her head. Made up of enormous numbers of curls, its appearance fascinated Corelle.

Corelle thought she had understood at last. "My thanks. We would like to see the house. Please."

The woman shouted something, and a man appeared from the rear of the building. The woman stood and took a small packet from a drawer in her desk, and the man took her seat as she turned to Corelle. "Please to follow."

"We have a trunk. Can we leave it here?"

The woman's face told Corelle she had not understood, so Corelle went out and pointed at the trunk.

The woman gave a nod of comprehension. "Is leave in here."

Pettra said something to the woman in Vyrrmod, and the woman replied. Pettra whispered, "Help me, Jorinda," and they pulled the trunk into the building. They smiled at the man before they returned to the woman. "I asked her if we could leave it here. In truth, I think I asked her if we could sell it to her, but we managed between the three of us." She smiled at Corelle, and the woman set off at a brisk pace.

She led them to a three-storey house on the side of a small hill. It had a circular staircase that swept around the entrance lobby, which extended the full height of the house. A door on either side of each of the landings led to the rooms. A parlour and a scullery made up the biggest part of the ground floor, with another small room that might serve as a making room. On the first landing, they found two bedrooms and a privy, and the top floor had a large bedroom with views across the rooftops to the harbour, a privy, and a smaller room Pettra thought she could use to store her clothes.

They did not need such a large house, and Corelle would have preferred to find something smaller and less expensive. The view over the harbour enticed them both, however, and the house entranced Pettra. In view of the language difficulties, it seemed easiest to agree to take the house, and they returned to the office to sign some parch and pay some rent. After some discussion, they decided to revisit the docks and change some of their Dur coin into Vyrrmod coin and return to pay the rent.

Corelle paid four passes' rent in advance, loath to have to return to the office again until her grasp of the Vyrrmod language improved. The woman arranged another cart to carry the trunk to the house, and they moved in. The house already had furniture, but Pettra began to plan new soft furnishings and bed covers the moment she closed the front door. They had a home for now, and only time would tell how long they stayed in it together.

CHAPTER 6
CORELLE

Corelle used some of her making pins to hang Deineike's sketches in the small room on the ground floor and moved the small table under the window to get more light for her making. As she finished, Pettra entered the room, dressed in a magnificent red silk gown with a low, fitted bodice, above which her breasts protruded in a provocative way. The tight skirt flared from her narrow waist across her hips, and the dress had a split from ankle to mid-thigh on one side. She had brushed her hair and applied some colour to her lips and eyelids. She looked spectacular, and Corelle felt the familiar tingle of lust.

Pettra's husky voice betrayed her own arousal. "This is the dress I had made with your coin. The one I wanted you to make for me for the ball."

"I had the right of it. It is far too racy for such an event. It is remarkable, nonetheless."

Pettra licked her lips and ran her hands from her waist up to her breasts. "It excites you?" She rubbed at one of her breasts, and a nipple hardened to press against the taut material.

Corelle's breaths quickened. "That it does."

"Do I excite you?" Pettra continued to caress her breasts.

Corelle pulled her close and kissed her, their tongues entwined in a passionate dance. Pettra moaned and thrust a hand between Corelle's legs as she pressed her other hand on the back of Corelle's head. Clumsy from their kiss, they knelt on the floor and Corelle pulled the skirt of Pettra's dress up her thighs. Her finger excited Pettra until she cried aloud and shook with the fulfilment that crashed in waves through her body. Pettra tore at the waist of Corelle's trousers and pushed them down over her hips. As Corelle kicked them from her, Pettra moved lower and teased her with her tongue until Corelle could hold back her passion no longer.

They pleasured one another on the floor of the making room for close to an hour before they lay sated in each other's arms. "It seems I do." Pettra kissed Corelle on the side of her head as she whispered the words.

"You do what?" Corelle felt almost too sleepy to reply.

"Excite you."

Corelle stroked her hair. "That you do. I curse myself for it, but you can arouse me in heartbeats."

"Jorinda." Pettra heaved a remorseful sigh. "Do not despise yourself for your desires. I doubt Deineike would wish you to die a lonely, frustrated old woman."

Corelle pondered the idea. She could not say what she thought Deineike would make of the situation that had developed with Pettra. She would wish for Corelle to be happy, but the betrayal had been so soon and so complete, Corelle's guilt threatened to overwhelm her. On top of her guilt, Corelle did not feel happy with the relationship even though Pettra excited her with such ease. Pettra was far more years than her, and although she had so far resisted any urge to press Corelle to strike her as they lay together, Corelle could not shake the menace of that violence from her mind.

Corelle rolled away from Pettra, determined to avoid the awkward conversation, uncomfortable that they discussed

Deineike so soon after they had made love. "If we are to stay in such a large house, we will need coin. I can take some making work to help. It should be safe enough in this land, in truth. I imagine you have no skills that might bring some coin into the house?"

"I could sell myself, if any would pay." Pettra's cheeks coloured, and she gave an embarrassed laugh, as if the jest had been somehow mischievous.

"They would pay." Corelle recalled she had made a similar jest to Deineike once before, in Vjort. She shook the thought from her head. Pettra had not intended to wound her with the comment, and Corelle should not judge the older woman by her own failures and self-hatred.

"I brought coin." Pettra seemed to take Corelle's reluctance to pursue the jest as concern over the issue of the coin. "Raolos has adequate, and I felt he owed me a share. He never kept much in the house, but he had a small amount hidden. He thought nobody knew its location. He thought wrong." She laughed, a childlike laugh as though she had taken a pastry from the scullery without her mother's knowledge.

"We will survive. We have plenty of coin for now." Corelle gave Pettra a smile of reassurance. "If things turn dire, we can always sell some of your clothes. I am certain you have sufficient to clothe most of the women of this land."

"You are a tease. But I love you, nonetheless."

"The dress is spectacular." Corelle rose and went up the staircase to light a fire in the privy, despite the warmth of the day. She desired a bath after such a long voyage. A pump in the privy filled the tub, even three storeys from the ground, and it relieved Corelle she would not need to carry pails of water up so many stairs.

Once she had lit the fire and hung a pail of water over it to heat, she wandered into the large bedroom and placed the few clothes from her pack into the drawer of a cabinet against one wall. She smiled as she gazed at Pettra's trunk, which stood near the bed, the lid open. Pettra had packed it to the brim with clothes. Doubtless the dress had been at the top of the pile, since the other clothes did not appear to have been disturbed. The trousers and white tunic lay discarded on the bed.

Pettra came up the stairs, and Corelle called out that she heated water for a bath. Pettra said she would follow Corelle and bathe also, and Corelle poured the first pail of water into the tub, then filled another. When she returned to the bedroom, Pettra had pulled clothes from the trunk and arranged them on the bed.

"Where will you store all these clothes?"

"I am not sure." Pettra did not look around, her attention focused on some organisation of the clothes by a system Corelle could not discern.

"Why do you need so many clothes?"

Pettra turned and flashed a quick smile at her. "Why does the sky need so many lights at night?" She returned to the trunk and the clothes.

At first, Corelle dismissed Pettra's question, but she reflected on it. Why did the sky need so many lights at night? She imagined they were a form of lantern or some such, but who lit them? "Why *are* there so many lights in the night sky, and what are they?"

Pettra froze, an elaborate dress in her hands. After a time, she replied. "I do not know."

The mystery lay beyond Corelle's capacity to resolve. She heated more water until she felt she had enough in the tub, placed another pail on the fire, cast her clothes from her, and slid into the tub. She realised she had no soap, so she yelled to Pettra. "Do you have soap?"

Pettra appeared in the doorway. "Do I have soap? What a ridiculous question. Of course I have soap." She laughed, produced a large bar of soap from behind her back, and dropped it into the water with a small splash. She still had the dress on, and Corelle looked away as her sex tingled again. Pettra kissed the top of her head and returned to her trunk.

The soap had a rich perfume, unlike any Corelle had ever used before. She shook her head and washed herself as fast as she could. She did not wish too much heat to disappear from the water before Pettra used the tub. She stood, but there were no cloths to hand to dry herself with, and she shouted again. "Pettra, are there any drying cloths around?"

Words that sounded like, "You are hopeless," came from the bedroom. A few moments later, Pettra came in with the white tunic Corelle had been wearing. "I could find none. We will need to purchase a few necessities. We ought to have thought this through with more care." Her innocent smile suggested their lack of planning did not concern her.

"You drove practical thoughts from me when you decided to wear that dress." Corelle dried herself with the tunic. "Let me top up the hot water, then you can bathe while I search the house further."

While Pettra bathed the voyage from her body, Corelle investigated the rooms on the floor below. She found no cloths and returned to the privy. "I can find no cloths. Do you wish to use my tunic, or shall I run out and try to obtain something more suited to a Duchess?"

Pettra splashed some water at her. "Bring me a tunic. I will be as common as you for a day." Her laughter tinkled in harmony with the water that dripped from Corelle's hair onto the stone tiles of the privy.

They dressed in clean clothes, and Pettra gathered up the ones they had discarded to wash them in the water from the tub. She carried them downstairs to find somewhere to dry them while Corelle wondered how she would empty the water away. She saw only one way to remove it; to scoop it out with a pail and pour it into the basin beneath the pump. The laborious task irritated her, and to her further frustration she noticed a rubber stopper on the bottom once she had almost emptied it all, which she had not noticed when she filled the tub. When she pulled the stopper out, the rest of the water drained by itself. Why had she not checked for such a thing before she had used the pails? She cursed her foolishness and went down the stairs.

Pettra had opened a door at the rear of the house that gave onto a small courtyard. She had arranged their clothes on a line strung across the courtyard. "We should find a market or a shop and buy some provisions, I think." Pettra wore a simple blue cotton dress with large white spots for a pattern. It flared down from her hips but fitted snug across her bust. It seemed all Pettra's clothes were designed to accentuate some part of her figure.

They found a shop nearby that sold basic food and household items. They learned of a market between the house and the docks, although there would be few stalls, if any, this late in the day. They resolved to visit the market the next day and provision the house. Pettra cooked a simple meal from the items they had bought from the shop. They sat on the couch together afterward, and Pettra folded herself into Corelle's arms. Pettra wished to find a means to hang her dresses, and they agreed to seek out a craftsman who could assist with a piece of furniture or some arrangement in the room off the bedroom.

"I am happy here already." Pettra gave a sigh of contentment.

"It has only been a day."

Pettra kissed Corelle's hand. "I know this. I never felt this happy with Raolos, not through all the years I spent with him. I do not ask you to say the same. I know you loved Deineike very much and would prefer to hold her in your arms at this moment. I am happy, nonetheless."

Corelle kissed her head. "My thanks."

The next day, they arranged for a rail to be constructed in the small room off the bedroom, and Pettra found some device that would hang her dresses from the rail. She bought a large stock of the devices and badgered Corelle to make her more dresses. Corelle approached some of the local garment shops and showed them some of her making. Although she obtained the promise of some work when the garment shops became overwhelmed, she could find no steady work. She did not want to start her own making business, uncertain she would settle in Vyrrmod.

On their third day in Arkkyd, Pettra produced a key for her house in Ort and asked Corelle to secure it somewhere. Corelle sewed it into the seam of her pack, as Styrrach had done with the key to his trunk, but she felt her stitches were more discreet and would be difficult for any but a trained eye to spot.

Corelle scribed a letter to Raolos and sent their address as a courtesy lest he worried about Pettra's welfare. In the letter, she painted an idyllic picture of the house and told him Pettra appeared happy.

Before their first pass in the house had elapsed, Pettra cried out for Corelle to hurt her while they made love one night. She apologised at once and claimed it had been a mistake made in the heat of her passion. Corelle accepted the apology and the explanation, but a few days later, Pettra again asked Corelle to hurt her, and this time she did not apologise.

They discussed the urges, and it soon became apparent to Corelle that, although Pettra had suppressed her desires, she still longed for violence as much as ever. She seemed to wish it more since she had been starved of it for such a long time. As another pass turned, the demands became so insistent, physical contact between them all but vanished.

To Corelle's joy and surprise, a letter arrived from Wilash. Raolos had contacted him and asked him to travel to Alcmouth with Klordia, where the new Bailiff had offered them both positions in his employment. Wilash had taken charge of the Magisterial section of the Bailiff's Offices, and Klordia had been made the

Senior Tally Master. Wilash pointed out no woman had ever been appointed to so prestigious a position, and all Dur talked about it. Klordia performed so well, none could question the decision, however, and they both seemed happy in their new roles.

It pleased Corelle to learn of their happiness, but she did not share their bliss. Her relationship with Pettra had deteriorated at a rate that surprised her. They did not often lie together, and if they did, Pettra begged her to do things to her that horrified Corelle. They remained amicable outside the bedroom, but they shared little physical contact.

The weather defied Corelle's comprehension. Most days were either warm or hot, and there had been no sign of any change to the season after more than two passes. Some days grew so hot, she did not dare to venture outside the door. Her pale skin burned in moments if she did so, and she found it difficult to adapt to such warmth and long hours of bright sunlight. Pettra scoffed at her, spent hours out of the house, and her skin turned deep brown. She did not become as dark-skinned as the people of Vyrrmod, but she had lost the pallid colour of Durfolk.

Corelle's grasp of the language had improved, but Pettra's exceeded hers by some margin. Pettra could converse with almost any of the local people with little difficulty. One day she returned from a trip to the market with a large cask of red wine she said originated somewhere deep inland of Arkkyd. The wine had a pleasant taste, and Corelle enjoyed a goblet of it in the courtyard as Pettra fussed over some food in the scullery.

When Corelle went into the house, she could not find Pettra downstairs, so she went upstairs. Heavy breaths came from one of the bedrooms on the first floor, and when she pushed the door open, Pettra pleasured herself on the bed. Pettra turned her head toward Corelle but did not stop. Corelle closed the door and went downstairs, where she poured another goblet of the wine and sat in a chair in the parlour.

Things had taken a sorry turn. The small joy Corelle had once found in her time with Pettra had vanished in the blink of an eye, it seemed, and their physical life had become all but non-existent. The wine slid down her throat until Pettra came down the stairs, her cheeks flushed, her hair dishevelled. She spoke to Corelle as she entered the room. "Are you hungry?"

"Not as hungry as you, I see this." Corelle could not resist the barb.

Pettra stood next to the chair, her hands on her hips. "What do you mean by that?"

"You know what I mean. I saw you sate your hunger."

Pettra glowered at her. "You will not touch me. How else am I to satisfy my desires?"

"I will not lie with you for reasons you are aware of. If you can satisfy yourself, then I see no issue with the situation. You are content, and I am not pestered to hurt you."

"Jorinda, you know I love you. I would prefer to lie with you than to touch myself. You must know this." Pettra sighed and sniffed as tears pooled in her eyes.

"You are an attractive and desirable woman, and you excite me. These things you ask me to do, I find unattractive; repulsive even."

"I repulse you?"

Corelle resented the way Pettra chose to interpret what she had said. "Do not twist my words. You do not repulse me. This violence you crave repulses me." Corelle had emptied her goblet, so she rose, refilled it, and sank into the chair, light-headed from the wine.

"You would rather drink that wine than pleasure me, it seems." Pettra's voice dripped with sarcasm.

Corelle could not keep the anger from her voice. "The wine does not beg me to hurt it."

"I cannot change my nature. I tried. I believe you know this, but I crave this pleasure and grow frustrated that you refuse to indulge me, though it costs you naught to do so."

"You know nothing of what it costs me." Corelle glared at Pettra.

"You have wrought unimaginable violence. I ask for so little, yet you refuse. How is it you can do the things you do to others, but will not please me? I love you, at the least."

"What is scribed, must be. You are free to return to Raolos if you find me unacceptable company."

Pettra stared at her for a moment as fury turned her face a bright red, then pulled her hand back and slapped Corelle's face. "How dare you speak to me so? I gave up my life to be with you. Do you find it so simple to discard me and order me back to a husband whom I do not love, whose illegitimate son, to my humiliation, I have raised as my own all these lonely, dark years? Are you a monster?"

Corelle raised a hand to her cheek and felt the warmth as blood surged to the spot Pettra had struck. She did not raise her voice, but she felt a familiar surge of tension spread through her body. "Many have died for less. You should be more cautious before you let your hands fly." She drained the goblet.

"Do you threaten me?" Pettra raised her voice when Corelle did not reply. "Do you?"

"I warn you of the dangers, nothing more. You did not give me the same courtesy before you struck me."

Pettra spoke in a horrified whisper. "Who are you? Never have I seen you be this hideous. You are like another person. This is not the Jorinda I love."

Her temper ready to boil over, Corelle at last raised her voice to a shout. "I am not Jorinda." Pettra started and took a step backward. Corelle stared at her, and Pettra flinched back another step. Corelle refilled her goblet and sipped at the wine as she stared out into the darkened courtyard.

After a lengthy silence, Pettra spoke through sobs. "Do you wish me to leave?"

"You are free to come or go as you please." Corelle's tongue felt thick, and she struggled to string her words together.

"You are in your cups." Pettra sounded disdainful. "There can be no other excuse for your atrocious behaviour."

"I am the atrocious behaver? You are the one who struck me."

Pettra did not reply immediately. "I do not think 'behaver' is a word."

Corelle wheeled on her and spilled some of the wine. "I do not care what you think about how I speak."

Pettra's eyes bored into Corelle's. "Very well. I will retire. You may sleep where you will. Good night." She turned and ran up the stairs, and the sound of her sobs receded as she climbed them. She slammed the bedroom door, and Corelle could no longer hear her cry.

Corelle muttered as she refilled her goblet. "Good night." She sat in darkness and tried to mull over what she should do, but she could not marshal her thoughts. Pettra had the right of it. She might be in her cups, but she believed Pettra had driven her to it. She sat in the darkened room and sipped at the wine. When she stood again, her balance betrayed her, and she fell backward into the chair.

She woke to another sunny morning. Her head pounded, and the stale taste of the wine filled her mouth. She stood but felt nauseous. How much of the wine had she drunk? Her face hurt where Pettra had struck her. She collapsed onto the couch and fell asleep again.

CHAPTER 7
CORELLE

Corelle woke as Pettra entered the parlour, her eyes red rimmed from tears. Pettra said nothing as she passed Corelle and headed for the scullery. A few moments later she returned and placed a cup near Corelle. "Water. I suggest you drink it." She turned and went out into the courtyard.

Corelle did not have the energy to drink the water. She lay, miserable, on the couch with a headache the like of which she had never endured before. Her stomach roiled and she felt she would fetch up at any moment.

Sleep took her again, and Pettra glared down at her when she woke. "You look awful, you fool. Why did you drink so much?" The fire had died from her voice

"It numbed the pain of your attack."

Pettra loosed a mournful sigh. "Jorinda, I am sorry I hit you. I am sorry I pleasured myself. I burned for you and could not resist some satisfaction. You spoke to me in such a horrible way. I think you also owe me an apology."

"I am not Jorinda." Corelle used her anger to hide her shame at the excessive amount of wine she had consumed. "As for any apology you feel you are owed, you will be disappointed. You asked if I am a monster. I am, Pettra. I am a monster. You once told me you found my hideousness attractive, but now you seem revolted by it."

"I said no such thing. I said I felt a violence about you that appealed to me. It stems from my desire to be hurt during lovemaking, not from some need to be abased and insulted where I ought to find love."

"Abased?" Corelle did not recognise the word.

"Humiliated, then, if this is easier for you to understand."

Corelle snorted. "Why use words I cannot understand? I know not why people must do so. Deineike used to…" She fell silent. Had she criticised Deineike, her beloved Deineike, whom she missed more than she could find words to explain? Her head ached too much to arrange her thoughts with any purpose.

Pettra stared down at her. "Jorinda, I do not wish to continue this argument. I think it best I go out and leave you to sleep or recover. I hope you feel better soon." She turned and ran up the stairs. A short time later, she came downstairs and left the house.

Corelle slept the morning away and drank the cup of water as her condition improved. The nausea passed, and she refilled the cup from a pitcher in the pantry. Unsure how things had turned so wrong so fast, she lay on the couch again. They had been content for a pass or so, yet not quite two passes later, they had become sundered, and Pettra had struck her.

Could the relationship be repaired? Did Corelle even want it repaired? She had not wanted to bring Pettra south with her in the first instance, but she had weakened in the face of the threat Pettra had made to take her own life. Corelle felt trapped, buried beneath the weight of yet another poor decision. The wine had brought some relief, although she paid a severe price for that relief today. This must be the punishment for her betrayal of Deineike when she lay with Pettra within a few days of Deineike's Pyre. Corelle deserved all that came her way.

Pettra had not reappeared, and Corelle rose and checked the pantry for some food. She ate some bread and cheese, felt somewhat improved afterward, and sat in a chair as morose thoughts crowded in on her. Pettra had not returned, and the day would soon turn to night. Corelle had not left the house all day, so she wandered out into the courtyard for some fresh air. When she returned to the house, she poured herself a goblet of wine from the cask. Only her and the wine together in the house, and the wine held its tongue, until the following morning at the least. She laughed at her jest and returned to the chair.

When darkness fell and Pettra did not come home, Corelle feared some harm might have befallen her. Several goblets of wine had left Corelle unsure whether she could walk if she needed to leave the house and search for Pettra. The time slid by unmarked as she rose from the chair to refill her goblet or relieve herself. The lantern cast formless shadows of the furniture on the wall.

At last, the door opened. Corelle watched as two Pettras entered the parlour, but when she closed one eye to help her focus, one of the Pettras disappeared. Pettra's cheeks appeared bright red, and Corelle asked her, "Have you run home?"

"What? Are you in your cups again?"

"You. Have you run?"

"That I have not. Why?"

"Cheeks are red."

Pettra raised a hand to her face. "Oh. That I have, I apologise. I realised it had grown late, so I ran back."

"Back?"

"I have been with a friend. Why are you in your cups again?"

"It helps me mind my own business." Corelle laughed at her own jest.

"What? I cannot understand you. You are worse than last night. Did you not learn your lesson this morning?"

In response, Corelle made a noise with her lips that sounded as though somebody had broken wind, and she laughed at the hilarity of the sound. After a time, she composed herself. "I will be all right."

Pettra stood near the doorway, stared at her, then spat, "Good night." She ran up the stairs while Corelle sipped at the wine and tried to make the sound again with her lips. She giggled whenever she made it, but she could not always control her lips well enough to repeat it.

Corelle woke slumped in the chair. The goblet had fallen from her hand and wine had stained the carpet. The sun had not peeped over the nearby rooftops, the morning still early. Her head pounded, her mouth had become as dry as sand, and her tongue stuck to its roof. Her vision blurred, and the lantern had gone out. She tried to reach the couch, but had to run to the basin, where she fetched up, loud and violent. She lay on the scullery floor and fell asleep.

"What in the Five Cities?" Pettra's voice woke her. The sunlight hurt Corelle's eyes, and she closed them again straight away. "Have you slept on the floor?"

"Go away." It took some effort for Corelle to speak.

"Did you spill wine last night?" Why must Pettra shout? Every word pounded on Corelle's skull like a smith's hammer, and her sighs of frustration rushed around Corelle's ears like angry winds. "You are hopeless. I will clean it, but you must clean yourself up. You are covered in vomit."

Corelle heard Pettra move around but still could not tolerate the brightness of the sun. At last, she forced her eyes open. Pettra knelt next to her and shook her head as she pulled Corelle upright, then moved behind her. With her arms under Corelle's own, she grunted as she lifted her miserable lover to her feet. She led Corelle to the couch and laid her on it.

"You are a disgrace. I will light a fire and fill a tub. You must clean yourself up."

"Where did you go last night?"

"Out with a friend, as I told you."

"Your cheeks are still red."

"Are they? I had not noticed."

"I recall your face looked this way once before, after I had struck you."

Pettra sucked air through her teeth. "What do you care?"

"You lay with another? One who gave in to your desire for pain?"

Pettra kept silent for a time, then repeated the question. "What do you care?"

It surprised Corelle to find she did not care. "I do not. I care only that you would lie to me. I do not deserve that."

"You jest, do you not? You spoke to me worse than you would an animal, you threatened me—"

"You struck me."

"That I did, and I am mortified. I have also apologised. For the last two nights you have become incoherent from the wine I now regret I bought. I spent some time with a friend, as I have told you. Beyond that, you deserve no explanation. You threatened to kill me, Jorinda."

"I am a killer, after all else." Corelle laughed again. The last few days had turned her into a jester without peer, it seemed.

Pettra sighed. "You should rest. I will light a fire and you may bathe when you can rise from this couch. You must change your clothes also. They are horrible. We will discuss this further when you are in a better mood. You must not drink while we talk."

"You do not order me around. I do not answer to you."

Pettra did not reply, and Corelle soon fell asleep. When she woke again, Pettra watched her from a nearby chair, an accusatory expression on her face. Corelle disliked the look. "What?"

"Do you plan to spend the rest of your life in the house? Will you never go out again?"

Corelle sat up. "What hour is it?"

"After the midday. How do you feel?"

"Terrible." Corelle saw no point in a lie.

"You look worse than you feel, then. That is some relief, I imagine."

Corelle looked down and saw yellow stains on her tunic. "What is this stain?"

"You fetched up on yourself. You do not remember this?"

"I fetched up in the basin."

Pettra shook her head. "If you intended to, then you missed. You fetched up on yourself and the floor."

Vague recollections came back to Corelle. "I spilled some wine."

"I have cleaned it up as best I could. I will work on it further once the carpet is dry again."

Corelle looked down into her lap, consumed by shame. She mumbled a response. "My thanks."

"Why do you do this to yourself, Jorinda?"

Corelle's shame burnt to a crisp in the fires of an anger that sprang up within her again. "You drove me to it, with the arguments. You did not tell me you would be out so late."

"You would make this my fault? How is that possible?"

Corelle did not have the energy to continue the argument or maintain her fury. She sat, sullen, on the couch and gazed out at the blue sky through the window at the front of the parlour.

"Can you make it up the stairs? The water will be hot. I will fill the tub if you can climb the stairs. You need to clean yourself up. You stink. I believe you soiled yourself as you slept on the scullery floor."

Corelle nodded in misery. Had she done the things Pettra

accused her of? She could not believe it. Pettra must seek some revenge for the argument, nothing more. The older woman went up the stairs, and Corelle rose and walked to the staircase, unsteady. Afraid she might lose her balance, she crawled up the stairs one by one, and it took a great deal of time to reach the bedroom. At the top of the stairs Pettra waited and watched, a disdainful look on her face. Pettra helped her out of her clothes and guided her into the tub. "Do not drown." Pettra seemed unable to resist the barb as she carried Corelle's clothes down the stairs.

The water soothed Corelle, and she felt better by the time the water cooled. She stood and climbed out of the tub, clean again. She dried herself with a cloth Pettra had left next to the tub and found some clothes to wear. When she went down into the parlour, some bread and cheese on a platter sat on a small table near the couch.

"You should eat." Pettra gestured toward the food. "You have eaten almost nothing for two days."

Corelle waved a dismissive hand at her and sat on the couch. As she nibbled at the food, she realised how hungry she had grown, and she finished it all as Pettra watched her.

"What?" Corelle felt uncomfortable under Pettra's gaze.

"We must talk. Things have been difficult between us for some time, but these last two days..." She seemed to run out of inspiration.

"I told you I did not wish you to come."

"That you did. Do you now wish me to leave?"

Corelle shrugged. "I do not care. I cannot tell you what you must do. You are a grown woman."

Pettra turned away as she sighed her bitterness into the room, then returned her attention to Corelle. "How have things turned so awry between us in fewer than three passes? I have loved you and asked for little enough from you. Why do you despise me?"

"I do not despise you. I despise what you ask me to do. I brought you with me on the promise you would not ask it."

"I promised to try, and try I did. I still desire it."

Corelle shook her head in exasperation. "And I do not wish to succumb to it. I fear to. I know the things I am capable of. Do not awaken the creature that lurks within me."

"Then what will we do?"

Corelle shrugged. "You have someone you can lie with who gives you what you wish, it seems. Go to her. Lie with her and let her cause you pain. If she kills you…" She hesitated, and Pettra looked down at her lap. "I have warned you of the risks. You are old enough to make your own decisions."

Silence filled the room for a considerable time. "Did you turn on Arella or Deineike as you have turned on me? Did you treat them with such contempt?"

Tears sprang to Corelle's eyes. She had turned on Arella enough to take her life in the interests of her own self-preservation. When Deineike saw the mariner who had killed her mother, aboard The Friendship, Corelle had burned with rage and could scarce talk to her for days. Her unstable temperament made her unfit to be in the company of others. Ashamed to make the admission, she whispered, "That I did."

Pettra also began to cry. As she sobbed, Corelle thought back on all the pain she had brought to the people whose lives had crossed her own, a ball of destruction that rolled through the land and shattered all she came into contact with. Her devastation spared nobody. Arella, Deineike, Raolos, Pettra; she had caused them all unimaginable agonies.

Corelle stood, poured herself a cup of water, and drank it in the scullery as she stared out into the courtyard. When she turned, she realised she could not see the cask of wine. "Where is the wine?"

"Gone. I curse that I brought it into this house."

"By what right did you dispose of it?"

Pettra looked up at her as tears poured down her face. "I bought it. I am free to dispose of it as I will. It has brought you nothing but a sharp tongue and painful mornings. It has brought me misery, and I have removed it."

"It brought me peace, whatever else you ascribe to it. For a short time, I could forget the horrors of my life."

Pettra frowned. "This is no way to live, in your cups, hidden away from reality. Can you not see this?"

"And this existence is the way to live, is that your argument?" Corelle waved her arm around as if to point out all the wrongs in her life.

"We had happiness. I did, at the least. We can again, I believe. I will try again to suppress my desires, but you must not drink your-self into oblivion every night."

Corelle's anger drove her spiteful response. "That is not your decision to make. I take orders from nobody."

"That is unfair." Pettra wiped at her eyes.

Pettra had the right of it. Why had Corelle become so angry at Pettra? Did it come because she had lain with another? That seemed unlikely. While Pettra craved the pain that appealed to her so much, Corelle had no wish to lie with her. She had never wanted Pettra to come with her, of course. Yet here they were, and Corelle could not calm her temper. Every word Pettra spoke rankled, and had for many days, even before the vitriolic arguments of the last three days. After all else, Pettra deserved to be treated with dignity. Whether Corelle could give her that dignity, she did not know. Raolos had not listened to her even as she told him as much. Pettra had refused to hear Corelle tell her she did not wish to be with her and threatened to kill herself unless Corelle took her south with her. The weight of everybody's expectations had grown too great for Corelle to bear without Deineike to help her.

Her anger calmed as she considered the unfairness of her

words, but she feared she might become enraged again at the drop of a word or gesture from Pettra. Some time alone and out of the house might be good for her. "I need to go out for a walk. Alone." A single, accusatory tear trickled down Pettra's cheek as she watched Corelle cross the parlour and leave the house.

CHAPTER 8
CORELLE

orelle wandered in the direction of the market, aimless and miserable to her core. The day had slipped away, and few stalls remained open for business. An hour passed before she turned back toward the house. She felt calmer, and as long as Pettra did not pursue the argument further, she might hope to remain so. Ahead of her, a shop that sold food and wine had not yet closed for the day, and as she studied the shelves, she saw a cask of the same wine Pettra had brought home three days ago. On a whim, she bought the cask. Pettra had thrown the wine out, but Corelle believed it would be a good thing to have a cask in the house. If the arguments began again, Pettra might drop the matter if Corelle poured a goblet of the wine.

When she returned to the house, she smelled food. Whatever Pettra had cooked while she had been out, it had a delicious aroma. Pettra turned as she heard her enter the scullery. The smile vanished from her face when she flicked her eyes to the wine cask. "You have brought more wine home?"

"That I have." Corelle pointed at the pot over the fire. "What is that? It smells good."

Pettra gave her a weak smile that could not reach her eyes. "My thanks. I found some mutton and have made a broth with some tubers and vegetables. I hope it will be tasty. I am not a wonderful cook."

"You are better than me. I imagine I would live on bread and cheese if I lived alone." That had not been the entire truth; she had cooked well enough while she lived in the farmhouse with Taro, but she felt Pettra deserved some joy.

Pettra smiled again. "It will be ready soon enough. Let me put the wine in the pantry." She held out her hands.

Corelle hesitated, then passed her the cask. "A goblet of it might be pleasant with the meal." A hopeful plea as Pettra carried it into the pantry.

"That it might." Pettra spoke from within the pantry. "One goblet might match the mutton well."

Corelle sat in an armed chair and watched Pettra dip a spoon into the broth, then blow on and sample it. "How is it?"

"You can have a small amount if you like. Let me know if it needs more seasoning to meet your tastes."

"I have simple tastes. I am sure it will be fine."

Pettra turned and nodded. "Where did you walk?"

"Toward the dock, for a while. Then I turned and came back."

"Such a lovely day. Not too hot." Pettra nodded, as though to confirm her opinion of the temperature.

Silence reigned for a while. Pettra stirred the broth from time to time before she ladled some into each of two bowls. She brought one bowl to Corelle with a spoon and some bread then brought her own meal over. Corelle sipped some of the spicy broth from her spoon. The flavour of the mutton shone through the other ingredients, delicious and satisfying. She placed the bowl on the floor, and Pettra gave her a curious glance.

"I will bring us each a goblet of wine to go with the broth."

Pettra pursed her lips, then nodded. "Is the broth good?"

"That it is." Corelle poured two goblets of wine. She handed one to Pettra, and they ate in silence until they had emptied the bowls. Corelle sipped at the wine as she ate. Her goblet had almost been drained by the time she had finished the broth.

Pettra gave her a warm smile. "There is more if you are still hungry."

"My thanks, I do not require more."

Pettra took Corelle's bowl from her and rinsed both the bowls and spoons in the basin beneath the pump. She drained her goblet and rinsed it also. "Are you finished with your goblet?" She did not turn to face Corelle.

"I may have another later."

Pettra stood at the pump and seemed to gaze out at the darkness as it folded the house in its grip, then she turned back to the fire, where a pot of heated water hung. With a cloth to protect her hand, she picked up the pot, poured some water into the basin, washed the dishes, and dried them with a cloth. When she had done, she sat in a chair. "Shall we go to bed?"

"It is early yet."

"I do not wish to sleep." Pettra sounded coy.

Although Pettra had promised to try not to beg for pain, Corelle felt reluctant to take the risk, and she did not want to lie with Pettra at the moment, after all else. The arguments were too fresh in her mind, and she thought if they lay together, and Pettra asked her to hurt her, they would argue again. She stood and refilled her goblet. Pettra said nothing further.

Corelle sat and sipped at the wine as Pettra lit the lantern then hovered near her chair. "I will go to bed. Will you join me?"

"Soon." Corelle smiled up at her, noncommittal.

Pettra sighed. "Jorinda, please do not drink any more wine tonight."

Corelle gazed at her. "Why not?"

Pettra shuffled her feet and stared down at them. "I do not wish another argument. I have asked you not to drink any more. I go to bed. Good night."

"Good night." Corelle watched Pettra climb the stairs, drank two more goblets, then with a sigh, she climbed the stairs and lay in the bed next to Pettra. Pettra turned, wrapped her arms around her, and nuzzled into her neck. Corelle turned away and lay silent with Pettra's arms still wrapped around her.

Pettra kissed Corelle's back and whispered. "I love you."

"Good night." Corelle heard Pettra fall asleep, but sleep seemed reluctant to come for her, and when it did come, it brought more nightmares.

The next days proved difficult. Although Pettra made every effort to maintain the unstable peace in the house, Corelle became more disaffected each day, and she could not determine what had changed to make her so unhappy in the relationship. She drank several goblets of the wine each night, although Pettra urged her not to. The cask soon emptied, and Corelle bought another. She thought she had gained weight, and her trousers did not feel as comfortable as they had at one time. She must have eaten too much in recent days, and she vowed to cut back on her food. In an attempt to control her weight, she went for a walk each day as soon as she had risen and dressed. Pettra did not seem to suffer the same fate. It may have been luck, or that the older woman had grown more used to large meals because of her high society lifestyle.

They had not argued for a sevenday when Pettra said she intended to visit a friend that evening. Corelle shrugged and said she hoped they would have fun. She suspected Pettra lay with the friend, whoever she might be, but she no longer cared, if she ever had. Once Pettra left, Corelle brought the cask of wine out of the pantry and set it beside her. She lit the lantern and sat in the chair as she drank the wine and thought back over her life. For much of the time, she thought of Deineike. The agony of how much she missed the dark-haired woman seared through her mind and brought tears to her eyes. Corelle guessed Deineike would be disappointed in her. She had broken her vow when she killed again after the Pyre, had betrayed her when she lay with Pettra, and had now become all but estranged from the woman she had brought south against her better judgement.

They had been in Vyrrmod for almost four passes, and the rent would soon fall due on the house again. There seemed to be only two seasons in this land: hot and hotter. In almost four passes, she could recall only three or four days of rain. Corelle's knowledge of the language had improved, and she could converse well enough and buy goods from the market and local shops. Arkkyd held little appeal, and the arguments with Pettra had grown wearisome. She would stay one more pass, then move on.

She had drunk a significant amount of wine by the time Pettra returned. She seemed surprised to find Corelle still in the parlour, and she stood in the lobby and gazed into the room.

Corelle's voice sounded coarse in the tense silence it broke. "How is your friend?"

"You are in your cups." Pettra sighed and looked down, but she did not enter the parlour. She wiped at her eyes.

"You shed tears for me?"

"That I do not. I will go up to bed."

"Again? Have you not just climbed out of one?" Corelle could not resist the barbs, though she recognised them as unkind.

Pettra stared at her in sadness. "You are horrible when you are like this. You become a different person."

Corelle sneered. "If you spoke the truth, I would become a pleasant woman indeed. I am a monster at all other times."

Pettra shook her head. "You slur so much, I cannot even understand you. Good night."

"Good night." Corelle blew her an ironic kiss, and Pettra climbed the stairs.

The night turned into another endless round of self-incrimination even as Corelle tried to hide from it in her goblet. She loathed herself and all she had become, had hated herself for years. Since they had arrived in Arkkyd, Pettra had brought out the worst in her, and try as she might, she could no longer control her vicious tongue. Pettra deserved better, and Corelle thought she should leave, so Pettra could find joy with her new dalliance. As soon as they argued, the worst of Corelle's nature took over, and she could not contain the barbs she hurled.

At long last, sleep shut down the contradictions in her mind, and she awoke as the sun came through the window. Her stomach drove her straight to the basin where she fetched up, then crawled back to the couch and tried to sleep again. Pettra came down the stairs, stood in the lobby, and gazed in at her. Something about her face looked unusual, and Corelle sat up and squinted at her.

Pettra shook her head, and her tone reminded Corelle of her mother's admonishments when she had misbehaved as a young girl. "You suffer again from too much wine. Will you ever learn?"

"Come closer, I cannot hear you."

Pettra hesitated and stood in the lobby for some time. With a sigh, she walked into the parlour. Discolouration around one of her eyes, which had swollen, made Corelle gasp. Her eyebrow had a large cut that bled even as she stood in the parlour. Corelle stood, concerned. "What is that injury to your eye?"

"I fell." Corelle heard no conviction or truth in Pettra's mumbled reply.

Corelle took her hands and stared at her palms. "That is untrue. No other cuts or grazes suggest a fall. Who did this to you?"

"That is not yours to know." Pettra spat the words out, then looked down. "I wished it."

"Pettra, I have warned you. There is danger in these abnormal games you play. You must be careful."

"You do not care what I do. Do not feign concern, who refuses to heed my advice about your wine consumption."

"The wine does not threaten to kill me."

"It will if you do not stop. You have gained weight, and you are not yourself."

"I have gained weight because I eat too much. I have determined to eat less."

Pettra gave a derisive laugh. "You eat next to nothing. You lie to yourself about the effect of so much wine, nothing more."

Corelle slumped back onto the couch. Her head hurt and the argument worsened the pain. "Be careful Pettra. That is all I ask." She sighed and lay down again.

"Your concern touches me." Pettra had vitriol in her voice.

Corelle waved an arm at her and closed her eyes. When she woke, she could not find Pettra. The parlour smelled of stale wine, and she headed out of the house for some fresh air. At the office where they had rented the house, she paid the rent for another pass. As she wandered the streets, she decided to leave Arkkyd before the pass she had paid for ended. The city brought her no joy.

She returned to the house and sat in a chair with a goblet of wine late in the day, and Pettra came down the stairs. As the older woman passed the parlour on her way to the door, Corelle called out to her, and she turned. She wore the dress she had worn the first day they had moved into the house. "Your friend will enjoy that dress, I am sure." Corelle could not keep the sarcasm from her voice.

Pettra shook her head and opened the door. Once she had left, Corelle went to the pantry. Nothing more than a dribble trickled into her goblet. With a muttered complaint to herself at the oversight, she set out for the shop, but it had closed, which confused her. She felt certain she had bought wine there later in the day than it appeared to be, but today the shop had closed early. As she wandered further in search of another shop, she saw a tavern.

That would do as well, she decided, so she entered the tavern and ordered a goblet of their best wine. Old habits die hard, and she took a seat at the far end of the tavernroom. She faced the room, had a solid wall at her back, and reached down to check for her dagger out of instinct.

Once she finished the first goblet, she ordered another. With her head bowed, she thought once more of Deineike, and a shadow fell over her. "May I join you?" The man spoke the language of Dur. Without a glance at him, she reached down to her boot and pulled out her dagger. She placed it on the table and trusted it would send the message she did not desire any company, the least of all that of a man.

The tavernroom fell silent at once, and Corelle glanced up. The man before her looked familiar. He wore an immaculate tunic of fine making and trousers to match. He spoke again in an alarmed whisper. "Please pick up your weapon without delay."

"You threaten me?" Corelle thought she recognised him, although she could not recall where from, and he spoke Dur.

"That I do not." His reply surprised her, as the people of Vyrrmod did not use the usual Dur phrases of agreement or disagreement. They preferred a simple "yes," or "no." It remained a strange custom to Corelle even after more than four passes in the land. In truth, no word for "yes" existed in Dur. "Our custom dictates that if a weapon is placed before another, it constitutes a challenge. My wife would be distressed if I am returned to her in small pieces."

Corelle felt she had heard the phrase before, but his identity continued to elude her. "And?"

"And if I pick it up, I accept the challenge. You would kill me, I know this. If I leave, I am a coward, and my business interests would be damaged by my new reputation. If you take the weapon back, you are a coward. I suspect your business interests in Vyrrmod would be affected less by this outcome than mine." He gave a dry laugh. "Please, Corelle of Dur, take back the weapon. I know you, and respect is due. My name is Rakulaj, although you seem to have forgotten me."

She remembered him now—the merchant from the ship in Ort, although he looked different somehow. Nonetheless, she picked up the dagger and returned it to her boot. She could not kill him over some foolish custom, and he had been an unwitting ally as Corelle and Pettra had sailed south at no cost. "Sit, if you wish." She waved a hand at the chairs opposite her.

"My thanks."

She waved the innkeep over. "Two goblets of wine, please." She pushed four gilks across the table.

Rakulaj pushed it back toward her. "You need not pay for your drinks in this tavern." His laughter dispelled the remain of the tension Corelle's dagger had created.

"Oh? Why is that?"

"Because I own this tavern, and respect is due, although you appear to be in poor condition at the moment."

Corelle arched her eyebrows. "You own this place, and happen to be here on the night I stumble into it? That is quite a coincidence." She placed little trust in coincidences.

He laughed. "It is no accident, as you have guessed. Once I heard you had sailed to Arkkyd aboard one of my ships, I circulated your description around my businesses and those of my friends. When you arrived here, the innkeep recognised you and sent for me."

Corelle frowned. "Why did he send for you rather than ask me to visit you?"

"Your reputation, my dear Corelle. I prefer to handle my own business and not involve my staff in conversations with killers. As it turns, that decision appears to have been wise."

Corelle could not argue with his logic. She did not know how she might have reacted had the innkeep tried to persuade her to meet with someone in a strange city. Trust seemed to have vanished from her life along with her manners. She nodded at Rakulaj and sipped at her wine.

He seemed to guess she had no comment on the matter. "Tell me, Corelle of Dur, is all well with you and your wife?"

"She is not my wife. How do you know of her?"

"You voyaged to my land aboard my ship. In truth, little turns here I do not learn of. I am… influential, I believe the word would be in your language."

She grunted, but curiosity gnawed at her. "Tell me more of this custom."

"There is little more than I have told you. Once the weapon is placed, there are only three outcomes. It is wise to be wary of who you place your weapon before, of course. He may be more dangerous than you believe. Or she, for respect is due."

"No respect is due to me." Corelle laughed, though her laughter dripped with irony. "I am a monster, it turns. A killer who cannot even protect those she loves."

"This tale speaks of tragedy. You had some part to play in the death of Styrrach, I take it?"

"That I did. I opened him up and stole his tomorrows from him. Too late, curse me. He had already killed the woman I love."

"This is indeed tragic. I regret this outcome. I believe that translates as I intend. It is the deepest expression of sorrow we have. I apologise if it sounds less sympathetic in your tongue."

"My thanks." Her mournful response must suffice, and she drained her goblet before she reached for one of the two the innkeep had delivered.

"Her death has affected you a great deal, I see this. You drink to forget your pain. It will not work, my friend. Trust me. I own many taverns, and I see many who try to escape their worries down this hole. It will spit you out and leave you more miserable than you were before you began."

She snorted. "Did Pettra pay you to say that?"

"This Pettra, she is the woman you arrived with? I have not met her, though I should like to meet the woman who travels with Corelle of Dur."

Corelle laughed. "She is in the bed of another as we speak. I regret I am unable to give you directions to that bed."

Rakulaj tutted. "Come, these recent events cause you pain, but I do not see before me the Corelle of Dur who spoke to me in Ort that day. What can I do to aid you?"

She looked into his eyes. "How is the new Bailiff?"

His happy smile would have been adequate response, but he elaborated regardless. "Excellent. Trade has never been better. Mariners clamour to sail my ships to Dur, men who would not venture there for double pay under Styrrach's trade arrangements. I am happy, I am richer than ever, and I have you to thank."

"It would help me if you told me one of your masters threw Glailam, the previous Bailiff, from one of your ships into the depths of the sea, which swallowed him down to the bottom. He avoided the justice I gave to Styrrach."

Rakulaj nodded his head, slow and thoughtful. "You feel he played some part in the death of the woman you loved?"

"I love her still. He played a part. He had a major role in Styrrach's enterprise. I am sure you already know this."

He nodded again. "I know this. I am puzzled as to how he had any involvement in the death of your love, if Styrrach killed her as you claim."

She wondered whether she should order another goblet of wine, but Rakulaj had not yet touched his, so she might drink that instead. "Styrrach ran the Guild, and the Guild killed those who hindered his ambitions. He killed most often at the behest of the Portreeves or the Bailiff, who ordered Durfolk killed, and through his Guild, Styrrach wielded the dagger that took those lives."

Rakulaj pursed his lips and looked thoughtful. "I knew nothing of this part of the enterprise until this moment. I find it distasteful one in so high a public office should have blood on his hands." He sat silent for a moment and his intense stare bored into Corelle. "Come. I have some news that will help you, although it may not please you." She raised her eyebrows in a silent question. "Glailam took ship to these very shores not six passes ago. I regret to inform you nobody cast him into the blue of the sea, but I do know where he travelled."

"How do you know so much?"

"I am influential. Little turns in Vyrrmod that does not come to the ears of Rakulaj in time." He smiled. "I have a good friend in a city not three days' ride south of Arkkyd, and he tells me your former Bailiff lives well in this city. He has guards and rents a large house there. This friend is an Upholder in that city, and he often sees our friend who is not our friend in a local tavern. He likes to game. Cards, dice, any wager it seems."

An Upholder as an informant? The Upholders of Vyrrmod were the equivalent of the Portreeve's men in Dur. Corelle guessed that across all lands, coin loosened tongues that ought not to be loose, even those in authority. She had seen that in abundance through Styrrach's ownership of the Bailiff and Portreeves. It worked the same here, it seemed. "Why have you not let Raolos know this information? Glailam is sought in Dur and a noose awaits his neck."

He shrugged. "I did not know of his complicity in all matters, as I have told you. I have not exchanged names with your new Bailiff. I do not reveal all I know to any to whom respect is not due." He smiled.

The customs of Vyrrmod appeared as complex as the laws of Dur in which the Duke had taken such obvious delight. "Will you tell me the name of this city, or must I deduce it myself?"

He hesitated. "Tell me, Corelle of Dur. If Glailam entered this tavern at this very moment, what would you do?"

She answered without hesitation. "I would strike him dead."

"Alas that you would, for if his guards did not kill you in turn, the Upholders of Arkkyd would hang you. Murder is frowned upon in Vyrrmod."

"I deserve to die for all the ill I have wrought."

He tilted his head to one side and frowned at her. "Few would say they deserve death for all they have done. You seem almost to wish for it." She did not reply. "Very well, I cannot be complicit in a murder."

"You will not tell me where he is?" Anger bubbled within her.

"This I did not say. I have already talked to you of a means to your end. Indeed, I almost fell victim to that means when I first spoke to you."

She nodded as comprehension dawned on her. The challenge. She need only persuade Glailam to pick up a weapon, and she would be within her rights to end his miserable existence. "He has played a part in the death of the woman I love."

"Then justice is appropriate. Proceed with care, Corelle of Dur. Respect is due, and I would be disappointed to learn you swung from a rope in the fair city of Yantogi."

She half rose, but he held out a hand. "Stay a while. Finish my drink for me, for I have no taste for red wine. Then go home, make peace with your friend, and ride for Yantogi in the morning. Can you speak our language? Dur will be uncommon inland."

Corelle replied in Vyrrmod. "I speak some of your language."

He nodded and laughed. "Your pronunciation is atrocious, of course. But you are understandable, at the least." He tore a button from his tunic. "On this tunic is my sigil. Show it to Undilk, an Upholder in Yantogi, and he will be happy to assist you."

"My thanks." Corelle took the button from him. "Respect is due."

He bowed his head. "One other thing. Any ship you see that carries this sigil at the stern is owned by me. This button will ensure passage for you on any of those ships. I will make it so. Good luck, Corelle of Dur. Respect is due."

For the first time in many days, a joyous smile sprang to her lips. "Your help is appreciated, Rakulaj of Vyrrmod. I am in your debt."

"It is so. I will not promise never to request your aid in payment of this debt. For now, it pleases me to aid you, for respect is due." He rose and bowed, and she did likewise. He left with no further words, and she sat and pulled his goblet toward her, though she ought not to drink any more, she reasoned. She would face a long journey in the morning and would prefer to wake refreshed and not in need of a rush to the basin or the privy to fetch up. She stared at the goblet for a time, then raised it to her lips and took a sip, stayed in the tavern until she had drained the wine, then offered the innkeep some of her coin, which he refused with a smile. She meandered back to the house and pondered how fortunate she had been to visit Rakulaj's tavern that night. That good fortune would not go to waste. More blood must be spilled in payment for Deineike's life, then she might turn her mind again to her vow to herself when she had killed Arella. She could see no prospect of further joy in her relationship with Pettra, and there would be nothing left to keep her from the fulfilment of her vow once she had killed Glailam.

Back at the darkened house, Corelle checked all the rooms. Pettra had not returned from whatever dalliance she had become involved in. Corelle climbed into the bed and fell into a sleep where no nightmares plagued her.

CHAPTER 9

KRAGE

K rage and his four guards stood and watched as the dockworkers struggled with the weight of his two trunks as they loaded them onto the strange, flat vessel. Sweat drenched them before the trunks had been loaded.

Krage glanced at Mauvlin. "Will this vessel carry us across the river?"

"That it will. It is used for that very purpose. It carries goods and equipment along the river for local people when required. It can pull up to the riverbank where no ship can find a place to rest."

Krage doubted his Senior Aide. To his eye, the vessel looked little more than pieces of wood nailed together that floated on the surface of the water. Needs must, however, and the trunks, it turned, were too heavy for any rowboat that could be found. The trunks contained coin as well as his personal belongings, and he would not abandon them.

He had decided not to sail to Ort, unsure it would be safe for him to land there, and he would find it as difficult to get his trunks across the river in Ort, in truth. Here, at the least, the flat vessel could be pressed into service. Such a vessel might not be available in Ort.

The dockworkers had loaded the trunks onto the wooden platform, which proved to be the easiest part of the trip for Krage. It refused to remain still and offered precious little to hold onto when it came time for him to board. He felt certain he would be tipped into the river in front of his men, who stood on the vessel and urged him to step onto it. They assured him they would prevent him from any fall into the river. His courage threatened to desert him, and he feared to take the first step. That step almost proved disastrous as the wretched platform chose that precise moment to move on the water. It drifted away from the riverbank and almost sent him headfirst into the Alc, but two of his men grasped at him and pulled him aboard without ceremony, where he sprawled ingloriously on the wood.

He lay on the rough planks, all dignity lost. "What is this thing called?"

One of the two men who operated it replied. "A lighter."

"Never again will I set foot on one." Krage's men helped him to his feet, but he sat straight down again as the vile thing tossed about on the surface of the water with such violence, he reasoned they would all be thrown off, trunks included.

Someone threw a rope from the dock, and it struck Krage in the back. He turned and glowered at the man who had thrown it before he muttered to his men, "If we ever return here, that man is an honour gest."

The two operators took hold of the oars, one each side, and the lighter moved away from the bank. It had so little stability, Krage could see no way it would not be upended by the current in the middle of the river. Corelle had killed him after all else, with no need of her blade. She had driven him onto the device that would send him to the bottom of the Alc.

Despite his reservations, the lighter made it to the eastern bank, although it did indeed try to throw him into the water multiple times, bitter cold water that splashed up onto them every few moments. It dripped from them all by the time one of the operators, who seemed unfazed by the instability of the device, leapt from it with a rope in his hand and tied it to a tree. The ground took a gentle slope down to the river where they had come to rest, and Krage shuffled forward on his behind until he reached the front of the lighter, then stood and leaped onto solid ground.

His men struggled with the trunks until both were safe on the riverbank. Krage refused to approach the lighter again, and neither of its operators helped, despite the exorbitant fee they had charged to carry them across the river. He should order his men to kill them, he thought. As much as the prospect tempted him, he wished to draw as little attention to himself as possible now he no longer enjoyed the protection of the Portreeve.

The lighter returned across the Alc as Krage recovered his composure. The incident had embarrassed him, but he must now re-assert his authority, lest his men doubt his strength. "We will need five horses. The coin in the chests will ensure we have a comfortable journey and life, and it cannot be left unguarded." He did not intend to share his wealth with the men when he fled Dur, unless he needed to pay for protection, but it suited him for them not to realise that at this point. "I will go with one other to find some town or other in this wasteland. We will return with horses. The others will remain here and guard the chest with their lives."

Mauvlin offered to travel with him, and while Krage thought his Senior Aide would be the best person to keep him safe, he would also be the best man to leave in charge of the trunks. Krage had no desire to return to the trunks to find large quantities of his coin spirited away by his own men, the rest tipped into the river. He turned to one of the others. "Your name?"

"Ifor."

"You will accompany me. Mauvlin will protect our coin."

Styrrach had believed fear had no equal as a means to engender loyalty, but Krage preferred to suggest all involved were part of the same grand design, hence his use of "our" for coin that, in his mind, belonged to nobody but him.

Krage and Ifor walked for at least two hours before they came to a village, so small it did not even warrant a sign to announce the name of the place. A large man came out of a home, and Krage called out. "You there. I wish to purchase horses. Do you know of anybody hereabouts who might have some for sale?"

The man stopped and stared at Krage. "Westfolk, I reckon."

"We come from the west of Dur, that is true. But we are Durfolk like you."

"Durfolk you may be, but you are not like me."

The man's churlish attitude baffled Krage, and he sighed. "Be that as it may, I need horses. Is there anywhere nearby I might buy some?"

The man stroked his chin. "Old Palder, out to the farm there, he has some horses. Not sure if he wants to part with them, mind."

"Where is this farm?"

"Back aways, where you came from. You must have passed it if you have come from the west somehow."

Krage sighed. He had no wish to return toward the river unless he could be sure he would obtain the five horses. "Are there no horses here, in…"

The man appeared not to notice that Krage had offered him the opportunity to reveal the name of the village. "That there are, but I do not say any of them are for sale. Try that house there." He pointed to a small, low home painted in a bright red colour. "He is wealthy, might have some business with Westfolk. Good day to you."

He appeared to be out of tolerance for them and moved off without a backward glance. Krage stared after him for a moment then turned, approached the house the man had indicated, and rapped impatient knuckles on the door.

A short, plump woman opened the door. Her dark lank hair hung below her shoulders, and she pursed thin lips as she looked them over with suspicious eyes. "What I do you for?"

Krage hesitated, unsure he had understood the question. If he quizzed her about it, he might alienate her, since it seemed people from the west found little favour on this side of the river. He decided to ignore the bizarre phrase and summoned up his warmest smile. "We understand you might have horses. We have need of some and would be prepared to buy any you will part with." He came straight to the point. The day slipped away, and he had made little progress.

She nodded, but he could not tell whether it meant they had horses for sale or only that she had understood him. "We have horses, but we uses them to travel around. We have three, and there are three of us. I cannot sell them, see?"

Krage resisted a temptation to push the woman backward and demand she speak their language in a way he could understand. "I would be prepared to pay you well. You would be in a position to buy far better animals from… wherever you buy horses in these parts."

"Desperate, are you?" A smile of contempt sprang to her lips. "Westfolk, by your clothes. On the slip from the Portreeve over to Zhanghar, I warrant."

Krage turned to look at Ifor, who stood in silence behind him. He had nothing to say to Ifor, but he wanted to control his temper and not strike down the woman and everybody else in this miserable stain on the land. He turned his attention to the woman again. "I will buy your horses if you will sell them. It is a simple proposition. Will you sell them?"

She chewed at one of her thin lips. "How much will you pay?"

Krage had no idea how much a horse might cost, so he guessed. "Ten regals."

"For all three? One alone costs more." She snorted, wiped at her nose with the back of a hand.

"*That cannot be true,*" Krage thought. Horses could not be worth ten regals. What a ridiculous price for such idiotic animals. "I meant ten regals for each." He fought to keep irritation out of his voice.

She chewed at the lip again. "Twelve."

Krage turned to look at Ifor again, but the man shrugged his shoulders. He must know no more about horse prices than Krage himself. He returned his gaze to the woman and stared at her without a word for a time, then leaned forward to speak, his voice low and quiet. "Ask me why I run from the Portreeve." He wanted her to hear, but nobody else.

She seemed taken aback by the question. "I meant nothing by that. None of mine what you run from. If you do."

He moved even closer and whispered in her ear. "I did not steal a loaf of bread."

The woman gulped, and the colour drained from her face. "Ten it is." Hurried words, the look of fear in her eyes. Krage had played a high hand. Durfolk had little experience with threats of violence, explicit or implied, and he had suspected his words would make her nervous.

He counted thirty regals from the pouch at his belt, and she led them round to the back of the house, where they found the three horses in a tidy shed. She helped them put saddles and bridles on the horses, and he and Ifor mounted one each. Ifor took the reins of the other in his hand. "My thanks. I hope you find excellent animals to replace these."

She did not reply and Krage did not wait to see if she found her tongue again. He rode out past the house and turned the horse toward the river. He had ridden no more than a handful of times in his life and had chosen the smallest animal in the hope it would be the easier to control. It seemed docile enough, content to plod along at a pace Krage found comfortable.

They found a trail that led off the path and Krage gambled it would lead to the farm the man had spoken of. They rode down the trail, little more than bare earth worn into the grass by the passage of feet and hooves.

Old Palder was well named. Krage believed him the oldest person he had ever laid eyes on. He had a faint, wheezy voice, and Krage had to listen hard to hear his words. He agreed to sell them two horses for eight regals apiece, and Krage wondered whether he should kill the woman and take back his thirty regals on the way eastward.

"I has five, rides none of them these days." Old Palder watched them struggle with the two horses' tack. "In truth, these others will die soon unlessing someone takes them off my hands. Too old to farm now."

"Quite." Krage ignored the man's dreadful grasp of his own language as he passed the reins of two of the horses to Ifor. Once he had returned to the saddle of his own mount, the last horse's reins in his hands, they rode back down the trail. Forty-six regals on horses. Outrageous. He would have killed the old man and stolen all five of his horses had they spotted the farm trail the first time. The body might never have been discovered, but they had been seen now, and there would be witnesses if word ever reached civilisation. He contented himself with the thought that forty-six regals represented a tiny part of his wealth and rode on.

They distributed the pouches of coin across all five horses. The light had all but gone before they finished, and they would doubtless find no accommodation at the nameless village. Krage suggested they should ride further, but the others resisted the idea. To ride in the dark on paths none of them knew presented many dangers. If a horse put a hoof into a hole and fell, it could break a leg, which would be the end of the horse. Horses' legs could not be reset, and horses with broken legs were killed. Even to Krage, who admitted he was little more than a cold-hearted killer, that seemed cruel and unnecessary, but they assured him it would be a kindness to the animal. Horses had fragile legs that broke with such ease and such terrible consequences, they could not be mended.

With no other choice, he agreed, and they slept on the ground beneath the black skies of the Eastlands. His first ever day east of the Alc had been horrendous. If they found no improvement, and soon, he might even welcome Corelle's blade at his throat.

CHAPTER 10
CORELLE

Corelle sprang awake at the sound of the door of the house as it closed two floors below her. Alone in the bed, she slid from the sheets and pulled her dagger from her discarded boot. Crouched beside the bed, Corelle listened as footsteps dragged themselves up the stairs. Whoever climbed toward the bedroom made no attempt to disguise their movements and seemed to labour to ascend the stairs at all.

The light through the open door turned darker as the person approached it and blocked the early morning light that slipped into the house through the window on the landing. Pettra entered the bedroom, slow, her head down. Corelle exhaled and slid the dagger back into the boot, then stood beside the bed before the shuttered bedroom window. She saw straight away Pettra had been hurt. Her dishevelled hair looked a mess, blood dripped from her nose, and the corner of her mouth had swollen and turned red. An ugly red welt ran from each corner of her mouth around her cheeks. She moved with difficulty and looked exhausted as she bent forward to place her hands on the bed. Each of her wrists bore a red welt, and bruises covered her arms.

"Pettra? What has turned?" Corelle's heart raced from anxiety at Pettra's condition.

"Nothing. I brought it upon myself." Pettra moaned, fell onto the bed, and lifted her legs from the floor with great effort and many groans. More welts could be seen around her ankles, and she wore no shoes.

"Who did this to you?" Pettra did not answer as tears sprang to her eyes. Corelle ran to the privy and pumped water onto a cloth before she returned to the bedroom and wiped some of the blood from Pettra's face with care as the older woman lay motionless. "Pettra, I am worried. What turned?"

"I told you. I requested such treatment. You know this. You know I crave it." Pettra closed her eyes, and tears ran down each side of her face.

Corelle gazed in disbelief on the injuries Pettra had suffered. "What woman could do this to another?" She had, in part, directed the question at herself.

Pettra whispered a weak response and closed her eyes. "No woman did it."

Corelle frowned. "You lay with a man? A man did this to you?"

"That he did."

"I thought…" Corelle blinked in confusion. Pettra had lain with a man? Corelle believed Pettra left Raolos because she no longer wished the attentions of men. Why would she abandon a good man such as Raolos for one who would treat her with such brutality?

She ran down the stairs, brought a cup of water to the bedroom, then raised Pettra's head gently to tip some into her mouth. Pettra managed a feeble smile. "My thanks. I will be fine. I need to sleep. All will be well."

"I fear to leave you in this condition."

Pettra's eyes sprang open. "Leave?"

"I ride today for Yantogi, a city three days from here. Glailam, the Bailiff who worked with Styrrach, lives there."

Pettra stared up at her in apparent disbelief. "How do you know this?"

"I met with an old friend last night. He did not treat me… No matter. He told me."

"Why do you go to see this snake?"

"I do not go to see him. I go to kill him."

Pettra tried to sit up, but Corelle held her down, careful not to press too hard and injure her further. "You will be hanged."

Corelle shrugged. "I deserve nothing less. There is a custom here that may mean I can kill him and not be hanged for the deed. I will roll the dice. He will pay for his part in Deineike's death."

Pettra closed her eyes again. "What of me?"

"You should heal these injuries and return to Dur. I am certain Raolos will take better care of you than I can. Or your friend here."

"You will leave me? I love you." Pettra's tears intensified.

"You do not love me. You lie with others. This does not suggest love. You have been infatuated."

"You will leave me."

This time it had not been a question, and Corelle did not know how to respond. "I fear to, now I see you in such condition, but I must. I must kill Glailam. I cannot bear the thought he might move on, and I miss my chance. This is my one chance to kill him. I am sorry." Corelle longed to offer a more detailed explanation, but she had already told the full tale.

"That you are not. You are pleased. You have never wished to be with me. You used me, and now you abandon me, even injured as I am. You are vile. I hate you." She covered her eyes with a hand.

"I am sorry Pettra. Please return to Dur once you are able. And please do not visit this man again. He might kill you."

Corelle glanced at the window, surprised by how far up the sky the sun had risen. Pettra had stayed with the man all night. To leave Pettra in such pain worried Corelle, but she doubted she could do much to help her, in truth. Further arguments would compound Pettra's misery, so Corelle threw her clothes into her pack and carried it down the stairs. The remains of her coin were still in the pack, and Pettra had sufficient of her own coin to make the journey back to Dur. Still, she left some coin on the table in the parlour, a feeble attempt to salve her conscience as she abandoned the older woman in a time of need.

Corelle ran back upstairs to check on Pettra, who had climbed into the bed and appeared to be asleep. Her dress lay crumpled next to the bed. As Corelle gazed in misery on the battered woman, she reminded herself she had stayed with Deineike in her hour of need and should do the same for Pettra. Deineike had gone to the flames, and vengeance must be taken for her death, so Corelle shrugged and descended to the lobby. *"I choose Deineike's vengeance,"* she told herself. As her key locked the door behind her, she pushed her guilt away. Let it consume her later. For now, she must avenge Deineike's death. A passer-by gave her directions to a stable where she could rent a horse.

Her skills on horseback had improved little, so she requested a docile mount, paid the hire charge for the horse and some tack for a sevenday, and set off south. As she rode, she decided to return to Arkkyd once the deed had been done, collect her making materials and Deineike's sketches, then travel onward to some other land. Vyrrmod might yet deliver justice, but the land held no happy memories, and she would seek satisfaction or death elsewhere. With luck, Pettra would have returned to Dur by the time she came back to their house. Corelle hoped Pettra would find happiness but doubted she would. Tragedy surrounded her, not the least her perverse desire for pain, and Corelle could not shake the thought it might lead to her ruin, another woman who said she loved Corelle led to a desperate end by those words.

The sun blazed down as the horse carried her southward toward whatever fates waited to be written in Yantogi.

CHAPTER 11
PETTRA

Pettra woke later in the day, exhausted and unable to leave the bed. Her life had collapsed around her. The arguments with Jorinda had been horrible, and she had been despondent as she strove to resolve them, only to drive further wedges between them. Her promise to try to avoid any requests for the pain when they made love had been kept, but the need for it burned in the core of her, and she could no longer control the urges.

It broke her heart to watch Jorinda drink herself to oblivion, and she blamed herself. Jorinda hid from her in the bottom of a goblet. At her wits' end, she had gone out to see a man she had met on his stall at the market two passes ago. His charm and friendliness had drawn her to him, and she returned often to his stall to pick over the trinkets he sold. They struck up a friendship of sorts, and he had always been respectful. As the bitterness with Jorinda escalated, she had confided in him, told him things had turned awry, and he had offered her a sympathetic ear at any time. After a few meetings, he told her his address.

On the first night she had visited his house, she had intended nothing more than to cry on his shoulder about how horrible

Jorinda had been to her throughout the arguments. One thing had led to another, and to her surprise he had kissed her. As she felt the tingle of desire in her sex, she wondered if he might strike her if she lay with him, and she could find some relief from the urges that gnawed at her. If she sated those urges with him, she might be able to repair the damage done to her relationship with Jorinda and would not need to seek the violence in bed with the woman she loved.

He had seemed surprised when she urged him to hurt her but gave her cheek a gentle slap. She begged for more and he hit her several times. The excitement peaked inside her as the pain coursed through her. It scintillated her, far more enjoyable than anything Raolos had ever done to her. To Pettra's disappointment, Jorinda had noticed the reddened cheeks his blows had caused, and the cat was out of the sack. She had resisted the urges for several days, and things remained calmer between her and Jorinda.

Jorinda's consumption of the wine did not lessen, and Pettra grew both anxious and vexed by it. After a time, with no sign Jorinda wished to lie with her, she went to the man again. He had been more prepared for her requests this time and had hurt her much more. At one point he had punched her in the eye. As she walked home and wiped at blood from a cut above her eye, she wondered if the violence had been excessive, but it had aroused her more than she had expected. The next morning, Jorinda noticed her eye and appeared concerned. Her words that Pettra should not pursue the dalliance further fell on ears that would not hear them, and Pettra desired the pain more than ever.

On the third night, she wore the dress Jorinda had paid for. It had aroused Jorinda when they had first come to Vyrrmod, and she felt certain the man would also find it irresistible. He had, but the violence escalated beyond anything she had been prepared for. He took her into his bedroom, called her repulsive names, told her she dressed like a courtesan. He slapped her so hard, he knocked her across the room. For the first time, the pain did not arouse her, but he pulled her from the floor by her hair and threw her onto the bed like a sack of tubers. After he rolled her onto her stomach, he tugged the dress from her, pulled her arms behind her, and bound them with something. She tried to protest, but he punched her in the arm and ordered her to be silent.

He pulled her around and sat her on the edge of the bed as he took his trousers off, shoved his manhood into her mouth, and made her stimulate him until he shot his juices down her throat. The bitter, salty taste repulsed her, but he forced her to swallow it.

She cried and said she wanted to leave, but he wadded some cloth into her mouth and bound it in place with another strip of cloth. After he bound her ankles, he pushed her onto the floor where she landed hard and banged her head. For a time, she lay there alone, frightened and in tears. She struggled against the bonds but could not free her wrists.

When he returned, he had removed his clothes, and he pleasured himself above her until he shot his juices over her body. On the floor, she wished he would let her leave, but when he returned a second time, he had one more humiliation to inflict on her. He dragged her to the bed and made her kneel, pushed her face down onto the bed, pulled her buttocks apart, then pushed his manhood into her rear passage. Her muffled screams at the agony that seared through her did not stop him as he pounded into her, and he only pulled himself away when he had emptied himself once again into her. The act broke her. Her tears stopped. She had journeyed beyond tears, and rational thought escaped her for a time.

He pushed her to the floor and collapsed on the bed. She lay there all night, frightened, despondent, distraught, and certain she had come to her ruin. If only Jorinda would come, kill him, and rescue her before he slit her throat. No salvation came. When he awoke, he unbound her and asked her if she had enjoyed it, and she nodded, desperate not to anger him. She pulled her dress on, and he followed her to the door. "Come back soon." As she left, he kissed her on the cheek as though the night had been no more than a few pleasant hours between two friends.

Her legs were sore and stiff and would not run to her house when she begged them to. She fetched up at the corner of his street. The sun peeped above the eastern city skyline as she reached her front door. Pettra hoped Jorinda would care for her and give her the chance to apologise. She would never again beg for pain during lovemaking. Jorinda had been right; the dangers were immense, and the night had gone far, far beyond anything Pettra had wished for. Worse, he had believed she craved the extreme brutality he had visited upon her. How could anybody enjoy such terrible punishment?

Jorinda appeared concerned at first, then devastated Pettra with news of her plans to leave. Pettra would be alone the morning after she had endured the worst night of her entire life. What had she done? Her desire for pain had almost cost her life and had driven away the woman she loved, left her alone, battered, and with no prospects. Jorinda had urged her to return to Raolos. That would humiliate her almost as much as the treatment at the hands of the market stall man.

Jorinda left as Pettra pretended to sleep. She had no strength left to attempt to detain her lover and felt an emptiness in her heart she had never known before. Although she had told Jorinda she hated her, she did not. Despite Jorinda's constant insistence to the contrary, Pettra loved the younger woman. For much of the day and the night that followed, Pettra slept. Jorinda did not return, though Pettra ached for her to reappear in the bedroom. Each time she heard a sound, she raised her head from the pillow, hopeful Jorinda returned, but her hopes were dashed every time.

The next day, she did not leave the bed other than to relieve herself. She cried enough tears to refill the Torr Sea if somebody had drained it beforehand, and she cursed herself and the dice she had rolled. The woman she loved had left, she suffered terrible pain, and she found blood on the bedsheet. It seemed possible the man had damaged something inside her when he had violated her in so repulsive a manner.

On the second morning after Jorinda had left, Pettra heard a knock at the door. Jorinda had returned. She descended the stairs in agony and tried to call out, to tell Jorinda she would reach the door soon. Nothing but a croak emerged from her lips. Another knock echoed through the lobby before she reached the locked door at last. She fell to the ground in tears—she had left her key in the bedroom. Another knock came, and she croaked, "I must bring the key. Please wait. Do not leave."

"I will wait."

The deep voice had not been Jorinda's. Could it be the man from the market? It did not sound like him, but fear gripped her and constricted her chest, her breath trapped in her lungs. "Who is it?"

"A courier. I bring a letter from Corelle."

Jorinda had scribed her a letter. "One moment." Pettra pulled herself up the stairs, grabbed the key, and returned to the lobby where she pulled the door open.

The man stood and stared at her, then turned away. She wore no clothes, and she had not realised it. "Are you all right?" Those marks—"

"I am fine. You have a letter from Corelle?"

"That I do not. I have a letter for Corelle. This is her home?"

She must have misheard him, or he had played some cruel jest on her. Tears sprang again to her eyes. "That it is." She held out her hand for the letter, he placed it on her palm, and she pushed the door closed. Slow, dejected, she dragged herself back up to the bedroom. She fell onto the bed, broken and wracked by sobs. After some time, she studied the letter. Wilash had sent it, and she tore the seal and opened it. Her horror intensified as she read each line.

Klordia had been killed. She had not come home from work one night, and despite extensive searches she could not be found. They found her naked body dumped at the door of the Bailiff's Offices at first light, her throat slit in the way Jorinda had slit throats in the Guild. Wilash exhorted Jorinda, or Corelle as he called her in the letter, to return to Dur and assist him to find the killers and dispense justice. The slit throat had been intended as a message, Wilash suggested, although Pettra could not imagine what the message could be.

Raolos appeared ready to turn a blind eye to Jorinda's presence in Dur as long as he did not see her, and she used discretion in any justice she dispensed. Pettra gasped. The "justice" Wilash sought was death. He had summoned Jorinda back to Dur to kill for him, to avenge Klordia. Pettra had never met Klordia, but she had heard stories of her. Jorinda had never liked her, it seemed. Wilash, however, had been a good friend to Jorinda, and to her first lover, before Deineike, and had Jorinda been here to read the letter, Pettra thought she would return to Dur to help her friend.

She dropped the awful letter, went to the privy to relieve herself, and gazed at herself in the reflecting glass. Black and purple bruises covered her battered body. Angry red strips on her face, wrists and ankles showed where he had bound her. When she turned, blood caked the backs of her thighs and dripped from her rear passage. The man had damaged something, she felt more certain than ever.

Scribing tools stood on the cabinet she carried the letter to, and she read it again. Raolos had been right. Jorinda would always be a killer. She had abandoned Pettra so she could kill the Bailiff, and Wilash had scribed a letter to implore her to kill on his behalf. Death followed Jorinda wherever she went. Death pursued her and begged her to be its companion across land and water, and she loved it, though she would never love Pettra. She had gone, driven away by desires Pettra could not control and that had brought her terrible injuries. Pettra picked up the scribing tool and scribed on the parch under Wilash's signature, "J. I love you. P." Then she added the address of the market stall man. At the bottom of the parch, she scribed, "I hope R can forgive me."

Pettra left the letter on the cabinet and forced her battered body out to the landing. Death followed Jorinda, and more awaited. She climbed, unsteady, onto the flat rail of the balustrade, then raised her arms out from her sides and leaned forward. The tiles of the lobby floor rushed up to meet her.

CHAPTER 12
CORELLE

orelle reined her horse to a halt at the outskirts of Yantogi. She had spent two nights in inns and had not pushed the horse too hard. Early on the morning of the third day, she had set out on the last part of the journey. The city spread out before her in the mid-morning sunshine, large and radiant in the hot sun, most of its buildings built from the same pale-coloured bricks as in Arkkyd. She kicked the horse forward and rode toward the centre of the city. She imagined she would find Undilk at the local version of the Portreeve's Offices. She did not know what the title of the Portreeve's equivalent might be here. It had never occurred to her to find out, and they had not had any cause to visit him in Arkkyd. Since Undilk served as an Upholder, Corelle guessed he worked from some central and important building.

Before she embarked on her search for Undilk, she found an inn and rented a room for the night. She stabled the horse and left her pack in a trunk in her room. With both of Wilash's daggers tucked in the waistband of her trousers, she went back to the street. Despite her reasonable grasp of the Vyrrmod language, she received nothing but blank stares in response to her requests for directions to the city square. Mayhap the city had not been built around a central square like cities in Dur. Questions about where the Upholders could be found yielded better results. Not long after the midday, she entered a large, impressive building, inside which a woman sat at a desk in the entrance lobby.

"Good day to you." The woman spoke in Vyrrmod as she glanced up at Corelle.

"And to you. I seek Undilk."

The woman nodded. "May I ask with what *akhtinta*?"

Corelle did not understand the word "akhtinta" but imagined the woman had asked why Corelle wanted to see Undilk. "Friend." She had confidence in the word.

"Your name?"

"Corelle." The name would mean nothing to Undilk, and he would not recognise her as a friend. She could not, however, call herself Rakulaj, and there seemed to be no alternative to her own name.

The woman said something Corelle did not understand, but she gestured to some chairs nearby, so Corelle sat on one of them and waited to see what would turn. The woman stood, opened a door behind her, spoke in hushed tones to some unseen person beyond, then sat behind the desk again and smiled at Corelle.

Time passed, and Corelle wondered whether her lack of ability in the language had resulted in some confusion that meant the woman had not sent for Undilk at all, but as she considered another approach to the woman, a man appeared from the door behind her desk. He had the usual Vyrrmod dark skin, a tall man with black hair cropped close to his skull. His remarkable features appeared as though they had been chiselled from some dark rock. He spoke to the woman, and she pointed to Corelle. He approached, a quizzical expression on his face. "You are Corelle?"

Rather than trust to her Vyrrmod, she handed him the button.

He glanced at it and nodded his head before he handed it back to her. "You are a friend of Rakulaj?"

"That I am." She nodded in support of words she did not quite trust.

"How can I help you?"

"Speak in private?" She hoped she had asked the right question. Other ears should not hear what she wished to know.

"Ah." He nodded. "Come." He led her across the lobby and through a door into a small room. "Private." His smile bonded them in an as-yet unknown conspiracy.

"I seek Glailam. Bailiff of Dur." Again, she hoped she had said what she intended to.

"I know of him. Why do you seek him?"

"Friend." Corelle forced a smile to her face. "From Dur." He need not know Glailam would die if she met him.

He stared at her and seemed to wrestle with something he saw or suspected. "You are Corelle of Dur?"

She bit at her lower lip. Had she not said as much already? "That I am."

"We know of you. Rakulaj"—another word she did not understand; it sounded like *hyarget*—"you." What had been the word she had missed? Loves? Hates? Desires? Her blank expression must have told him she had not understood. "Respect is due." He had spoken in shaky Dur.

She smiled. "Respect is due."

He held up a hand. "You are known. I am nobody."

The strange reply might mean something to the people of Vyrrmod, but not to her. "Glailam?"

"Yes. Tonight, here." Had he attempted to keep his Vyrrmod simple so she could understand? He had failed, unless Glailam would, in truth, be at the office tonight.

"Glailam here tonight?" She pointed to the floor.

"No." He laughed as he used the unfamiliar negative, as all people of Vyrrmod did. "You. Me. Here tonight."

Had he asked her to lie with him? That could not be what he meant. He must wish to meet her here tonight. She pointed to him, then to herself, then to the floor.

"Yes. Tonight."

"When?"

"Tonight." Another smile.

Corelle doubted she had the patience to pin him down to a more precise hour, so she decided to sit on the chair in the lobby until he came for her and outlined whatever plan he had. She nodded her agreement.

"Good." He opened the door and held it for her as she re-entered the lobby. "Later, here." He walked toward the desk and returned through the door he had appeared from.

She sat on the same chair, and the woman glanced up at her. "Do you need help?"

"I wait for Undilk."

"He has left." She seemed confused.

"We have arranged a further meeting later."

The woman nodded and carried on with whatever she had been about before. Corelle had spent many hours motionless as she waited and watched nothing happen in preparation for her gests in Zhanghar. The wait today would be no hardship as she had a chair and had no need to lie in mud or squat in a shop doorway in bitter, cold winds.

The hours passed. The shadows in the lobby changed as the sun crossed the high window above and behind her. She watched the last of the sun fight to remain in one low corner of the lobby, then it had gone, and the soft shadow light that comes to any space when the sun has left for the day bathed the lobby. Undilk did not reappear, and still Corelle sat motionless on the chair. From time to time somebody entered the lobby and spoke with the woman. Some of them sat near Corelle until some other person came and took them away to other parts of the building. She watched them leave later, sometimes shown back to the lobby by the person who had collected them, sometimes alone. Some took parch away with them. Corelle did not listen to their conversations; they were not her business.

The woman placed some parch in a drawer in her desk and tidied the scribing tools on the desk surface. She appeared ready to leave for the night, and Corelle wondered if the woman might shoo her out of the lobby. Corelle worried the Offices might close as the woman left, but she did not glance Corelle's way when at last she stood and went through the door behind her. Moments later, an older man came out of the door and sat behind the desk. He wore the same olive-green tunic Undilk had worn, no doubt the uniform of the Upholders. He inclined his head toward Corelle but did not speak to her. She smiled at him.

An hour after the woman had left, Undilk emerged from the door behind the other man. The men spoke for a moment, then Undilk approached her. "You are ready?"

She nodded and followed him out of the building. The hour had grown later than she had realised as she sat in the lobby. Corelle followed him, cautious, as he walked through the streets of the city, and she peered around to ensure they had not been followed. Though she had no reason not to trust Undilk, her natural sense of caution did not permit her to relax.

When a large tavern appeared ahead, Undilk stopped and turned to her. "What will happen next?"

Corelle did not feel she could place him in an awkward position where he might need to respond to an unpleasant situation. Rakulaj had sent her to him, though he had known what she intended, so she rolled the dice and decided to tell him the truth. "I will challenge him."

He nodded, and a serious expression sprang to his face. "He has wronged you?"

"He and another killed someone I love." Her grasp of his language would not permit a more detailed explanation.

"A worthy challenge. Come."

He led her into the busy tavern. Corelle made no attempt to approach the counter or buy drinks. She checked her waistband for both of Wilash's daggers and pushed through the crowd behind Undilk. He stopped next to two burly men, both too pale-skinned to be Vyrrmod folk. Undilk did not look at Corelle, and she tried to imagine what would happen next. A great commotion broke out ahead of her, so she pressed on through the crowd.

Several men sat around a large table. Each of them had coin on the table before them and cards in their hands. Other cards lay on the table. It seemed they played some form of game for coin. Rakulaj had mentioned Glailam often gambled in a tavern, and she found him easy to pick out, his pale skin out of place among the darker skinned Vyrrmod players. She moved closer and observed. A large stack of coin sat on the table in front of him, but she could not discern whether he had enjoyed good fortune or played with an inordinate amount of coin every night. He laughed and chatted with the other players and his grasp of Vyrrmod appeared well advanced compared to her own.

Corelle saw no others who might be Durfolk other than Glailam and the two she had first noticed, and she guessed they must be Glailam's guards. Undilk still stood beside them and now watched her with intense interest. She wondered if the guards would be a complication, but she had not come here for them, so she returned her attention to the former Bailiff. He lost a hand, a large sum of coin, but he seemed unconcerned and laughed as the winner scooped the coin from the centre of the table. Corelle had no idea what game they played. She knew nothing of card games, and they did not interest her, since they relied too much on chance. Since she had joined the Guild, she always focused on the highest probability of a favourable outcome, and card games offered none of the assurance she preferred.

She controlled her breaths and rehearsed the gest in her head. It would be simple and quick, and she would leave afterward without delay. The less attention she attracted after she had killed in so public a place, the better. The number of witnesses discomforted her, but Rakulaj and Undilk had convinced her the challenge ensured she could kill without any fear of being hanged. In truth, as long as Glailam died, her own fate mattered little to her.

Several of the players stood from the table among jeers and laughter. Some drifted away, but they left their coin at their places. It seemed they had taken a break. The time had come. Glailam would not leave the table alive.

She pushed past a small group of men and stood next to Glailam. Deep in a conversation with the man next to him, he did not notice her as she slid both daggers into her hands and held them tight against her legs.

She called his name, soft but confident. "Glailam." He half-turned toward her, though he still spoke to his neighbour. "Glailam." She said it again, louder.

He turned in his chair and gazed at her, a curious expression on his face. "Do I know you?" He spoke Vyrrmod.

"I have a gift for you." She replied in Dur, and she placed the dagger from her left hand on the table before him. A silence fell around her and spread through the room like a wave that crashed, soundless, onto the shoreline. In the periphery of her vision, every head turned toward the table.

"What is it?" He glanced down at it. He had switched to Dur to her relief. Part of the deception required that few of the patrons understood their conversation.

"Pick it up and see." A shout came from behind her. She ignored it.

He glanced at her and gave a nervous laugh. Did he know about the challenge? He moved a hand toward it and the noise of a commotion built behind her. He glanced up and tried to peer around her as if to see what turned.

She pressed on. "Pick it up. It is a gift from Styrrach."

At last, he lifted it from the table and stared at it in apparent confusion. "I do not understand." He looked up at her. "What is it?"

"It is your ruin. My name is Corelle, and this is for Deineike." Her other dagger slashed across his throat, and his blood spurted out onto the table. Men jumped back in shock and surprise. He stared at her in fury as his life left him, and he slid to the floor beneath the table. She snatched the other dagger up from the table where he had dropped it and bent down. She used his tunic to wipe the blood from the dagger that had killed him, then leaned forward to whisper to his already dead body, "Tell Styrrach I hate him."

When Corelle stood and turned, Glailam's guards bristled before her, anger in their eyes. Undilk, along with some other men, stood between them and Corelle and appeared to hold the guards back. The challenge seemed genuine; nobody clamoured for her to be hanged, and they seemed to protect her from Glailam's vengeful guards.

One of the men shouted at her in Dur. "Corelle, you worthless jade. You are a coward. You tricked him."

"He should have been more aware of the customs of this land." Her eyes narrowed as she spat her reply.

"I challenge you." He screamed the challenge at her in Dur, then switched to Vyrrmod. "I will challenge her." The room fell deathly quiet again. Undilk glanced at her, and she shrugged, unconcerned. He moved aside, and the guard approached the table.

He reached behind him and pulled out a long dagger with a serrated blade. The fearsome weapon had been designed to intimidate first, then kill those it did not intimidate with one swift blow.

The blade had been designed as a brawler's weapon, not for use in the stealthy work Corelle excelled in. Corelle smiled at it, then stared into the man's eyes. "Nice dagger."

"I will use it to split you from your crotch to your neck. I will carve you into little pieces when you are dead. You will have no Pyre."

She shrugged. "Do you plan to kill me with the dagger or talk me to death?"

He snarled at her and lowered the dagger to the table with great drama. The instant it touched the table, her hand shot out and snatched it from his fingers. She drove it upward into the underside of his chin and gave it a vicious twist as she pressed it deeper into his head. A quizzical look came into his eyes, and she stood on the tips of her toes to whisper in his ear. "Be careful who you challenge."

He sank to his knees as absolute silence settled on the room. He collapsed forward, hit the table, and scattered the coin around the floor. Somebody fetched up and the bilious smell assailed Corelle's nostrils. She glanced at Undilk, who stared at her open-mouthed. Glailam's other guard glared at her, and she raised her eyebrows at him in a clear question.

He hesitated and she stepped closer to him. She spoke in Dur again. "I imagine there is much coin in his home. If you wish, you can take it all, or I can kill you here. All I need is your decision." He gave her another hateful stare, then wheeled and pushed through the crowd until she lost sight of him.

The crowd found its voice, and the babble of excited talk rose to fever pitch. Undilk pulled at the sleeve of her tunic. "You made a good challenge. Respect is due." He had slipped into Dur. "Leave now, I suggest."

She inclined her head. "My thanks." Corelle pushed her way through the crowd. Lest the other guard had made the wrong decision, she kept a watchful eye around herself.

People grabbed at her and shouted things she did not understand, but she pressed on through the crowd until she saw the door. Once outside, she moved away from the tavern as fast as she could. Darkness had cloaked the city while she had watched the game and awaited her chance, and she melted into the shadows as she made her way back to her inn. Splatters of blood covered her, but she avoided the few people she saw. She had a room at the rear of the inn on the ground floor, and she hurried through the rear door and into her room.

Once in her room, she gave in to the tension that coursed through her. She collapsed to the floor with her head in her hands. Deineike had been avenged, and Glailam and Styrrach had both been killed. Nothing more remained to live for. She pulled the daggers from her trousers and held them in her hands. The one that had killed Glailam still had a great deal of his blood on its blade and handle, which did not satisfy the perfectionist in her. She rose and took some time to clean it in the water bowl. She used one of the inn's cloths, then dropped the cloth into the blood-red water and sat on the bed with both daggers in her hands.

Pettra's face came to her mind; not the peaceful, pretty woman Corelle had first met at Raolos's house, but the battered, bruised face she had left behind in Arkkyd. Guilt washed over her, and she hoped Pettra had taken her advice and left for Dur. If she had not, she might still need help, so horrific had her injuries been from whatever the man had done to her that night. Corelle sighed and decided to return to Arkkyd the next day and ensure Pettra had either gone or needed no further help with her wounds. She lay back and closed her eyes, and she watched blood spurt from Glailam's neck in her mind's eye. The anger faded from his eyes as his life pumped out of him over the table.

As sleep took her, she muttered, "I hate you both."

CHAPTER 13
KRAGE

Krage reined his horse to a stop and gazed at the sign before him. Dust caked him, and every bone and muscle in his body ached. How he smelled, he could only guess. The others stopped beside him.

Ifor turned to Krage. "What does it say?"

"You cannot read?"

"That I cannot."

Krage heaved a large sigh. "My friend, it says 'Estway Farm.'"

Krage had not killed the woman who charged him ten regals for each of her horses, then doubtless bought three more from Old Palder for eight or less. They had ridden south-east and stopped at any town or village with an inn, and where locals said they could not reach another that day. Krage refused to spend another night on the ground after that first dreadful one.

The path became a road, and the road became wider. They passed ever larger numbers of travellers, and at long last they reached Dur City. Krage thought the ride had taken a tenday, and they had passed through the edges of the Forest of Dur, staggered by the size of the mighty Ortwood trees. The trees had been so tall,

Krage thought they must scratch the clouds above, and so wide that to walk around one took so many steps, he lost count. From the far side of the tree, he could not see any of his four guards, even if they lined up their horses head-to-tail.

They lingered in Dur City for four days. Krage spent an hour in a tub on the first night, called non-stop for more hot water, and still felt he had not washed all the dust of the journey from himself. They all drank more tankards of ale that night than any of them could remember, and the next day they all paid a terrible price for the over-indulgence.

Dur City had been larger than he had expected. It had been built in a terrible position; so hard to reach, he could see no reason anybody would try. There seemed no reason for it to be a city in truth. He suspected its people had been born there and never left, for few enough of the population could have come from other cities. They would have to trek for day after endless day across the dusty, soulless Eastlands to reach it.

The city boasted a substantial population, and the industry to support the city all lay in the city itself. No trade could move into or out of the city without a journey that would render any profit non-existent relative to the cost and effort involved in the trans-portation of the goods. Small wonder the city had never been part of Styrrach's organisation.

After four days, they resumed their ride south. The road became narrower, and the road became a path, and still no end could be seen. On a clear day, they could see Mount Belram far off in the distance, but to Krage's eyes, it never came any closer, and he despaired. Once again, it seemed Corelle had killed him without need of her deadly art. He believed he would fall from his horse, dead from old age, long ere they reached Estway Farm. The remote location had been a motivation for its purchase, but Krage had not appreciated how far it stood from anywhere. He imagined the journey would have been easier from Ort, and he wished he had not decided to avoid the town. He had acted out of concern for his life, but the path to the farm from the north seemed determined to claim it anyway.

They had turned west at a town called Solgarn after they had been informed the town of Yerrsun, where Krage knew the farm to be located, lay little more than two days' ride away. Before they arrived in Yerrsun, Krage had seen the sign that announced their arrival at the entrance to Estway Farm and had stopped, jubilant. At last, the arduous journey had ended. Krage had no idea how long it had taken them to reach the farm. He had lost count soon after they left Dur City.

The large farmhouse had a sizeable barn at the rear. It came as no surprise to find the farm wore an air of abandonment. No animals could be seen, and no crops grew. Twilight had fallen, and Krage did not know how much further Yerrsun might be, so they stabled the horses in the barn, entered the house, and made ancient cots ready to sleep in.

The next day, he sent one of his men into town to arrange some provisions. They could not find a cart, and Krage instructed the man to be discreet, but to find someone who would bring provisions sufficient for a week out to the farm. By then, he hoped others would reach the farm and they could decide what to do.

The man returned late in the day. He had found a woman prepared to bring food out to them. The town lay almost half a day's ride away, so it would take a merchant a full day to drive a cart out and back. It disappointed Krage the town lay so far away, although it did not surprise him. Privacy mattered to the Guild.

The next day, Krage sent Mauvlin into the town to see the Portreeve and ask him to pay a visit to them at the farm. Krage would not risk a trip to the town if he could avoid it. The lives of his guards could be expended; his own could not. The Portreeve might be happy to keep them informed of strangers or threats in the town, in exchange for coin. Krage guessed coin would buy anything in these lands, little more than a destitute cousin to the Dur he knew, west of the River Alc.

As it turned, the Portreeve, Rognakk, had been associated with the former Portreeve, Carshan, whom Glailam had moved to Torric. Rognakk welcomed them and agreed to serve Krage as desired, and the Portreeve left the farm with far more coin in his pouch than when he arrived.

Krage settled into the humdrum of daily life at the farm, ever wary. He waited for others to arrive, and the days blurred together.

CHAPTER 14
CORELLE

Corelle left Yantogi the morning after she had killed Glailam. As she rode north, she thought back to the day she had entered Orgel's shop, a carefree loner, unconcerned about the problems of Dur, a girl who knew nothing of lands beyond Dur's shores and believed murder did not exist. How much she had changed in… how long? She tried to calculate. She thought she was seventeen years when she met Arella. Two years later, Arella was dead. No, three years. She had forgotten they had spent almost a year in Ryl and Zhanghar before she joined the Guild.

Six passes after she had killed Arella, she had met Deineike and they had travelled together for more than a year, always in the shadow of Styrrach's vengeance. At the end of that time, Deineike also lost her life. Two women dead because of her in the space of little more than two years. An inconceivable reality. She was now twenty-two years and had the weight of so many deaths on her conscience. Not the least of those deaths were Arella and Deineike, both dead because they had loved her. Inconceivable and unbearable.

One night out from Arkkyd, in her cups, she had been asked by the innkeep to return to her room when she had stumbled and fallen in the tavernroom. She had scattered the tankards of three men from their table and had attempted to offer them coin to replace the ale, but between her limited grasp of the language and her inebriation, she had been unable to make herself understood. She had become frustrated, and one of the men had yelled something at her. She had reached for the dagger in her boot, but hands had pulled her to her feet, held her upright, and the moment passed.

Corelle had staggered back to her room and collapsed onto the bed as tears again poured from her eyes. She had pulled out the dagger and pressed it against her throat, despondent beyond reason, but had hesitated when she thought of Pettra. The wine had taken her into a deep sleep, and she woke with the dagger beside her on the bed and her own vomit down her tunic.

Coated in dust from the ride north, her body ached from the journey. Even this far into the day, her head still ached from last night's drink. Her shock after she killed Glailam and his guard, and the terrible state of Pettra when she had returned to the house the morning Corelle had left for Yantogi, crushed her spirit as her horse trudged toward Arkkyd. Soon after the midday, Corelle returned the horse and tack to the stable in Arkkyd and hoisted her pack over her shoulder.

Dejected, she trudged toward the house. Rivulets of sweat trickled through the dust on her face and arms, and the heat stole the breath from her lungs. The door remained locked, and a smell crept from the house. Death had been her constant companion for years, and she recognised its vile stench as soon as it assailed her nostrils. She scrabbled in her pack for the key and opened the door.

"Oh, Pettra." Corelle closed the door behind her and whispered in sadness and horror. Pettra's body lay on the lobby floor, surrounded by a pool of dried blood. Flies buzzed around her, and her head lay twisted to one side at a gruesome angle, her arms and legs splayed in unnatural positions. The marks and bruises from the night of violence stood out against her grey flesh. Pettra always wore her hair tidy and coiffed, but now blood matted it, and it lay strewn about her face and the open eyes that stared at Corelle, full of accusations. Corelle slid down the door and sat on the floor with her head in her hands. Tears gushed from her, and she screamed in anger.

She lost track of how long she sat there and cried. Another woman had told Corelle she loved her, and another woman had died as a result. Had Pettra fallen, or had she been thrown to her death? Had she become so despondent when Corelle had abandoned her, she had jumped from the upper floor? The man who had done so much damage to her might have killed her, as Corelle had warned. The only person who could tell the truth of the matter lay dead nearby, and Corelle accepted full blame for her death. She had destroyed Pettra's life, and now it had ended. "I hate you." This time, she whispered to herself.

Outside, it grew dark, and Corelle dragged herself to her feet and climbed the stairs, weary and miserable beyond her capacity to find words for. She reached the bedroom and lit the lantern. A parch lay on the cabinet, and she picked it up and read it. She cried aloud again, slumped to the floor, and leaned back against the bed. Yet another death on her account, Klordia gone and Wilash devastated.

Corelle wept bitter tears, filled with her hatred of herself. Like that hatred, the tears came and came and seemed reluctant to ever cease. Why had she been born? All she had brought into this life had been horror, death, and misery. Nobody who met her emerged unscathed from the encounter; either dead, or their life turned so awry it could never be pieced back together again. Resentful of all she had become, she contemplated the fact that if she had made good on her vow after she had killed Arella in Zhanghar, Deineike,

Pettra, and now Klordia might still be alive. Corelle should die now, before another woman had the opportunity to seal her doom, to say those terrible three words that would write her irrevocable fate.

Why had she abandoned Pettra in her most desperate hour of need? Corelle accepted the truth; no worse monster than her ever existed, and she wandered out to the landing, morose, inconsolable. She gazed down on Pettra's broken body, and a tear splashed onto the rail of the balustrade. Pettra's notes at the bottom of the letter suggested she had jumped, desolate and alone, rather than been killed. Even in the darkness of her final moments, she had scribed those terrible three words, and they had brought her ruin. Corelle whispered down the staircase to Pettra, "I am sorry," and she hoped the words would somehow seep beneath the door of the house and come to the ears of Deineike, Arella, Klordia, Wilash, Raolos; anyone she had ever wronged.

Why had Pettra scribed an address on the bottom of the parch? Corelle's brow knit as she pondered the significance of the address. Might it be the address of the man who had harmed her? Could it be Pettra's plea for vengeance from wherever she had travelled to afterward? Corelle had left Arkkyd to exact retribution for Deineike and returned to find a request from Wilash for her aid in vengeance for Klordia. Did Pettra also ask her for revenge? Could this be all Corelle had become? The hopes and dreams of the little girl who stepped from the carriage each night to be swept onto the dance floor by a beautiful blonde woman, all distilled into a creature who existed only to kill without mercy, to exact revenge or punish some transgression on others' behalf?

She had forgotten the address, so she returned to the parch and studied it again. She had walked that street many times in the last few passes. Would she find answers there? Might she discover some clue as to what had passed on the night Pettra did not return home, or what had taken place while Corelle had been away?

Another thought came to her. She owed it to Raolos and Raopul to let them know Pettra had died, and to pass on to Raolos Pettra's last plea for forgiveness. Corelle's throat caught as she choked on the thought of the grief the news would bring to them. They deserved to know, and only she could tell them, harbinger of doom in all its guises, and she vowed to scribe a letter to them. She would visit the address Pettra had scribed first and seek answers that might help her break this terrible news to Raolos and his son.

The issue of Wilash's request remained. Should she abandon him and his desire for vengeance, or should she sail for Dur and kill again in the endless cycle of vengeance all who touched her had need of at some point? Why had somebody framed Klordia's death as though it had been at Corelle's hand? There could be only one explanation. The Guild sent a message; some of them remained and wished her dead. They were not alone in that wish. She wished it also. Wilash too, she imagined.

At that, she wiped the tears from her eyes. She would go to the address Pettra had left and determine what she could, then she would sail for Dur. Wilash could break the terrible news to Raolos. If she could help Wilash, she would. If she died as she provided that help, so much the better. The fewer people who had the opportunity to meet her at some point in the future, the better. They would be spared a terrible fate.

She opened Pettra's trunk, took her coin pouch from it, and added its contents to the coin in her own pack. She pulled out the bloodied tunic she had worn when she struck down Glailam and dropped it on the floor, then folded Wilash's letter and placed it in the pack. Nothing remained in the house she wished to take other than Deineike's sketches, but as she noticed Pettra's discarded dress beside the bed, she picked it up. Blood spattered it, and the rear of the bodice had been torn, some of the hooks lost as though it had been ripped from her body at some stage of the events that had led to her injuries.

Corelle dropped it on the bed and noticed more bloodstains on the bedsheet. What had turned for Pettra that night? She must know. On a whim, she pulled her trousers and tunic off and pushed them into her pack before she pulled Pettra's dress on. Pettra had been taller than her, her breasts smaller. Corelle could not quite fasten the damaged bodice and only managed to close enough hooks that it would not slide down and expose her. The tight skirt restricted her movement, and she could not understand how Pettra had moved in it at all. Pettra's hips had been fuller than Corelle's, but the dress remained tight enough to require smaller steps than she would take otherwise. The dress smelled of the fragrance Pettra favoured, and tears came again to Corelle's eyes as she breathed in the dead woman's scent.

She gathered up Deineike's sketches, thrust them into her pack, and left the house. She locked the door behind her and dropped the key on the short path that led to the street. Despite the constraints of the dress, she walked as fast as she could, although she reasoned she could never wear so restrictive a garment for any length of time and would change back into her trousers at the first opportunity. Why had she donned the dress at all, unless it had been guilt, or some wish to retain some trace of Pettra?

Corelle made use of the cover of the darkness as she walked with more caution down the street Pettra had pointed her to from wherever she had travelled to afterward. At last, she stood before a small one-storey house. Paint peeled from the windows and door, and the house had an air of poor maintenance. Without hesitation, she rapped on the door with her knuckles. She heard movement inside before the door opened and spilled lantern light onto her.

The man who stood there seemed familiar. Tall and slender, he had short, jet-black hair and a crooked nose, as though it might have been broken at some time. "Can I help you?"

"Do you know Pettra?"

"I do. A lovely woman. You are a friend of hers?"

"I used to be."

"I have not seen her for some days. Is she well?"

The conversation in his language had been simple enough for Corelle to understand and respond to this point. "You killed her." The accusation might not be true, but she decided to see how he reacted to the news.

He stood in silence, to all appearances stunned by the charge, and did not respond for many moments. "That is her dress."

"That it is. Her blood is on it, spilled by you." Corelle's lips peeled back from her teeth in an involuntary snarl. There could be no question; this had been the man Pettra had visited that night. How else would he recognise the dress?

"No, no. Everything I did, she requested. Who are you?" He seemed to recover his composure. It surprised Corelle he only now wondered who she might be. His claim to innocence did not sit well with her. Pettra had asked him to hurt her doubtless, but Corelle guessed he had gone far beyond anything she desired into a realm of pain that had shattered her sufficient for her to take her own life. All that turned that night had turned at his hand, and it had inflicted terrible hurt on Pettra. Corelle had poured oil on the flame of Pettra's agony when she had left her to pursue her own agenda, and it had cost Pettra all her tomorrows.

Incensed, she pushed the man backward. Though he stood far taller than her, she caught him unawares and he stumbled backward two steps. She followed him and slammed the door behind her.

"What are you about?" He gave a panicked shout as she bent to her boot. Her blade came up in one deadly motion from boot to neck, and he tried to scream, but his life pumped out of him onto Pettra's dress too fast as the familiar vermilion ribbon opened across his throat. With detached indifference, Corelle watched as he fell to his knees and reached toward her as if he begged for help from the woman who had wrought his ruin. He fell sideways, and a pool of blood spread around his head. Corelle cleaned her blade on his trousers. His blood now soaked the dress, mingled with Pettra's, and Corelle pulled it from her and dropped it over his body. She pulled trousers and a tunic from her pack and wandered through his house once she had dressed again.

Unlike the exterior, he kept the inside of his home neat and clean, and she found no evidence of whatever he had done to Pettra that night. Corelle could no longer remain in Vyrrmod. Nothing would connect her to the death of the man, but Pettra had also died, and the authorities would be certain to seek her in connection with that death. She washed the blood from her face and arms at his basin. Satisfied she would draw no attention to herself, she stared at her face in the reflecting glass. A hint of her youth stared back at her, but lines around her eyes and mouth belied her twenty-two years, and flecks of grey could already be seen in her dark brown hair. A killer's remorseless eyes stared back at her, and behind them a mind that loathed her, filled with self-recrimination. She could take somebody's life with no regret, but she regretted she lived.

In an outburst of rage, she smashed the reflecting glass with the handle of her dagger, and her image shattered into myriad pieces, as broken and destroyed as Corelle herself. She wheeled, picked up her pack, and left the dead man on his floor. Despondent, she closed the door and walked away in the shadows of a sultry night.

CHAPTER 15
CORELLE

The docks buzzed with activity even at this late hour, as ships sailed with the tides and not the sleep schedules of the citizens of the lands they frequented. Rakulaj's sigil flew on banners at the stern of the first ship Corelle boarded, and she asked for the master. The ship would soon depart for somewhere she had never heard of, but he thought The Merchant's Mistress, moored further along the docks, might sail for Alcmouth.

On a different night, Corelle might have smiled at the ship's name. Tonight, she had no humour in her, and when the Mistress's master confirmed he would sail that night for Alcmouth, she showed him Rakulaj's button and obtained passage in a small, comfortable cabin. The master welcomed her aboard like an old friend; Rakulaj had been true to his word. How long that would last once news of her infamy spread throughout Vyrrmod, she could not guess. She would be long gone by then, and dead, she hoped. She collapsed into the bunk and cried herself to sleep.

Unbearable nightmares assailed her. Pettra fell from a tall tower and shattered into small pieces as she hit the floor. Each piece changed into a gaming card in the air and fell to the ground. Blood covered every card, and they all had, "I love you," scribed on them in Pettra's hand.

"What have you wrought?" Deineike's voice came from behind Corelle, and when she wheeled, Styrrach had Deineike's severed head in his hand. Deineike's head spoke again. "Arella has need of me." Glailam swept Styrrach's head from his shoulders with a sword in the shape of an enormous member. He thrust the member toward her, and Arella appeared before her, impaled on Glailam's manhood. As Corelle wept tears of blood, Klordia rose from Styrrach's corpse.

Klordia spat familiar words at Corelle. "You will bring nothing but darkness to her door, and she will never again know joy if she remains with you." A gash opened in Klordia's throat as soon as she uttered the words. Coins spilled from the wound instead of blood. Klordia reached toward Corelle, and her hands clenched and unclenched. "Are you the monster you appear to be?"

"That I am." Corelle looked down, dejected.

All the faces in the nightmare appeared behind Klordia and spoke in unison. "I love you."

Corelle sat upright in the bunk. Her breaths came in rapid shallow gasps, the nails of her clenched fists dug into her palms, and sweat ran in rivulets down her face. She climbed from the bunk and dipped a cup into the pitcher of water on the vanity cabinet. She guzzled the water and stood stationary in the darkness. The wind whistled through the ropes, nets, and sails above her, and the Torr Sea splashed against the hull of the ship as it ploughed northward through the swell.

She heard voices in the wind, and they cried her transgressions. Had she lost her mind, after all else? Her entire life seemed nothing more than a tragic garment of chaotic making, and that making unravelled more with every corpse that fell at her feet. She had killed so many people, she could not count high enough to reckon them even if she could remember them all. Why had Arella not run away with her from Ryl? They could have fled west to whatever lay beyond Dur where they could have lived a happy life together. The Guild would never have found them, and Corelle's garment making skills would have kept them in some comfort.

Instead, they had sailed to Zhanghar and all that followed. Now she sailed again to Dur, no longer certain who she had become and with a litany of repulsive acts of violence as her legacy. Women who had loved her lay dead behind her like footprints in the sand.

She dressed and went up onto the deck. As she emerged from the door, a mariner shouted a caution from above her. Small lanterns had been affixed to each mast, but darkness covered the deck, and although she did not understand what the man had said, she guessed he had urged her to be careful not to fall in the dark. It would matter little to her if she fell overboard. Life wearied her, and she wearied of death. In her case, one had its hand in the glove of the other, and she could not separate the two.

Corelle sat at the bow of the ship, which had reached deeper water and pitched up and down in dramatic fashion as it crested each wave. Water sprayed up from the bow, and the air smelled of salt. Corelle relished it. It smelled more pleasant than death, and she wondered whether she might become a mariner. At some point, she would speak to the master about it.

She sat embroiled in her misery for some time. The sky lightened, and the sun poked its head over the horizon to her right as it greeted all beneath it on land and sea with the promise of another day. For Corelle, another day of torment and guilt lay ahead, and she could do little enough to change it.

The ship pitched downward at a steep angle, and she slid forward. She felt no fear as the sea drew nearer, but as the ship climbed the next wave, she slid to a halt short of the rail.

"You have not fallen in?" The voice came from behind her, one of the mariners.

"That I have not. If I do, leave me. I will swim to Dur."

"You can swim this well?"

"That I cannot. I cannot swim at all." She let loose a bitter laugh.

The mariner did not return her laugh, and he went about his duties. The sun seemed in a hurry to climb the sky this morning, and she gazed out on a vast expanse of white-capped blue. She could see nothing but water from one horizon to the other. Corelle wondered how far the sea extended. She had never seen any journal that explained what lay far beyond Dur. She believed a few lands might lie to the north, and she knew for certain other lands lay to the south. The east and west remained mysteries to her.

As the sun climbed overhead, she lay on the deck and dozed. A shout woke her with a start, and she sat up to see what had turned. Several of the mariners had gathered at the rail, and Corelle scanned the sea beyond them. The surface of the water boiled, and she used her feet to push herself backward in fear. Without warning, an enormous blue creature appeared, and a plume of water rose from it. The mariners shouted and cheered. Corelle rose with a gasp and wandered over to where they gathered.

One of them turned to her, a huge grin on his face. "Blue giants." He might not have used the actual word "giants," but Corelle had to admit the title would be appropriate. The giant had a long, beak-like head, and its mouth looked as long as the ship. It had an eye behind its mouth, on the side of its head. Corelle had never seen anything like it, and she felt sure it must be the largest creature that could exist anywhere. Had she not seen it with her own eyes, she would not have believed anybody who described the size of the blue giant.

Her mind flew back to a nightmare she had endured once, aboard a ship to Alcmouth with Deineike. Arella's face had adorned an enormous fish, which had slit her throat with its tail. Could the fish in that dream have been one of these giant creatures?

The animal had a large, flat tail that it flicked up and down. The tail splashed enormous quantities of water into the air, then the giant disappeared beneath the water again. Another tail broke the surface beyond where the first creature had been, then flicked down again to send a huge plume of water into the sky. The spectacle enthralled Corelle and took her breath away.

At once, the water near the ship boiled, and one of the giants burst from the water into the air. Corelle took a startled step backward. Could the creature fly also? Most of the giant's body rose out of the water, but it fell back down to the surface with the largest splash of water that could ever have been seen. As the creature fell into the water, a vast wave raced toward the ship, and someone shouted, "Wash inbound."

The wave lifted one side of the ship, and Corelle fell and slid down the deck along with two mariners. She slammed into a mast that knocked the breath from her body with a whoosh. The ship righted itself and rocked from side to side. The two mariners seemed fine, although one of them had sustained a cut to his arm.

The master rushed down to the deck and stood over Corelle as she fought to suck breath into her lungs. "You live?" He spoke perfect Dur but appeared concerned.

"That I do." Her stomach felt tender, and she reasoned she might develop a healthy bruise where she had clattered into the mast.

"This is good news." He extended a hand to pull her to her feet, and she leaned forward with her hands on her thighs as she gasped and sucked air down her throat. "Please hold the rail if the blue giants are near."

The creatures had been called giants, after all else. "They are magnificent." Corelle struggled for breath to form the words.

"Yes, they are, but their games can be dangerous to ships, as you have seen." He had used the Vyrrmod word for "yes", which still sounded wrong in Corelle's ears, and she reminded herself the master did not speak as Durfolk would.

Corelle hungered for more knowledge about the incredible creatures. "Is there a chance they would eat the ship? They are large enough to swallow it whole, I believe."

He laughed. "You might find it hard to believe, but the creatures they eat are smaller than a span."

Corelle gasped, incredulous. "That cannot be. The giants are enormous. To be sated, they must eat more of such creatures than there are lights in the night sky."

"They do. They eat vast numbers of them every day."

"How many of these creatures are there, then?"

"The giants, or their food?"

"The tiny creatures." She could scarce believe what he had told her. It must be a jest he played on those who did not often sail on the deepest seas.

"If you began to count them today, you would not have finished before the sun had burned out and the seas frozen."

Corelle could never hope to grasp the concept. Such vast numbers of creatures lay far beyond any ability of hers to comprehend. In truth, the size of the blue giants had bewildered her. The life of a mariner must be remarkable indeed. "How would I become a mariner?" Her breath had almost returned to normal.

He laughed again. "You have the stomach for it, I see this. You do not fetch up in the roughest seas, and I hear you do not eat the bread." She made a face of disgust that brought more laughter. "I know of no woman who sails the seas. It would not be easy for you to persuade the mariners to accept you."

Such barriers would present no obstacle to a determined woman. Few would believe a woman could become a ruthless killer, yet she could kill the entire crew as they slept and doubted any could prevent her. "If a woman wished to become a mariner, what must she do to accomplish this?"

He gazed at her, his laughter gone, replaced by a serious expression. "Your name is known to us, and respect is due. If all I hear is true, then Corelle of Dur might be the first woman to ever become a mariner. Little enough is required. Some physical strength and common sense, for the most part. Understand the way the sea moves and how we sail upon it, of course."

She nodded. "How does one obtain such knowledge unless one is already a mariner?"

He smiled. "An excellent question. You may have the attributes required, yet it is a hard life. Lengthy periods away from home, poor rations as often as not, the risk you may drown, be ship-wrecked, or die of thirst, becalmed. Poor pay, worse conditions. Rough, vulgar companions for long periods, most of them accom-panied by a dreadful smell. It is not for all."

"I see." He did not make it sound an attractive proposition, although she reasoned it could be no worse than the profession she followed.

"What work do you do?" It seemed he had guessed her thoughts.

She looked away. The giants had moved further from the ship. Their paths had crossed, but they now headed for different destina-tions. Corelle so often headed in unclear directions, she reasoned the life of a mariner must be preferable to that of a murderer. "I am a killer."

He pursed his lips. "Does this employment pay well?"

He thought she jested, it seemed. "That it does not. No home to call my own, no companions, vulgar or otherwise, the risk of death at every turn. Fear and hatred in the eyes of all you encounter. It is not for all."

He lowered his voice. "For some years, a token existed."

"I have travelled under this token. The token's threat came from a man called Styrrach." The master nodded, as though he knew the name. "I killed him."

He drew in a sharp breath. "We carried another to Vyrrmod six or seven passes ago. Glailish his name, I think."

She corrected him. "Glailam. He is now dead."

He stared at her, but his face betrayed no emotion. After some time, he bowed and turned. He walked toward the aft deck but stopped after four paces. He did not turn, but he said, "Become a mariner." He walked on.

The days passed with little variety, but a fresh agony visited Corelle. The longer the ship ploughed through the waves, the more she craved a goblet of wine. If she slept through the day, she woke in a sweat, whether she had endured a nightmare or not. She could not understand the desire that knotted her stomach, but she regretted she had not brought any wine aboard. When she asked the master, he had a small amount available, and he allowed her a goblet once a day, but no more. She did not wish to push for more, but the goblet failed to satisfy her, and her anguish increased.

As she watched the mariners work around the ship, she saw routine in much of what they did. They checked equipment, raised or lowered sails according to the winds. Nothing about their work looked beyond her. She imagined more must be involved whenever they prepared to leave from or arrive at docks, but once they were under way, little changed from day to day unless some unusual weather occurred, such as the storm they had encountered on the voyage to Vyrrmod.

They saw no more of the blue giants, and after a sevenday, Corelle saw a smudge on the horizon ahead that grew until it became the unmistakeable shape of land. One of the mariners confirmed they had almost arrived in Alcmouth. Despite her banishment from Dur, she had returned in fewer than five passes. Although she doubted she could help Wilash track down Klordia's killers, she would do all she could. News must also be delivered to Raolos that would be sure to devastate him, although Wilash's letter made it clear the Bailiff would not permit her to meet him.

As the sun sank low in the west, the ship docked in Alcmouth. Pack in hand, she sought out the master. "Respect is due." She gave a bow.

"Respect is due, Corelle of Dur." He matched her bow. "Look to your safety."

Corelle turned to stare at the busy docks. Her safety mattered little to her these days. The master's words should have been addressed to all who had encountered her. For Arella, Deineike, Klordia, and now Pettra, the caution had come too late.

CHAPTER 16
CORELLE

orelle left The Merchant's Mistress behind. Memories of Torric came to her, when she and Deineike had been unable to understand the names on the sterns of the southern ships. These days, she could understand some of the names of Vyrrmod ships. In an ironic twist, she could no longer return to that land for fear she would be hanged. The same restriction applied to Dur, in truth, but she had been allowed to return under specific conditions, and now she stood again on the docks at Alcmouth.

Once she had found accommodation at in inn near the square, she asked for some parch and scribing tools and scribed a letter to Wilash. The letter told him she had arrived and asked him to come to the inn, The Warm Hearth, as soon as he could. She walked through the square to the Bailiff's Offices, entered through the Ortwood doors, and handed her letter to a woman seated at a desk in the lobby with a request for it to be delivered to Wilash without delay, then left and returned to the inn.

Rather than go to her room, she went straight to the tavernroom and ordered a goblet of wine. As usual, her table commanded a view of the entire tavernroom, and her wait for Wilash began. She had drunk little wine aboard the ship, and she craved it now more than she had aboard the Mistress. Three goblets later, Wilash entered the tavernroom and looked around. His eyes fixed on her as she sat and watched him. He looked unhappy but well. He had lost some weight since she had last seen him in Ort, and it suited him. Grey threatened to overwhelm his dark hair, and he wore far better clothes than the mundane items he wore before he met Klordia and became an important part of the Bailiff's Offices.

He had two guards with him, dressed in the distinctive yellow tunics of the Bailiff. Wilash made for her table, and as the guards followed him, they glanced around at the other patrons in the tavernroom. Corelle approved of their caution, but she had already determined no threat existed in the room. She stood as he approached, and he swept her into his arms. He began to cry and held her tight.

"I am sorry Wilash. Poor Klordia. It is all my fault."

"That it is not." He struggled to form words through his tears. "It is the fault of Styrrach, who unleashed this torment on Dur in the name of his greed." He pulled back. "My thanks that you came." He sat on the settle next to her, and the innkeep came over. Wilash ordered a tankard of ale and a goblet of wine for Corelle. His guards hovered nearby, out of earshot of their conversation but close enough to react if things turned awry. "Pettra is not with you?"

Now tears sprang to Corelle's eyes. "Pettra is dead." The words caught in her throat and appeared reluctant to be spoken.

Shock reduced his voice to a whisper. "What? Dead? How?"

"She fell from the upper floor of our house. Rather, I think she jumped. She killed herself, I believe."

"Killed herself? Why?"

The innkeep returned with their drinks and Corelle waited until he had passed out of earshot before she replied. "The why of it is difficult to tell, and much of it might taint her memory. I do not know the full story, in truth. I failed her, as I failed Arella, Deineike and Klordia."

He laid a hand on her arm. "I cannot tell you the depths of our grief when we heard of Deineike's death. We all lost a remarkable woman, and her loss devastated us. Her like can never be replaced."

Corelle wiped tears from her eyes with the back of a hand. "My thanks." She looked away from him for a time. When she had composed herself, she turned and gave him a weak smile.

Wilash drew in a long, thoughtful breath. "It must be Glailam." Corelle gave him a confused look. "He must be behind the murder of Klordia. Who else? He and Styrrach worked together, and he will have lost much when you and Raolos tore down their enterprise."

"Glailam is dead."

He pursed his lips, and comprehension filled his eyes as water fills a basin. "You killed him?"

"He lay hidden in Vyrrmod, a land to the south."

"I have heard of it. Much trade comes from Vyrrmod to Dur."

"He hid, but not well enough. A friend pointed me at him, and I took him."

He sat in silence for a time. "Still, Klordia may have died by his orders, given before you killed him."

Corelle conceded he might have the right of it. "That she may. If so, she is avenged. Regardless, others carried out the deed, and they know of my work. Why else would they slit her throat so? It is a message, as you have guessed."

"We have encountered many sorry turns since you arrived in Zhanghar with Arella. Many whom we loved are lost, and we cannot wake from the nightmare, it seems." He sighed and took a sip of his ale.

"What motive did they have to kill Klordia?"

"They wish to flush you out and kill you, my guess."

With a shake of her head, she said, "I would welcome it, in truth. So much bloodshed and pain. I tire of it, Wilash. This life cannot be borne. It is too painful."

He placed an arm around her and squeezed her, gentle, soothing. "You have strength and can cope with much. You survived the loss of Deineike, which I confess I thought would kill you. They will not find you so easy to throw into the flames."

"Are there any other clues, or information that might help me?"

"A letter arrived some days after Klordia's murder. It read 'You are next. C.'"

"They strive to cast her death as my work. I imagine you are right; they wish to flush me out. They may also wish to kill you, however, and I am pleased you are guarded."

"Who do you believe is behind my wife's murder?"

"You married? You had not told me."

"That we did, in Dur City. I wish you could have been there. You and Deineike, both."

She laid her head on his shoulder. "As do I, Wilash. As do I."

"Who then?"

"The Guild, my guess." Corelle had turned over all the possibilities in her head but found no other explanation. "Who knows my methods and would also know you? Members from Zhanghar, I reason."

"Torric also, since I spent time there. Alcmouth too. Styrrach sent me there, and they saw your handiwork on Sky."

She considered the list of Guilds. "I feel Alcmouth is the less likely. For the most part, they scattered after Styrrach arrived here. Synna told me this before I left. I killed at least three, and the two who were with Styrrach when he attacked us at The Duke's Seat also died. Few would remain, my guess."

"I agree." He sipped at his ale. "Synna tells me he has found no trace of any Alcmouth members in the city since Raolos became Bailiff."

"Torric or Zhanghar members then, my guess." Corelle could not understand why the Guild members still pursued them with such fervour. Styrrach and Glailam had enriched themselves, and she could have understood their anger at her. Both had now been killed, however, and while the other Guildmeisters might hold a grudge, it seemed reckless to pursue the issue now all had been exposed and torn down.

"Torric would be my guess. They have no love for me there. I threw their Senior Aide into the dust, and he wished me killed on the spot. Styrrach ordered me shrouded in Alcmouth as payment to them, I am certain."

Corelle had finished her wine, and she caught the innkeep's eye and ordered another when he bustled over to them. "It is certain they will watch you. Nobody suspicious has entered the tavernroom since you arrived, but if their plan is either to flush me out or kill you, they will watch for opportunities, we may depend on it."

"I am to be the bait, then?"

"Is Synna available to aid with this enterprise?"

"That he is, as long as you are both discreet. Raolos cannot be compromised. If he knows you are here, he is obliged to arrest you."

Corelle nodded. "I understand. Send Synna to me in the morning, and we will hatch some plan to watch for those who observe you. Do not venture out alone, I beg you. Your life is in danger if they do seek to kill you."

"I am guarded at all times. Do not fret over me." He gave her a smile of reassurance as she drank her wine.

She reached behind her back, pulled his dagger from her belt, and placed it on the settle between them. "Pettra returned this to me. I now return it to its owner. It killed Glailam if that brings you any joy."

"You did not kill him with your own dagger?"

"This is its equal and has seen less use. I used this blade to slit his throat."

He nodded in approval. "It has done great work. I have no need of it though, and it may serve you better than me."

"You should be armed. You told me that the first time I encountered you in this very city."

He laughed. "That I did. Very well, I will carry it. My thanks." He slid the dagger into his belt. "Now, I must away, and you also. You have drunk more wine tonight than I have seen you drink before."

She forced a blank expression onto her face. "Two goblets only."

"Three." Had he counted? "You already had one when I arrived. And that one is empty already." He touched the empty goblet. "Is all well?" He sounded concerned.

She sighed, a dejected breath of air, empty of all hope. "Can anything be well in my life, Wilash? I feel the weight of my guilt over the deaths of three lovers. Who can bear such a burden?"

"I understand." He laid a hand on her arm. "No answers lie in the bottom of a goblet, Corelle, I know this from bitter experience. I cannot offer you any words of wisdom to salve all your hurts, but neither can a pitcher of wine."

Corelle nodded at the truth of his words, even as she desired another goblet. He said he would inform Raolos of Pettra's death, and of her final request for his forgiveness. She told Wilash the number of her room and urged him to send Synna to her early the next morning. They embraced, and he left with his guards. She sat at the table for a few moments, then summoned the innkeep.

The next morning, a knock at her door awoke her. Her head throbbed, her mouth felt dry, and she still wore yesterday's clothes. She scrabbled around for her boots, which lay strewn in two separate corners of the room, kicked off the night before in her intoxication. She took her dagger and stood beside the door. "Who is there?"

"Synna." His familiar voice comforted her. She pulled the door open, and he entered. He looked on her with a curious expression. "This room smells like a tavernroom, and you look awful."

She snapped straight back at him. "It is good to see you also. I took a little wine last night. Have you never done so?"

He brought a soft smile to his face. "It is good to see you, even in such circumstances. I thought I would never see you again."

"Our time together has been fraught with danger, it seems. More awaits, from all Wilash told me last night."

"Klordia's murder shocked us, and Wilash took it hard. Raolos also. She excelled in her role as Senior Tally Master. She opened many eyes and many doors for other women."

"You have heard the news concerning Pettra?"

"That I have. Wilash told me this morning. More terrible news. She took her own life? That is a terrible thing."

"I take the blame. It proved a mistake for me to take her south with me. She needed somebody other than me. I did attempt to convince Raolos of this."

He nodded, glum. "That you did. What drove her to such desperate lengths, however, is a mystery to me."

"Raolos must never know this, but the violence she longed for played a part. She sought it with another, and that other served her rough treatment. I had left to kill Glailam when she had need of my help to recover from injuries he had inflicted, and she received the letter from Wilash before I returned. I cannot guess what passed through her mind in those days. I abandoned her, which may have distressed her beyond her capacity to endure."

"A man?" His expression turned curious. "I thought...." He left the sentence unfinished.

"As did I."

"Raolos is devastated. He must tell Raopul, and I do not envy him that task."

She wiped at her eyes. "I can only imagine Raolos's pain. I avenged her, curse me. I ended the life of the one who hurt her so much. None of this must come to Raolos's ears." Synna nodded, and she continued. "We must formulate a plan to flush out whoever is behind Klordia's murder and arrange for them to swing from a tree as soon as we can."

"Have you given the matter some thought?"

"That I have. They must watch the Bailiff's Offices, since that is where Wilash spends much of his day. They must have taken a room over a building in the square, my guess. We need to locate that room."

He nodded in agreement. "How can this be done?"

"Are we authorised to act on Raolos's behalf?"

"I work for him, which gives me the right. I also have letters that confirm anybody who acts on my request also works for the Bailiff's interests. The letters do not name anybody but me and must in any event be destroyed at the conclusion of our business."

"I will find a vantage point above a business on the square. The letters should enable me to persuade a business owner to grant me access to a higher floor. Today I will watch for any suspicious activity. With luck, we may at the least learn where they are hidden, since they must change the watcher at whiles."

"It is a weak plan, but your plans have always been thus." He smiled.

"Mine may be weak, but yours are non-existent." Corelle laughed, comfortable with the bond that had been re-established between them. "Now tell me, did Raolos apprehend any of the Portreeves and Guildmeisters involved in Styrrach's scheme?"

"That he did. New Portreeves serve here as well as in Zhanghar, Torric, Ryl, Vjort and Ort. Ibie is the Portreeve in Ort." Corelle smiled, happy at the news. "Raolos hanged the Portreeves in Zhanghar and Ryl, but the others were not caught. Those in Vjort and Ort could not be hanged in truth since no evidence could be found that linked them to the Guild. We apprehended no Guild-meisters, nor any Guild members. The citizens are outraged by the murder of Klordia, a high ranked member of the Bailiff's organisation. They call for justice, and Raolos is determined to deliver it. For Wilash, as much as any other reason, I believe."

It disappointed Corelle to learn so few had been taken. "I had hoped he would deliver more justice, but I have also delivered some, at the least."

"I hear this news. It is my belief Klordia would have become a Portreeve in time. Raolos took her murder hard. In so short a time, he came to depend on her financial skills."

"Very well. What is scribed, must be. Hand me the letters and let me be about my shaky plan."

He passed her a parch and she read it. It authorised any who carried it access to any reasonable request in the name of the Bailiff and carried both his signature and his seal.

As Corelle readied to leave, he held her back. "Tell me how Glailam died."

She paused before her grim reply. "With my face in his eyes and my name in his ears."

"That is as it should be. You did Dur a service."

"I have served Dur better than I served the women who loved me. Meet me in the tavernroom tonight at the sundown, and we will plan our next action based on what I can learn."

"You do not wish an earlier meeting? The sand falls."

"That it does, but we must not rush our actions on the dictates of the hourglass. This must be handled with care and discretion. I will take no satisfaction if I can do no more than slit a throat or two. I wish to know why they act, and who orders it. It may be we can throw back a small fish as bait for others much larger if we roll the dice well."

He nodded agreement, wished her luck and left. Corelle used some paste to sweeten her breath. Her head still pounded, and her stomach roiled. She drew in a sharp breath and headed for the square.

CHAPTER 17
KRAGE

A tenday after Krage arrived at Estway Farm, Priu and two of his men arrived from Ryl. Krage embraced Priu. They had run Ryl together for many years and had become friends as well as colleagues. The two others, it turned, represented the entire complement of Ryl. The Guild there had always been small, and when they had been forced to shroud one of their members some years before, they had needed an extra member for a time. That member had been Arella, and her arrival in Ryl set in motion the things that led them to this hole in the middle of nowhere, about to flee before the Bailiff's noose caught up with them.

Another delivery of food had been arranged, but with the arrival of Priu, Krage faced a dilemma. Three more mouths to feed meant they would need more food sooner than he had anticipated. He spoke to Priu about their options—they could head south and live well for the remainder of their days or wait a little longer in case Sisnop came also.

Priu wanted to leave the next day, but Krage argued that since his letters to Sisnop suggested they all meet up at the farm, they should wait a day or two longer. Priu begrudged the courtesy but agreed it would be polite to wait. The journey from Torric would be lengthy for Sisnop and Gillar. If they sailed to Ort, the ship alone would consume more than a tenday, plus the time required to ride from Ort. As they had not yet arrived, either they would not come at all, or they had sailed somewhere on the southern coast of the Eastlands and rode north, which Krage believed would involve a substantial ride.

Priu said that if Sisnop came that way, they might meet him on the road south, and they could turn and head south with him, then all sail south together from whatever port served the coast. Krage argued that would be hard on them, more so if they met them almost at the farm. The harsh ride, repeated straight away without opportunity to rest, would take a toll on them Krage could not bring himself to impose.

In the end, their indecision led them to stay at the farm much longer than a few days. Krage judged he had been at the farm almost a pass before Sisnop arrived. They had indeed sailed to Eastport, a port on the southern coast. The ride north had taken them two tendays, Sisnop thought, and they arrived exhausted. Sisnop had his Senior Aide, Gillar, with him, as well as Carshan, the Portreeve of Torric, and eight of Sisnop's men. Krage could not disguise his surprise the Torric Guildmeister had brought so many men.

"I needed guards." Sisnop sounded put out.

"As did I, yet I only brought four with me. The cost to maintain such a large cohort will soon drain your coin."

"I have plenty of coin, have no fear. I ran Torric, not Ryl." Sisnop sneered as he replied. "Besides, I brought only seven from Torric, my entire force. Another joined me at Eastport. He had come from Alcmouth, and he recognised me. He told me of some further developments that may be of interest." Krage raised his eyebrows in curiosity. "Corelle has left Dur. It seems she sailed south aboard a ship bound for Vyrrmod. Another went with her, a woman. They left from Ort, and somebody spotted them board the ship. Word had reached Alcmouth through friends not long before this man left the city."

Krage considered the news. Corelle had left, but that did not mean she would not return. He longed for her death for all she had wrought, all that had brought such hardship to him and the remainder of the Guild. He had been forced to flee and endure lengthy horse rides to the middle of nowhere to avoid the noose, and all thanks to her.

Sisnop had more news. "Raolos is the Bailiff now. Glailam fled after Corelle killed Styrrach, it seems."

The news irritated Krage, but he had not changed his opinion about Styrrach's failures. "Styrrach led us to this turn. He should have ensured Corelle died in Zhanghar, as he promised me. Then he failed in his attempt to woo Raolos into the operation, and now that fool is the Bailiff. Curses."

"I do not disagree with you, but I see opportunities still. The Guild is damaged, but it is not broken. We are still alive, and we are in charge now, in essence. We have good men with us and can return to our operations. We have always operated in secrecy, and with the threat of violence, old partners may still be persuaded to enrich us as before. We would be even richer. We would be in total control."

Krage did not care for the idea. It seemed far less risky to flee south. Raolos had undone all their trade agreements, he argued.

"That is the reason we must return, and soon." Sisnop remained optimistic, it seemed. "Before this new way of business becomes normal, at the least. We can reverse our ill fortune if we act. Portreeves can be bought, even when Raolos has replaced them all, as he is sure to. Torric and Zhanghar can be ours again. Torric, at the least. It is not on the Alc and is less well thought of by those who reside in enormous homes in the capital. There is plenty of coin for you and me there, Krage, I assure you. We might even bring Vjort into the organisation, something Styrrach strove for."

Krage could see the attraction, but he also saw great risk. He cared little enough what became of Sisnop. They belonged to the same organisation, but he knew little of the man from Torric. His own life, however, he guarded with great jealousy. "I will think on it."

"Do not delay, I urge you. The sand falls. If Raolos's new trade agreements become normal, we will find it harder to restore the proper order."

Some days later, news came to them that Raolos had appointed a woman as his Senior Tally Master. All Dur talked about it. To add insult to injury, the woman turned out to be the wife of Wilash, the Guild member who had knocked Gillar from his horse in Torric. Gillar became enraged and wanted to ride to Alcmouth there and then with every member from the farm and strike them both dead.

Krage had been about to inform Sisnop he disliked the plan to re-build the Guild, and he would sail south with Priu and their men. As he listened to Gillar's incessant tirades against Wilash and his wife, however, the germ of an idea formed in his head. It would keep him in Dur a little longer, but the reward would be priceless, and too tempting to ignore.

To send all their men to Alcmouth in an attempt to obtain revenge for Gillar would be futile; ridiculous even. The woman could still be killed, however, and bring about the promise of something far more important to Krage than revenge on Gillar's behalf against some man who had knocked him from his horse. More fool him, Krage thought, that he allowed this Wilash to get the better of him.

The true exquisiteness of the death of Wilash's wife's murder lay in her death at their hands. Styrrach had killed Corelle's lover in Alcmouth. If the Guild killed this woman, whatever her name might be, how could Corelle not reappear from whatever hole she lay in? How could she not seek vengeance for the death at the Guild's hands of another woman associated with her? Such a simple yet beautiful plan, and Krage did not believe the jade could fail to come in search of them. If she came after them, he could be done with her once and for all, and good riddance. Once she had been killed, the south awaited, and a life where he need not look over his shoulder ever again.

He had become rich under Styrrach's scheme and had grown richer by the day until Corelle killed Styrrach. That frustrated him, but he still had plenty of coin, most of it Styrrach's before his death. No man could have everything, after all else.

Sisnop rejected the idea. It would be too dangerous to entice Corelle back into their lives. It invited disaster. If Krage did believe the Guild's days had come to an end, then let them all ride away now, take a ship south and live a good life. No need to invite Corelle to harm that outcome as she had done so many times before.

Of course, Gillar liked the idea, and when Krage suggested they might not only kill the woman and Corelle, but Wilash as well, Gillar chomped at the bit to lead a team to Alcmouth as soon as possible. Sisnop found himself outnumbered, since Priu sided with Krage. Krage had won the argument. Now he needed a plan to make it all come about.

In the end, Sisnop devised the plan. They would send a team to Alcmouth. Four men, no more, since no more would be needed. They would kill the woman—they were killers, after all else. They would slash her throat, in the same way Corelle used to fulfil her gests, then send letters to Wilash to suggest Corelle had killed his wife. He would not believe it, of course, but he must send for her, with his wife dead and the Guild certain to be behind her death. The team would watch and wait until they saw Corelle, then they would lure her into a trap and bring her back to the farm in bonds.

Krage believed Corelle would come to Wilash's aid. They had

worked together to thwart the Guild's earlier attempt to kill the same woman in Alcmouth, if the stories were true. Every aspect of the plan brought more benefits. Krage instructed Priu to select three good men and leave as soon as could be arranged, though it disappointed Gillar he would not be a part of the operation. Priu and his team left the farm, but Gillar could not be satisfied, and now he and Sisnop outnumbered Krage, who found himself caught in the same trap he himself had sprung days before.

Gillar insisted he would lead another three men to Alcmouth. They would not intervene unless necessary. They would monitor Priu's team, ensure the woman died, and Corelle re-appeared. They would then assist Priu's team to capture Corelle. Four men may not be enough; she had proved elusive thus far. Eight men would be too many for her, however. Krage resented the implication Priu could not perform the task, but Gillar and Sisnop would not be dissuaded, and another four men left the farm.

The wait for the return of the two teams and Corelle began, and Krage lay awake at night as he devised a long, painful death for her.

CHAPTER 18
CORELLE

orelle stood at the entrance to the square and gazed at the throng of people who wandered around the cobbled surface. A small market operated in one corner, and a garment maker's shop stood close to it along one side of the square perpendicular to the Bailiff's Offices. If Corelle had wished to watch the Bailiff's Offices, she would have taken up position opposite them, so a shop at one side of the square would give her a good view of the shops and taverns across from the Offices where the watcher might lie. She wandered through back streets until she could enter the square into the hectic market, filled with shoppers who crowded around the stalls. Most of the stalls seemed to sell clothing, jewellery, and other trinkets rather than foodstuffs.

From the shadows, she watched for a time to satisfy herself nobody circulated around the market, hidden in the crowd, their attention on the Bailiff's Offices and not the goods on the stalls. Confident the crowd in the market swirled around like water as it runs down a drain, she waited until a tall, handsome man passed her, then fell into step beside him. Any casual observer would take them for a couple who entered the square on whatever business occupied them. He stopped at a stall and looked at a well-made tunic. Corelle commented on the high quality making. He glanced at her and smiled, as a husband might do if his wife ventured an opinion on the tunic he studied. She stayed close to the stalls and glanced at them as she moved toward the garment shop. Nothing about the way she moved would draw any attention as she opened the shop door, took two steps inside, then turned.

Corelle watched the square for a few moments. Nobody came close or peered through the door at her. From behind her, she heard a polite cough, and she turned to face the man behind the counter; the owner, she imagined. She showed him the parch and asked if he had access to an upstairs room with a window that looked into the square.

He did, but he appeared reluctant to let her use the room despite the letters. His shop sold good quality making; not fine, and not as good as her own, but better than many people in Dur would ever wear. Corelle opted for flattery. "Your making is remarkable. I have some skills in making myself, though I am nowhere near your equal. Has the Bailiff ever called in to your shop?"

"That he has not." Corelle had guessed as much. Raolos measured his worth by his clothes and would demand finer making than this man's.

She tutted. "I wonder if he could be persuaded to favour you with some business. Of course, if you are not interested in such a customer…"

She had played a high hand. Moments later, she arranged a chair in the room above the shop, set back from the window so she might see but not be seen. The window had not been cleaned for some time, but she had a decent view of the buildings opposite the Bailiff's Offices.

All morning, men in the yellow uniform of the Bailiff and the red of the Portreeve moved backward and forward across the square. As the midday drew closer, she became more vigilant. The midday would be the perfect time to change one watchful pair of eyes for another. A beautiful summer day had the square thronged with people. Corelle had avoided the Dur winter and spring while she had been in Arkkyd; there had scarce been a cold day throughout her time in the southern city. It seemed she had returned to Dur at the perfect time to continue her enjoyment of the warm weather. With each summer, she aged herself a year, so she arrived in Dur a year older than when she had left. She was now twenty-three years.

Those trained to move in stealth, unnoticed, do not move the way a regular person moves. They glance around and take detours, some instinct born out of necessity. They are lithe, more cat than horse, and hold their bodies in a permanent state of readiness. Though Corelle could move unobserved by most, she could not guess how she might blend into a crowd if a trained eye watched for her.

A man entered the square opposite her and headed straight for a tavern across from the Bailiff's Offices, and she leaned forward as she recognised the characteristics she had looked for. Head down, he changed course to avoid a Bailiff's man headed for the Offices and confirmed himself to Corelle as a Guild member. As he moved, he remained poised, balanced and ready to flee if he could, fight if it turned to such an outcome. He wore plain dark, inconspicuous clothes, not the bright summer attire of most people in the square, and they stood out, different.

He entered the tavern and Corelle waited. A short time later, a similar man emerged and headed across the square, the reverse journey his accomplice had taken. Guild members, no question about it. The Guild watched Wilash, and when a Guild member watched a person for any time, death followed; today or in a pass, it would arrive once an opportunity presented itself. A great many other people came and went from the tavern, but none resembled the two who had piqued her interest. She noticed movement at an upstairs window, and a face peered down. Corelle wondered at such a novice error until she noticed a buxom woman in a low-cut dress approach the tavern. The allure of plump breasts had betrayed the watcher further.

She watched for around two hours. Of all who entered and left the tavern, none looked suspicious, and the man who had entered at the midday did not emerge. Their eyrie had been discovered. Now she needed a plan that would lead her and Synna to whoever had ordered the vigilance.

As the sun slipped down the sky, she went back down to the shop and enquired about a rear exit. She did not want to roll the dice and leave from the front door where the Guild might see her. The owner showed her to the rear door, and she headed back to The Warm Hearth.

At the tavern, she ordered a goblet of wine and sat at the same table as the previous night to await Synna. It baffled her the Guild would go to such extravagant risk and effort to kill Wilash or her. Their business had been cast down, and those who pulled the strings should have fled south as Glailam had done. Why they waited in Dur, bent on reprisals, she could not fathom.

Synna entered the tavernroom, headed for her table, and she outlined all she had seen. He shared her belief she had seen Guild members. "You had a flimsy plan, but you have turned it to your favour as ever." He shook his head and smiled.

She squirmed, uncomfortable at the slight praise, anxious to divert the conversation away from it. "It is clumsy, this plan of theirs. Why they expend such energy on this lost cause, I cannot fathom."

"Revenge for the death of Styrrach, my guess, and for the slight in Torric. Wilash has told you this tale?"

"That he has, but I am uncertain so simple a motive would drive such elaborate work. They have framed Klordia's death as though I killed her; they observe the Offices. It is too much effort.

Some other motivation lies behind these actions, but I cannot see it."

Synna sat quiet for a time. "Regardless, I feel it is time for another of your weak plans." He smiled again as he spoke.

As she had sipped at her wine, she had given the matter some thought and come up with some ideas. "Wilash will leave the Offices without his guards. The Guild are bound to follow if they intend to kill him. We mark any who follow him and apprehend them."

He pursed his lips. "Weak, even by your standards." He shrugged his shoulders. "We do not know they will follow him. He may not be their mark. If they look for you, they may hold their vigil. If they do follow him, they might have a way to summon reinforcements. We could take two or three, but we do not know how many we face. Wilash is in danger if they come in large numbers. Even if only one of them follows him, and Wilash becomes mixed up in some group as they leave a tavern, the Guild might strike before we can intervene. It is risky. I do not like it."

Corelle gave a defeated sigh. "You are correct. This is a risky plan. I have another."

"Let us hope it is better than your first." A smile flickered on his lips, teased her.

She summoned the innkeep and ordered another goblet of wine. Synna raised his eyebrows but said nothing. "Wilash comes out alone and crosses the square. The watcher's attention will be drawn to him at that moment, and we can slip into the tavern unseen. Wilash can return to the Offices and safety as we do so. We can then find the room the member is in. It is at the front on the first level, in the centre of the inn's front wall. We persuade him to reveal such information as we can extract."

Synna chewed his lip. "Fraught with danger. We do not know whether the Guild man has assistance in the tavern. He might prefer to die rather than risk the Guild justice he would be owed if he told us anything. You reach for clouds with both plans. What is the next?"

"I have no other cloud to reach for, but you reach for no cloud at all, as ever." Corelle heard the irritation in her voice. "If he prefers to die, we wait. His relief will arrive at some point and may be more talkative."

He shook his head. "Your schemes are always tenuous at best. But I can think of none better, and of the two, I prefer we enter the tavern. Wilash is exposed to less risk this way, I feel."

"Then we are agreed?"

He sat, deep in thought, for some time. "That we are. When do we execute this plan?"

"Tomorrow morning. Three hours after the sunrise."

"Not earlier?"

"You must first brief Wilash, and the later we leave it, the more the Guild member will be anxious for his watch to end. He may be more careless." Both points had been accurate, but in truth she did not wish to rise too early in case she felt unwell from drink. It seemed she felt that way most mornings these days.

Synna's brow creased. "Guild justice." He seemed to have returned to his earlier comment. "Do you believe there is such a thing?"

His question astonished her. "Of…" She paused on the brink of her confirmation, mindful of the story about the non-existent Debtor's Gaol. "Why would there not be? We both knew Styrrach's nature."

He shrugged. "I never saw it dispensed. Did you?"

She had not. "Arella once killed a recruit who could not endure the initiation, but that man did not receive Guild Justice."

"Is it a myth? Is shrouding the only Guild justice?"

Corelle could not unravel the truth, and if Guild justice did not exist, then Arella need not have died. Corelle could not endure further guilt over the death of her lover. "This is unimportant. We have a plan. Are you committed to it?"

He heaved a resigned sigh. "Very well. I will explain to Wilash in the morning, and I will leave the Offices by the rear exit. If any follow me, I will lose them."

"Meet me at the pastry shop outside the square. You know it?"

"That I do. Curse them. I have become captivated by the buns with the cream in the centre."

"Deineike and I were fond of such pastries also." Corelle smiled, relaxed now their business had been completed. "Now, will you have a drink with me?"

"That I will, then I will away. A good night of sleep is good preparation for such tasks, I find." He fixed her with a pointed stare, but she ignored the implication of his words.

Corelle ordered a goblet of wine and a tankard of ale, and they reminisced for a time on their lives in the Guild and the events that had passed since the day she had first seen him in the garden opposite Raolos's home in Ort. Despite his words about a good night's sleep, she ordered another goblet once he had gone, and she drank it alone. When she stared into it, Deineike's face swam in the red liquid, a reproachful look on her face.

She finished the wine and headed for her room and a sleep riddled with nightmares. When she became intoxicated, the nightmares either did not plague her as often, or she could not remember them. The sunrise woke her, exhausted and miserable, and she lay in the bed, cried to herself and cursed the fates written for her. Dressed in simple clothes, she spent some time with a whetstone she had bought in Arkkyd, which she stroked across the blade of her dagger against the prospect things might turn awry.

Corelle walked to the pastry shop on another bright, warm morning. She bought one of the pastries Synna had mentioned and had eaten half of it when he appeared. He also bought a pastry, and they ate them as they studied their surroundings.

They finished the pastries, and Corelle continued to turn over all possibilities in her mind. "Wilash will not stay out of the Offices for long with no guards?"

"That is what I urged."

"Let us find a sympathetic corner where we will be hidden from the tavern but can see the Offices then. The hour is almost upon us."

"Let us roll the dice." Synna checked his dagger, hidden at his belt. Corelle pulled her own from her boot and placed it at her belt, and they took station at a suitable corner to wait for Wilash to emerge from the doors of the Bailiff's Offices. The magnificent Ortwood doors stood open across the square from the tavern. It amazed Corelle how many people entered and left the ornate Offices as they watched.

Synna nudged her when Wilash appeared in the doorway and strode into the square. No guards followed him as he turned to his right and moved toward the market in the corner of the square. Synna and Corelle walked without hesitation to the door of the tavern. They kept close to the buildings and trusted the Guild member's attention remained focused on Wilash.

As Synna ducked into the tavern, Corelle glanced toward Wilash. He had stopped and had his hands in the pockets of his trousers. He pulled the contents out, then thrust them back in anger and turned back toward the Bailiff's Offices with a shake of his head. It had been the perfect performance of one who has forgotten something—coin or some other important item. Corelle smiled at his effective act and ducked into the tavern.

No customers sat in the tavernroom at such an early hour, but the innkeep stood behind the counter and wiped a tankard with a cloth. He looked up as they approached him. Corelle smiled at him, and he returned the smile. He drew in a breath to speak, but Corelle spoke first. "We work for the Bailiff. Who uses the room upstairs?"

He looked perplexed. "Nobody. We are a tavern, not an inn. There is a fine inn—"

Synna growled at him. "We do not seek an inn. We seek the man who uses your upstairs room."

His eyes flicked to a closed door at the side of the tavernroom, then back to them. "Nobody is upstairs that need concern the Bailiff, if you do indeed work for him." They both wore plain clothes rather than the yellow tunics, and Corelle thought it not unreasonable he might doubt their claim. It seemed he covered for the Guild, however, and whether because he had been a part of Styrrach's enterprise or because he feared to betray such a deadly organisation could not be guessed.

"Do you know the name 'Styrrach?'" Corelle kept her voice low and even.

He hesitated, and his eyes flicked to the door again. Corelle guessed it led to the stairs. He might hope for a Guild member or two to appear from it and strike down the two people who asked such awkward questions. "This name is familiar to me for some reason." He sounded guarded.

Corelle pulled her dagger from her waistband and laid it on the counter. He stared at it for a moment, and his face lost some of its colour. "What is your name?"

"Feuyelk."

"Feuyelk." The name felt strange on her tongue. Mayhap he had not been born in Dur, although he spoke the language with no noticeable accent. "This dagger spilled Styrrach's innards from his stomach." His face grew paler, and he took half a pace backward. "We have business with the man who watches the square from your upstairs window. You need not pay with your life for your connection to these people, but you may be assured, I will not hesitate to add you to the list of Guild members I have killed." She picked up the dagger and returned it to her waistband.

Feuyelk gulped. He had a prominent throat protrusion, and it bobbed down and up again, unmissable and unmistakeable. He feared her and might wonder whether he faced a greater threat from her or the Guild. In the end, he seemed to decide his potential ruin now stood before him, while the Guild were elsewhere at this moment. He pointed at the door his eyes had flicked to. "Up the stairs behind that door."

Corelle smiled at him and waited as Synna approached the door, pulled it ajar, and peered through the gap. He turned to her and nodded. Corelle glowered at the innkeep. "We will be here for a time. I would be disappointed if I returned to the tavernroom at some point, and you had left."

He nodded, and she turned to the door, which Synna had pulled open. Only the fates knew how many Guild members hid in the room above the inn, but Corelle and Synna were about to learn, and the price of that knowledge might well be their lives.

CHAPTER 19

CORELLE

Corelle sucked in a deep breath as she joined Synna at the door, through which a short passage led to a staircase. Slow and cautious, they ascended the stairs, kept as close to the wall as they could. Stairs often creaked but were less liable to make any sound at the edges rather than the centre of each step. Several doors opened off the landing. They ignored the doors on the side that did not face the square, which left four that might hide the Guild member. The movement she had seen the previous day had come from closer to the centre of the tavern, and they focused on the two centre rooms for now.

Synna listened at one of the doors for a time, then shrugged. He repeated the process at the other and gave the handle a gentle turn. Without a sound, the door opened a crack, Synna peered through, then opened the door further as Corelle stood to one side of him, dagger drawn. He pushed the door all the way open, stepped into the darkened room, bent low, then moved to one side and crouched motionless in the room. Corelle waited on the landing to allow time for his eyes to adjust to the darkness in the room. That darkness suggested closed shutters, which meant nobody watched from the window. After all else, if there had been anybody in the room, they would have challenged Synna by now. In her mind, the other room held their mark, but she waited for Synna to confirm her suspicion.

He stepped forward and a small amount of light appeared as he opened the shutters a little so they could inspect the room. The dusty room appeared to be a storeroom that contained some crates and a large bale of cloth. Some empty pitchers had been stacked in one corner, and some lay, haphazard, around the floor. Synna shook his head, and they moved to the next door.

Synna tried the handle, and it turned, soundless, but the door did not open. "Locked." At his whispered explanation, Corelle nodded, beckoned to him to move away from the door.

She leaned close to whisper into his ear. "We could attempt to force the door, although we might fail if some heavy item is pushed against it. All surprise would also be lost. It is only an hour from the midday, and yesterday at that hour a replacement came to the tavern. That may happen again today. We could hide in this other room and emerge as whoever is within unlocks the door. We would need to act fast; there would be two of them."

"Or more. We do not know how many wait within."

She nodded. "True enough."

"We could ask the innkeep for the name of the man who waits inside, if he knows it, and call to him. We might fool him into opening the door."

She smiled, amused. "You have a plan at last." He gave her arm a gentle push. "We will lose surprise if we try this, if the innkeep even knows the man's name. If there are more than one in the room, things might turn ill for us."

"Then we wait, it seems." He wore a wry grin as they returned to the darkened room and debated whether to close the door. It might alarm a Guild member if he noticed it had been opened, and he might investigate, but if they left the door closed, it might hinder them. They decided closed would be the lesser of the two evils and began the wait.

Corelle and Synna found it no hardship to remain silent and motionless for an hour, so they stood near the door and listened for sounds. Voices rose up from below that suggested some patrons had entered the tavern. The hour dragged past, and no sound came from the stairs or the landing. They exchanged glances but did not move.

At length, they heard a door below them close, and feet ascended the stairs. The person who came up them did not use caution, and it seemed the innkeep had not betrayed their presence to whoever would soon reach the landing. Synna placed a hand on the door handle, and they heard a distinctive knock on the next door along. Corelle guessed the knock had been pre-arranged as there were two quick, short knocks, then a delay followed by four knocks with longer gaps between them. Another gap, then three quick knocks seemed to complete the routine.

Synna held up a hand to Corelle to indicate she should wait. A key turned in a lock, and footsteps followed before a door closed. Confused, Corelle whispered. "Why do we not move?" She leaned into Synna to ensure he heard her soft yet urgent question.

"Let the other leave, then we repeat the knock. Fewer to deal with."

Corelle nodded at Synna's plan; the fewer Guild members they needed to confront, the better. They heard no voices from the room next door, and before long the door closed, and the key turned again. Feet moved down the stairs and the ground floor door closed. They slipped from the room and stood before the door. Synna repeated the knock that had been used earlier. After a brief silence, a voice called through the door. "What?"

Synna placed a hand in front of his mouth and spoke, quiet but audible, Corelle hoped. "He came out earlier. Forgot to tell you."

The man inside did not reply for a moment. "Any sign of her?"

"She may have watched from the market. I am not certain, but I can point out the shop she entered so you can keep an eye on it." A further silence followed, and Corelle hoped the man in the room had not spotted the blatant discrepancy in the tale Synna had spun. With every heartbeat, she feared the man had unravelled the contradiction between Synna's claim he had not been certain he had seen Corelle yet could point out the store she had entered. To her relief, the key turned. As soon as the door opened a crack, Synna pushed it inward and rushed through, Corelle close behind him. The man who had opened it had been struck in the face by it and staggered backward a few steps. He fumbled at his belt as Synna and Corelle ran toward him, but he froze as two daggers pointed at his throat. Synna patted at the man's waist, pulled a dagger from his belt, and tossed it into a corner of the room. The window looked out onto the Bailiff's Offices across the square, and a chair had been positioned a step back from the window. A small table sat to one side with a pitcher and a cup on it. Discarded food remains lay scattered around the chair.

The man stared at Corelle. "I know who you are."

"Then you know I will not hesitate to send you wherever you travel to afterward if you do not give us the assistance we seek."

He turned to Synna. "I do not know you."

"Like you, I worked for the Guild. Now I work for the Bailiff. My name is Synna."

"What do you want of me?" The man's face had turned pale, and his gaze turned to Corelle often, although he glanced away each time.

Corelle's soft words could not disguise her menace. "You fear me?"

"I do. You have wreaked havoc on the Guild for reasons unclear to me."

"The reason is that Styrrach sold me to the Portreeve. They call it shrouding. When it suits their purpose, they cast us aside like a discarded tunic. Styrrach meant that to be my fate, but I avoided it, and now I plan to burn down any who stand in my way." She glared at him.

He gasped. "They sold us? The Portreeve hanged Guild members in Torric. You claim Styrrach had some hand in this? It is difficult to believe."

"Yet it is true. What does it benefit me to lie to you? You know my reputation. I could kill you with ease and would shed no tears. I tell you the truth. What you make of it is of no concern to me."

He glanced at Synna. "You would let her kill me? You are a brother Guild member."

Synna loosed a sardonic laugh. "I would let her kill you. If I tried to stop her, she would kill me also. I am not ready to travel yet. Are you?"

"That I am not." The man swallowed hard. "What do you wish to know?"

"Who is behind the death of Klordia, and why did they kill her?"

He exhaled. "I cannot answer the second part of your question. The Guild has not changed. We are told what to do, not why we do it. As for the first part, the order came from Sisnop and Krage."

"The Guildmeisters from Ryl and Torric?" Corelle recognised the names.

"Krage became Guildmeister in Zhanghar when Styrrach left. He took over there, and Styrrach took over here. Krage and Sisnop ordered her death, and instructed us to watch this other, Wilash. If an opportunity to kill him presented itself, we should kill him. If you appeared…" He did not elaborate.

"I have appeared." She flashed him a grim smile.

He looked down, muttered. "That you have. Wilash incurred Sisnop's wrath when he cast Gillar to the ground after we had failed to apprehend you. He is owed Guild justice, but he avoided it, even though Styrrach assured Sisnop he would be killed." He shook his head, looked at Corelle again. "That sat ill with Sisnop, in truth. You may have pleased him when you killed Styrrach."

Synna elaborated. "Styrrach did plan to kill Wilash. He sold him to the Portreeve here, chosen for shrouding. Corelle intervened, and he lives."

The man stared at Corelle. "Sisnop has a grievance against you also. You killed three of our couriers."

"Hiw." She spat out his name. "He meant to rape me and the woman who travelled with me, the one whom Styrrach killed. I rejoice that I killed him and the imbeciles he travelled with. I would do so again if necessary."

"He always had an unsavoury attitude toward women, I know this." The man sounded sad, to Corelle's surprise. "Nonetheless, you are marked for Guild justice for that and for killing Styrrach. Krage despises you. He had some fondness for the woman you killed in Zhanghar, it turns."

"Arella. I cannot forgive myself for that act." Corelle pulled herself together. It would not do to concede any weakness to the man. "How many members are here in Alcmouth?"

"Four. Neither Krage nor Sisnop are here, although Priu, the Senior Aide from Ryl, is with us."

"Where are the Guildmeisters?" The man's tale implied nothing more than a ragtag band of Guild members remained in Dur.

"I do not know for certain. They are on a farm somewhere south of Dur City, I believe."

Corelle thought she detected a hesitation in his answer. He had lied. She needed other answers first, however. "What is the objective of this group? Simple revenge? You expect us to believe this?" Corelle thought the risks great for something as banal as revenge.

He shrugged. "I have told you all I know. If we can, we are to slit Wilash's throat. If you appear, you are to be taken to them, alive if it proves possible."

Had Corelle caught him in a lie? "Taken where? You say you do not know where they are."

"The Senior Aide from Ryl will tell us, if we capture you." Uncertainty in his voice suggested he had lied again, but why?

"How did they know I would come at all?"

"They did not, my guess. They rolled the dice, and they felt it worth the chance, I believe. They were right, after all else. You have come. And now it seems I will not share in any bounty that may be available."

Synna stepped closer to the man, snarled. "Did you kill Klordia?"

"That I did not. I swear I speak the truth. Priu killed her. We seized her as she walked. At that time, I did not know she would be killed, I swear. I believed her to be a hostage, to be used to summon Corelle. Priu used her and slit her throat. He made us watch. None of us agreed with it but had no will to intervene. After all else, you know as well as I what would have turned had we done so." He hung his head. "I believe he enjoyed it, and he told us he had killed her because he believed Wilash would be more inclined to summon you if she had been killed. A sorry turn."

"They have sent four of you to take Corelle? That is all?"

"That it is. We did not know you aided her. Four would be enough, they thought."

Synna laughed. "Four would not be enough, you may believe that."

Corelle laid a hand on Synna's arm. "They might. They are all trained killers, and I am no brawler. One at a time from darkness, that is my method. Four at once? I doubt myself."

Synna shook his head. "They might be enough to kill you, but they wish you alive, so he says."

The man confirmed it. "That they do, if it can be achieved."

Corelle agreed with Synna. "I would not permit them to take me alive. Four might kill me, but they would not find it easy to subdue me. I would die before I allowed them to use me and serve me up for Guild justice."

Synna looked again at the man, thoughtful. "You have told the truth? There are but four of you?"

"That I have. I swear it."

Synna shook his head and spoke almost to himself. "There are more. Some system keeps them hidden from one another. They would not risk that such a prize might slip through their fingers if they value your capture so much. How they manage it, I confess I do not know."

Corelle understood little of the plan. "Nor why. Why go to such lengths to capture me? All is undone. Why do they not take their coin and flee, as Glailam did?"

The man frowned. "Coin?"

"The Guild enforced justice at Styrrach's behest. He enriched himself through manipulation of prices of goods imported from the south. Others gained from it; Guildmeisters, Portreeves, the Bailiff. Senior Aides also, my guess. We were toys in their game, and they would cast you aside for shrouding if it suited their aims. Raolos tore the trade scheme down, and when I killed Styrrach, that put an end to it, or so I thought. I also killed Glailam, the Bailiff, who had been in league with Styrrach."

The man let out a soft, low whistle. "You are formidable."

"That I am. And now your fate must be determined. I have one more question for you. The other three with you. Where are they hidden?"

He hesitated. "You know I will be marked for Guild justice if I tell you this. I would prefer a quick death at your hand, for I must die either way, it seems. I am caught between doubt and uncertainty."

She pondered his words, so similar to Synna's earlier. The threat of Guild justice hung over all who had been in the Guild, yet none could say what it involved. Its threat alone assured obedience. Did it even exist, or had it been nothing more than another ruse? It hung over them all like a dark cloud, and she understood how a swift death at her hand would be preferable to Guild justice to this man, as it had been to Arella. "When will you be relieved?"

He seemed surprised by the question. "If Wilash leaves, I follow him to his home. At some point after dark, another will come here. If I am gone, they come to Wilash's home and relieve me there. If not, I am relieved here."

Corelle turned the situation over in her mind. "For two years Styrrach and now these others have tried to kill me. They have failed and they will continue to fail. Tell us where Krage lies hidden and where the other three are and you may leave."

He shook his head. "I cannot run as you have. I do not have the will for it. I do not wish Guild justice."

Corelle crossed the room and picked up his dagger. "Synna, can you leave us alone for a time?"

Synna looked worried. "I am not comfortable with this. I work for Raolos. I cannot condone torture and murder. I will not leave you alone with him. We are to be discreet, or do you forget?"

"I do not forget. I only wish to talk to our friend for a time. I have things to say to him a servant of Raolos should not hear."

The man looked at Synna, terror in his eyes. "Do not leave me alone with her. She is terrible."

Synna's eyes did not leave Corelle's as he replied. "That I will not."

Corelle glared at Synna. "You stretch our friendship. I will have justice, and I will understand why Klordia died. Do not stand in my way." She slid her own dagger into her hand and held them both out before her. Synna's hand moved to his belt, and Corelle shook her head, took a pace forward.

"Wait, wait." The man intervened, to Corelle's relief. "I will tell you where they are, but you must give me your word you will let me go. I will flee, although they will be sure to seek me." He shook his head, trembled. Still afraid, it appeared.

"You have my word." Corelle still stared at Synna as tension crackled between them. "Tell us, then leave. We have never seen you. You do not exist. Do not cross my path again. Ever."

"Krage is on a farm east of Ort, in the Eastlands. I do not know its name. It lies beyond a large town, called Yatsun, or some such. Priu and the other two are in the poor quarter. A house on Torric Street, number eight. They are there. We threw the owner of the house into the Alc. Priu killed Wilash's woman at the house. Swear to me you will let me leave."

Corelle put her dagger back into her belt and reached into her pocket. She pulled her pouch out and handed the man some coin. "Take this and leave. We will give you time to flee. None will ever know we learned anything from you." Synna still glowered at her in anger.

The man took the coin and ran from the room, and Synna shook his head. "What turned then? You would kill me in the pursuit of whatever it is you seek?"

She laughed. "Synna, relax. I bluffed. I would not hurt you unless you threatened me. I could not convince him unless I convinced you. I apologise, but we needed the address, and I saw no other option."

He sighed, either from relief or comprehension. "You played the part well, I admit. Please do not spring surprises such as this on me without prior warning again. I feared you would kill me."

She smiled. "Come, we must unravel what we have learned and decide what we do with this information."

"Our best option is to capture the relief man here, with the help of some of Raolos's men. We can then attempt to take the other two at the house on Torric Street. I remain convinced there are others who may watch that house, and it may not be an easy task."

She laughed. "That is a certainty. I fear the one we released also. Would he betray us?"

"I believe they would kill him anyway, as an example."

"Still, it may be wise for me to follow him for a time to ensure he does not run to them. You can organise Raolos's men, and I will meet you all back here before dark."

He nodded, and she hurried down the stairs and out of the tavern. Which direction would the man take? Toward the docks, she guessed. She did not know where Torric Street lay, but the poor quarter stood between the square and the docks if he made for the house. She hurried off toward the docks and soon saw him ahead. He seemed in no rush, and he often stopped to stare in shop windows. He doubled back, then spun on his heels and continued on his way. She guessed he worried that she or some other followed him.

He turned into an alleyway, and she hurried to the entrance and peered around a wall, crouched close to the floor. He had stopped halfway down the long alleyway and turned to face the way he had come. He must suspect somebody followed him. Corelle saw no way to enter the alleyway without being seen while he checked in her direction. If she allowed him to reach the end before she entered it, he might slip away. She could not wait there all day until darkness fell and concealed her. She stepped into the alleyway.

He called out. "I knew it. You never intended to allow me to leave."

"Did you lie to us? Do you run to warn them?" She moved toward him.

"That I do not. I flee, as I agreed."

"If you believed I would kill you, why did you reveal all to us?"

"If you speak the truth, they have betrayed us all. I prefer a swift death at your hand than Guild justice, and you can then repay some debt for all those who were hanged by the Portreeve at Styrrach's behest."

Corelle sighed, frustrated by every aspect of the complex situation she found herself in. "I do not wish to kill you. I spoke the truth about all we discussed. I followed you to make sure you do not warn your companions."

"They would not permit me to live if I told them I had been in a room with you but ran in fear. I do not head for Torric Street, I head for the docks where I hope to find passage away from here."

Corelle mulled over his words. She believed he told the truth; the Guild would be unlikely to see his failure to capture her as anything other than betrayal. She must roll the dice. "Go. I wish you luck, but do not let our paths cross again."

He nodded. "My thanks." He turned and walked off down the alleyway. Corelle also turned and headed back to the tavern to await Synna and the Bailiff's men.

CHAPTER 20
CORELLE

Corelle climbed the stairs of the tavern. Synna had already arrived, along with four of Raolos's men in the bright yellow uniforms of the Bailiff's office. Synna raised his eyebrows in curiosity as she entered the room, and she shook her head. "I do not think he has warned them."

"That is good. What is the plan?"

"I do not trust the innkeep. I will wait in the tavernroom and follow the Guild member up the stairs so there can be no interference. You wait here with the door locked until you hear the knock. We will capture him, and Raolos's men can take him into whatever custody may be found."

"Such as a gaol?" Synna winked at her.

He had not forgotten her embarrassment on the night in Ort when her mistaken belief in the existence of gaols had caused her severe embarrassment. "Curse you." She allowed herself a smile. "I will be less inconspicuous in the tavernroom if I am with a man. Are there any clothes to hand that are not these dreadful yellow items?"

"My tunic will suffice." Synna glanced at the four men. "You are around my size. We will swap tunics, and you may sit in the tavernroom in Corelle's embrace." He laughed, and the man gave her a shy smile. Synna and the man swapped tunics, and Corelle checked they all understood the plan before she and the man went down to the tavernroom. Corelle bought a goblet of wine and a tankard of ale. They sat at a table with a view of the door, out of the line of sight of anybody who entered the tavern, and settled down to wait.

Corelle sipped at the wine. It had a rich, plum flavour. The man did not touch the ale. "Take a drink. You must blend in."

"I am on duty. We are forbidden to drink ale when we are on duty."

She sighed, exasperated. "These are special circumstances. I do not ask you to become inebriated, but at the least sit with a tankard before you that is not full to the brim." He took a small sip and set the tankard down.

Corelle shook her head. He must be stubborn, she imagined. She drank half her wine as the light faded outside. She wondered how long they would have to wait for the Guild member to arrive. She laid her head on the arm of Raolos's man, to all appearances a couple who enjoyed a drink together at the end of the day. He sipped a little more from the tankard.

He muttered to her under his breath. "We should talk, I imagine."

"That we should. My name is Corelle."

"I know who you are. You are banished. Much is not clear to me, but Synna tells me we search for Klordia's murderer. Such a terrible thing. I liked her. I am happy to be involved and look forward to seeing the killer hanged."

Corelle could not suppress a quiet laugh. "You meant it when you said we should talk, this is clear. I wish justice for Klordia also, and we may keep Wilash safe at the same time."

"He is a good man. He is in charge of our division, the Magisterial Division."

"He is an old friend. Our pasts are best not discussed, however." She smiled to herself as grim memories came to her.

"I hear tales around the Offices. Some say he used to be a ruthless killer. Others say the Duke banished you for brutal murders. Men, women and children, I have heard. You will kill anybody who stands in your way."

Corelle mused on her reputation. She had not sought it, and it had been based on half-truths, it appeared. Under no circumstances would she kill a child, of course. She had killed men and women both; she could not deny it. "Reputations always last, whether they be true or no. I must correct the story, however. I have never killed a child."

He sipped more ale. "You killed a woman who carried a child, as I heard it told. In Zhanghar, I believe."

Corelle sat up and stared at him. "How did this outrageous tale spread itself?"

"You say it is not true?"

"That I do. A woman in Zhanghar..." He must mean Arella. Who had attached the fallacy she had been with child to the story though? "She carried no child." Did she?

"Then the story is untrue, my guess." He glanced at her. "I apologise that I repeated this untruth."

She opened her mouth to reply, but a man entered who had the unmistakeable manner of a Guild member. She buried her head in the man's chest and whispered, "He has entered. Hold me, so he does not see me."

He wrapped his arms around her and clutched her to him as he whispered a question. "The one who passed the counter?"

"I can scarce breathe, much less see." He loosened his grip, and she twisted her head as the Guild member opened the door at the bottom of the stairs. The service of his many customers kept the innkeep busy, and it seemed he had not betrayed them. She pulled herself free of her companion's grasp and stood. With her dagger concealed at her side, she crossed the tavernroom and stood at the bottom of the stairs, Raolos's man with her. He pulled the door closed behind them. The Guild man had reached the top of the stairs, and he gave the pre-arranged knock.

Corelle did not move until she heard the key turn in the lock, then she stepped onto the first stair as a voice said, "Who are…" With that, the Guild member came into view, ran down three stairs, saw her, and stopped. Synna followed him but paused at the top of the stairs.

The Guild member pulled a dagger from his belt, and Corelle stared into desperate eyes. "Drop the blade. There are six of us. You are undone."

He smirked at her. "I may die, but I might kill you first. Are you ready to journey wherever you travel to afterward?"

She returned his smirk. "Hiw and Styrrach thought much as you do now. They were wrong."

"They were not me." He moved down the stairs, slow and guarded, as she advanced toward him at the same time. "I will take my chances." He lunged at her and thrust his dagger at her heart.

Corelle had anticipated the attack and turned sideways. His dagger came up short in any event, but it would have missed her. Hers did not miss him as she stepped forward and drove it deep into his side. Movement behind him caught her eye as Synna attacked him also. She pulled her dagger from her victim's side and slashed upward at his throat, and a gash opened from his collar bone to his ear. He cried aloud and pitched forward down the stairs to land with a heavy thump at the feet of Raolos's man, who stared down in horror as blood pooled around the Guild member's body.

Corelle scurried down to the Guild member's fallen body, checked his neck, and found a weak pulsing. He stared at her, hatred in his eyes, and she smiled at him. "Farewell." The life fled from his eyes as she spoke.

Synna's voice came from the stairs. "Is he dead?"

Corelle did not glance around as she replied. "That he is."

"That disappoints me in so public a place."

A voice called through the door. "What has turned?"

Raolos's man replied. "Nothing. Go about your business." He leaned against the door in case any tried to open it.

Corelle returned to Synna's comment. "It disappoints me also, but it could not be avoided. He would not be taken alive."

Synna bit at his lower lip before he responded. "After all else, you cannot be found here with his body. You must leave. Go to your inn. I will come there for you when we have arranged things here."

Corelle saw sense in his words and nodded to the Bailiff's man, who opened the door enough for her to squeeze through. Some blood had splashed on her tunic, but she ignored any who stared at her as she headed for the door. An eerie quiet had fallen on the tavernroom, and she guessed the patrons had heard some noise of the incident, mayhap as the Guild member fell down the stairs.

As she walked back to her inn, she reflected on the information they had learned through the day. The first man's story did not quite ring true. He may not have known the motives of those who gave him orders, but simple vengeance could not be the motivation for such an elaborate scheme and Klordia's brutal death. Something more lay behind this, and she could not unravel it. It gnawed at her without respite, like a rat will chew at a long-dead creature. Their next move must be to visit the house on Torric Street. At least two Guild members would be there. Others might also show up, if a second group did indeed exist as Synna believed.

The words of Raolos's man also nagged at her. He had implied Arella had been with child when she had died. That could not be possible, of course; she did not care for men and Corelle believed she had not lain with any. She gave an involuntary smile at the thought it had not been her who had impregnated her lover. The words the Guild member spoke earlier came back to her then. "He had some fondness for the woman you killed in Zhanghar, it turns," he had said. Krage had been Arella's Guildmeister in Ryl. Might they have lain together? Corelle did not believe so, certain Arella had never desired to lie with men.

Corelle shook her head but could not align the jumbled thoughts in her mind. Little of it made sense, but little enough had ever made sense in her life, in truth. She must hope they could capture Priu, the Senior Aide from Ryl, at the house and pry more information from him. As the lights of her inn drew close, she wondered why she had come here to pursue these men. Vengeance? Retribution? She laughed out loud. There could be no retribution for her. If that had driven her here, it had been a fool's errand. Guilt? It consumed her. Every beat of her heart condemned her in her own mind. Did she seek death as payment for that guilt? Raolos might hang her, or Krage might give her Guild justice if either of them caught her, but she could not accept she had returned to Dur in search of either of those outcomes. Vengeance, then. What other excuse could she find for her return to Dur?

Corelle paused at the door to the inn and wondered how long it would be before Synna came for her. She had time for a goblet of wine, she believed. So far today she had drunk only one, in the tavern in the square, and she had left that unfinished when the Guild member had entered. She craved another, and once more it alarmed her. The words of Pettra and Wilash came back to her. They had both warned her not to seek answers at the bottom of a goblet. Pettra had said that to drink as Corelle did would kill her. With an ironic smile, she realised she could think of worse ways to die. A few patrons still sat in the tavernroom as Corelle sat at a table that faced the room and ordered a goblet of wine.

There might yet be more work for her blade this night, and she wished to be alert and not in her cups. Small sips of the wine should see it last until Synna arrived, but he had not arrived before she stared at the bottom of the empty goblet. As she stared into it, she fought the urge to call the innkeep over and order another. She had always drunk wine, since her early teenyears. Her parents allowed her a small goblet of wine at mealtimes from time to time, but never had she drunk the quantities she now consumed. She could not decide whether it had become a concern, but it amazed her how easy it had been to become reliant on it to calm her. It took the nightmares away, and that gave her reason enough to drink.

Corelle sighed, laid her arms on the table, and rested her head on them, her eyes closed. Pettra's broken body filled her mind, surrounded by her dried blood on the floor in Arkkyd. Had Corelle's consumption of wine driven Pettra to the fate that befell her? Corelle could not deny her treatment of Pettra had been terrible. She had said horrific things to her and even threatened her. What had come over her, to treat Pettra this way? She had no answer. Another wine might help.

"Corelle, are you all right?" Synna sounded anxious.

She looked up. He stood before the table, concern in his eyes. Several men in the Bailiff's yellow tunics stood behind him. All eyes were on her, and she swept her hair back from her face. "I am fine. I dozed for a few hours while I waited for you." She sweetened her jest with a gentle laugh. "I thought I might go to bed. I feared you had forgotten me." She could not tell them the truth about the anguish that ripped her apart every moment of the day.

Synna moved around the table and sat beside her. "Then wake yourself, for we must hurry to Torric Street before those we seek can slip away."

Corelle raised a hand and squeezed her temples. "We cannot march over there with this army. If you are right, and another group is here, they will watch for signs of problems or some indication of success. These yellow-chested birds will sing a song of escape to our enemies long before we reach Torric Street, my guess."

"What then? Another Corelle plan is about to appear, I suspect." Synna's eyes twinkled.

"You and I should go alone. Leave the men behind."

He sighed and shook his head. "That will be fine if there are only two of them, as we have been led to believe. We do not know the size of the force we face. I am not ready to die, and I will have failed if I let you die."

"Then have them follow, some distance back. If other eyes watch us, they cannot fail to recognise me and follow us. They may not notice this horde that trails behind." Corelle felt certain the Bailiff's men would be spotted in their unmistakeable, bright yellow tunics. Then again, there may be no other group, and they worried over nothing. Time alone would tell.

"I am not certain they could be far enough behind to remain unseen, yet close—"

Corelle's impatience interrupted him. "By the fates, Synna. I will go alone if you prefer. They do not seek you; only me. This debate wearies me."

His face wore his hurt surprise. "I…" He seemed lost for words for a moment, then appeared to gather his thoughts. "Very well. They will follow behind. Let us hope this plan of yours works."

Corelle had not intended to snap at him, but his bruised sentiments must wait for another time. "Then let us leave now. The sand falls, and I am anxious to act."

CHAPTER 21
CORELLE

Synna gave the leader of the Bailiff's men his instructions. He emphasised they must not be seen nor heard and must not follow close enough to allow either, then nodded to Corelle. They walked out into the night and headed toward the poor quarter. Synna hugged the shadows, but Corelle motioned for him to join her in the middle of the street. "We must be seen. They must see us and follow us, if they exist at all." She remained unconvinced they would be observed.

She kept a watchful eye on every door and alleyway they passed but saw nothing to suggest they were watched, other than the few citizens they passed, most of whom hurried past them. One man threw them a hearty greeting as he staggered past them, and Synna whispered to her. "A friend of yours?"

"I do not know him. Why would I?"

"He is in his cups, and you seem to have developed a fondness for wine."

Corelle gave a frustrated sigh and glanced up at the lights of the night sky. "I enjoy a goblet of wine if that is what you intimate.

Why that should lead you to believe I am familiar with everyone in the land who also takes a drink, I know not."

He walked in silence for a time, then spoke. "I am sorry. I tried for a jest, and a poor one as it turns."

"Think nothing of it. No apology is needed." Had Synna tried to provoke her, or had she over-reacted? Twice in a short time she had felt her temper heat up within her. He had proved a loyal friend, more than competent as a colleague in violence. She sighed and changed the subject. "It cannot be far now."

The streets had turned rougher, the houses smaller and not as well maintained. They had reached the poor quarter. Synna's soft, breathy whisper eased the tension that hung in the still air between them. "Torric Street lies ahead. I have seen no sign of anybody who paid us any attention or followed us."

"Neither have I. We may be unobserved, after all else."

They stopped at the corner of Torric Street and peered down its length. It seemed unremarkable, as would be expected. The Guild would not choose to hide out somewhere that would attract attention. The closest house had the number two painted on its door in crude strokes of brash yellow, while across the road, the first house had no visible number. A small sign attached to the wall of the house next door had a faded red number three painted on it. It seemed one side of the street had been numbered with even numbers, the other odd.

Corelle leaned close to Synna and murmured into his ear. "Four houses down." He nodded confirmation, but a further thought occurred to her. "We do not know whether there is a rear door. There is an alleyway behind us." Guild houses had no more than one exit in her experience, but from what the man at the tavern had said, this house may have been chosen in haste.

Synna exhaled. "Have we lost all our skills? We are here, and yet we are as unprepared as could be. We have no plan, and we know nothing about the house."

Synna's words might lie closer to the truth than Corelle felt comfortable with. She had become careless. She vowed to do better in the future, for all any vow of hers held any worth. "Let us check down the alleyway at the least."

They slipped down the alleyway. All the houses on Torric Street had both front and rear doors, and Synna sighed. "This is not good news. We will be separated if we cover both doors. If there are more members in the house than we have been led to believe, whoever enters must do so alone and will be in great peril."

Corelle tutted. He had the right of it, but she would not admit defeat. "I will enter through the front door while you watch here. I will take my chances."

His terse reply cut through the night air. "That you will not. You might be slain, and those we seek away into the night, and I might never know until Raolos's men arrive. We must wait for them and do nothing until they are here."

She slapped her thigh in anger but could not fault his logic. "I will watch the front door, at the least. You watch here. When the others arrive, we will enter." Her half-formed plan had led them so close to answers, but mistakes had been made, and more errors might cost them dear. If a second group watched them, they would slip away like mist in the morning as soon as the Bailiff's men arrived. She tutted in annoyance.

Synna agreed with her, so she returned to the front of the house and sauntered past it, to the untrained eye no more than a neighbour on her way to her work or a shop. She cast a quick sideways glance at the house as she passed. No light shone from within, but that did not surprise her, since shutters would have been closed over the windows. The Guild did not care to be observed.

A thought struck her then. The Guild did not care to be observed, but it also did not use houses with two exits as its hideouts. One exit would be simple enough to protect. More doors required more guarding. Double the exits meant double the risk, so why had they chosen this house and not the Guild house on Water Street? She stopped. They had been told Krage and Sisnop had not come to Alcmouth. Priu and those with him might not be as skilled as others, which might explain the unusual mistake with the doors and might suggest they could be careless in other ways. They may not even post a guard inside the house.

The rationale seemed thin, but on a whim, she approached the front door and listened at it. She heard no sound from within, so she turned the handle with care. It gave off a squeak, loud to her ears, and she faced the dilemma of whether to back away or proceed. Anybody within who could hear would now be on their guard. Hesitation could cost her life, so she committed to her plan, turned the handle the rest of the way, and pushed open the door. As it swung away from her, she slid to one side of the doorway and waited for a curious head to peer out into the street, her dagger in her hand.

Nobody appeared, so she crouched down and glanced through the door. Her head would be lower than anybody inside might expect, and if the occupants launched an attack, Corelle hoped to gain vital time while they adjusted their aim, but the dark interior slumbered in silence, with no hint of shadowy movement. She stepped inside and crouched with her back to the wall, then waited, motionless, while her eyes adjusted to the darkness inside.

That darkness changed to a dim light, enough moonlight to permit limited visibility. The room must be unoccupied, or she would have heard somebody by now, and they would doubtless have attacked her. The faint light from the door showed a narrow parlour with a few chairs and little else. No trained killers stood in the room with daggers in hand, so she stood, still pressed against the wall.

Corelle took a careful step and checked for noise from each floorboard before she trusted her entire weight to it. Step by step she crossed the room with only the chairs for company. A closed door led off the parlour, but she ignored it and moved straight ahead. A staircase and a door that might be the rear exit loomed through the gloom at the far end of the parlour. She listened with an ear pressed to the rear door but heard only the sounds of the night, small creaks from the building, and the faint beat of her own heart in her ears. Time to choose; one of the doors, or the stairs. Without Synna, she did not dare to ascend the stairs. Of the two doors, she believed the one she had listened to would be the rear exit, which would lead to Synna and a second dagger in case things turned awry.

Slow and careful, she turned the handle. It did not squeak, but the door had been locked. By a stroke of fortune, the key sat in the lock, and she pulled the door open and gazed out at Synna, his dagger raised. She held a finger to her lips for silence, then beckoned him to enter the house. He shot her a look, part question, part accusation, but he entered the house and closed the door behind him with care. As Corelle had done, he stood motionless while his eyes adjusted to the murky interior. She waited until he felt comfortable. Why invite catastrophe into the operation for the sake of a few heartbeats?

Synna glanced around. He pointed to the door Corelle believed led to another room, but she shook her head. The Guild members appeared careless, reckless even, but Corelle did not want to push their luck too far. The door might be rigged to make a noise or might have something pressed against it. To open it invited attack. The stairs, too. They would be noisy and would alarm any upstairs if they slept there. She imagined she felt the sting of Porl's hand as it struck her in the Zhanghar Guild building when she tried to fix the squeak of the stairway there. Any attempt to sneak upstairs seemed destined to wake all the occupants of the house.

An idea formed in Corelle's mind. She reached for the rear door and turned the key to lock it again. She beckoned for Synna to follow her, retraced her steps to the front door, and pushed it closed. A key protruded from that lock also, and she turned it. A lantern stood on a table, and she struck the flint that lay beside it. Light sprang up and illuminated the room. Synna wore a concerned expression, but she smiled at him.

She placed a hand on the back of a nearby chair and raised her eyebrows at Synna before she scraped the chair along the floor, no attempt at silence. At the sound, Synna raised a finger to his lips, but she ignored him. The noise had been intentional, part of her plan.

They waited, and before long, a tired voice came through the ceiling from above. "Jeg, is that you?"

Corelle beckoned for Synna to follow her, approached the other door in the parlour, turned the handle, and pushed it open. She stepped inside and crouched low, but the small room held nothing but a battered couch in one corner near a fireplace. She turned as the voice from upstairs called again for Jeg to confirm he made all the noise. Synna stood nearby, a quizzical look on his face. She grabbed a handful of his tunic and pulled him into the room, then pushed the door almost closed. She dragged Synna next to her beside the door, on the hinge side, and used one hand to press him back against the wall, a finger to her lips.

They heard muttered complaints from above, then the floorboards creaked. Somebody moved across the ceiling above their heads, then came down the stairs. Corelle had been right; the stairs creaked and groaned like a worker at the end of a hard day's work. The feet hesitated as they reached the ground floor. Corelle imagined the man looked at the lantern, gazed around the room, then saw the door ajar. The feet moved closer, and the door swung inward half a pace.

"Jeg, what in the Five Cities are you about?" The owner of the voice pushed the door further open. As his shadow spilled into the room, Corelle shoved the door into the man with all her strength. The door hit him hard, and he cursed. Synna hurried around the door and had his dagger at the man's throat before he could recover his composure.

Corelle stepped out and pulled the man into the room the same way she had pulled Synna. She slammed the door shut and heard somebody else above climb out of bed and move down the stairs, in more of a hurry than the first man. In the smaller room, blood poured from the man's nose, and Synna's dagger had drawn a thin red line of blood from his throat. The man stared at Corelle as though he saw a vision as she pressed herself against the wall beside the door, this time on the handle side.

The door opened, and Corelle thrust her dagger against the throat of the second man in a heartbeat. She hissed, "Be still or die. You know who I am."

"That I do, jade." Pride and resistance flamed in his eyes, and she flicked her dagger upward to slice into an ear. He howled with pain.

Corelle snarled. "Do not delude yourself with thoughts of heroism. Many who thought themselves my equal or better now fill the bellies of whatever creatures feasted on their unburnt remains." Synna frowned at her, and she stifled a laugh. The line sounded terrible, she knew, but it had come to her, and she had been unable to resist its questionable charm.

"What of Jeg and Argull?" The man had a deep voice that resembled the growl of an animal, she thought.

"Dead. Are you Priu?" He gave an almost imperceptible nod. Corelle's blade remained pressed to his neck, and blood ran down his neck and shoulder from the ear she had cut. "Where are the others?"

"Dead, you told me." Spit flew from his lips as he spoke, his fury evident in his eyes.

"Not them, the others who came here also."

He snorted "Others? There are no others."

She gave a sardonic laugh. "Krage sent only four to capture me? I do not believe you."

He glowered at her. "You are not all you believe yourself to be."

"Yet here you are, beneath my blade." She laughed again.

He gave a small, derisive laugh of his own. "I would rather die than tell you anything."

"You will die, my guess. It matters not, after all else. The Bailiff's men come to take you to the gallows soon, and afterward we leave to kill Krage and Sisnop."

He tried to scoff, but doubt tinged his words. "They are well guarded. You will not find them easy to take."

"On a farm? I think not, unless they are guarded by muttons or milk cows."

She laughed and he squirmed against the blade in anger. "We have eyes in Yerrsun." She heard his vitriol in every word. "Your movements there will be known long ere you can act. Guild justice will be hard on you. You have set yourself against us at every turn."

She gave no indication they had already known the nearest town to the farm, albeit one of the men had misremembered its name, but it pleased her he had fallen for so crude a bluff. The training in Ryl must have been inferior to that in Zhanghar. "I set myself against nothing. Rather, you set me against yourselves, when you chose me for shrouding." He said nothing in reply, and she turned to the other. "What of you? Do you know where these others skulk, afraid to show themselves until you need their aid? They leave you to take the risks and seek to enter the fray at the end to claim all the glory. Why protect them?"

He looked downcast. "I do not know their whereabouts. I did not know others had come to Alcmouth until you…suggested it."

"Come. The Bailiff's men will be here any moment. Tell us what we wish to know, and I will release you through the rear door. You will be hanged for Klordia's murder otherwise."

His eyes widened. "I did not do that. He did." He nodded his head toward Priu.

Priu spat at the man. "Shut your mouth. Do you wish Guild justice?"

The other gave an ironic laugh. "I am a dead man either way. All is destroyed. Styrrach is dead, the Guild is shattered, and you have cost me my life."

Fists pounded on the door and heralded the arrival of Raolos's men, and Synna pushed the Guild member into the couch. He sat, despondent, and stared at the floor as he pinched the bridge of his nose in an effort to stem the flow of blood. Synna ran to the front door, unlocked it, and the yellow tunics of the Bailiff soon filled the room. They pulled the two men out into the parlour and slapped manacles on their wrists.

One of the men nodded to Corelle. "They will hang before morning."

"Raolos might consider some leniency for this one." Corelle pointed a finger at the ordinary member. "He may be prepared to swear he saw this other kill Klordia."

"That will be for Raolos to decide." Raolos's men dragged the Guild members out to the street.

Synna sat in one of the chairs in the parlour. "Success, and yet failure." He sighed and looked downcast.

"Indeed. We are little further forward, and if another group had been sent here, they must have seen all and fled."

"Do we abandon our search for them?"

"That we do. Go home and sleep. Tomorrow, I will head for Yerrsun. That is the only information we gleaned from all that passed today. I will invent a plan on the road."

Synna looked up at her, and thought creased his brow. "I will see whether Raolos can spare me. I will come to your inn if he can. If not, then tread with caution. They will be forewarned, if you have the right of it. They will expect you, and we do not know how many they are."

Faces swam before Corelle's eyes. Deineike, Arella, Pettra, Klordia, Taro. She stared at Synna, then spoke a soft reply. "I know how many of them there are."

He raised his eyebrows. "How many, then?"

She gave a grim smile. "Not enough."

CHAPTER 22
CORELLE

Corelle awoke to the sound of knuckles as they rapped on the door of her room. She guessed the hour was still early, although the effective shutters allowed almost no light into the room. Her clothes lay folded on a table beside the bed. She had not drunk any wine last night on her return to the inn. The tavernroom had been deserted and dark, neither customer nor staff visible, and she had retired to bed in frustration.

The knocks came again, and Synna's voice called out, muffled by the heavy door. "Corelle. Do you still sleep?"

She shouted back at him. "That I do. Go away, if you value your life."

Synna laughed. "Rouse yourself, I bring news."

Corelle groaned. Curse the man. Why had he turned up in the middle of the night? "Go away."

"I have pastries."

She slapped a hand to her forehead. "You try to bribe me now? I hate you." She crawled from the bed and dressed. When she tugged the door open, Synna had taken a step backward down the hallway as though fearful of her reaction to his early visit. The smell of fresh baked pastries came from a small sack in his hand. She turned, stomped into the room without a word, and tugged the shutters open. The hour was not as early as she had thought. A bright, warm summer's day greeted her as the shutters abandoned their vigil against the light that now poured into the room.

She turned. Synna had sat on her bed and worked hard on one of the cakes with the delicious cream centre. Another of the cream centred cakes had been placed on top of the sack, and she grabbed it for herself and settled in the sole chair in the room. "What news?" A mouthful of the delicious pastry turned her words to mush.

Synna wiped some cream from his face with the back of a hand. "Raolos bids me travel to Yerrsun with such help as I can find." He paused, then, "It infuriates me, this game we play, how he pretends you are not in Dur even as he knows full well you are. Regardless, he has heard nothing of Yerrsun, but we have learned it lies three days' ride to the east of Ort, or many days ride north from Eastport."

"Eastport?" Corelle had never heard of it.

"Some little town east of Alcmouth, it turns, along the coast. A small dock, a couple of taverns, and a Portreeve nobody has ever heard a word from. Eastport." He took another bite of the cake.

"It will be faster to sail to Ort and ride to Yerrsun, I think." Corelle turned over his news as she worked on the last of her pastry. "Are there more of these?"

Synna looked ashamed. "There were. They disappeared on the way here. There is a fresh bun though."

"A bun? You ate all the cream pastries and left me a bun?"

"And a cream pastry. That pastry tempted me, let me assure you. You should be grateful for that."

"I hate you." Corelle reached for the bun. Fresh baked and still warm, it had overtones of cinnamon. It tasted delicious, but compared to the cakes… "I hate you."

"More news." Synna licked around his mouth as though he

quested for some last trace of the cream. "Priu has drawn his last breath. The testimony from the other member convinced Raolos. He hanged Priu at first light. The other is banished. A better outcome than he deserved. With luck, you will find him at some other time, and there will be harsher justice."

Corelle gave him a non-committal nod. The other man mattered little to her. Priu had killed Klordia, and he had been hanged. She would have preferred to slit his throat herself, but Raolos's men had arrived, and the moment had passed. "How did Wilash respond to Priu's death?"

"He claims justice is served, but I believe he would buy you a goblet of wine for every additional death you bring to any involved."

Corelle nodded and did not doubt it for a moment. She remained determined to bring further justice for Klordia, Arella, Deineike, and Pettra. The price rose with the death of every friend, and those involved must pay. As must she, she reminded herself. Afterward.

The pastries had gone. Synna sat on the bed and swung his legs back and forth. He had no pack she could see, and she wondered how he intended to manage for fresh clothes on a journey that would take the better part of a tenday before they came to Yerrsun, and longer to complete once they arrived. "Where is your pack?"

"Downstairs. I left it with a comely woman who greeted me."

Corelle smiled as she took simple pleasure from Synna's appreciation of the woman. Corelle believed her to be the daughter of the innkeep but did not know for certain. "You burden me again. I must keep you alive so you may pursue a friendship with her on your return, my guess."

He smiled back at her. They held a tenuous grip on life, the consequence of the work they undertook. Life could be assured only until the next breath they took. Beyond that, no guarantees would be asked or given. "Indeed." He smiled. "Where is yours?"

He had criticised her unready state in so polite a manner, and she laughed, amused. Corelle crammed her few belongings back into her pack, careful not to damage Deineike's sketches any more than she already had done, then picked it up. "To Yerrsun, and whatever we find there." She cast a final glance around the room before they descended the stairs, and Synna collected his pack from the woman. He smiled at her and blushed when she returned it. The exchange entertained Corelle, and she turned away in order not to embarrass either of them with her grin.

She paid for her room, said she hoped to return soon, then they set off for the docks. Corelle studied their surroundings as they walked but nobody appeared to show any interest in them. They spoke little, and soon enough the docks came into view. The sun sparkled from the surface of the river. Several masts stretched toward the blue sky as Corelle and Synna entered the docks, and she hoped at least one of the ships would travel to Ort on the next tide.

The Torr Sea lay to the south, and the docks had been built north of the sea somewhat, in the wide mouth of the Alc as it made its way into and out of the sea with the tides. Somewhere far to the south, Pettra had lost her life. Corelle wondered about the custom in Vyrrmod. Did they hold a Pyre? Would somebody give Pettra a Pyre and a Sending? Justice of a kind had been served for Klordia, but none for Pettra, unless the death of the man who had hurt her counted as that justice. Corelle believed nothing but her own death could atone, and she longed for it with every breath she took. In truth, she should die young for all she had done in her life, but vows to end her own life lay broken and scattered behind her. Unless somebody else killed her, her death might elude her for many years. She had not yet found the courage to end the one life whose blood might pay some of the debt owed to so many who had died as a result of her existence.

Corelle stopped outside a tavern. She wished to buy a cask of wine for the voyage north, but now it came to it, she felt embarrassed to admit it to Synna, and she gave him a sad smile. He responded with a confused one of his own. Her raised hand suggested he should remain outside as she ran into the tavern, found the innkeep, and persuaded him to sell her a cask for a price she imagined he had inflated. It would doubtless be of a poor quality, here on the docks, where the rough and tumble of mariners, courtesans and dock workers made up the daily life.

Synna raised his eyebrows when he saw her emerge with the cask, but he said nothing. They approached the dockside, and Corelle voiced her thoughts. "The Dur ships, the two-masters. They are more likely to be headed for Ort than the southern traders, I think." Synna nodded in silence, and they wandered along the dock and called up to the mariners on the decks until they found a ship headed for Ort. Corelle had never seen such a small ship on the river, and the name painted on the stern, Journeys End, seemed bizarre to her. Synna laughed and explained the play on words. Corelle had not appreciated a small squiggle between the Y and the S would change the definition of the name so much, although she doubted Synna had the right of it. Deineike would know, she thought sadly. Even if Synna had been correct, she doubted the ship's owner had intended to make the pun. It seemed more likely to have been a mistake by whoever had painted the words rather than a clever jest.

They boarded, and Synna paid for passage. As they walked to their cabins, he said Raolos had given him some coin for the trip. Corelle had a tiny cabin, two bunks and two chairs the only contents. It had no window, the door had no lock, and no trunk had been provided for her belongings. With nowhere to hide all the coin she still carried, she took her pouch to Synna's room, but he had no trunk either. They agreed they had no option other than to trust the mariners not to steal the coin, though they both expressed some doubt such men could be trusted. Corelle returned to her own cabin, laid the pouch at the bottom of her bunk, and spread the pouch's contents as flat as she could before she remade the bed. She laid her pack on the blanket above the coin, the best she could do to disguise its presence.

In the common room, she found a cup and took it back to her cabin so she could drink the wine as they sailed, then decided to go up to the deck and watch the ship set off for Ort. She took her usual position at the bow of the ship and sat cross-legged on the deck. As the sounds of activity grew louder, she turned so she faced backward and could watch the mariners as they coiled ropes, pulled on lines that extended from the sails, and readied themselves to haul in the lines that ran down to the dock. Each man seemed to know his precise duties, and she saw nothing she thought would be difficult to learn. Officers barked orders, men leapt to tasks in response, and the ship slid out into the river and headed north. The sails filled with wind, and soon the little ship made good speed as it skipped along the water. The activity on the deck reduced once they were under way, though mariners coiled the lines and laid them on the deck at the front and rear of the ship.

Synna came out of the cabin area and sat near her for a time. They spoke little, nothing more than a few words of observation as the land slipped by on either side of them. Corelle guessed they sailed the widest part of the river, based on her recollections of previous journeys. As darkness fell, Synna went in search of some food, but Corelle sat at the bow until long after dark. At last, she rose and returned to her cabin, where she poured some wine into the cup, and sat on one of the chairs as she sipped at it. She had been correct about the low quality of the wine. The harsh, almost bitter taste suggested it had not been worthy of the price, but it would suffice. At first, she intended to drink only enough to drive the nightmares from her, but as the ship pressed on toward Ort, she drank more than she had planned to and had become intoxicated by the time she climbed into her bunk. Something at the bottom of the bunk, underneath her blanket, pressed against her legs, but she felt too inebriated to investigate. She kicked it aside as best she could. It jingled, and she remembered she had hidden her coin there, giggled at her own foolishness, and soon fell asleep.

Her condition the next day had become all too familiar, and she tossed in the bunk, restless, too ill to get up. She battled the urge to fetch up, her head pounded, her throat felt as dry as sand, and her eyes hurt. The ship wallowed in the water, but it appeared to have no effect on her condition; her stomach roiled without any encouragement from the river. She had no idea of the hour, but the occasional voice passed her cabin door. At some point, she reached down inside the blanket, pulled the coin pouch out, and dropped it to the floor. Her tunic lay next to the bunk, but she still wore her trousers. She could see only one of her boots, and she hoped Synna would not come to her cabin.

A knock at the door woke her, and, to her disappointment, Synna asked if she needed assistance. Corelle ignored him and stayed silent but imagined he would peer round the door at some point. She pulled the blanket over her head and hoped he would leave. The door might have opened, but Synna said nothing, and she fell asleep again. She felt little better when she woke. With great reluctance, she dragged herself out of the bunk, pulled her tunic over her head and searched for her other boot. To her dismay, she realised she had worn it to bed. She ran her fingers through her hair, and they tangled in many knots. Where had she put her hairbrush? In her pack, she imagined. She pushed her clothes around without enthusiasm until she found the brush, then sat on the bunk and ignored the pain as she dragged it through her hair until she felt satisfied she had tamed all the knots.

With a deep breath, she headed for the deck. The shock of the wind in her face refreshed and revitalised her, despite the cold of a grey day with a hint of rain in the air. She missed the warm, summer day she had left behind in Alcmouth yesterday as she wrapped her arms around herself for some warmth and made for the bow. Synna already sat there, and he glanced up as she sat down.

"What hour is it?" Her voice sounded croaky even to her.

"Around the midday."

It amazed her the hour had grown so late. He must have guessed wrong; the sun could not pierce the heavy grey cloud above. He might be mistaken.

The uncomfortable silence unsettled her. They often said little enough to one another, but she sensed some judgement from him, unless she felt guilty she had drunk so much wine. "Something is amiss?"

"I should ask you the same." He turned to face her. "You look terrible, and you smell like a tavernroom."

"I drank a little more than I realised, I think." A barefaced lie.

His head bobbed once. It might have been a nod, or some reaction to the movement of the ship. "Does this happen often?"

She tutted. "An impertinent question. I do not seek your approval for my actions."

He held up a hand. "Then so be it. You have gained weight, however, and I must be sure you can perform if it comes to a fight, that you have not slowed down."

She stared at him, open-mouthed. Had he called her competence into question? "Do you know how much blood I have spilled?" Venom had crept into her voice.

"That I do not. Much, my guess."

"Then you should not doubt me. I could kill you in the blink of an eye, whatever doubts you hold about me."

He shook his head. "You are unfathomable. At times, you are easy company, but there is unpleasantness in you."

Her lips drew back from her teeth as her anger grew. "Forgive me. One would think my life of ballgowns and attentive suitors would have made me a nicer person." She turned away in a sulk and watched the water as the ship sliced through it with ease. Another episode of temper, but Synna had angered her with his words, and she felt justified in her rage. She made no effort to break the silence between them as the vessel carried them north toward a town Corelle felt she had visited more times than she would have cared to, and never to any good purpose.

CHAPTER 23

CORELLE

Corelle lay back on the deck, weary. She had no sooner done so than Synna spoke again. "I grew up in the poor quarter of Alcmouth with an oaf of a father, in his cups more often than not. Somebody killed him when I was young, a fight over a hand of cards. An accident, they said, the misfortune of a brawl in a tavern while intoxicated. One punch and no more, but his head smashed into the floor, and he never woke again. My mother did her best to take care of us. She took in laundry from the better parts of the city, cleaned floors, whatever she could find."

He paused, and Corelle turned to gaze at him as he fiddled with a sleeve. "I became a thief at a young age, stole anything I could lay my hands on; food from stalls so we could eat, anything I could sell for a few groats. I killed my first man in my early teenyears, an attempt to pick a pocket turned awry. The man produced a knife, but I took it from him and killed him with it. I weighed little more than a sack of tubers and never grew tall, but my speed and toughness saw me through those times. Somebody suggested I should meet a man called Styrrach who might find me some work. The rest…"

Synna fell silent again, and Corelle could not understand why he had told her this story. "I had no privileged childhood, any more than you did. Less so, my guess. Yet I do not spit threats at my friends as you do. It is unfathomable, as I have already said."

"You had a difficult life. You had a low hand and played it as well as you could. You have emerged to a better outcome than many might have in your circumstances. Do not expect pity or sympathy from me. You have guessed right; I enjoyed a comfortable childhood, with parents who loved me, and no shortage of coin. Then I met Arella. From that moment, through nobody's fault but mine, my life has turned as black as the darkest night. Blood and death stalk and manipulate me. You cannot know what gnaws at me. You cannot understand, for you are not me."

Synna shook his head. "I know what gnaws at you, although I accept I cannot understand it. How you bear it, I cannot say, and I admire your resilience. I do not believe I could have done so. I would have ended my life, I am certain."

"Empty words. At times, they have sprung to my own lips with similar ease. It is not so easy to act on them. The mind invents ever more plausible reasons to delay. I may live forever, and forever promise myself I will kill myself as soon as I avenge the next person whose life I have destroyed."

"You find the strength to cope with these things in the wine? Is that what you say?"

His earnest gaze pierced her, and she looked away, ashamed, then sighed, resignation more than misery. "It may be. I turned to drink when the arguments with Pettra grew unbearable. I should never have taken her south with me."

He seemed to contemplate her answer for a few moments before he replied. "I have never drunk much, the occasional tankard of ale and no more. I cannot imagine any answers lie at the bottom of an empty tankard. You would be more likely to fall over than strike me today, it seems to my eye. That is dangerous by itself, but excessive wine must affect other things—judgement, speed, perception."

"Synna. You mean well, I am certain. But please—leave me be. I am a conundrum to myself. You can never unravel me. Do not strain our friendship and press me in directions I do not wish to go."

He gave a heavy sigh. "I have never doubted your capabilities. In a dangerous spot, I must trust your skills will not desert you. My own life might depend on it."

"Then trust. I will not let you down. Now, let us speak no more of this. I apologise for my outburst earlier. You are right; there is part of me I cannot control, and it is quick to anger these days. Klordia's death has compounded my guilt, to say nothing of poor Pettra."

Synna gazed off to the side of the ship for a while. After some time, he spoke again, a friendly tone to his voice. "I do not think I have ever travelled so fast on the river. Either this ship has remarkable speed, or the wind pushes us along with some extra strength."

She nodded. The small trees and fields raced past at a pace she had never noticed before. She glanced up at the sails, which billowed above them. "The wind, my guess. We may reach Ort sooner than we anticipated."

"Have you eaten today?"

The question caught her by surprise. "That I have not. In truth, I am not hungry."

"You should eat something." His soft voice carried encouragement.

"Have you eaten the bread they carry on these ships?"

He pulled a face of distaste. "That I have, when I journeyed north on The Jorinda. It is as vile a bread as I can imagine."

Corelle gave a soft laugh of agreement, then recalled the incident long ago when she had tricked Wilash into eating it. "Wilash has a taste for it."

Synna looked staggered by the revelation. "That he does not. I refuse to believe anybody can enjoy it."

"He does." She looked down, consumed by the memory of that journey. Both Deineike and Klordia had been killed since that voyage. How could that be? She shook her head.

Concern in his voice, Synna laid a hand on her arm. "Something troubles you?"

"That it does, but there is little to be done about it, I fear. Let us see if we can find something edible in the common room."

Corelle drank little wine that night, somewhat bashful over the confrontation with Synna, and she wished to avoid feeling so dreadful the next day, in truth. Despite how long she had slept that morning, she retired to her bunk early, exhausted.

The following morning, she met the master in the common room. He confirmed strong winds from the south had helped the little ship, and he thought they might arrive in Ort late the next day. It would be one of the fastest voyages he had ever had, he told her. Synna nodded when she relayed the news to him later that morning. To her relief, no awkwardness lingered from the previous day's conversation, and Synna did not suggest Corelle felt so much better because she had not drunk to excess the night before, although he must have noticed her liveliness throughout the day compared with the day before.

That night, however, she drank more and again felt intoxicated when she collapsed into the bunk. She could not explain it, but once she started to drink, she could not stop, continued until inebriated, then needed to sleep. The next day, she felt terrible and had to find a pail as she fetched up through the morning. She decided not to spend any time at the bow of the ship as she could endure no more recriminations from Synna.

Corelle went to the common room at one point and found some meat and cheese she could take back to her cabin, along with a little fruit. She ate the food mouthful by slow mouthful, pleased it stayed down, for she had feared she would fetch it straight back up. Miserable, she took Deineike's sketches from her pack and looked through them until a knock came at the door, and she looked up and called out for the person to enter.

Synna peered round the door. "I thought I would check on you. I have not seen you at all today."

"I desired no company. I would be poor company today, in truth." She let out a miserable sigh.

Synna seemed to notice the sketches. "You sketch?"

"That I do not. Deineike used to, although she was terrible."

Synna seemed contemplative for a moment. "I will leave you with her memory." He turned to leave.

"Synna." He stopped and looked back at her. "My thanks."

He smiled and left the cabin, and tears ran down her cheeks. She packed the sketches again. They had become battered. She must find a way to store them that would protect them, since her pack appeared unsuited to that task.

Melancholy drove her to take some fresh air, so she walked to the bow but did not sit as had become normal. The wind rippled the surface of the river as it stretched out ahead of the ship. The river had no worries, she guessed. It ebbed and flowed with the tide and had no responsibilities. If somebody chose to jump into it, it had no obligation to tend to their safety. If heavy rains came, it left its banks and spread where it wished with no guilt, and only returned to its course once the myriad tributaries that flowed into it no longer overfed its gluttony. It felt neither happiness nor sadness. It shed no tears, nor did it laugh. It seemed an idyllic life.

It would be easy to embrace that life, she reasoned. She need only jump from the ship and join the river in a permanent union. All her cares would be behind her. Nobody would ask her to kill for them again. She leaned over the rail and watched as the ship ploughed forward, fascinated by the splash of the droplets as the sharp point of the bow parted the water. When she leaned forward further and stared down into the water, it seemed to whisper to her. *"Come to me. Abandon your cares. I will tend to you."* She sat on the wooden rail, swung her legs over the side, leaned forward, and watched her feet as they dangled over the river.

Hands grabbed her arms, and a gruff voice came from behind her. "Dangerous that, miss. You can fall right easy, then down to Helchik's treasure with you."

She turned. A mariner held her tight with his large hands, faded etchings all over his hairy arms. "Helchik?"

"The ruler of the seas. He keeps his treasure down deep, way under the waters. People who go in, they go down to him. Some say he claims them as part of his treasure."

"Ruler of the sea? I have never heard of this."

"Few have unless they ply the waters for their coin, miss. Now, why don't you come back aboard? I'll catch it from the master if you go down to the treasure. Like as not he'll refuse to pay me for the voyage."

Corelle had lost count of the number of times she had sailed. It would not be many compared to these mariners, but it staggered her nobody had mentioned this treasure story to her before. Not that she believed it, of course, but it had been a quaint story. She swung her legs back over the rail and stood on the deck. "I will not go to Helchik tonight." She gave the man a smile.

He nodded and left her alone, although she noticed he did not wander far. She wondered whether he realised she had contemplated a jump from the ship, or whether he thought she had sought a thrill, to ride with her feet over the river. No matter, the moment had passed. Corelle would not be added to the treasure. She would return to her cabin and be tormented by thoughts of the four women whose faces had been forever burned into her memory, then fall into nightmares. The prospect did not appeal, but what else could she do? She spoke to the mariner as she passed him. "I will get no better offer." He nodded his head and smiled as though he had understood.

A little wine remained in the cask, and she finished it alone in her cabin. It seemed possible the wine's low quality may have contributed to worse after-effects than she might have felt had she drunk a better wine. She lay on the bunk until sleep took her.

Tonight's nightmare had never come to her before. She stood before a door. A wall ran away on either side of the door as far as the eye could see. From behind the door, Pettra's voice cried, "Let me out."

Corelle turned the handle, but the door had been locked and had no key. She bent to it and fiddled with her dagger until she heard the tongue of the lock clear the groove in the door frame. When she pushed the door open, another wall ran away from her, a fresh door set into it, and from behind it, Pettra's voice called again. "Let me out."

As before, the door would not open, and she pried the lock open with her dagger. Once more, a wall ran away from her and once more, a door had been set into the wall. Again, Pettra called to be let out, and again Corelle opened the lock with her dagger in confusion. Why did the walls continue to appear? She should be back where she started by now, she believed. Her dagger opened the lock again and repeated the entire scenario.

Over and over, the same thing. Corelle opened the door, but instead of Pettra she found another door to unlock. When at last her eyes opened to free her from the nightmare, sweat soaked her. The nightmare had not been violent or bloody, but she thought it had been the worst nightmare she had ever had. She hoped it would never be repeated.

Corelle trusted they would reach Ort later that day, as the master had suggested. With the wine gone and the nightmares back, she felt ready to leave the ship. So much time had been wasted on ships in the last year or so as she waited to reach one destination or another. It bored her.

She mentioned the nightmare to Synna as they sat together at the bow later in the day and asked him what he thought it might mean. Most of her nightmares had been simple enough to unravel, and almost all involved the death of someone close to her in some hideous way. Corelle believed such nightmares to be the work of her guilt. This one made no sense to her, and to her frustration, Synna could not fathom its significance either.

As the last light of the day faded, Corelle saw the outskirts of Ort ahead of them. Relieved they could leave the ship, she retrieved her pack and watched the buildings grow ever denser. They had reached Ort, and she waited, impatient for the ship to dock and a ramp to be raised up. She hurried down the ramp and stood for a moment to allow herself to become accustomed again to the firm ground beneath her feet. Synna did not appear desperate to leave the ship, and she thought she might wander off to find an inn. He appeared at the top of the ramp and his eyes swept the dockside until he saw her. His cheerful wave surprised her, not at all what she had expected. She beckoned for him to join her, and he wandered down the ramp.

She spoke as he drew close. "We should find an inn."

He pursed his lips. "Could we not cross to Eastort tonight and stay at an inn there? We would have a good start tomorrow this way. It seems better to me."

She considered his point. He had the right of it; it would save time in the morning, but she did not know whether the rowboat still plied its trade so late in the day. It had almost grown dark, and it might be dangerous to cross the river in such a small boat in darkness. "Let us see if the rowboat still crosses this late."

A sign at the rowboat dock said the boat had left earlier for its last journey of the day and would set off again from Eastort at the sunrise the next day. They found an inn on the docks, reluctant to wander far, determined to rise early and take the rowboat on its first return journey. They took two small rooms on the first floor, at the rear of the inn. The small, three-storey building came nowhere near the quality of the finer inns Corelle had been staying at since she helped herself to Styrrach's coin. Her pouch felt far lighter these days, and she guessed she could not make the coin last much longer.

Corelle dropped her pack on the bunk and headed down to the tavernroom. As she sat at a table with a goblet of wine, she realised she had made no attempt to hide her coin. She had been in such a hurry to reach the tavernroom, it had slipped her mind. Synna may have had the right of it. The wine might affect her judgement, after all else.

With a shake of her head, she dismissed the thought and ordered a second goblet of wine. The low-quality wine reminded her of the cask she had drunk on the ship, also bought in a dockside tavern. She gazed around her. Four women sat in the tavernroom. The men appeared to be dock workers for the most part, finished for the day. She saw no mariners, and she wondered what made any given tavern appeal more to different types of workers. Three of the women appeared to be courtesans and the other wore rough clothes like those of the dock workers, as though she also worked on the docks. Precious few women did, but Deineike had worked in a tally house in Vjort and found the work none too difficult, although she had been a tall, muscular woman, unlike the one in the tavernroom tonight.

Corelle lost interest in the woman as she started on her third goblet. Synna entered the tavernroom and gazed around himself as the innkeep poured him a tankard of ale. His gaze met Corelle's, then slid to the table and the goblet. He carried his ale over to Corelle's table and sat opposite her.

He took a sip of his ale. "I hope we can rent horses in Eastort."

Corelle had not considered this difficulty. "We must be able to.

The rowboat cannot carry horses, and people must cross here to ride to Dur City and other towns in the east."

He sipped again. "I hope so. It will be a lengthy walk if we cannot."

She pondered his words. "I wonder why there is an Eastort and an Eastport. They are easy to confuse, I imagine."

Synna looked into his ale. "They may be, though they are far apart. One may not know of the other."

"Eastort is clumsy on the tongue."

"That it is. More so after several drinks."

Corelle pouted. "I have only had three."

He held up his hands. "My apologies. I meant that comment as a jest, not as a barb aimed at you."

Corelle sighed, frustrated. She seemed to have become so sensitive these days. She drained her goblet. "Three will be my lot for tonight. I will await you in the morning and we will discover whether we ride or walk to Yerrsun." He returned her smile. "Goodnight, Synna."

"Sleep well. I trust the nightmare will not plague you again."

He had wished in vain, and Corelle opened the wearisome doors again all night until she woke in the morning drained and dejected. She lay on her cot, listened to a light rain fall outside, and whispered to herself. "Please have horses. I have no energy for a lengthy walk in the rain." Then she dragged herself out of the cot, splashed some water on her face and headed downstairs to begin the journey to Yerrsun.

CHAPTER 24
CORELLE

The unseasonable strong wind that had carried them north in so short a time made the river choppy. The rowers fought against the wind and the current to keep the little boat on course, and the five passengers gripped the side. The little craft wallowed from side to side in the rough water in the middle of the river as though it tried to cast them all down to Helchik's treasure. Corelle wondered how Wilash had endured the rowboat a second time when they were summoned to Raolos's service. They may have travelled to Alcmouth via Eastport to avoid a repeat of the experience.

Many of the passengers fetched up into the water, and even Corelle sighed with relief when at last they were across and on firm ground again. Synna shook his head in obvious displeasure. "What an unpleasant journey."

"Let us hope further unpleasantness can be avoided, and we can rent two horses. Or even one."

"One?"

"It will be no unpleasantness for me if you are forced to walk."

Synna laughed at her jest. "Come, faithless friend, let us see how many horses we can find. I will settle for a large dog if a horse cannot be found."

Now Corelle laughed, and they had not walked far from the small dock before they saw a livery stable. Synna negotiated for two sturdy horses complete with tack. Corelle insisted one of the horses be docile as she remained a poor rider despite her time on horseback in Vyrrmod. Synna paid the stable keeper, and they set off eastward. A light rain still fell, but ahead of them the sky promised better weather later in the day.

The directions they requested from the stable master proved unnecessary. Only one road led away from Eastort, and it headed east. The man had confirmed the road led to Yerrsun, to the north of Mount Belram, and some villages lay along the road with some meagre accommodations. Corelle's mind wandered back to the journey south from Taro's farm, when she and Deineike had been obliged to spend many nights on the hard ground under a thin blanket no matter the weather. She no longer wished to travel in such a manner.

At first, they rode in silence, but as she thought about the coin Synna had spent, given to him by Raolos, she asked about the vast sum of Styrrach's coin she had left with the new Bailiff.

"He has put it to excellent use, in truth. He bought large houses in each of the five cities and made them available as accommodation for street urchins. A friend of his oversees the operation in a new division of the Bailiff's office Raolos has created. He has yet to expand the operation to the larger towns, but I believe he intends to. Reports say fewer urchins are seen on the streets these days. He has told me he intends to create a new post attached to each of the houses that will work in the poorer quarters and encourage women to seek help if they find themselves with a child whose father's identity might be… difficult to establish. He has done well, I think, and has great ambition to do better."

Corelle nodded in satisfaction. Raolos had already done more than she had the imagination to envisage, and he seemed bent on more. Styrrach's ill-gotten gains had turned to some good, after all else. "He is a good man."

"That he is. He has named the operation 'House of Deineike,' in honour of her time as an urchin herself."

Corelle's throat tightened, and her eyes stung as she fought back the tears. She had shed tears enough in the past year. They were treacherous companions who promised to assuage guilt but failed to deliver. What purpose tears served, Corelle did not know.

The rain stopped, and they encouraged the horses to walk at a decent pace and even trotted for some stretches, though they did not wish to over-exert them. As the sky cleared, the enormous Mount Belram stretched up to the clouds, far above the smaller mountains that surrounded it. Wispy smoke drifted up from the highest point of its cone and mystified Corelle. "Why does Mount Belram smoke?"

"I confess, I do not know." Synna shaded his eyes with a hand as he peered to the south. "I do not think I have ever noticed the mountain before today, and I know nothing of it."

Corelle shrugged and resolved to ask at whatever inn they stayed at tonight, and they rode on. They did not stop to take lunch, as Deineike had always been keen to do. They pressed on until, late in the day, they saw a small village ahead of them.

Synna reined to a halt and glanced backward at the sun, low in the sky. "Should we stop here or press on? A fair part of the day remains if we wish to continue."

Corelle thought for a few heartbeats. "Let us stop. We do not know when we will encounter another inn, and parts of me already tire of this beast."

Synna snorted. "Little more than two hours have you ridden it."

"Your knowledge of the passage of time appears as scant as your knowledge of the mountain. Seven hours, my guess. I long for some respite from this saddle." Synna opened his mouth to reply, but she interrupted him. "Do not say a word. I do not like to ride, and my behind aches. If you breathe one word about my behind, I will stab you in yours and leave you unable to ride at all."

He laughed, then nodded. "Very well, let us find some accommodation palatial enough for your needs."

They rode on. But for a few houses each side, they might not have been in a village at all. They had passed almost every house and worried they would not find an inn, but at last they saw one, set back from the road. It looked little more than a tavern, a rail outside with two horses hitched to it, and a sign that read "The Eastlands Inn." In the area between the inn and the road, a small carriage might stand if its passengers desired a break from their journey. They saw no sign of a stable, so they fastened the reins of the horses to the rail and entered the inn. The door opened into the tavernroom, where two weather beaten men sat at a table, a tankard before each of them. At a small counter in one corner of the tavernroom, a short, jittery young woman fiddled with the tankards stacked behind the counter.

The two men looked up as Corelle and Synna entered. One nodded in welcome, and Corelle smiled at him. The men wasted no more time on them and resumed their conversation, and the woman turned from her tankards as they crossed the tavernroom toward her. She paused, surprise on her face when she noticed them.

Synna greeted her. "Good evening." The woman chewed at her lip but did not answer. "We seek accommodation for the night, if you have any." The woman still said nothing, and she favoured Synna with a blank stare.

"She is simple." One of the two men behind them had spoken, and Corelle turned her attention back to them. "Cannot hear, we think. Never get a word out of her, nohow."

Synna turned his head toward them. "Then how does she run the inn?"

"She does not run it." The other man took over. "Her father runs it. He only leaves her here if he has an errand to run or such."

The first man muttered. "That he does, curse him. Woe betide you if you drain your tankard while she is there. She can no more fill a tankard than fly, but will she let you fill your own?"

The other shook his head. "That she will not."

Corelle let out a breath of frustration at the men's long-windedness. "Do you know whether the innkeep will be gone long?"

"Hard to say." Back to the first man. Did they take it in turns to speak? "Could be he will. Could be he will be back before you can say your name."

Corelle could not contain another frustrated sigh. "Corelle is my name. Synna, my friend."

The man nodded. "My mistake. I did not ask for your name, friend. That is no more than an expression we use hereabouts."

He did not offer either of their names and Corelle raised her eyebrows in astonishment at such unusual manners less than a day's ride from Ort. Isolation must make these people less friendly. She imagined few enough folk from the east would bother to ride the little rowboat to visit the large town to the west. "You keep to yourselves over this side of the river, I imagine?"

"That we do." The second man again, or mayhap the first. They looked alike to Corelle. "See few westfolk here, to tell you the truth. Large group came through here from somewhere to the east not twenty days since, and some of them rode back east in a hurry yesterday."

The other corrected him. "Day before. Seemed to me like they ran from something—you, for all I know. Had their tails betwixt their legs, whatever it was chasting them."

"Chasting?" Synna frowned.

"Chasting. Do you fancy westfolk have a better word for being chased?"

Synna stared at the two men as though they had spoken

Vyrrmod, and Corelle felt obliged to respond. "That we do not, but I assure you, we are not the ones chasting the men. We travel to Yerrsun to bring news of our mother's death to our sister there."

"Closer to two passes than twenty days." Corelle stared at the man who had spoken, confused.

The other mumbled, grudging. "You may have the right of it. Long time ago, after all else."

Corelle guessed they meant the two groups who had travelled to Alcmouth to kill Klordia. It sounded as if they had all travelled together, which did not gel with what they had been told in the tavern in the square. "They rode through two passes ago, all together, is that correct?"

"I cannot say they all rode together. I do not know how many of them there are, altogether. More went than returned. More than that, I cannot swear to."

Corelle exchanged a worried glance with Synna. Why had the Guild member, Jeg or Argull, lied when he said he did not know about the other group? If they had travelled together, then he knew they were there, something he had denied, even with his life in peril. That would be something they could discuss in privacy, she decided.

"Why does it smoke, the mountain?" Synna's question took Corelle by surprise.

The men laughed. "Because it is asleep. Hope it does not wake while you are out this way."

"Wake?" Corelle had not known mountains could be asleep or awake.

"When it wakes, it does more than smoke. It belches out fire and rocks, and worse. You run if it wakes, you hear? If you run fast enough, you might even live."

Corelle shook her head in disbelief. "Then why do you live here, where it might wake and kill you?"

One of the men rubbed a chin, thoughtful. "Like as not you

would be fine here. We are a day or two from it. Yerrsun is closer. You might be in danger there. If you wander too close and wake it, you will not live to regret your impetuosity."

Corelle struggled to believe the man, other than the fact she could see no point in the invention of such a fantastic tale. At that moment, another man entered the tavernroom. He stopped for a moment to take in the scene, then moved toward them. "Ah, visitors. Forgive my daughter, she does not hear, nor speak."

"Think nothing of it." Synna, it seemed, had regained his composure and power of speech. "We enjoyed our conversation with our two new friends."

The innkeep glanced at the two men. "Those buffoons? You did well to understand them. They are unable to put three words together to form a sentence."

"Buffoons?" One of the men looked at the newcomer, wide-eyed. "That is a fighting word, brother." All three men burst into gales of laughter, while Synna shook his head, and Corelle glanced around to see whether hordes of people lay hidden as they watched some inconceivable jest played at hers and Synna's expense.

"They are your brothers?" Synna had bewilderment in his voice and on his face.

"That they are, I am sorry to admit." What the men had said earlier no longer made sense. Why in the Five Cities could they not help themselves to ale if their brother owned the inn?

"They want a room for the night." One of the seated men took it upon himself to explain their visit.

"That will be no problem." The innkeep smiled.

"Might be they will pay you, too. Westfolk."

The innkeep laughed and turned to Synna. "Just the one room is it, sir?"

"Two." Corelle hurried to correct him.

The innkeep hesitated. "Two it is. Out here, we stay out of other folks' business. No city ways out here."

Corelle could not accept their customs could be so different this side of the river. "You are less than a day from Ort."

"Ort is a town." This from one of the men at the table.

Corelle gave up. "You have the rooms? My friend will pay."

The innkeep gestured to his daughter, an elaborate series of movements with his hands that took several heartbeats. "My daughter will show you to your rooms."

Corelle glanced at the girl, who reached behind the counter, came out with a shawl, and wrapped it around her shoulders. "You speak to her with gestures?"

The innkeep had no time to respond before one of his brothers spoke. "No other way to talk to her."

For a heartbeat, Corelle wished she could wake from what must be a nightmare. The girl motioned for them to follow her and moved toward a door at the rear of the tavernroom. "Can we stable our horses?"

The laughter returned, louder than when the innkeep had insulted his brothers. In time, the innkeep calmed enough to speak. "You won't need a stable for them. Nobody will steal them, not from outside my inn. No rain will come for days now, and if the mountain wakes enough to spit at us here, horses will be the least of your worries."

"That they will." One of the brothers managed to gasp words among his laughter.

"Our horses have been out there for three days." The other brother this time.

"Four."

The innkeep joined in his brothers' fun. "A tenday, it feels to me, you are such bad company." They all collapsed into laughter again.

Corelle and Synna followed the girl out of the door and across a bare patch of ground to a cabin where the girl pushed the door open and gestured inside. When Corelle stepped in, she saw five doors and guessed they led to five rooms. She turned to ask the girl which rooms they should use, but she had gone.

Synna whispered, as though afraid the brothers might hear him. "What in the Five Cities?"

"I do not know. Strange beyond anything I have ever encountered. Am I asleep? Is this one of my nightmares?"

"If it is, then I am in it also, tormented as much as you."

Corelle sighed. "We can take any room we wish, my guess." She pushed a door open and entered the room, small, with a single cot, a chair and table, and a small vanity stand with an empty pitcher on it. A chamber pot sat under the bed. A small, shutterless window looked west, where the sun had disappeared. She went back out, opened another door, and found an identical room that faced east. Of the other three doors, two were rooms, one of which Synna had claimed. A privy with a pump lay beyond the fifth door. She filled her water pitcher, and Synna's also, then kicked her pack under the cot, sat on the chair, and stared out as darkness folded the Eastlands into its embrace.

Some wine would be pleasant, but she did not want another encounter with the oafish brothers. After no more than a few moments, she lost the battle with her need and wandered back to the tavern room. Nothing had changed. Corelle thought the beard of one of them bushier than the other, so she decided to call them Bushy and Sparse, since they appeared to be in no rush to let slip their real names. The daughter sat on a trestle at a table next to theirs, a pitcher and a cup before her.

Corelle asked for a goblet of red wine, which produced much laughter. The innkeep thought he had some and scrabbled around under the counter for some time before he came up with a cask covered in dust. "Some westfolk passed through and left me this, hundreds of years ago now. I hope it is still all right." The comment amused Bushy and Sparse, who roared with laughter. The innkeep had no wine goblets, so Corelle settled for a small tankard, not the full-size things the two men drank from. He poured the wine into it. "Shall I add the cost to your room, miss?"

She waited for the laughter to subside before she replied. "That would be the civilised thing to do."

"Civilised?" Bushy yelled. "Big word, that. That a fancy word for westfolk?" She recalled an old phrase from Ryl. *"If you cannot beat them, you are as well to join them."* She roared with laughter at his jest but fancied she could not be heard over their own raucous guffaws.

Tears rolled down the innkeep's face. "What is your room number?"

"I do not know. I took the first room on the western side."

"Oh dear." The innkeep looked mortified.

"Oh dear." Either Sparse or Bushy shared his regret.

"What?"

The innkeeper gave her a serious stare. "That room is reserved for the Duke. He arrives later."

She saw the jest too late, which compounded the laughter. She felt the heat in her cheeks, and she gazed around the tavernroom as she fought her temper. As the laughter abated, she sipped at the wine. To her surprise, the wine had a delicious flavour, fruity and full-bodied. Whoever had left it had more taste than these rubes, it seemed. "How much will this swill be?"

After a brief pause, either Bushy or Sparse said, "I like her. She has spirit."

"That she has." At the least, both of them had grown fond of her.

The innkeep smiled. "I do not quite know what to say. Look, it came to me free, I cannot very well charge you for it now, can I?"

"That you can, and you will. My companion works for the Bailiff and will pay for it, along with the rooms."

Bushy and Sparse's laughter almost defeated the innkeep's attempt to reply. "Best be on our top behaviour tonight, brothers.

We have the Bailiff's own aides in the Duke's room, as it turns."
The laughter took an eternity to die down. Corelle joined in, since
she saw the funny side of that jest.

Bushy yelled at her. "Here, come sit with us." She had no wish
to join them, but did not want to appear rude, even among such
unpolished gems as these. "You can tell us about the Bailiff and his
fancy ways."

With a resigned sigh, Corelle carried her wine to their table and
sat next to Sparse, her back to the wall.

CHAPTER 25
CORELLE

The three brothers and Corelle talked and drank for an hour or more, and the conversation became louder with each new round of drinks. How the innkeep intended to account for the drinks, she neither knew nor cared. Synna would pay in the morning. She enjoyed the wine, but the conversation brought her less satisfaction. At times, the brothers became so lewd, Corelle worried about the young girl, who still sat at the adjacent table, until she remembered they had all claimed the innkeep's daughter could not hear.

Synna joined them after a time. He watched Corelle like an anxious parent, and he seemed to disapprove of the amount she drank. By now it did not matter to her, as she had drunk sufficient to lose any inhibitions she might have had were it not for the wine. The two brothers seemed unaffected by the ale they consumed, which Corelle thought remarkable if they had drunk without pause for four days as they claimed.

Synna endured some banter about his work with the Bailiff. He denied it and claimed Corelle had spun a tall story. The brothers asked her what work she did, and she said, "A killer for hire." Synna gave her a hard, expressive stare. The reply brought extensive laugher and many jests about how they must not turn their backs on her.

The innkeep asked how much she would charge to kill Bushy and Sparse, and she said she would be happy to do the job for free in payment for their jests at her expense. Bushy would have none of it. "Try it. You are so tiny, a strong wind would knock you down."

Synna's face had reddened, and he looked concerned. "This jest has run its course. Tell us instead what you do for work."

Sparse burped, then answered. "We do as little as we can get away with."

"We are drinkers for hire." The predictable laughter at Bushy's jest ensued. Corelle had grown tired of the laughter and the jests and struggled to retain the focus of her gaze. She wondered whether she should pull out her dagger and slaughter them all.

When she stood, she stumbled and almost fell. The innkeep would not serve her any more wine, and she became annoyed. Synna intervened in the argument and insisted he take her to her room. He would not leave, and she soon fell asleep, still in her clothes.

The morning brought the usual remorse, along with another headache and bilious stomach. Synna had left her room, and Corelle lay on the cot and cried to herself. To be a killer had always been a difficult load to carry, to have brought about the deaths of so many who had not deserved it, but when she added the angry, incoherent inebriate she had become last night, the package became hideous even to her. Once, she had been a clandestine killer. Now she boasted of her nature in public and offered to kill all who stood before her, friend or foe.

A knock on the door interrupted her self-loathing, and Synna's voice asked if she had woken. She called him in, and his gaze piled further recrimination upon her. "Corelle, you need to do something about this."

Corelle looked away. She feared he had the right of it but had been powerless to stop herself last night. If the innkeep had continued to serve her, would she have killed the brothers? Their constant banter and jests had rankled her, but they were harmless enough. After all else, she had said she would be happy to kill them.

"Corelle?" Synna touched her shoulder, gentle and concerned.

She shrugged him off. "I will be ready in a moment. You should settle with the innkeep and check our horses are still outside."

He sighed, then left the room. Weary to her bones, Corelle dragged herself to the privy and resisted the urge to fetch up. She stumbled again, exhausted, then collected her pack and headed out through the empty tavernroom.

The sun already warmed the morning, and to her surprise it had climbed higher in the sky than she had expected. She had slept overlong. Synna and the innkeep stood by the two horses. The brothers' horses had gone and Corelle threw her pack onto her mount and avoided eye contact with the innkeep. Synna and the man exchanged soft words, then Synna pulled himself onto his horse.

The innkeep had an inexplicable sadness in his voice. "Farewell. Safe journey."

She pressed her heels to the flank of her horse and rode after Synna in a sulk. They did not talk for some time as they plodded through the morning. The Eastlands were different to the Northlands. Other than the range of mountains to the south, where Mount Belram continued to smoke, much of the land seemed to be flat, but dry and dusty, with none of the lush green fields of the Northlands. Almost no wind blew, and the smoke from Mount Belram climbed straight up to the sky like a stone column. Much of the land either side of the road appeared to be scrappy farmland. Occasional fields of muttons or milk cows broke up the patchwork of crops that grew in abundance around them. Corelle did not recognise any of the crops and wondered how they could grow in such dusty soil. They passed an occasional house and some lanes she guessed led to farmyards. They met nobody as the day wore on. Synna did not stop, and he did not slow or ride beside her. He left her alone with her headache and her dark thoughts.

The sun warmed her back as the day progressed. The warmth should have been pleasant, but it brought her no real joy. She had spent the journey in contemplation of things she had already brooded on for more hours than could be reckoned, and nothing had changed. Each day followed the last, and she could find no peace. If she had dug a pit in which to bury her own inadequacies, she had achieved nothing more than to dig ever deeper as she added failure after failure like extra holes in a belt.

A small knot of buildings ahead might be a village or town. She hoped Synna would stop, but the late start had cost them time, and he might press on further. As they approached the collection of buildings, however, he slowed, and she caught up with him. He sounded terse, irritated. "This is the last village before Yerrsun. Yerrsun is a long day's ride from here. We can rest here and face a long day in the saddle tomorrow, or we can ride on, sleep on the ground, and face a shorter journey."

She did not wish to sleep on the ground tonight or any night. "Let us break our journey here."

"We must leave early tomorrow in that case. It is a full day's ride to Yerrsun. The innkeep gave me this information. It surprised him how intoxicated you allowed yourself to become last night."

"That need not concern him. I trust he charged you for the wine I drank."

"That he did."

"Then he is none the worse for the encounter, and much of his long-forgotten cask of wine is gone. The rest of it, I guess, he will again ignore until it becomes undrinkable."

Synna sighed. "This cannot continue, Corelle. I would rather go on alone than endure nights of intoxication from you, followed by churlish words and days where I must tread with feathery steps around you, lest you erupt into some rage and threaten me."

"I did not ask you to accompany me. You came of your own intent."

"That I did, for the friendship I bear you and Wilash both. I wish to see justice for Klordia. Unlike you, I cared for her."

She snapped her head around. "You suggest I did not care about her?"

"That I do not. You cared about her, but you did not care for her. They both told me of the tension between the pair of you."

"No doubt all the blame sits at my feet." She heard the bitterness in her own voice.

"That it does not. It stung Klordia she had been so abrupt with you. I believe she came to understand the weight that crushes you and regretted she did little enough to alleviate it."

The debate came to an abrupt end when they spotted an inn called "Belram's Shadow," and Corelle thought the name apt. "Are there other inns, or will we spend the night in the shadow of the mountain?" She remained angry about the conversation but felt no urge to continue it.

"There is but this one. They have a stable, at the least."

They reined to a halt outside the inn and fastened their horses to the long rail that ran along the front of the building. Several other horses had been tied there, and more patrons sat in the tavernroom than The Eastlands Inn. To Corelle's relief, Bushy and Sparse did not seem to have moved on to this inn to continue their aggravation of her. Synna arranged rooms and space for their horses in the stable, and a boy in his teenyears led them through the constant buzz of conversation in the tavernroom to show them to their rooms.

Corelle sat on the cot in yet another room in yet another inn and wished for Deineike to walk through the door and make everything right again. She sighed, wandered to Synna's room, and knocked on his door. He pulled it open, no expression on his face. "Let us find some food. I am hungry." She smiled, anxious for the tension between them to dissipate.

"That you must be, for you have eaten almost nothing since Ort." He smiled back at her and stepped out into the corridor.

"I will take no wine tonight." She spoke in a quiet voice and half hoped he would not hear her and hold her to it.

He nodded. "My thanks for that." He had heard her, after all else. The words had been spoken now, and they had been heard. Corelle would honour them. An early start would be easier if she did not suffer from the after-effects of copious wine the previous night.

They entered the tavernroom and ordered food, simple fare when it came, but plentiful. Corelle felt ravenous. Synna had the right of it; she had eaten precious little for two days. She gulped her food down and stabbed her fork into an extra tuber from Synna's plate. He glared at her while she laughed as she ate it.

After they had eaten, he suggested they take a walk around the village. Outside, darkness crawled over the land in pursuit of the sun as it fled west, and the village turned out to be bigger than they had first thought. They chatted about this house or that shop and found themselves back at the inn within an hour. The sky had turned dark, with a bright, full moon above them. Corelle gazed up at it and recalled the time she had asked Deineike whether one day people might fly in the sky with the birds. Deineike had not thought so. If it were possible, Jorinda would fly to the moon and hope she could live out her days there, alone and in peace. It would disappoint her to arrive and find others already lived there.

They may already do so, she thought, although how they came there in the first place she did not know. "I will go to my room early, I think. A long ride is best prepared for with a good night's sleep."

"That it is. An excellent idea."

They walked through the tavernroom and parted at Corelle's door with a brief goodnight. She lay on the cot, tired still from the previous night and the ride, and sleep soon took her.

Early the next day, she woke and rose from the cot to wash herself in the water on the vanity stand. She could not recall the last time she had taken a bath and guessed she smelled atrocious. From her pack, she took a clean tunic, pushed the discarded one deep inside. Then she went in search of something to eat before the long ride. Synna emerged as she ate some cold meats and fresh baked bread, still warm from the oven. With a plate of food from the table where it had been laid out, he joined her and appeared relieved to find her already up and about.

The hour was still early as they set off again. They hoped to reach Yerrsun before dark, so they rode at a brisk pace. Corelle pondered for a time on the absence of another inn between the Belram's Shadow and Yerrsun. If the distance could be covered in a day, why not? Another night in a rustic village would add nothing to the charm of the journey from Eastort.

As the morning passed, she reflected on all they had learned about the situation they rode toward. Precious little, in truth. They would need some help and could ask the Portreeve what he knew. The influx of a large group of men who lived a guarded life must have attracted some attention.

Corelle brooded on the words the Bailiff's man had spoken to her as they had waited in the tavern for the arrival of the Guild man she had killed. How had he heard tales of her, in Alcmouth? More important, how had he come to learn of the death of Arella, far north in Zhanghar? She created a list in her mind of those who knew of her background and might have said something. Wilash, Raolos, Synna, Klordia. Ibie also, she thought. A short list.

Time to see what Synna knew of the conundrum. "I must ask you a question." Synna turned to face her. "In Alcmouth, one of Raolos's men told me he had heard the tale of when I killed Arella."

"That is not a question."

"I had not finished." She aimed a playful swipe at him. "Did you mention it to him?"

He hesitated a heartbeat. "That I did not."

She stared at him and searched for untruth but saw nothing to suggest he had lied. "Somebody did, my guess."

"What does it matter? It is not a slander. The things you speak of are true. Of late, you seem to revel in your status, in others' fear of you. I would think it pleased you when he knew of your reputation."

More lay behind his words, she felt sure of it. "He did speak a slander, in truth."

"Oh? How so?" He shifted in his saddle, seemed uncomfortable.

"He accused me of the death of a child."

Synna rode on in silence for a time, and she waited for his response. "I do not believe you would sink to that, although I would have believed it at one time. I do not think you would kill a child by design."

"Your words dance to a melody I do not care for, Synna. Come, let there be no lies between us. The man suggested Arella had been with child. I suspect you know something of this."

His heavy sigh did nothing to dispel the notion that he kept some part of the story from her. "It would be best for you to put his words from your mind. He is a soldier. Who knows the tales they invent and spread among themselves as they strive to appear more informed and battle-ready than the rest?"

"Synna, I beg you. Do not hide what you know from me. If you know something of this, then tell me."

"I…" He stared into her eyes. "I think it best you do not hear it at all. If you must hear, then you should hear it from he who said it."

"Hear what? Synna, tell me."

"This knowledge cannot benefit you in the least, Corelle. It is painful to me, what little I know of it. I fear it would devastate you."

"Tell me." Corelle had shouted as frustration got the best of her. She balled her fists, and tears welled up in her eyes. A heaviness had settled on her heart. Others knew some tragic detail she did not know and had never known, it appeared.

Synna lowered his head and wiped at his eyes with the back of a hand. After some time, he looked at her with pain-filled, red-rimmed eyes. "Arella carried a child when she died."

Corelle pulled on the reins, and her horse stopped. She had become light-headed, could not believe the words she had heard. Whispers came from her as her throat constricted. "It is not possible. More than that, it is a lie." She stared at Synna, and the truth hit her like a slap on the cheek. "Wilash. He told you this." Synna said nothing, but he did not need to. His face told her she had guessed right. "Why does he spread this tale? It cannot be true. Does he seek revenge for my clashes with his wife? Why does he tell these lies to all who would hear?"

Synna looked devastated. "I regret I said anything."

"He told me he loved her. He had… I cannot believe it. Why would Arella lie with him? She did not care for men."

"I do not believe Wilash fathered the child. Another, he said."

"But why does he tell this tale? It cannot be true."

"He had drunk too much ale, in truth. He blamed you for Klordia's death, at first."

"I had travelled to Vyrrmod, far to the south. It could not have been me."

"I did not say he accused you of her murder, but he blamed you for everything that turned. He had become intoxicated and filled with anger and grief. Corelle…" Synna stopped.

"Tell me all. You cannot stop now." Corelle struggled to find the breath to force the words from her lips, shocked by all she had heard.

"Raolos and I took him to a tavern. Klordia's death left him distraught. He lashed out at you and said you had caused all that had turned awry in his life. Then he said you did not even know the full horror of all you wrought, that Arella had become with child, and you had, in all likelihood, been shrouded because of that. She could not flee with you with a child in her belly but could not bear to tell you the truth, so she begged you to kill her, and the child with her."

Synna sat before her on his horse, but Corelle did not see him. She saw Arella in the darkness of the room above The Ship's Yard, heard her own lover exhort her to take her life. She had been with child? How? It could not be possible. She shook her head, but Synna's words would not be cast from her. "How?"

"How?" He seemed puzzled.

"How did she come to be with child? Did Styrrach take her against her will?"

"He did not say who. 'Another.' He said no more than that."

Her head swam, her vision blurred, and she feared she would fall from the horse. When she dismounted with difficulty, her legs would not support her. She collapsed on her haunches on the dusty road, her head in her hands. Each new day brought fresh horrors to her. How could she be expected to endure such grief? Her life had tested her beyond her capacity to survive. She looked up at Synna as tears streamed from eyes grown all too accustomed to them and whispered familiar words. "Kill me."

He shook his head, his own face wet with tears. "You have asked me to kill you before today. You know I will not."

"I can bear no more. I am spent. Kill me, or I will do it myself."

Synna jumped from his horse and held her. He pulled her dagger from her boot, and she tilted her head back. "Strike. Dispatch me as I did her."

"I cannot." Synna pulled her head forward onto his chest, his arms around her. "I am sorry Corelle. I wish with all my heart I had never heard this woe-begotten story. It seems Raolos's guards overheard, and the rumour spread."

She cried into his chest, her body shook, and she could not control the tremors that wracked her. Deineike's death, Pettra, Klordia; all had stemmed from the horrific words she had heard for the first time today. Arella had betrayed her and lain with a man and had died rather than confess the truth. That disloyalty set in motion events that had eaten away every scrap of decency Corelle had possessed and turned her into a brutish, despicable monster. She screamed into Synna's tunic, all her pain contained in the loudest scream of her life.

He held her tight and made "shh" noises as though being silent might heal this latest rend in her heart. They sat in the road, the warm sun unable to penetrate the cold bleakness of Corelle's state of mind. How long, she did not count. Her tears subsided, and still Synna held her.

She groaned into Synna's chest. "Why me? Why so much tragedy in one life? Do I deserve it?"

"That you do not. None do. Unkind fates have been written for you."

She sneered. "Unkind? Well, poor me. Life has been *unkind* to me." She spat out the word "unkind" as if she might purge her anger, remorse and shame with it.

"I apologise." Synna stroked her hair. "A poor choice of word." He relaxed his grip on her, held her chin in his hands, and forced her to meet his eyes. "We will unravel this. All of it. I swear to you; I will not turn from you until all is resolved, though it cost me my life. Answers may lie in Yerrsun, and if not, we will slay all who had any hand in any of these events. Then we will return to Alcmouth, and Wilash can tell you the full story. Until then, we are in the Eastlands, and we must ride on if we are to make Yerrsun before darkness falls."

She sniffed and wiped at her eyes. "You need not stay with me. You have duties to Raolos."

"You saved my life that night in Ort. I owe you my life, Corelle, and you did not need to intervene. None would have blamed you if you had let them hang me, not even me. You are hard-headed, and you can be as angry as a cornered dog, but I will aid you."

"A cornered dog?"

He smiled. "I forgot. You are from Ryl."

She managed a weak smile. "Help me up. We must continue to Yerrsun. Let us hope we find some resolution there for all these puzzles I cannot fathom."

He stood and helped her to her feet. He held her dagger toward her, handle first, but pressed her for reassurance she would not take her own life with it. She promised that until they had some information from Yerrsun, she would endure his company without any attempt to open her own throat. The dagger back in her boot, they mounted their horses and rode for Yerrsun, faster than earlier in the day.

Night had fallen before they reached the centre of the town. It seemed smaller than Ort, but as big as Vjort. They found an inn on the square and Synna arranged rooms and care for the horses. Corelle felt drained of all her energy from the journey and from all Synna had told her, and she went straight to bed.

She dreamt of Arella. The beautiful blonde-haired woman stood before her with her stomach distended. Corelle reached her arms out toward Arella and a ribbon of red gushed from the throat of her first real lover. It flowed down over her breasts and turned her bloated stomach red.

Deineike appeared behind Arella, burnt almost beyond recognition, and her blackened lips formed bitter whispers. "Why? You burned me alive."

"That I did not. You died."

"That I did not. I fell asleep, no more." Deineike's insistent denial tinged with anger saddened Corelle.

At that, Arella screamed, and her stomach burst. A baby fell to the floor and stood, unsteady, its gaunt, hawkish face unmistakeable as that of Styrrach. He turned, climbed up Arella's leg, and forced his erect member into her. He yelled, "More babies," and he turned to gaze at Corelle as his excitement grew. "I love you." Arella gasped as he cried the three words. Behind them, Deineike crumbled to blackened ashes, then blew away in the wind.

Corelle screamed and sat upright in the bed. The horror of the nightmare pounded in her head, and the door burst open. Synna stood there, silhouetted by light from outside the room. He had his dagger in his hand. "Is all well?"

"That it is. Another nightmare." Corelle buried her face in her hands, shaken by the trauma of the dream.

"The doors again?"

"Arella this time."

He nodded, his mouth set in a grim line. "Try to go back to sleep."

Corelle lay back as he closed the door, but she could not face sleep and the prospect the nightmare might return. She lay awake until the sounds of the day began: footsteps passed below her window, market stallholders shouted, somebody walked past her door. The smell of fresh baked bread floated up from somewhere, and she leapt from the bed to fetch up into the chamber pot. What fresh horrors awaited today, she could not tell, but she could bear little else. She splashed some water on her face, pulled on her clothes.

Time to seek answers and to repay some debts. When she opened the shutters, a cloudless blue sky brightened the square, and the Portreeve's Offices stood across from the inn. That would be a good place to start, and woe betide any who came between her and the answers she sought. She pulled her dagger out of her boot and examined it. *"Still sharp enough to spill blood,"* she thought. Blood would be spilled today, she felt certain of it.

She went downstairs, then out into the square toward whatever fates were written.

CHAPTER 26
CORELLE

Corelle had taken no more than ten paces when she stopped. The Portreeve would be unlikely to see her if she presented herself alone, while Synna had papers from the Bailiff that should help, so she turned and went back into the inn. Synna had not come down to the tavernroom, so she went up to his room and knocked on the door. She heard movement, and he pulled the door open. He wore only trousers, his long hair dishevelled. It seemed he had still been asleep.

"Rouse yourself, layabout. Work awaits." Corelle hoped a cheeky smile would turn her words into a jest.

He yawned. "What hour is it?"

"I know not. The hour to be up and about in search of answers. Dress yourself and meet me in the tavernroom." Corelle went back down the stairs where a man cleaned the counter. She asked for a cup of water, and he found a cup, handed it to her, and pointed to the privies. From the pump there, she filled the cup, gulped it down, and refilled it. She sat on a settle in the tavernroom and sipped at the second cup until Synna entered the room. She placed the cup on the counter. The man had gone, so together she and Synna walked out into the sunlight of Yerrsun's square.

A market had been set up in one corner, and they wandered past it. It spilled out into a smaller area attached to the square, and they found a large collection of stalls that sold all manner of foodstuffs and dry goods. They did not linger at the market but carried on until they stood before the Portreeve's Offices, the inn behind them across the square.

Although not as grandiose as the buildings in the cities, or even Ort, The Portreeve's Offices looked impressive in the small town. Synna wondered aloud why a town such as this would exist so far east, but Corelle reminded him the fifth city of Dur, Dur City, lay to the north. They knew little of the Eastlands, but Corelle imagined a substantial number of people lived in this part of Dur who felt little connection to the Duke or the rest of the land.

They walked through the Ortwood doors that seemed to be a standard feature for Portreeves and all in authority, and a young woman flashed them a warm smile. Synna showed her the letters, and she became deferential, asked them to wait, and disappeared through a door behind her. When she returned, she brought a wiry man with her who asked them to follow him. The Portreeve's meeting should end soon, he explained. The aide would ask him to see them as soon as he became free.

They sat on chairs and waited. Time slipped by, and they speculated the Portreeve had not been in a meeting at all but had tried to impose his importance. He would not be so rude as to refuse a request from the Bailiff, but he might wish to cast himself as a powerful man in the town.

After a lengthy wait, the aide reappeared and summoned them to follow him again. He led them down a corridor and pushed open an Ortwood door. They walked through the aide's office and beyond into the Portreeve's own office, smaller than Raolos's, and with less luxurious furniture. Nonetheless, it exuded power and wealth. The Portreeve stood as they entered and beckoned to a couch to the side of his desk.

He introduced himself as Rognakk, a stout man, not much taller than Synna, whose deep black hair receded from his forehead, its colour so intense, Corelle had never seen the like of it. His small hands fluttered all the while, and his heavy jowls suggested he enjoyed the finer things in life, and in good quantity. His dark eyes flicked from Synna to her as they sat. "How can I be of assistance to the Bailiff's trusted envoys?" He seated himself in an armed chair. "I am at your disposal. Ask, and it shall be so."

Corelle thought his words carried little sincerity, doubtless nothing more than lip service to the man for whom he worked. "We seek a group of men, and we believe they have hidden out on a farm nearby. Have you heard any talk of their presence here?"

He rubbed his chin in thought. "A group of men, you say. Please, what sort of men?"

Synna answered his question. "Not the sort you would wish to meet. The unsavoury sort."

"I see. I take it you seek to bring these men to the Bailiff's justice?"

Corelle replied. "The reasons we seek these men, we keep to ourselves, but we may have need of your men."

He sucked air across his teeth. "Of course, the Bailiff's authority is not to be questioned, but the town of Yerrsun is mine to tend long after you have left. You understand I wish no unpleasantness that might upset the people of such a quiet town."

Corelle's mood would not tolerate officiousness or obstruction. "We have no desire to upset your citizens. Those we seek are dangerous, and your town will be safer once we bring them to justice. We will request your help if we feel we need it. In the meantime, I ask again whether you know anything of these men."

"I fear I know nothing of them." His smile did not extend to his eyes. "There is, however, one who might aid you. His name is

Minarko. He is old and has lived his entire life in Yerrsun. Little turns here unless he knows something about it, and his knowledge of the town and its surrounds is second to none. He might give you some information." He stood. "I will have my aide give you directions to his home. If that is all…"

Corelle shot Synna a glance. He shook his head and shrugged his shoulders. "Our thanks." She stood and headed for the door. Rognakk instructed his aide to provide directions to Minarko's house and the door closed behind them. Armed with their directions, they left the building and stood in the square again.

The Portreeve had aroused Corelle's ire. "That pompous oaf. Does he think he can trifle with the Bailiff's own emissaries?"

Synna laughed. "That he does. I thought him obsequious and arrogant. Something more though, I felt, as if he intended to obstruct us."

"I thought so also. Obsequious?"

"He grovelled, but without sincerity."

"An excellent word for him, but we waste time on a buffoon. We should visit Minarko right away." They set off and followed the directions given to them by the aide, and they found Minarko's home by mid-morning. His run-down house had seen no paint for many years. Long grass grew in a small garden in front of the house, and the dilapidated fence, a gap where a gate might once have stood, seemed on the brink of collapse. They walked to the front door and Synna rapped on it. The sound of movement came from within, and the door opened. It unleashed the pungent aroma of someone who washed so infrequently, it might no longer be possible for them to be clean again. A bundle of filthy grey rags with bony hands and feet and a gaunt, bald head stared at them.

The man spoke, his voice wheezy, feeble. "Strangers. Out-of-towners. What do you want from me? I have no coin if that is what you seek."

It amused Corelle that he took them for thieves. "Keep your coin, old man. Are you Minarko?"

"That I might be, if I know who asks."

Synna clutched the letters in his hand. "We serve the Bailiff and seek information on a group of men who came to the area in the last pass or two."

The man laughed, a dry laugh that crackled from his lips and exposed too few teeth in his mouth. "Few who knock at this door claim to be from the Bailiff. An audacious story."

Corelle imagined the tale might seem tall to the old man. "The truth, whether you believe it or not. The Portreeve sent us to you with promises you knew all that turned in Yerrsun."

"Rognakk sent you here? A weasel of a man. I dislike him. The sound of his name alone persuades me to distrust you." He moved to close the door, but Synna shot out an arm and held it open, and the man cried out. "Will you attack an old man?"

Corelle spat out her answer. "That I will, if you force me to." Synna tutted at Corelle's response. "Your opinion of Rognakk is irrelevant, even if I am inclined to agree with you. Do you know anything of these men? They will be numerous, I imagine. Secretive also. They are dangerous, so if you know of them, I caution you to stay clear of them."

He studied her face, then shifted his gaze to Synna. "I sense you speak the truth. You are a good man, I think. This one…" He turned his attention to Corelle. "There is terrible violence in you. This surprises me, for you are a woman, and a small one. I would have feared you in my younger days. Now I mark time until this life ends, and I do not fear death."

She sighed, irritated by his chatter. "Do you know anything of these men?"

He gave one sharp nod of his head. "I believe I may have heard a rumour or two. I am indeed Minarko, and there is little in Yerrsun I know nothing of. There is a farm half a day to the east. Long years it lay empty, they say. Those who owned it vanished in the night, and it fell into disrepair. I hear it is inhabited again, though I know little of the new occupants. Some say they are secretive, as you suggested they might be."

Synna nodded. "My thanks for this information."

Corelle did not think Synna had stressed the danger of the people at the farm. "Those who told you this; if you see them again, advise them not to approach the farm or any who live there. They are dangerous, as I have said."

Minarko stared at her. "That they are. Not as dangerous as you, I think." Corelle huffed and turned to leave, but Minarko spoke to her back. "Try the markets. I hear there is one who goes out that way. A woman. I know her name, but I will not do all your work for you." He laughed again, and she heard the door close.

They headed back toward the square, and Synna said, "A strange fellow."

"In many ways, for sure. His woeful hygiene standards turned my stomach."

Synna laughed. "I doubt we smell much better. We should both take a bath later."

"Time enough for baths when we know what we face and how we deal with it."

The midday approached by the time they returned to the markets. The wait for the Portreeve, then the walk to and from the old man's house, had taken longer than Corelle had expected, and it frustrated her. They moved from stall to stall and asked women who worked on each if they knew anything of a farm that lay half a day to the east, an innocuous enough way to open a conversation. They could not be certain whether the woman sold them items from her stall or had become involved in a dalliance with one or more of the Guild members. If she did lie with some of them, Corelle and Synna must ensure she did not warn Krage they searched for the farm.

After they had wandered the market for a time, they found the woman, who ran a vegetable and fruit stall and said she had received several orders from what she described as Estway Farm. She appeared happy to chat to them and confessed she had been surprised they ordered her goods. Estway Farm ought to have grown sufficient fresh food to sustain the occupants for the most part. She believed she had won the business because she had been the only one prepared to spend an entire day to drive out and back on her cart to deliver the goods, but she charged extra for the delivery, and so far, they had been happy to pay.

Corelle pressed her on how often she delivered to the farm. It seemed orders were irregular. Someone would come to the stall and request the goods they needed, and the stallholder would gather them together and drive out once she had obtained everything they wanted. Deliveries would often be more than a sevenday apart, and she had been out there two days ago.

Corelle asked how many people were at the farm and the woman pursed her lips in a thoughtful gesture. "I have seen five. All men—no women."

Synna asked whether they carried weapons, and she thought again. "Not that I could see. I do not profess to know much about such things." Her smile lit her pretty face and made her brown eyes sparkle. Her light brown hair hung down her back, and she stood no taller than Corelle, with a slender body and small hands that bore the callouses of hard work.

"Of course." Synna blushed, and Corelle looked down, so her amused smile did not embarrass him further.

An older woman came to the stall to buy some vegetables, and the stallholder turned her attention to the customer. They appeared to know each other and chatted together for some time. The older woman handed over some coin, but the stallholder pushed her hand away. "Today there is no charge. The vegetables are not as fresh as I would like."

"Are you sure?" A look of surprise sprang to the older woman's face.

"They will make a fine broth, but I cannot charge you for them." The stallholder smiled, and the older woman gushed her thanks as she left.

Although Corelle knew little about vegetables, she could see no fault with the goods on the stall. The stallholder seemed to notice Corelle's inspection of the produce and gave a chuckle. "You are right, they are fine. That lady lost her husband a pass ago, and I suspect she finds coin a little tight without him. I do what I can."

The stallholder's compassion drew a small nod of approval from Corelle. "I am Corelle. This is Synna."

"Vamma." The woman held out a hand, and Corelle shook it for a heartbeat, then Vamma extended it toward Synna. He held it for some time before he released it.

They had all the information they needed. Vamma had described the farm and its surrounds and had given them detailed directions on how to reach it. Like much of the Eastlands, the land around the farm sounded flat, which would make it difficult for them to approach the farm unseen. Synna seemed reluctant to agree to Corelle's suggestion they should continue about their business, but as they left the stall, Vamma called out to them. "I will be at The Yerrsun Tavern when I close my stall here. It is the best tavern in the town for a meal and liquid refreshment, if you would both like to join me."

Corelle and Synna exchanged glances. Corelle wanted to ride out to the farm then and there, but they would arrive in the dark and accomplish little. They would then need to ride back to the town late and in darkness, into the early hours of tomorrow, and to ride in the dark would be treacherous. Synna, it seemed obvious, wished to visit the tavern with Vamma, so Corelle said they would see her there, and they wandered back to their inn.

"You seem taken with her." Corelle smiled as they walked.

"She is a pleasant person, and kind, it seems."

"That it does. She is pretty, also."

"Is she? I had not noticed."

Corelle slapped him on the upper arm. "You are a terrible liar. You could not take your eyes off her."

"I admit it. She is pretty." He blushed as he spoke, and the widest smile Corelle had ever seen sprang to his face. "Very pretty."

"Then I wish you luck tonight. I will not come along. I will be in the way, and I do not wish to be a distraction for you."

He walked with his head down for a time. "What will you do instead?"

She shrugged. "I know not. I may explore the town. I might find a different tavern, where the women are open to the pleasures I enjoy."

He glanced at her. "Please remember my words, and go easy on the wine. As for a dalliance, I wish you luck."

Corelle had never gone in search of a dalliance and did not know how she might go about such a thing. There would be great risk if she missed her guess and said the wrong thing to a woman in a tavern full of men. She doubted she had the courage to take the chance, so she smiled in reply. Her comment about the dalliance had been no more than a jest. Synna's jab about the amount she might drink had stung her, but she felt Synna had been right to say it. Though the midday had not long passed, she craved a goblet of wine already.

Corelle suggested they explore more of the town until Synna left to meet Vamma. A small river tinkled over some large stones not far from the square. A large tree spread its branches over the bank of the river at that point and offered a shady spot to sit and while away some of the day. They discussed their next steps and determined to ride out to the farm at first light. They would ride as far as they felt they could approach unseen, then move closer on foot to observe the farm. She hoped they could guess the number of men present and, more important, confirm they belonged to the Guild.

They expected Krage and Sisnop to be there, and Gillar also. Two Guildmeisters and one Senior Aide. The Guildmeister and Senior Aide from Alcmouth had not survived, and the Senior Aide from Ryl had been hanged. Corelle had killed Porl, which left a maximum of three officers, plus an unknown number of members and even a Portreeve or two. If Portreeves travelled with Krage, they might have some of their more loyal men with them as guards. There could be a substantial force at the farm. An excellent plan would be vital if Corelle and Synna intended to survive the encounter.

The issue of why the Guild continued this vendetta against her and Wilash still eluded Corelle's comprehension. Some rationale nagged at the back of her mind, but she could not bring it to fruition. It seemed Krage and his colleagues had become reckless also, careless at the least. The murder of Klordia in Alcmouth had achieved next to nothing, and Corelle would not have included it in any plan of hers. She would also not have risked exposure as they did whenever they sent men into town to order mundane groceries. Such sloppy work baffled her.

The sun dropped in the sky, and Synna wanted to return to the inn and bathe before he met Vamma. Back in her room, Corelle lay on her cot for a time, then decided a bath might help her also. Once she had dressed again, she decided to go out and find a quiet tavern for a goblet of wine or two. As she wandered, she noticed The Yerrsun Tavern and could not resist the temptation to peer within to see how Synna and Vamma got along. She opened the door, but to her surprise, a hallway led to the tavernroom. Most tavern doors opened into the tavernroom, but this one had a different design, so she walked down the hallway, opened the tavernroom door a crack, and peeped in to see if she could catch a glimpse of Synna and Vamma.

"Do you spy on us?" Vamma's voice from behind made Corelle jump.

She closed the door and turned to face her accuser. "Not at all. I wanted to see how the meal…" She felt the heat in her cheeks. Vamma had caught her, and no ready lie sprang to her tongue to save her.

Corelle liked Vamma's bright clear laugh even as it mocked her. "He is good company, and generous with his coin. I am disappointed in the night, however."

That disappointed Corelle also. "How so?"

"I invited you both, yet you did not come, detained on business, Synna said. Yet here you are, and you peek through a door at us."

Corelle felt her cheeks flush even more. "I did not wish to be a horse outside the traces."

Vamma laughed. "Come. Join us. We will see whether there is room for a third horse to pull this cart."

Corelle raised both hands toward Vamma. "I could not impose. Synna…"

"Synna will not mind, I am sure."

The unexpected outcome left Corelle miserable. "I think he might."

Vamma would not accept Corelle's refusal. "I insist. I shall go home at once otherwise and leave you and your friend here together."

Corelle sighed. "I will stay for one goblet, no more."

"Excellent. Come, I will show you to our table. I doubt you could see it from your little hidey hole here." Her wicked grin both teased and humiliated Corelle. She had been caught and exposed as a peeper who spied on Vamma and Synna from the shadows. The outcome horrified her, and Synna would be furious. The evening had got off to the worst possible start and doubtless could not be redeemed. She pulled the tavernroom door open and beckoned to Vamma to go first.

CHAPTER 27
CORELLE

As she followed Vamma to the table, Corelle thought her cheeks must be the brightest red they had ever been. Although Vamma showed no sign of annoyance, Corelle felt mortified to have been caught in the act. Synna showed no surprise, but no anger either. Vamma laughed as she told him how she had caught Corelle in her effort to see how the evening went, and he laughed. He did not seem put out, however, and invited Corelle to sit next to him. They had not yet ordered any food, and both he and Vamma insisted she sup with them.

Corelle ordered a goblet of wine and Synna asked for food for all three. The server brought her a pleasant wine, not the quality of the one at The Eastlands Inn, but smooth and fruity, with a dark red colour. Vamma also drank red wine, and two empty goblets had been on the table, which the server had taken away when she brought Corelle's wine. Synna had drunk less than half of his tankard of ale.

Vamma continued to be chatty and told them all manner of information about the characters of the town and the best shops for food. Corelle and Synna asked her to recommend a pastry shop, and she told them of one four streets from the square. She claimed it sold the best cakes in the Eastlands. The server brought them a delicious spicy broth with meats and tubers in it. Fresh bread served to mop up the remnants of the gravy, and all three plates were emptied before the server returned to collect them. While they had eaten, Vamma had drunk two more goblets and insisted Corelle keep pace with her. Synna frowned when Vamma waved for two more goblets, but he said nothing.

Although Corelle knew she should leave, she found Vamma excellent company, and she needed conversation with another woman. It had been some time since she had enjoyed a civil discussion with a woman that did not develop into an argument, and she found Vamma attentive and easy to talk to. More wine came, and Vamma drank at an impressive rate. Synna struggled halfway through his second tankard, and his cheeks turned red. It seemed he had spoken the truth when he told Corelle he did not drink much.

In one corner of the tavernroom, some minstrels began to play, greeted by raucous applause. Vamma explained they were the most popular minstrels in the Eastlands, and folks would travel from far out of town to see them perform. They appeared often at The Yerrsun Tavern, it seemed. They struck up a sprightly tune and Synna asked Vamma to dance with him. She agreed without delay, and they took to an area in the centre of the tavernroom where people had cleared the tables and chairs to fashion a makeshift dance floor. Synna swept Vamma around and Corelle had to admit it to herself; he danced well. His prowess surprised her, and she recalled a dance on the ship north to Ort after Styrrach had attacked them in Alcmouth. How had she not recognised his ability that day? Her own dancing left much to be desired next to Vamma and Synna's.

They returned to the table when the music ended, their breaths heavy, their cheeks red, and beads of sweat on their foreheads.

Corelle praised Synna as soon as he took his seat. "You are a remarkable dancer."

Vamma agreed with her. "That he is." Synna looked bashful and mumbled half-hearted thanks. As the minstrels struck up another tune, Vamma reached a hand across the table to Corelle. "Dance with me." Corelle thought she saw something in the pretty woman's eyes that might have been an invitation to something more than a dance.

Corelle shook her head, guarded and concerned. Her reluctance to hold hands with Deineike in public had cost her the opportunity to enjoy some of the physical moments men and women took for granted, but nothing had changed. Despite the night with Pettra, she still feared to be seen to hold a woman or touch her in public, and she would feel uncomfortable if she danced with Vamma.

"Come along." Vamma laughed. "One dance."

Corelle shook her head again, more assertive. "I am a terrible dancer. I have both feet in one boot on the dance floor."

"That matters not. Synna, persuade her to dance with me." Synna glanced at Vamma, then turned to Corelle. Corelle gave him a pointed glare in the hope he would take her side and not badger her to dance with the stallholder.

He seemed to catch her meaning. "I have seen her dance, and you are fortunate indeed she will not dance with you. She resembles a mutton as it falls off a log."

Vamma screeched with laughter and turned to Corelle. Something in Corelle's demeanour must have registered with her, and she drew in a sharp breath. "I apologise." She smiled. "I should not have pressed you to something you felt uncomfortable with. I will buy you another wine as recompense."

"Recompense?"

Vamma laughed, glanced at Synna. "Compensation."

Synna helped himself to Deineike's jest, as men seemed wont to do. "She is from Ryl." Vamma laughed again.

"I have never been to Ryl. We must go there together one day." Vamma waved an arm that might have included everybody in the bar, but her eyes were locked on Corelle's.

To Corelle's embarrassment, not only had Vamma caught her as she peered round the door, but she appeared to be more taken with her than Synna. More goblets of wine appeared, and Corelle could no longer meet Synna's gaze. She stared down into the dark red liquid in the hopes she might find some means of escape from an uncomfortable situation. None appeared, so she took a sip.

Synna coughed. "I am weary. I believe I shall retire."

Vamma had other ideas. "That you will not. I wish to dance more, and since Corelle refuses to dance with me, you must stay."

Synna yawned, although Corelle cringed at his lack of skill as an actor. He rose, but Corelle laid a hand on his arm. "Stay, Synna. It is I who should go. I have intruded on your evening."

He stared at her, seemed about to speak, then looked away. He slumped back into his chair and seemed pensive.

Vamma stood. "I must visit the privy." She headed out through the door Corelle had peeped through.

As the door closed behind her, Synna turned to Corelle. "I believe she has left us to resolve this conundrum."

"She seems nice. I am sorry I have dampened your evening."

"You have not, but if you continue to drink at this pace, you will be in no state to head out to the farm in the morning. That is my sole concern. That she has eyes only for you, I can accept, since that will not change no matter how much I brood on it, and you did nothing to encourage it."

Corelle turned one side of her mouth down, remorseful. "A sorry turn. I regret I came here now."

"I will leave. Let the dice fall as they may. Please, do not drink so fast, I beseech you. You have already had more than enough."

She nodded at him, noncommittal, reluctant to make the promise but anxious not to anger him. "I am sorry."

"Do not be, but please do not make me sorry in the morning."

Corelle felt wretched. She wished to drink more but did not want to disappoint Synna, whose hopes seemed to have been dashed, as they both now believed Vamma showed more interest in Corelle than him. She should leave, but before she could, Vamma returned. "More wine?" Corelle nodded, unhappy but unable to refuse.

"I take my leave. Ladies, enjoy your evening." Synna strode from the tavernroom.

Vamma giggled. "Oh dear. Have I disappointed him?"

"That you have. He is most taken with you."

"He is a wonderful man, and a fine dancer. On another night, I might have taken him home and enjoyed his company all night. Tonight though, I did not desire it."

Corelle nodded, uncertain of what Vamma meant. "He will be fine. He does not bear grudges."

"Tell me the real reason you would not dance with me. I do not believe this tale of a mutton that eats logs."

Some of the wine Corelle had sipped snorted from her nose onto the table as she laughed. She wiped at it with the sleeve of her tunic. "I believe he said, 'Fell off a log.'" Vamma giggled. "Are you inebriated?"

"That I am. What of it?" Vamma sat upright and looked into Corelle's eyes with pride. "But do not deflect me. I asked you a question, and I will have an answer."

"Or?" A line had been crossed. They had entered territory with only one outcome, the jests little more than a disguise for the irresistible sexual tension that crackled in the air between them.

"Or I shall buy you more wine. Synna makes it obvious he does not approve that you drink so much."

Corelle sighed. "You are right, and he has good cause. I am a terrible dancer, but above all, I am afraid to dance with a woman. As a child, I dreamt I danced with a woman; my lover. Everybody admired us. The truth is less palatable. For two women to touch, much less dance, is unacceptable in Dur."

"Unasettable?"

Corelle snickered. "I did not say that. I said unacapt..." She paused, and Vamma laughed loud, unconcerned as heads turned to look at her. "Curse you."

"You are inebriated also, it seems. How do you know it is unacceptable?"

"What is?" The conversation confused Corelle, and she sipped at her wine.

"For two women to dance together."

"Because I have loved a woman. Loved her with all my heart."

"Where is she?"

"Dead. She died." Corelle choked back tears.

"That is a sad thing to hear." Vamma laid a hand on Corelle's arm, all sympathy.

"You do not know the full sadness of it."

"Then tell me. I would like to hear it."

Corelle wiped at her eyes. It would be too painful to open up recollections of Deineike. The wine dulled her memory, but Vamma had opened wounds that would never heal and seemed determined to pick at them until they bled more. Corelle could not endure it, even more so after the words Synna had chilled her heart with yesterday. "It is too sad." She had slurred the words. "I cannot tell it. Not now."

Vamma stared at her, compassion in her eyes. "Come to my home, and dance with me there. None will see but us."

"I cannot. If I am not on my horse at the sunrise, bright of eye and..." She had forgotten the rest of the phrase. "Anyway, Synna will kill me."

"I do not understand why you must ride out to the farm, nor why you show such interest in the people out there."

Corelle sighed her reluctance to go any further into the reasons she wished to visit the farm. "I cannot tell you, not now. Ask me when I have drunk less." She smiled. "Let us go to your home. I fear I have had more than enough wine. Take me away from the temptation to consume more."

Vamma's attention, however, had turned to the minstrels, who performed a slow, remorseful song with an evocative melody. The song told the story of somebody alone, lonely, and unhappy. The singer's crisp, clear voice carried the words of the song into the hearts of everybody in the tavern, but none more than Corelle. It seemed the song's words might have been scribed not about all the forlorn people in the land, but about her alone.

> *"There are people who are on their own,*
> *Like a road that winds in circles ends up back at home.*
> *There are dreamers in their lonely rooms,*
> *Like a tattered, half-made garment on a broken loom."*

Tears streamed from Corelle's eyes, and Vamma pulled her forward, cradled Corelle's head on her bosom, and stroked her hair. Corelle fell into the comfort, but old fears soon nagged at her again, and she sat upright.

"You miss her." Vamma had not asked a question, and Corelle could only give a miserable nod of her head, deprived of words by the sense of loneliness that washed over her as the minstrel's song stripped away all pretence she could survive without Deineike. "Come. This place has become maudlin. Let us leave."

Vamma helped Corelle to her feet. Corelle struggled to walk, and her level of inebriation surprised her. Had the wine been stronger than she was used to? Vamma did not appear to be affected anywhere near as much. She must be more used to the wine in this tavern. With Vamma's aid, Corelle staggered outside. The fresh air slapped her in the face after the heady atmosphere in the tavernroom, and she staggered, almost fell, but Vamma held her upright. The stallholder's life must be physical, Corelle thought. Vamma appeared far stronger than might have been expected from such a slight woman. "You are strong."

"You are intoxicated. I do not think I can carry you alone to your inn. My home is near. Come and sleep on my floor. In the morning you may be bright of eye, as you desire. I doubt it." She laughed again. Corelle enjoyed the sound and wanted to hear more. It soothed the beast inside her that threatened to dash her on the rocks of her fates. Without the laughter, she thought she might reach to her boot and end her life, so broken had she become, but when Vamma laughed, Corelle stayed her hand.

Corelle muttered, mired in her thoughts about Deineike. "Died because of me." The words proved difficult to form as they struggled along the street. Passers-by gave them a wide berth, although some threw Vamma a hesitant greeting as they passed.

Vamma soft reply almost disappeared in the inexplicable ringing in Corelle's ears. "Shh. Save your tale for another time when you have not had so much wine."

"Because of me." Through the haze of her intoxication, Corelle recognised the only thing she had wrought throughout her life had been destruction. "It all turned because of me."

"I do not understand you. You have such a soft voice, and your words are slurred. Some grief lies on you about the woman you lost, it seems clear. Do not torment yourself. Nothing good comes when we dwell in times long past."

Vamma stopped and fumbled at her waist with one hand as she struggled to hold Corelle upright with the other, produced a key from somewhere within her clothing, and pushed it into a lock. The door swung open, and Corelle swung toward the street, unable to retain her balance despite Vamma's arm around her shoulders. Vamma reached for her with both hands, but Corelle fell face first into the street and grunted as the fall drove the air out of her body.

Vamma knelt beside her, concern in her voice. "Are you hurt?"

"In so many ways." Corelle laughed, a short, ironic laugh that held no joy.

Vamma pulled at her. "We need to get you into bed." The stall-holder managed to pull Corelle to her feet with some difficulty. "You are a sorry sight." She sighed as Corelle swayed before her. "Come on, in we go."

Vamma helped Corelle into the small house. The front door opened onto a small parlour, lit only by the moonlight that shone through the door. Near a fireplace to the rear were three chairs around a table. None of the chairs appeared to match, and Corelle closed one eye so she could focus on the mystery of the mis-matched chairs. Stairs led upward to her left, and to her right she could see a small, battered couch. Little else furnished the room other than some shelves that held various small knick-knacks.

"Welcome to my home, as humble as it is." Vamma lowered Corelle onto the couch. "This will be your bed tonight, I think. The stairs…"

She left the sentence unfinished. Corelle lay down on her back and gazed up at Vamma. Again, she closed one eye, the better to concentrate on what she saw, and Vamma laughed. "Do not laugh at me." Corelle tried for a jest. "I am a killer. None mock me."

"You are a what?" Vamma laughed. "I thought you said 'killer,' though at the moment the only person you are fit to slay is yourself."

"You drank it also. Lossof wine." The words again proved diffi-cult to form. Corelle's tongue felt twice its normal size, and she appeared to have left her lips behind in the tavern.

"I did not drink as much as you. I can drink, but you race through each goblet as though death itself urges you to hurry so it might take you wherever you travel to afterward." Vamma turned, lit a lantern that brightened the room, then pushed the door closed.

"Death travels with me. I am its boon componi…" Corelle

waved an arm in the air. The word would not form; Vamma must determine her intent herself.

Vamma stared down at her, confusion on her face. "You talk of killing and death overmuch. What plagues you so?"

"Where would I begin that tale?" Corelle laughed the mirthless laugh again, squinted up at Vamma. "You are kind. All must love you. Synna loves you."

Vamma laughed. "Poor Synna."

"Where is he?" Corelle looked around the room but could not see her companion.

"Do you not recall?" Corelle stared at her, not understanding. "He left. You stayed."

"Why?"

Vamma laughed again. "You do not remember. I did not have the impact I hoped to. That disappoints me."

Corelle wrinkled her brow and tried to unravel the mysterious conversation. "What?"

"I did not desire him tonight. I did not desire any man, although most in the tavern would have served on a different night."

Corelle sifted through the jumble of words but could not find nothing that made any sense. "Of course they would. You are very attracive."

"If you mean attractive, then my thanks. But I did not desire them. A man does not understand a woman's body like another woman does."

"You should not say that. It is unsafe. People will think you are a deviant."

"Are you shocked to learn I have lain with women?"

Corelle snorted. "Why should I be shocked? I have already said I loved Deineike."

"Deineike? It is a pretty name. Tell me about her."

Corelle sighed in exasperation. How could she explain Deineike to this woman, even if she were not intoxicated almost beyond the capacity to speak? She laid an arm over her eyes. "She was Deineike." What more could she say?

Vamma sat beside her and stroked her hair. "Great pain lies on you, I see that. Something else I see. Something fearsome."

Corelle lowered her arm and gazed into Vamma's earnest eyes. "All fear me." The whispered words and the truth they carried brought her fresh agony.

"I did not say I fear you. I said you are fearsome."

Corelle gave a dismissive snort, then wiped her nose with a sleeve as mucus trickled from it. "Though not to you?"

"Not to me." Vamma leaned forward and kissed Corelle, a tender, warm kiss. Corelle blinked up at her, uncertain of the moment, and Vamma sat upright. "Not to me." She bent, forced her tongue into Corelle's mouth, and explored it. Her eyes closed, and she took Corelle's hair in each hand, eased her head up into the passion of the kiss. Corelle slid a hand to the back of Vamma's head and pressed them closer together as her own tongue danced past Vamma's into the other woman's warm mouth.

Corelle pushed at Vamma's shoulders to break their tongue's wild dance. "What of Synna?"

"I wanted you when you came to my stall. I wanted you when you entered the tavern. Synna is a good man, doubtless. Tonight, I want you." Vamma's eyes were half closed, her voice breathy.

Corelle's sex tingled. "Then take me." Vamma fell on her. Her calloused hands explored Corelle's body and tore at her clothes as Corelle begged her, "Take me where I may forget all this pain." Vamma's hand dived between Corelle's legs, and despite her intoxication, she gasped as desire engulfed her body. The other hand flicked at Corelle's nipples, and Corelle sank back into the couch and abandoned herself to the sensations Vamma's hands aroused in her. They kissed again, and their tongues battled for dominance. Corelle pushed two fingers inside Vamma's wet, ready sex. Vamma cried out as Corelle pumped her fingers in and out and refused to stop until she coaxed Vamma to a peak.

Vamma nibbled at Corelle's ear. "If you excite me so when you are in your cups, what will you do to me when you are in full possession of your senses?" As she nibbled at Corelle's earlobe, it sent spasms of lust through Corelle's body.

"Do not ask me tonight." "*Cause your death,*" would be the truthful response, but Corelle's desire spun out of control, and she wished to be sated.

"That I shall not, for I fear I am about to lose the power of speech." Vamma whimpered as Corelle's fingers teased her and drew her toward another crescendo. She rose, straddled Corelle, and urged her to drive her to the ecstasy she sought.

They gave and took pleasure from one another until Corelle could no longer continue, drained by her emotional response to the song and the subsequent exertions of lovemaking with Vamma. As they lay entwined on the couch, Vamma ran her hand across the ugly scars on Corelle's arm. "How did these happen?" she asked.

"Cookery accident." Corelle laughed at her own jest.

Vamma glowered at her as she muttered. "I shall ask you when you are capable of a response." Corelle did not care whether she did or not. The wine and the lovemaking had exhausted her, and she fell asleep with Vamma on top of her, a sweaty tangle of bodies and limbs.

Movement in the room woke her. She opened her eyes, but the daylight blinded her, and she closed them again. Her head thumped, and she groaned, her throat parched dry and her stomach bilious.

Vamma's voice made her jump. "You must rise. Synna awaits, and I must go to my stall."

"Synna." Corelle could scarce recognise her own voice as she croaked out her reply. "He will slice me open."

Vamma shook her, and Corelle forced her eyes open to look up into Vamma's serious face. "That he will not, but he is sure to be angry you are not there yet. Last night you said you would ride to the farm today, and the sand falls."

"I cannot rise, or I will die. Synna must go alone."

"Do not bleat. Rouse yourself. I must leave."

"Kill me. Synna will if you do not, my guess."

Vamma stared at her for a moment. "Rouse yourself." She spoke in a quiet, firm voice and pulled Corelle's arms until she fell from the couch.

Corelle lay on the floor, stunned that Vamma had dumped her there. "Are you deranged? I might have been hurt."

Vamma gave as good as she got. "More than when you fell into the street?"

"I did no such thing."

"That you did, and that you have forgotten does not change the truth of it."

Corelle's clothes lay scattered around the room, and she crawled to her tunic, pulled it over her head. As she struggled into her trousers, Vamma bent to pick up one of her boots, then stopped. Corelle also paused the fight with her trousers as she guessed what had alarmed Vamma.

Vamma looked over at her before she spoke, little more than a whisper. "You carry a knife?"

Corelle searched for a non-committal response. "The road is a dangerous place."

Vamma's forehead wrinkled. "Dangerous? What do you mean?"

Corelle tutted. It had nothing to do with Vamma whether she carried the dagger, in truth. It would be rude to appear defensive, however, and she wracked her brain for a suitable reply that would diffuse the tension. "There are..." Words failed her.

"Last night you said you are a killer. Does this knife have some part to play in that tale?"

Corelle heaved a frustrated breath. "The tale is a long one, and to tell it exhausts me. It must be even worse to hear, my guess. Please, let it pass now. I am in no condition to explain it to you, and I imagine Synna will use the dagger to put me out of my misery, after all else."

Vamma seemed to weigh her words, then she picked up the other boot and dropped both next to Corelle. "Very well. Tonight, at the tavern, before you are in your cups, you will tell me some part of this mystery."

"Vamma—" Vamma held up a hand to stop her, and Corelle sighed. Glum, she accepted defeat. "Tonight." At last, she overpowered her trousers, pulled them up, and fastened them. She pulled the boots onto her feet and sat up. As soon as her head rose above her waist, it pounded more than ever, and her stomach threatened to disgorge its contents at any moment.

Slow and careful, she stood, unwilling to trust her legs to support her. She leaned on the wall and heaved huge drafts of air into her body. She had no desire to explain her life to Vamma, but neither did she wish to argue. She had agreed to meet that night, with little or no intention she would make good on the arrangement. It had been a convenient way to escape the awkward conversation.

Vamma stood at the door, the key in her hand as Corelle stepped into the street. The sunlight scorched her eyes, and she squinted to reduce the glare as she cursed to herself. Vamma locked the door and reminded her to be at the tavern tonight. Corelle nodded in agreement and set off toward the inn where Synna doubtless awaited her, his fury immense.

Corelle had almost reached the inn before she lost the fight with her stomach. She hurried into a nearby alleyway and fetched up, fell to her knees on the ground as she heaved out the contents of her stomach. Why did the wine go in red but come out a lurid yellow-green colour? Items of half-digested food also came out, and they included things she felt certain she had not eaten. Pieces of her insides, doubtless. She seemed fated to fetch up her innards each morning until nothing remained inside her, and she died. Tears flowed down her cheeks as she knelt beside the rank evidence of another night of excess. She guessed her grief and guilt would soon be compounded by Synna's anger. Her stomach heaved again, and she knelt on all fours as she fetched up, heedless of any who passed by. Let them laugh; they had the pleasure to watch the last acts of a life turned more wrong than they could ever imagine.

CHAPTER 28

CORELLE

Synna sat in the entrance lobby of the inn and glared at Corelle as she entered. "Where have you been? Your bed has not been slept in. You look terrible. Again." His red face, narrowed eyes, and taut lips told Corelle anger boiled in his veins. "The sand falls, and we have riding ahead. You have delayed us. Why?"

She tried to summon indignation to respond to his questions, but she could not dredge it up past the shame that filled every part of her. She looked down at the ground. "I slept on Vamma's couch." He tutted, and she continued. "I will sweeten my breath and splash some water on my face. Then we may leave for the farm." He did not reply as she moved off, but she paused after a few steps. "I am sorry."

In the quiet of her room, she closed the door and leaned back against it with a heavy sigh. Her jumbled thoughts needed to be organised before she and Synna reached the farm. There would be time on the ride to consider what they might achieve once they arrived, but for now she had to admit to herself she had no plan or even a desired outcome. They rode east to investigate whether the

Guild were at the farm, but she had no idea how they might proceed afterward. That had been the case for all her gests, of course. Watch and wait, gather information that would lead to a plan of action. This would be no gest, however. They might find a large force arrayed against them, had limited assets in terms of assistance, and the element of surprise may not be on their side.

Corelle pushed herself away from the door and splashed cold water on her face. It refreshed her but did not relieve the terrible symptoms that resulted from last night's wine. The paste sweetened her breath, which must have been hideous. In the reflecting glass, her face looked pale, her eyes red-rimmed and shot through with bloody veins. The catastrophe of her hair might never be redeemed, so she swept it up into a horse's tail and tied it in a knot behind her head. That would suffice. Beyond that, any further rescue of it might require her to cut it all off and start anew. Her tunic had been stained by wine and vomit, so she pulled a fresh one from her pack.

Corelle gazed in abject misery on the discarded tunic. As a girl, her making had been so fine, a Portreeve's wife had commandeered a dress of hers and ordered several more afterward. How had the mighty crumbled, that she should now treat a tunic of her own making with such disdain, she would fetch up onto it? It defied comprehension. She wiped the tears from her eyes, steeled herself against Synna's further wrath, and headed downstairs.

Synna had left the lobby, so she went out into the street. She hoped the fresh air might help with the after-effects of the drink more than the stale air of an inn. Synna waited outside the door with their horses. He sat on his, the reins of her mount in his hand. He handed the reins to her without a word, and she hauled herself into the saddle with some difficulty. She glanced at Synna, who watched her tight-lipped, and she nodded her head.

They followed the directions Vamma had given them. Little more than an hour had passed when Corelle had to stop her horse and dismount to fetch up in the hedgerow. She wiped her mouth with the sleeve of her tunic, then pulled herself back into the saddle and pressed her heels to the horse's flank to walk on.

"This must stop." Synna had not followed her, and she reigned her horse to a halt and turned in her saddle.

"What do you mean?" She knew what he meant, but she feared to face either the truth of his words or the argument she felt could not be avoided.

"You are out of control. Wine renders you ineffective for the work we are here to perform, and it will kill you, I fear."

Her hackles rose. "Ineffective? Do not doubt me, Synna. I have lost none of my skills."

"Look at yourself, Corelle. You resemble a street urchin rather than a ruthless killer. You can barely sit on your horse and have to stop at every farm gate to fetch up."

"I have fetched up once." Anger burned at her like the bile that had burned her throat moments before.

"Once since we left the town. You were covered in it when you returned to the inn. I guess you had done so between Vamma's house and the lobby. Can you swear you will not do so again this morning?"

Corelle longed to say she could, but her stomach suggested it would be a falsehood. She looked down at the pommel of her saddle in a mixture of self-pity and self-loathing as her anger collapsed under the onslaught of her shame. "I am sorry."

He might not have heard her apology, for he gave no acknowledgment of it. "I cannot support you if this continues."

"You said you would stay with me not two days since."

"That I did, and I do not hand out such commitments unless I mean them. But you make it difficult. Indeed, you seem determined to drive me away in favour of the wine. If trouble comes this morning, I doubt you are in any condition to face it, no matter what you say." She glanced up at him and he shook his head. "I am here not only because of you. Raolos and Wilash need my help, and I will continue. But I warn you now; I am prepared to handle this thing without you if you continue to drink yourself into this state every night."

"It keeps the nightmares away." Tears again formed in her eyes.

He stared at her in silence for a time. "I understand, but this is not the way to escape those nightmares, Corelle, for it will kill you. If the drink itself cannot kill you, and I confess I do not know whether it can, you will find yourself in an argument, too inebriated to defend yourself. You will be killed in an alleyway by some buffoon who could not otherwise best you if he had ten hands, a dagger in each."

She stared at him as she tried to recover some pride. "I would welcome it."

He shook his head. "I know this, for you have begged me to end your life more than once. I doubt Deineike would wish this for you."

The mention of Deineike stung her and her ire rose again. "Deineike is dead. She left me to deal with all I have done, all I have become, alone and helpless."

His face reddened and his lips drew taut. "She did not leave you. Styrrach murdered her because of you." He raised an arm. "Because of *you*, Corelle." He stabbed a finger toward her as he spat out the word 'you,' then turned away from her, his breaths heavy with fury.

An awkward silence fell between them. Corelle felt both ashamed and angry. She had chosen this life, but she had not asked it to become so tragic. She had loved Arella and Deineike and had not wished either of them dead. Everybody blamed her for both deaths, even Corelle herself. It infuriated her it had been her lot to bring about so many unnecessary deaths. As ever, her guilt overwhelmed her fury, and her head fell forward as tears streamed from her.

With a long-suffering sigh, Synna kicked his horse past her, and she turned her own mount to follow him. She had to stop once more and dismount to fetch up. How could anything be left in her stomach to gush out of her mouth? The stale, acrid taste made her grimace as they continued toward the farm.

Vamma had given them excellent directions, and Corelle recognised a small copse of trees Vamma had described, close to the farm. Synna reined his horse to a halt, and Corelle waited in silence behind him. He turned in the saddle. "We will hide the horses in those trees and move forward on foot." She nodded in agreement.

They tied the horses to tree trunks and walked back to the road. It was past the midday, and the sun's heat fell on them from a cloudless blue sky, but clouds covered Corelle's heart, and no warmth penetrated it. Ahead of them, the road curved, and a shallow ditch lay to either side of it, dry now in the warmth of the summer despite the recent rains. Synna held up a hand for Corelle to wait. He crouched, moved forward with stealth and grace, then slid into the ditch. He stopped at the corner and beckoned for Corelle to join him.

They had a clear view of the farmhouse from the corner, fifty paces away across the flat, featureless land. It would be difficult to approach the house any closer and remain unseen, however, since no trees grew, only a few sparse shrubs here and there to provide any sort of cover. The shallow ditch ended a few paces ahead of them where it became nothing more than a barren verge along the side of the road.

Two men stood at one corner of the house. Guards, Corelle guessed. The men would see them if they moved forward, even if they crawled, unless the guards were distracted. It would be a huge risk to gamble that neither guard paid any attention to what turned around the farm. They could not move any further forward for now.

The farmhouse looked even larger than Raolos's house. She

imagined a great deal of coin must have been involved in the purchase of the house and its land. It rose three storeys, with red walls and a dark roof. Another large building lay behind it, a barn or something similar. Corelle gazed around at the countryside. She could see no ready way to approach the house unseen from any direction, although a small bank rose from the ground some way behind the second building. She could not be certain from this distance the bank would provide much protection from sight, and to reach it unseen would be a challenge, since the road did not seem to travel there, and the flat land would be no ally.

She whispered to Synna. "We cannot approach unseen by day."

"That we cannot. Could we kill the guards with crossbows?"

She stared at him, aghast. "Have you lost your mind? Can you even use a crossbow? I have never drawn one in my life. I do not know the range of such weapons, and we do not have them to hand. We also do not know these two are the only ones who watch. There are many windows, and there may be guards on the opposite side of the house."

He laughed, his hand across his mouth as if to disguise the sound. "I cannot form outrageous plans as you can. Mine are woeful and unachievable, it seems."

"We could bring the Portreeve's men out here."

He appeared to consider the idea. "We could, but we do not know for certain the Guild is in the farmhouse. There are guards, but that does not mean some rich merchant has not moved into the house. They often travel with armed protectors."

Corelle thought back to the encounter with Hiw and the merchant he travelled with, when Deineike had fallen from the horse and suffered terrible injuries. "The people they travel with are often incompetent and can be dispatched with little effort. Regardless, you are right. We need proof, and to obtain it, we must get closer."

"Could we ride Vamma's cart out here as if we brought supplies?"

Corelle pondered the suggestion. It had merit, but also considerable risk. "They would recognise me if I drove or sat alongside you. All Guild members have my description, as you know. I would need to hide in the back, under a sack or some such. Would they recognise you?"

He rubbed his chin. "I doubt it. I have never met any members from Torric or Ryl to my knowledge."

She turned to study him. "You look like a killer."

"My thanks." He gave a dark laugh.

She punched him in the arm. "Oaf. I mean you do not look like a stallholder. You are sinewy and move like one who has been trained in the ways of caution. I do not know how long you could fool them."

"I have a day to learn to be clumsy, then?"

She laughed at his jest. "What would we do, if we came back in the cart?"

"The cart is the extent of my plan. I hoped you would develop it in your own unique style."

Corelle raised herself up as far as she dared, looked around again for something they might have missed that would give them a more realistic plan, but saw nothing. With a resigned sigh, she agreed to attempt the cart tomorrow. There would be no problem while Synna drove the cart to the farmhouse, but it seemed impossible to avoid a confrontation once they arrived. They did not know the numbers they faced, and she thought the plan risky, but they had no other. They must find a way to make the plan safer with a higher chance of success.

Two more men came out of the house and spoke to the two who had stood guard. The first two entered the house and left the newcomers in their place. It seemed the guards had been changed. The other side of the house could not be seen, but no doubt there would be a door on that side the guards could use. At the least, they now knew they faced not fewer than four guards.

They returned to the horses and rode back toward the town. As they rode, Corelle wracked her brain for a workable way to make the cart plan work. Synna interrupted her thoughts. "Vamma's couch?"

She snapped her head around to look at him as she tried to understand the significance of his question. "I slept there last night. I told you."

"That you did, but why the couch? She made it obvious she desired you, so why did you sleep on her couch?"

Corelle had no more than patchy memories of the night. She could remember when Synna had left, but she remembered little of the events at Vamma's house. "I had drunk too much for the stairs."

"That you had, if this morning is any measure. You did not lie with her?"

Corelle felt trapped, with no desire to admit she had lain with Vamma, lest it dismay Synna, but neither did she want to lie to him. She could not bear either, but she had to choose. The truth would be the lesser of the two evils, she guessed. At least it would not rely on some elaborate lie that might be confounded by his better recollection of their time in the tavern. "That I did." A sad sigh accompanied her confession.

They rode on in silence for a time, but even as Corelle hoped he had abandoned the thread, he disappointed her. "This is ill news."

"I am sorry, Synna. I know you wished to become close to her. I did not ask for things to turn as they did."

He stared at her, inscrutable. "I am not concerned because she chose you over me. What is scribed, must be. I am worried for her."

The reply confused Corelle. "I will not hurt her."

"That you will not. I know this. But my concern is that when we leave here, she might have become fixated on you, as Pettra did.

She deserves a better fate than the one that will be written for her if you draw her into your web of ruin."

Perplexed and put out, Corelle felt the heat of anger in her face. "My 'web of ruin?' You think I spin this web on purpose, to destroy those who cross my path?"

"Calm yourself. I know these terrible circumstances are not your choice. Who in their right mind would choose the life you have lived, after all else? Can you deny that women who become close to you suffer through that closeness? In your heart, do you deny it?"

Corelle took a deep breath to begin her defence, but he had the right of it. She lived with the agony of it every day, every hour. "That I do not. You are right, but you have forgotten her situation. Vamma has a home and business here. Friends and family too, I imagine. I lay with her last night, broken by events that had turned, and at her insistence." Not the entire truth, but she remained defensive.

"What events?"

"A song, the wine, my endless guilt. I became distraught and too inebriated to walk alone to the inn. She offered me her couch, then offered me herself. In my intoxication, I did not refuse, and I would not have done so even if I had not been in my cups. She is an attractive woman."

"That she is. Will you see her again?"

"She wishes it. I do not, for the reasons you have already mentioned. I will need to now, however, thanks to this foolish plan of yours."

He gave a soft laugh, then fell silent for a time. "You did not reveal our purpose here, I hope."

"That I did not, although she asked. I told her to ask me when I was not in my cups, although I hoped no such opportunity would present itself."

"Please say you will not be in your cups tonight. Much depends on you being in control tomorrow."

She sighed; he had the right of it. "I will not drink tonight. I understand how dangerous tomorrow will be." She paused as a thought came to her. "It may be difficult to keep our business here from her if we ask to borrow her cart when we may not be alive to return it."

Synna gave a short, bitter laugh. "We will not be alive. That is guaranteed."

CHAPTER 29
CORELLE

Corelle frowned as she pondered Synna's words. "I do not think it certain they can best us. We know there are, at the least, six or seven of them. If there are no more, and with the element of surprise and our superior skills, we may come through it." Something nagged at her, as it had for many days since Alcmouth. "Why are they still here? There are at least two Guild-meisters whose skills may be rusted compared to the other members. They must know how risky it is for them to take us on."

"They do not know you are in Yerrsun."

He had missed her point. "I meant here in Dur. They must have amassed great wealth under Styrrach. Why do they not take it and leave Dur?"

"You have wondered this before. You have not reached any conclusion and are unlikely to unless they reveal it to you. You can ask them tomorrow. I am sure they will be reasonable men and will explain it to you. Then they will kill us." He laughed his bitter laugh again.

Corelle could not pin down the thought that skipped in her head like a leaf in a breeze, often near at hand, then caught on the wind and carried far from her. "Glailam left. What drives these others to remain?"

"Glailam did flee Dur, but it did not save him, in truth."

She snorted. "An accident. Pure luck. I am grateful for that one improbable chance, but I rolled sixes. It seems inconceivable I could find him as I did, even now he is dead. Something holds Krage and these others to Dur and drives them to trap and kill me. This conundrum eats at me as flies eat at carrion."

"A vendetta for the wrongs you inflicted on them, my guess. Wilash also. You forget they seek to kill him."

"That is too simple a motivation for such risks. They play a higher stakes game than that, I am certain of it. Wilash did little more than push somebody from a horse, after all else."

"You and he worked to bring down their enterprise."

"That we did, as did you, yet you are not threatened."

His shrug suggested the issue did not merit further consideration. "They do not know who I am. None from the Alcmouth Guild appear to be involved."

Corelle shook her head. More must lie behind the presence of the Guild at the farm, but it eluded her. The debate with Synna brought her no nearer to the answer, since he did not share her viewpoint. They chatted as they rode, the tension reduced, but Corelle did not return to the question that gnawed at her.

The sun had sunk low in the sky as they handed the horses over to the stable boy. The market in the corner of the square had all but closed, a few stalls still open, doubtless in hopes of some last coin from citizens as they hurried home from a day's work. Corelle went to her room and lay on the bed with no desire to see Vamma again, but she could see no way to avoid it in the circumstances. She went to Synna's room and asked him to accompany her, but he did not want to be the fruit in the vegetable patch, as the expression went. He reminded her of her promise not to drink and said he would head out to find some food. He urged her to report the outcome to him later.

When Corelle entered the tavernroom, Vamma had already arrived. She sat at a table with another woman. They both had goblets before them. Corelle hesitated and wondered whether Vamma had found another to dally with tonight, but their need of the cart remained, so she crossed to their table.

Vamma rose, kissed Corelle's cheek, and embraced her like a long-lost friend. The show of affection embarrassed Corelle, but she smiled as she sat down. Vamma introduced the other woman, but Corelle did not catch the name as she studied the room for any sign of danger. She thought it had been Zui. The name sounded strange to her, but the woman spoke with an accent and had dark skin like the citizens of Vyrrmod, so she may not have been Durfolk.

If Zui, or whatever her name had been, stayed in the tavern all night, it would be difficult to ask Vamma about the cart, but to Corelle's relief the woman rose and said she must go. Vamma and the woman embraced, and Vamma watched after her as she left.

"She is a friend?" Corelle asked out of politeness. She did not wish to pry and did not care, but it seemed appropriate to show some interest in the woman.

"That she is. An old and dear friend. We have helped each other through difficult times. Her husband is…" She stopped and blushed. "I do not care for him. Let us leave it at that."

Corelle did not understand. "I see."

"She is from Qagrue, far to the south. She has been in Dur for many years now."

Corelle had not heard of Qagrue. "What brought her to this… to Yerrsun?"

Vamma laughed. "Not all people like the hustle and bustle of the cities." Her eyes sparkled. "Some of us like the quiet life."

Corelle nodded, although she had lost interest in Zui as soon as she had been introduced to her. She felt confident her polite interest in the woman had been sufficient, and she moved on to the reason she had come. "Do you use your cart every day?" She realised she had taken the conversation in a clumsy direction, and Vamma's confused expression confirmed the notion. "I am sorry, I am rude. How are you? Did you have a busy day at the stall?"

Vamma summoned the innkeep and ordered two more goblets of wine. Corelle said she did not want one, but Vamma insisted. When the innkeep had gone, she turned to Corelle and favoured her with a suggestive smile. "That I do not. Well. That I did. Let us go home after this goblet."

Corelle struggled to unravel the answer, then realised Vamma had answered her three questions before the suggestive idea they go to her home. There could be no doubt about her intent with the suggestion they should leave. Beneath the table, Vamma stroked Corelle's thigh, her pupils dilated, a blush on her cheeks. She looked aroused and in need of satisfaction. Synna's face flashed through Corelle's mind. Business before pleasure, she decided.

The wine arrived, and Corelle sipped at hers. "Before we leave, I must ask a favour of you."

"Ask it." Vamma slid her hand to the top of Corelle's leg and dangled her fingers close to Corelle's sex. Memories of the nights in Syme's tavern in Ort, when Deineike had behaved in a similar manner, flooded Corelle's mind, and she choked back a sob. To her disappointment, Vamma noticed. "Is something wrong?" She looked worried and raised her eyebrows, her eyes fixed on Corelle's own.

"That it is. I am uncomfortable with public shows of affection, as I have told you." Corelle sipped at her wine again. "The favour I must ask is this. May we borrow your cart in the morning?"

Vamma's own goblet paused between the table and her lips, and she turned to face Corelle again. "Pardon?"

Corelle frowned—she had never heard the word used in the way Vamma had used it. She guessed it had been a request for clarification, but it sounded unfamiliar in that context. "I do not understand this use of 'pardon.'"

"We use it here to indicate we have not understood a person's question. I do not understand why you have asked to borrow my cart. Indeed, I may have misheard you."

Corelle sighed. It had been another clumsy moment. Had her tongue abandoned her? "I apologise for such a blunt question. Synna and I have need of a cart for some work tomorrow and wondered if we might use yours, since you say you do not use it every day."

Vamma turned to her wine again and took a healthy drink. "My cart? What work?"

"We must move some large items."

"I see." Vamma's voice suggested she did not see at all. She took her hand from Corelle's thigh. "Where must you move these… items to and from?"

"From here to Estway Farm. We will have need of it all day." Corelle decided to leave unsaid the risk they might not live to return it.

"The farm? You still have not told me why you are so interested in that place." Vamma looked annoyed, Corelle thought. This could not have gone any worse. "Have you driven a cart before?"

"That I have. Synna has also, and he will drive it." She did not know whether Synna had driven a cart, but she reasoned she should imply they would take care of it.

"What will you use to pull it?"

Corelle could not guess why Vamma asked so many questions. Why could she not either agree or disagree? Corelle would prefer for her to agree. "Your horse, or one of ours."

Vamma snorted. "I doubt your horses would be used to the exertion of an entire day spent in the harness as they pull a heavy cart." She drained her goblet and waved to the innkeep. It seemed the cart had driven her lust from her mind, and she spun her empty goblet between her hands.

Vamma's questions, and the last response in particular, irritated Corelle. "Is it such a big favour to ask, the simple loan of a cart?" She strove to keep her voice calm.

"That it is. It is essential for my business, and to lend it and my horse to two virtual strangers is an unusual request."

"Strangers? You were less reluctant to help yourself to my body last night." Corelle regretted the words as soon as she had uttered them. "I am sorry. I should not have said that. Please ignore my rudeness."

Vamma sipped at her fresh goblet and turned to face Corelle, her face a blank. "You are right. I took advantage of you last night. You ask me to trust you with my cart now, and that is a different matter altogether."

"We can pay you, if that is a concern."

Vamma's sigh did not fill Corelle with confidence. "Corelle, the coin is not the issue. What if something happens and it is damaged? My business will suffer. My livelihood." She drank again, and Corelle pushed her own empty goblet away from her. The innkeep had brought her another when Vamma had summoned him, and she sipped at it. Vamma stared into her wine as she continued. "At the least, tell me the truth. What is your interest in Estway Farm? I do not believe this tale of mysterious items you need to transport out there."

Corelle let out a sigh of frustration. "I cannot tell you."

Vamma drained her goblet again and placed it on the table, gentle, as though it were a fragile, delicate keepsake in need of special care. "You are a strange one, Corelle. I do not understand you. I have never met anybody like you, in truth. You are cloaked in menace. You are almost dangerous, I think, like a snake ready to strike at any moment."

Corelle touched her arm. "I will not hurt you. Please believe me."

Vamma's grim laugh suggested she had not anticipated the answer. "Anybody else would have gushed about how I had misread them, about how sweet and innocent they are. You assure me you will not hurt me and confirm my suspicions. There are some whom you would not hesitate to hurt, I think. I told you last night; you are fearsome, but you do not frighten me. Tell me Corelle—and be truthful. Have you hurt others?"

Corelle gazed into her eyes and decided to be honest. "I have killed people."

Vamma stared down into her empty goblet again for long moments before she raised her eyes and summoned the innkeep. Once the wines had been replaced, she turned to Corelle. "You said last night you were a killer, and now you confirm it. You must understand how this sounds, here in Dur. Zui tells horrible tales of violence and death in Qagrue, but here in Dur there is no violence. Did you kill these people in some far-off land?"

Corelle exhaled a long, heavy breath. "Some of them."

Vamma lowered her voice as though concerned the Portreeve might hear her and hang them both on the spot. "You have killed in Dur?" Corelle shrugged in response. "That is inconceivable. Who did you kill?"

"Vamma, it is dangerous to discuss these things. Can we not change the subject? Will you lend us your cart?"

"You wish to kill the people at the farm." Vamma gasped and raised a hand to her mouth. "You will somehow use my cart to kill them." Her eyes had widened, and a tear trickled from one of them. Corelle said nothing as she drained her wine. How many had she drunk? She had promised Synna she would not drink, but the evening had taken a turn that drove her toward inebriation, and she felt powerless to stop it. Vamma whispered. "I cannot allow it."

Had she spoken to herself or addressed Corelle? "You will not lend us the cart?"

Vamma looked deep into Corelle's eyes. "That I will not. If you or Synna have killed, that is no business of mine. I wish to keep it that way. I will not become embroiled in your violence."

Corelle pushed her goblet away from her and stood. "I understand. I am sorry Vamma. I did not mean to bring this darkness to your door." She must now break the bad news to Synna, and they would need a new plan.

Vamma reached up and grasped at her arm. "I said I will not lend you my cart. Negotiations for the loan of my body have not taken place. I feel the odds are more in your favour in this matter." She smiled up at Corelle, suggestive once more.

Corelle returned the smile. "You would lie with a killer?"

Vamma stood and whispered into her ear. "I would lie with you. Whether you are a killer is of no consequence."

Once they reached her house, they went up the stairs to Vamma's bedroom. She had little more than a small bed and some trunks in the room. In truth, the room resembled a great many of the bedrooms Corelle had been in. Vamma pulled her down onto the bed and thrust her tongue into Corelle's mouth, her passion evident in the moans that rose from deep within her. They enjoyed each other's bodies for well over two hours, then lay contented in each other's arms. Vamma pushed Corelle's damp hair back from her forehead. "I had the right of it." She kissed Corelle's sweat-soaked forehead.

"About what?" Corelle laughed, and Vamma slapped her behind.

"You are even better when you are not in your cups. You are… incredible. You have spoiled me for the few women of Yerrsun I sometimes entertain."

"My apologies." Corelle longed for sleep. The rigours of the day had exhausted her.

"How long will you stay in Yerrsun?"

"Not long, I hope. Longer, I imagine, now we cannot use your cart."

"I am glad about that," Vamma purred as she slid a hand between Corelle's legs, "but if you had thoughts of sleep, you were mistaken."

Corelle gasped as Vamma slid a finger deep inside her. "So it would seem." She kissed Vamma, their tongues again entwined in a passionate dance.

CHAPTER 30
CORELLE

As she had the previous morning, Vamma bullied Corelle out of bed earlier than Corelle would have wished. At the least, she had no headache or bilious stomach. She felt exhausted nonetheless; they had slept little. Vamma had an insatiable sexual appetite, and Corelle had struggled to keep up with her as she gave and demanded pleasure all night.

Another warm morning greeted Corelle as she walked to the inn lost in her thoughts. The outcome with the cart disappointed her, but in truth she had never had much faith in the plan, and they must now come up with another. Synna sat in the tavernroom with a plate of meats before him. She sat next to him and helped herself to some of his food.

"I asked you to tell me the arrangement, not steal my breakfast." Synna did not look up from his plate.

"That you did, but there are no arrangements to tell you. She will not lend us the cart."

Synna stared into her eyes. "Is there some reason I should know about?"

Corelle coughed, embarrassed by the confession she had made

the previous night. "I told her little enough, but I would not lie to her. She asked questions I could not evade if I told her the truth."

"You are permitted to lie, Corelle. Have you forgotten your training?"

She fixed him with a stare. "Would you have me lie to you?"

He glared at her for some moments. "Curse you." He returned to his food.

Corelle chewed on a piece of meat and thought about Vamma on her cart as she drove out to the farm with the provisions. At once, a question formed in her mind. "Why do they order provisions from Vamma?"

"She is the only one prepared to make the journey. She said as much."

"That she did. She also expressed surprise they did not grow their own food. It is a farm." She grabbed his arm. "It is a farm, but they are not farmers."

"We know this."

"Why do they come into the town? It is shoddy and reckless. The risks are enormous. They are killers, hunted by every Portreeve in the land at Raolos's orders."

"They must eat. Where else do they obtain food?"

Her frustration grew that he could not join together the points she had made. "That is what I mean. I have wondered why they remain in Dur. To remain here at the farm is another chance they take. Unless they take no chance at all."

He looked at her in confusion. "You have lost me."

"The Portreeve. He shows no interest in them and does not follow Raolos's express command to apprehend any who might be involved in Styrrach's operation."

"And...?"

"He might know them. He might have known one of the Portreeves involved in Styrrach's operation. That could be why they hide here and visit the town without fear. The Portreeve will not trouble them, for he is bought by them."

Synna looked thoughtful. "There is sense in your argument, but how do we find out? They are as unlikely to tell us as the Portreeve himself."

"The old man, Minarko. He can tell us how long this Portreeve has been in office. Did Raolos appoint him, or has he been here for long years? The latter, my guess. Raolos would not have thought to seek Styrrach's cohorts out here in the wilderness of the Eastlands."

They finished their breakfast and set off for Minarko's house. As they walked, Synna turned to Corelle. "My thanks."

"For what?"

"You kept your promise last night and did not drink."

She felt warmth in her cheeks. "I did drink, but not sufficient to be ineffective this morning."

He laid a hand on her arm, a happy grin on his rugged face, old before its time. "That is a start."

"You again?" Minarko asked when he answered their knock. "Can you not leave an old man in peace?"

Synna replied. "We are sorry to trouble you again, but we have more questions."

"Of course you do. Nobody visits me unless they wish to know something, did you know that?" They said nothing. "Has Vamma sent you here? Oh, do not look surprised. I know you found her after your last visit. You are imaginative, I will grant you. Very well, ask your questions."

Corelle wished he would chatter less when she had urgent need of answers, but she fought down her irritation. "How long has Rognakk served as Portreeve here?"

His face turned dark. "That weasel. He is unfit to be Portreeve of Yerrsun. This new Bailiff you purport to serve should sweep him back under the rock he crawled out from and install one who is competent here. Do you seek to bring him down?" His mood brightened as he seemed to reach his own conclusion.

Synna rushed to deny his deduction. "That we do not. We want to know how long he has been in office. Do not draw any conclusions, please."

The old man huffed. "A pity. Somebody should remove him from office. He is a weasel of a man."

Corelle thought a weasel must be some kind of animal, but she had not heard of it before. She had not pressed Minarko the last time they spoke, but today, her curiosity got the better of her. "What is a weasel, after all else?"

He laughed once, a short, derisive laugh. "Do they teach you nothing in the west? It is an animal, a pest, known to kill all manner of creatures. Dogs, cats, rabbits. Weasels are short of leg and skittish, like Rognakk."

Corelle stifled a laugh. "I see. You have not answered our question, I should point out."

"Should you indeed? How observant of you. Hmm, let me see now. It would be around four years ago Carshan left for Torric. Rognakk had been his assistant for some years, but the old Bailiff moved Carshan to Torric, and Carshan advocated for Rognakk to take over his position. Torric, mark you. Quite a promotion. Quite a promotion indeed." Synna and Corelle exchanged glances. "I see this news pleases you. Now you will please me and leave an old man in peace." They thanked him and walked down the path. Minarko yelled after them as they left. "Treat Vamma well while you are here, young lady. She deserves it. She is a good person, unlike you." The comment took Corelle by surprise, but she did not turn or respond.

As they walked back toward the inn, Corelle voiced her thoughts. "This Portreeve is in league with the one from Torric, I would wager all I own on it."

"That would be a poor wager to win, I imagine. Nonetheless, I agree. It is too much of a convenience not to be so. Did he take part in Styrrach's scheme?"

Corelle laughed at his jest, although he had the right of it—she owned nothing but a few clothes and the remains of Styrrach's coin. She weighed up all she knew of Styrrach's operation. "I doubt it. Yerrsun is not on the river and is a difficult place to reach. Rognakk is in thrall to this Carshan somehow, I suspect. But I do not think Yerrsun played any part in Styrrach's business. Carshan may be at the farmhouse with Krage, nonetheless. Did they not mention a Portreeve, the men in Alcmouth?"

Synna nodded his agreement. When they reached the square, they stopped at one corner. A large crowd bustled around the market. While she wondered what their next move ought to be, Corelle scanned the crowds in the square, and her eye caught a man who seemed out of place. He had glanced their way but looked away as soon as Corelle's gaze swept over him. She did not allow her gaze to linger on him. He wore a hooded cloak, despite the warmth of the morning, and his short, lithe body looked out of place among the shoppers and workers. He did not look like one of the regulars who swarmed around the market. As the Ryl phrase went, he stood out like a milk cow in a stable. "We are watched." As she spoke, she stretched as though tired.

Synna showed no alarm, but his eyes scanned the square once. "Where?"

She laughed and glanced at Synna, as if he had told her a jest. "Toward the market. Brown cloak."

Synna shook his head and waved his arms in front of him as though he refuted something Corelle had said. "I see him. Guild, there is no question."

"Let us separate and see which of us he follows, or if there are others. If he follows me and you see no other, follow at a distance. Do not be seen."

Synna pushed her and laughed, then walked away. Corelle

admired his craft and could see why he had been chosen to kill Pettra and Raopul. He might have been the best in Alcmouth as he had once claimed, she reasoned. She looked around as though she tried to orient herself. The Guild member did not follow Synna, and she spotted no other who did.

Corelle headed for the market and passed close to their new friend. To have circled around him might have appeared suspicious, but neither did she take a direct line toward him, lest he guess she had seen him. If she passed him within ten paces, it would seem as though she went about her business with no idea he watched her. He twitched as she drew near but held his ground. This man seemed terrible at his work. She fancied she could smell his nervous sweat as she passed him. Why had they sent this incompetent to watch them? Another mystery.

She paused at Vamma's stall. Vamma served a thick-set man, but as he left, she noticed Corelle. She stiffened, and the blood drained from her face. Corelle thought it a curious reaction but focused on the man who followed her for now. He fidgeted with some items at a nearby stall. Corelle had noticed the stall before. It sold trinkets such as necklaces, earrings and the like. A poor choice of stall to have stopped at, for almost everything on it would hold little appeal for a man.

She picked up an apple and held it out toward Vamma, whose eyes flicked from side to side. In different circumstances, Corelle would have wanted to know what troubled her, but she held out a groat in the other hand, and Vamma took it from her, slipped it into the pocket of her apron. "My thanks."

Had the Guild questioned Vamma about Corelle? That might explain the unusual behaviour. If she spotted the man, she might fear him, or she may worry Corelle might harm her in case she had revealed information about their activities. Corelle had no time to unravel that puzzle now. She turned, made for a tavern, and spotted Synna, who followed the man, well hidden in the crowd.

At that, Corelle stopped and bent to fuss at her boot. She slipped her dagger out into her hand. In the corner of her eye, the man stopped at a meat stall and inspected the meat.

The stallholder spoke to the man and distracted him, so Corelle rose and walked toward him at a brisk pace. Synna changed direction and closed on the man, who glanced toward Corelle and turned, then hurried away. She threw the apple as hard as she could, and it struck him in the back. He jumped and turned to look at her. Synna seized his moment to grasp the man's arm. As the man turned to Synna in surprise, Corelle reached him. She held her dagger to his side. Nobody who passed by would notice, but he could feel it.

Corelle spoke in her normal voice to allay any suspicions if anybody had noticed them. "Styrrach, old friend. Let us head into that tavern for a drink."

The man glanced between her and Synna, fear in his eyes. "You can do nothing here."

"Why not?"

"You would not kill me in the marketplace, with so many witnesses." Sweat beaded his forehead, and his body shook. His voice sounded more desperate than confident. "You would be hanged."

"Hanged?" Corelle laughed at his wild claim. "For the death of a man whom we know to be a killer? We carry letters from the Bailiff that instruct us to do just that. We work for him. No, my friend, I think not. Your friendly Portreeve could not hang us."

He gulped, and any vestige of confidence he may have clung to fell from him as Synna confirmed his predicament. "You cannot return to the farm now. We spotted you without difficulty. You have failed them. Do you wish Guild justice?"

A look of fear crossed his face. "What then? A quick death at the hands of the monster you travel with?"

Corelle answered his question. "Let us have that drink. We can discuss your options in a more relaxed atmosphere."

She watched him weigh up his choices. He glanced around, and she pressed the dagger against him to remind him he held a low hand. He nodded, and they entered the nearby tavern and took a quiet table in a corner. The innkeep took their orders and they waited in silence, the man in the corner, Corelle and Synna seated either side of him. Once the innkeep delivered the drinks, Corelle raised her goblet. "A toast to our new friend." Synna raised his tankard. They waited until the man raised his own, and they all took a sip of their respective drinks. Corelle insisted he hand over his weapon, a long-bladed dagger, crude and well used. She slid it into a boot.

Synna began the interrogation. "Tell us your name."

"I am Velbur. I know you." He spoke to Corelle before he turned to Synna. "I confess you are unknown to me."

"Let us keep it that way, for now." Synna gave him a wry smile.

Corelle pressed on. She embellished her story, the better to add to his discomfort. "Velbur, we will dispense with the request for you to tell us everything, since we already know much of your situation. We know two Guildmeisters, one Senior Aide, several members, and a Portreeve or two hide out at Estway Farm. We know the Portreeve here is in Krage's pocket. Do not look to him for aid. We will kill him and his men if necessary. We will turn the Yerrsun square vermilion with their blood if we must. Then we will kill you and all those who quake with fear at the farm, afraid to confront us. Do you doubt me?" He shook his head, and his face blanched. "That is good. Please, continue your ale." She gave him a warm smile. "You may have heard I kill at whim, or that I am a merciless monster. That tale has some truth about it, but I have also spared more than I have killed. Those who co-operate with me tend to live longer than those who oppose me." She could not look at Synna as she spun her fanciful tale. If they made each other laugh, the jig would be up. The man must fear them for her plan to produce results.

Velbur shook his head. "When your name is mentioned, mercy is never in the same room. You are a cold-blooded murderer, by all accounts. You seek to seduce me with these friendly words, have me betray my colleagues, then slit my throat in an alleyway somewhere."

"That I do not. I am a woman of my word if nothing else." It had been a lie, like so much of her life. Broken promises lay behind her, as abundant as her footprints.

Velbur had more to say. "Rognakk will hang you. You cannot kill all his men. There are only two of you, and this other may have never killed in his life. No doubt he is some gullible fool you travel with to deflect attention from your deviancy."

His words angered her, and she snatched a fistful of his cloak in her hand to tug him closer to her. "How do you know how many we are?" Spittle from her lips spattered his face. "Even if we are but two, we could kill this peasant Portreeve and all his men and not even break sweat. I am a monster, or do you forget? Has the Guild stood before my wrath? This Rognakk will stare at his entrails on his fancy desk as he dies." She released him, and he shrank back as sweat dripped from his forehead onto the table. She slowed her breaths and battled to control her temper. Synna watched on in silence. "It comes to this. Debts are owed, and I am here to pay them. Shall I begin with you? Were you in Alcmouth when Priu killed Klordia?"

"That I was not. I stayed here, at the farm. I had naught to do with that."

She nodded. That increased the likelihood their numbers were greater than she had hoped, but it made sense for Krage and Sisnop to keep guards at hand while they dispatched others to Alcmouth. "How many are at the farm? We know of Krage, Sisnop, and Gillar. Who else? Speak quick now. The sand falls."

He stared into the remains of his ale for some time, disconsolate, as though he wished he could jump into the ale and drown, to be rid of his tormentors at last. Corelle fought her impatience and sipped at her wine until he looked up again. "I will not tell you."

Corelle sat back and studied the man. He had answered out of bravery or fear. She had not anticipated Velbur would be more afraid of the Guild than of her, but she could play on that very fear to get information out of him. "Very well. You are free." She saw Synna draw a breath to speak and shot him a glance that stilled the breath in his throat. "I will ride a while with you, even. Once we are in sight of the farm, of course, I will slit your horse's throat and ride back to town. I do not wish them to catch me, but I do not care about you. Your fate will be written when they see me ride off, I think."

"Curse you. You are more of a monster than they say."

"That I am." Her cold smile reinforced the assertion. "That is history. We are interested in news, if you have any to impart."

He drained his tankard in one swallow. "Curse you. Will you not give me a quick death? Why must you torment me?"

He blinked in surprise at her sardonic laughter. "You think I torment you? Velbur, my friend, you have never witnessed Guild justice. You will long for a tankard of ale and my questions ere you die to that justice."

Wide-eyes and pale, he stared at her anew. "You have seen it?"

She leaned close to his face again. "I *am* it. Tell me what I want to know or suffer the consequences."

He stared at her with raw hatred in his eyes. "You have named three already. One Portreeve, as you suspected. He is from Torric. Carshan, his name." Corelle shot Synna a sharp look. "Gillar returned from Alcmouth a few days ago with news of what turned there."

Although they had made progress, he had revealed little more than they had already guessed. "How many members guard them?"

He sighed. "Ten. One from Alcmouth, the rest from Torric and Zhanghar."

So many. Fourteen would be difficult to take, even if Carshan could not fight. Velbur might be counted out, but that still left thirteen. They would need surprise and great fortune to take so many. Surprise now seemed unlikely, since they knew she had arrived in Yerrsun, and mayhap Synna also. The Portreeve's men might also aid Krage. She decided to confirm that Rognakk had revealed their presence in Yerrsun. "Krage sent you to watch us. You knew because the Portreeve of this town sent word?" His glum nod confirmed it.

She wondered if he had any insight into the issue of why the Guild remained in Dur. "Why do they remain here, in Dur? They must have amassed great riches. Why did they not flee, as Glailam did?" He shrugged. Her lack of progress frustrated her, and she slumped back into the trestle.

"You have heard of shrouding?" Synna took over, and Corelle shot him a grateful glance. She caught the innkeep's eye, and he brought another round of drinks to their table.

Velbur answered once the innkeep returned to his counter. "That I have not."

"The Guildmeisters selected members to sacrifice to the Portreeve to appease any cries for justice for our work. We were sold, handed over to be hanged."

Velbur's eyes widened. "Impossible. Why would they do this?"

Corelle provided the explanation. "They made a fortune and would do anything necessary to protect their income. Styrrach sold me in Zhanghar. The Portreeve's men came to capture and hang me, but I escaped."

"You lie." She saw the doubt in his eyes, nonetheless

"He confessed it to me, in the moments before I took his worthless life. All for coin. The Guild served as nothing more than a convenient way for them to remove obstacles to the improvement of their financial situation. The gests came from the Portreeve, who ran the business side of it. We were little more than disposable tools they could cast from them when the need arose." He shook his head but said nothing. "They hanged Priu. You know this. The citizens' outrage over any violent act must be assuaged so they can return to their peaceful delusions. We have told this tale to so many like you, we grow weary of it. No matter how many times we repeat it, there is a fresh queue of former members who wait for us to tell it again and again."

He fell silent and stared into his tankard as he shook his head in apparent bewilderment.

Corelle pressed on. "You threatened Vamma?" Little else could explain Vamma's reaction to Corelle's appearance at the stall earlier.

He sighed. "I like her, in truth. I saw you leave her home this morning, and we all know of your proclivities. It proved easy enough to draw the two lines together. I warned her you pose a danger to her, nothing more. I swear it."

"Proclivities?"

Synna explained it for her. "Appetites."

Corelle tired of Velbur. He knew little enough, she believed. His lack of skill suggested he was a low-ranked member of the Guild who might be marked for future shrouding. "Ride your horse south. Do not let me see you again. It goes ill for those I see a second time."

Synna objected, distress on his face. "Wait. We cannot let him go. He must answer for his crimes."

She shook her head. "His crimes are no worse than ours. He had no hand in Klordia's death. Like as not he will drift around the land until he is killed in a fight over a hand of cards or some such. He knows little more than we ourselves already knew."

Velbur stood. "I am free to go?"

"Begone." Corelle sighed as she moved to permit him to leave the table. He scurried out of the tavern.

Synna tapped his fingers on the table top. "I fear you have made a mistake."

Corelle gave Synna a furious glare. "What would you have me do? Kill him? Must I kill everybody who walks the land? It sickens me, the death, though it will not abandon me."

"Even so…"

"Synna, think. If we take him to the Portreeve, he will hang him. He must, to save face. If Velbur returns to the farm, Krage will kill him. He is no threat to us, and I do not wish more blood on my hands from another who has been used as part of the game Styrrach and his allies play. They know we are here, and they are too many for us to take."

"Then what is our next move?" Corelle turned over their limited options in her mind, but after a while, Synna went on. "I have a thought. We could return to Alcmouth and bring a substantial force of Bailiff's and Portreeve's men back here with us. We could capture them with such a force."

The plan did not appeal to Corelle. "That would take an interminable amount of time. Three tendays, my guess. I suspect the Guild would flee long before we returned."

"Would that be so bad, Corelle? One has been hanged for Klordia's death. That should serve Wilash's desire for justice, since the one they hanged killed her himself."

"He killed her. He did not order it." Even if it satisfied Wilash, it would not satisfy her. Priu's death did not atone for all that had turned.

Synna remained insistent. "If they leave Dur, everything they plot will be undone, will it not? I do not see their rout as a bad outcome."

He might have the right of it, but she still disliked the idea. "I cannot tell Wilash Klordia is avenged. She is not, any more than Deineike, Arella, or Pettra. More must pay, and something is afoot I cannot yet determine. They may leave now, but they may return in a few passes. They have stayed in Dur and taken great risks to lure me out. Whatever their scheme, I do not think they will abandon it in a heartbeat, as you seem to believe."

"You think there is something more to this, but I do not. I believe they intend nothing more than to kill you. They seek revenge on you for the destruction of their organisation, I am sure of it."

Corelle could not overlook her concern for Vamma. "What of Vamma? Velbur knows I lay with her. She might now be in danger. We cannot abandon her to them."

Synna frowned, lost in thought for a few moments. "There is something in what you say. Out at the farm, they may know nothing of your relationship with her. You have brought this danger to her door."

"You are right, and in being right, you convince me. I cannot abandon her. I must stay here."

"Then you will both die. They are too many."

Corelle shrugged. She had known that all along. Death, her boon companion, waited for her at some point. Today, tomorrow; who cared? She would welcome its embrace. It held no fear for her. She levelled her gaze at Synna. "So be it."

CHAPTER 31
CORELLE

Synna let out a lengthy sigh as Corelle sipped at her wine. At last, he replied. "You may make that decision for yourself, but not for Vamma. We must warn her, at the least. We might persuade her to leave Yerrsun. I can give her letters to grant her safe passage to Alcmouth. She can await you there if you return alive from here."

"We are not as close as you appear to think. She may have no desire to wait for me, and I am not sure I would seek her out even if she did so." Despite her protests, she could not deny the truth in his words. "We can warn her, however. You may have the right of it. She might leave, and that is the best thing for her safety."

"We will warn her now, then we should leave, with her if she will come with us, or together. She can leave when she is ready."

"I will stay. Something more turns, I am certain of it. You should go alone if you are determined to bring reinforcements. Come, let us visit Vamma at her stall and make our case."

They left the tavern and made for the market. They saw no sign of anybody who followed or watched them. The market appeared no less busy, and they waited while Vamma served two customers.

She smiled at them as they approached her stall, but with little warmth in the smile.

Corelle lowered her voice. "We spoke to someone today who had earlier spoken to you about me."

"That he did." Vamma remained silent for a heartbeat, then drew in a deep breath as though she had come to some decision. "He told me you are a dangerous killer. Is he right? Have you killed him?"

Corelle clucked her tongue in frustration. "You knew this already. I have told you I have killed." She did not turn to look at Synna, had no need to see him to sense his displeasure.

"He said you have killed for coin, but now you kill for fun. Even women you love. Have you killed him? You did not answer my question."

Corelle choked back anger at the things Velbur had said about her. "That we have not. There is more to the tale than his words suggest."

"I do not believe you."

"Which part?" Corelle grew more irritated.

"That you have not killed him. The other is simple to deduce."

Corelle sighed. "Why would I lie? We did not kill him."

Synna came to her aid. "She let him go, against my better judgement, in truth. She has a soft side. She is not all bad."

"I believe that, at the least." Vamma sighed.

Corelle carried on. "Nonetheless, you are now in danger because of me. I am sorry about that. I would have avoided it if I could. The men at the farm are killers also, and there are a great many more of them than there are of us, as you know. You must leave Yerrsun for a time, until this matter resolves itself."

"This is my home. My stall, my house, such family as I have, my friends; all are here. I cannot leave."

Synna growled stern words at her. "You must. You are in peril."

"I cannot, and I will not. All I am is in Yerrsun."

Corelle sighed with frustration. "Your ruin may be here also."

A woman approached the stall, and Vamma turned toward her, but she paused and turned to Corelle. "We all die, sooner or later. I will take my chances." She turned her attention to her customer.

Corelle gave Synna a look of consternation. The last person who told her they would take their chances had been the man at the tavern in Alcmouth's square a tenday ago or so. He met his ruin, and she took no comfort from the memory. Synna shot a weak smile of encouragement back at her, and they watched as Vamma served the customer before she returned to them and waved an arm as if to shoo them away. "I will not leave. You two will gain nothing if you stand there all day. You will not change my mind."

Corelle sighed. "You do not realise how serious this situation could be."

"That I do. I realise, but I do not care. This is my home, and I will die here. It is not mine to decide when that will be. What fates are written for me, I cannot see, and I will not tamper with. Now be off with you both. Come to my home tonight if you wish."

She turned to another customer, and Corelle's head sank forward. "She is stubborn."

"Where have I seen this virtue before?" Synna laughed.

As they walked toward their inn, Corelle returned to Synna's plan. "Will you leave today?"

He shook his head. "That I will not. I cannot make the next village today, after all else. I will leave first thing in the morning. I wish you would leave with me."

"How can I, when Vamma insists she will remain?"

"I understand. Be careful. There is no help for you here. The Portreeve is hostile to us and—"

Corelle interrupted him and snapped a finger against a thumb as an idea struck her. "The Portreeve. We will use his hostility to our end." Synna's blank stare told Corelle he had not understood. "We will go to him now, and we will tell him our work here is done. Tomorrow, we will ride west out of the town. We will ensure our departure is seen by as many citizens as possible."

Synna shook his head. "Leaving Yerrsun is an excellent plan, but I fail to see how this uses the Portreeve to our own advantage."

"Once we have left, he will waste little time before he informs Krage we are gone. They will relax and return to their routine."

"They will remain wary, I feel."

"For a day or so they may, I agree with you. Then their vigilance will reduce." The plan came together in her head so fast, she struggled to explain it.

"How does this help us though? I feel I have missed some key part of this plan. It feels more chaotic than any you have ventured before, and that says much."

"You will ride on to Alcmouth, as planned. I will turn aside and return to the farm across country, unseen and unsuspected."

"Where you will be killed as soon as they see you." Synna sounded exasperated.

Corelle had no room for doubt in her plan, as dangerous as it would be. "They will not see me. I will watch until you return if needs be. At some point, they will act. They cannot sit in that farmhouse for ever. In small numbers, I can pick them off."

Synna shook his head again. "The moment you kill one of them, they will know you have not left Yerrsun."

Corelle grimaced. The plan had caught up with her thoughts, and she had not considered this element. "I can use discretion in how I kill them."

"Discretion? What do you mean?"

"If I push one off a horse, for instance, he might have fallen."

Synna stopped, stared at her, and laughed. He laughed so hard, tears came to his eyes, and he doubled up with his hands on his thighs. Corelle watched him laugh, and her impatience and humiliation grew by the heartbeat. His laughter showed little sign it would end soon.

"What amuses you so much?"

Between gales of laughter, Synna replied. "Corelle, the deadly killer, feared by everybody, although she stands little more than belly high to a mutton, and all who oppose her are pushed from their horses to their ruin."

She stared at him open-mouthed, then the picture his words had painted became too much, and she also broke into laughter. They roared for some time, and each time one of them came close to some semblance of control, their eyes met, and they both collapsed into further laughter. They ignored the confused stares as people passed by until, after many moments, Corelle's laughter subsided, and she gasped, "I hate you."

Synna managed to speak through his own laughter. "There is merit in one part of your plan, at the least."

"My thanks for your great compliment."

"If we tell the Portreeve we will both leave, you can, at the least, return unseen. Your life will be somewhat less imperilled."

She favoured him with a sarcastic reply. "I am relieved you find something worthwhile in my idea."

"Come, we will visit Rognakk and lay down the bait." He turned and strode across the square in the direction of the Portreeve's Offices. Corelle hurried to catch him, and they walked side by side. "Let us hope we convince him."

She let out a short, sardonic laugh. "He is an imbecile. He will swallow every word we tell him, then send a rider to the farm as soon as we leave the room, desperate to curry favour with his masters."

"You are correct, my guess. Let the deception commence."

They insisted on an immediate audience with the Portreeve and waved Raolos's letters in front of the poor woman in the lobby until she rose and scampered through the door behind her. She returned and beckoned them to follow her through the door.

As they entered Rognakk's office, he stood and greeted them like old friends. "Always a pleasure to see the Bailiff's agents."

Corelle's smile matched the friendliness of his greeting. "We are grateful for Yerrsun's hospitality. Our investigations are complete, and we return to Alcmouth tomorrow."

If her announcement surprised him, he did not show it. "I trust all is well. It is important to us all here in the Eastlands that the Bailiff is satisfied with our endeavours on behalf of the Duke."

Synna reassured him. "Most satisfactory. Raolos will be pleased by all we report."

"Then I must bid you a fond farewell. I wish you safe travels to Alcmouth. It is such a long journey." He came around the desk and motioned to the door. He followed them out into the Aide's office and bade them farewell.

As they left the building, Synna whispered, "He could scarce wait to summon one of his men to ride to Estway."

"That he could not. He acted well though, I thought." She sniggered. "We must act at least as well in the morning, if the bait is to be taken."

"We could leave now."

Corelle shook her head. "We have told him we leave tomorrow. It would introduce complications if we act contrary to our words."

"Will you visit with Vamma tonight?"

Corelle detected no animosity or resentment in his voice. "I had not given it more thought. I imagine I will."

"Please be mindful of her. She remains in danger until we can apprehend Krage and his allies."

The thought dwelt her mind for much of the time. "I know this. I will watch over her."

They reached the inn. "That is good."

In her room, Corelle changed her trousers, since she had worn the same pair for several days. As she slid them down her legs, she remembered the soft leather trousers Deineike had worn when they had first met. They had proved impossible to dry and impractical for a trip across the countryside in the wet season, and Corelle had mocked Deineike at some inn or other for the poor choice. The memory made her smile. She had said, "Poor Deineike. No coin, and no trousers," or some such. The exact words would not come to mind, but she could recall Deineike's face, put out by the ridicule and the truth behind it. Corelle smiled again. It felt better to smile than cry when she remembered Deineike. At moments such as these, it seemed the pain had lessened somewhat, but an ache endured in her heart the smiles could not diminish.

Vamma ushered her into the house when she knocked on the door an hour later, then thrust her tongue into Corelle's mouth as soon as she closed the door. Corelle returned the kiss, and their tongues writhed and swirled in a now familiar routine. Vamma slid her hand inside Corelle's tunic, found her breast, and caressed the flesh. The soft, sensual touches sent ripples of desire through Corelle's body.

Corelle whispered as they pulled their lips apart. "Good evening."

Vamma smiled. "It will be, I am certain. First, I must ask you a question."

Corelle groaned. Her past spawned endless questions, it seemed, and they grew tiresome. She must find a life where nobody asked questions, where the past and all its secrets lay concealed. The thought of a mariner's life again entered her mind. When she had settled her debt with Krage, she might give it more serious thought. "Ask it as fast as you can. I ache for you."

Vamma's mouth twisted into a wicked smile, and she draped her arms around Corelle's neck. "Where did that man come from?"

Corelle sighed. She had feared the question would involve her past and the Guild, and so it had. "An enemy from long ago."

"Is he still your enemy?"

"That he is. I did not kill him, yet he remains my enemy. He is bound up with the organisation responsible for Deineike's death."

Vamma stared into Corelle's eyes and knitted her brows. "You said Deineike died because of you. You were in your cups, I realise that. You said it though, yet now you say this man is tied up in her death somehow."

Corelle sighed. "These people seek me. They have sought me without respite for over two years. They once had me in their grip, but they took Deineike's life in place of mine."

Compassion sprang to Vamma's eyes, and tears also. "That is… It must be unbearable."

"That it is." Corelle pulled Vamma close and buried her head in the hair that hung around Vamma's shoulders. "There are times when the pain and guilt overwhelm me. I would rather be dead than alive at those times."

Vamma stroked Corelle's hair. "Do not say such things." She kissed Corelle's cheek. "You came to Yerrsun to kill them?"

"To kill them or see them hanged for the things they have done. They are an itch that cannot be scratched. They are a plague on the land, and I must see them swept from it. I owe it to Deineike, and others." She pulled her head back and focused her eyes on Vamma's. "Though it may cost me my life to do so."

"Shh. Do not say that, I beg you."

"It is a risk I take, and I am prepared for it. I cannot allow your death because of me. Please leave with Synna tomorrow."

Vamma pushed Corelle back by the shoulders to give her a quizzical look. "Synna leaves tomorrow?"

"We both do. He goes to Alcmouth for aid. I have other tasks to perform, but I will ride with him some of the way. I would be happier if you rode on with him."

Vamma frowned. "You will leave also?"

"That I will."

"This is sad news. I will miss our nights. If you are back this way, please call on me."

"You will not go with Synna?"

"I will not go with him. I have told you this." Vamma pulled Corelle's head forward and kissed her. "Let us be upstairs. I have only one more night with you, and I intend to enjoy it."

Their passion for one another delayed Corelle the next day, and the morning had advanced before they prepared to leave the house. "I have some things to attend to at the stall, but I will be at the inn to say farewell soon." Vamma ushered Corelle out of the door.

Synna awaited her when she returned to the inn. He seemed agitated and the further delay as she pushed her things into her pack irritated him more. He tutted non-stop and grumbled about the hour. Corelle urged him to relax, and they went down to the tavernroom to settle with the innkeep.

As they left the inn, three men in the uniform of the Portreeve confronted them. The men stood side by side near the door. Beyond them, Corelle caught sight of Vamma as she walked toward the inn, and a few curious citizens had also gathered to see what turned.

As Corelle and Synna took a step forward, the Portreeve's man in the centre of the three held up a hand. "Corelle, you are required to answer to the Portreeve." Corelle raised her eyebrows in a silent question as she stopped. She did not intend to comply with the summons. He went on. "Come with us now, without any fuss."

She gave a derisive laugh. "On what grounds does the Portreeve compel a representative of the Bailiff of Dur to attend upon him?"

The man cleared his throat. Sweat dripped from him, and he seemed nervous. "You are a deviant. You lie with women."

Corelle turned to Synna and shot him a curious look, unsure she had not misheard. Synna shrugged and made a confused face, his mouth crooked and his eyes wide. More people had gathered around to watch events unfold. Corelle turned to face the

Portreeve's man again. "That is a crime here in the Eastlands? I am certain it is not a crime in the Bailiff's own home, but if you would care to travel with us, you may ask him yourself. If it is not a crime in his home, how can it be a crime here?"

"It is unacceptable behaviour to the people of Yerrsun."

"Unaccept…?" This inconsequential charge bewildered her, and she turned to the crowd. "Is it?" Her eyes swept their faces. Some looked down at their feet, many shook their heads, but none said they found it unacceptable.

Vamma spoke from behind the Portreeve's men. "What turns here, Dillor?"

The man who had spoken turned to her. "She lies with women. She must answer to the Portreeve." His voice took on an ugly tone as he continued. "You are no better, for you have lain with her, have you not?"

Vamma laughed and clapped her hands together before her face. She gazed around and said, "I have lain with at least four people in this crowd, you among them, and at least one of the women I see here. What of it?"

Synna leaned toward Corelle, whispered, "A virtuous woman."

Before she could question him, Dillor spoke again. "Corelle, will you come with me?"

Corelle's mind raced. She guessed Rognakk put on this festival on the orders of Krage, but she would not allow him to take her into custody on such a farcical charge. If she fell into the Portreeve's grip, she would doubtless soon enough find herself dispatched to Estway Farm and whatever justice Krage might inflict upon her. "That I will not."

"Then we must take you into custody by force."

She snorted. "Should you try, you will go wherever you travel to afterward. Do you wish it?"

For a heartbeat, Dillor seemed taken aback and cast anxious glances at each of his men, who had their hands on the short swords they each wore at their belts. Swords, it seemed, increased in popularity despite their poor utility in situations such as this. He faced her again. "You threaten the Portreeve's men?" He sounded surprised, concerned even.

"You threaten to take into custody the Bailiff's personal emissaries. Rognakk has seen the letters we carry. We act on Raolos's direct orders." It surprised Corelle that Synna had not spoken. He had remained silent throughout other than the whispered jest about Vamma's virtue.

Dillor's eyes did not leave Corelle's, but he hesitated, and a look of uncertainty flashed across his face. "You must come with us." He sounded almost hopeful.

"That I will not."

He pulled his sword from his belt and took a cautious step toward her. His men hovered nearby and seemed unsure what he expected of them.

Corelle tutted. He had drawn his sword, an escalation she had hoped to avoid. This man only did his job, and he acted on the orders of the Portreeve, no matter how ridiculous those orders might be. He had been placed in a terrible situation by others. Krage had brought this confrontation about, and Corelle wished to resolve it without more unpleasantness. She adopted a conciliatory tone. "Put away your sword, Dillor. It is unsuited to close combat and will not serve you in the work you ask it to do." He remained motionless, the sword extended before him. Tension crept into her voice. "If you wield your sword against me, I will take your life, and I will not hesitate to do so. Do not doubt me. I do not wish this, and I remind you again, I serve the Bailiff and the Bailiff alone. I do not answer to your corrupt Portreeve. Rognakk will be removed from office as soon as letters of impeachment can be drawn up. Now move aside. We have important work to do on the Bailiff's behalf."

A gasp rose from the large crowd that had now gathered. The

confrontation threatened to turn ugly, and none of the town's citizens might have seen its like before. It turned that more lay in the gasp than mere surprise at Corelle's bold words as Dillor snarled, his jaw set. "My father is not corrupt." He waited a heartbeat, his face reddened in anger, then he swung his sword high at Corelle's head.

Corelle ducked under the clumsy swing with ease, reached into her boot, and came up with her dagger in her hand. She stepped forward inside the arc of Dillor's swing so he could not aim a second blow at her.

She had no sooner risen from the crouch when blood splattered across her face, and she sensed movement from beside her. Dillor's face wore a quizzical look, and he dropped his sword, which clattered a mournful death song as it fell to the cobbled square. Blood poured from his throat, and he raised a hand to press on the grim wound that had opened up beneath his jaw. Corelle snapped her head to one side. Synna crouched beside her, his dagger before him as blood dripped from its blade.

Dillor sat with a heavy thump, then fell backward as the last of his life gushed from his throat and turned the cobbled square vermilion with its spent force. Corelle hissed under her breath. "Curse it Synna, we do not execute people in public for stupidity."

The crowd had fallen silent as Dillor had swung the sword, but now they cried aloud in anguish and shock. Dillor's two men stared at his body, then turned as one and ran across the square toward the Portreeve's Offices. Vamma stood close by, her hands over her mouth.

Synna whispered his answer. "He attacked you. You have killed for less."

Corelle shook her head. He spoke the truth, but this had been little more than a boy, the victim of cruel games played by crueller masters. She looked around at the crowd. Many of them seemed to be in shock, and several fetched up.

Corelle shouted to the gathered throng. "Somebody gather him up." Nobody moved. "He must be taken to his family, or his wife if he has one. I did not desire this tragic turn, but when the Bailiff's emissaries are attacked, they must defend themselves. The Bailiff will pay for this man's Pyre."

Two men hesitated before they stepped forward and bent to Dillor's body. Somebody shouted for Corelle and Synna to be hanged. Some murmurs of assent came from parts of the crowd, but someone else shouted they had been attacked. Another yelled, "They work for the Bailiff. They cannot be hanged for this."

At Corelle's side, Synna whispered, urgency in his voice. "We must go."

He had the right of it. Their continued presence could do nothing but worsen an already volatile situation, so they set off toward the stable to collect their horses. Vamma stood rigid where she had been as the unfortunate event had unfolded. Corelle took hold of her elbow. "Come with us. Word of this will reach the farm by the midday, and there may be repercussions for you."

"What turned here? What have you done?"

"It is tied up with the organisation I spoke of last night. You are in danger. All here heard the accusation you had lain with me, and you spoke in my defence."

"I will not go with you. I will come with you as far as your horses, no further."

"Then come, rouse yourself. We must away. I do not wish to aggravate this situation any more than has already turned." Corelle pulled at Vamma's arm, and the stallholder followed them to the stable where they set about the preparation of their horses.

Before she pulled herself up into the saddle, Corelle took Vamma into her arms. Tears flowed from Vamma's eyes, and Corelle placed a gentle kiss on each of them. "Do not cry."

"He is dead. I have lain with him, and he is dead." Vamma buried her head in Corelle's neck.

"I am sorry." Corelle could find no other words of solace. The confrontation had developed and turned awry so fast, even she could not understand all that had turned. "I must away. Farewell Vamma. Stay safe."

Vamma placed a hand each side of Corelle's head, pulled her close for a passionate kiss, and Corelle's sex tingled. With no time to succumb to such desires, however, she dragged herself up onto her horse and kicked it forward.

She heard Synna and Vamma exchange farewells behind her, then they were in the sunlight. Some of the crowd had dispersed, but many still stood there and talked in small groups. Corelle and Synna kicked the horses into a trot and rode through the square, away down the path to the west, and left Yerrsun behind them.

CHAPTER 32
VELBUR

Uncomfortable, Velbur shifted from foot to foot. He should have taken Corelle's advice and ridden away. Instead, he had ridden hard back to the farm, certain he could spin events in his favour with Krage and Sisnop. To his surprise, Krage had called him into his office alone. Sisnop had not been invited to attend the meeting.

Krage listened without a word as Velbur told him all he had learned; that Corelle lay with Vamma and travelled with another, a man. He did not recognise her companion, who had not spoken much. Even as the words left his mouth, he knew he had tripped himself.

Krage's intense stare brought beads of sweat out on Velbur's forehead. "You spoke with her?"

"That I did." Velbur tried to find a story that might save him from the hole the slip of his tongue had dug him into. "They took ale in a tavern, and I sat at a nearby table and listened to their conversation."

"What did they say?"

"They are here to pay debts Corelle believes are owed to the Guild. They know the names of some here already, you and Sisnop among them. They do not know our strength, but they know the Portreeve is bought."

"You learned much."

"I am a good listener."

"That you are. That you are. But you said you had talked to them, not overheard them. What did you contribute to the conversation?"

He had tripped himself again, curse it. "I passed the time of day with them, as anyone might do in a tavern. That is what I meant, in truth."

Krage steepled his fingers and stared at Velbur. He did not have the cold stare of Styrrach, and it did not unnerve Velbur as much. Velbur had seen Styrrach's stare only once. It had been directed at another in Torric, not at him. He had been grateful. Krage did not have the same menace, he felt. "Nothing more?"

"They spun some fanciful tale, said Styrrach had betrayed Guild members. Shrouding, I believe they called it. Beyond that, I learned nothing of their plans other than they know we are here. We should flee."

Krage raised his eyebrows, wide-eyed. "We should flee? Fourteen against two. You do not like these odds?"

Velbur gulped. Had he made himself look like a coward? "I do not. She is a monster. All say so."

"Tell me more of this shrouding."

"I have told you all I know." Velbur's misery increased. He had made a terrible mistake when he returned to the farm. He should not have mentioned the shrouding. Krage might have also shrouded Guild members. Why had Velbur not taken the chance of freedom the woman had offered him? He cursed himself for a fool.

"Excellent." Velbur had not expected Krage's bright response.

"A drink, I think. An ale. I have a fine cask of ale out in the barn. I keep it hidden from this rabble. Let us repair there for a celebratory drink, you and I." He rose from the desk and placed an arm around Velbur's shoulders. "You have served me well, and I intend to give you an appropriate reward."

CHAPTER 33
CORELLE

Corelle and Synna rode in silence for a time until Yerrsun lay far behind them. As the sun climbed overhead and began its journey to the western horizon, Corelle addressed the incident in the square. "He did not need to die. He looked little more than a boy."

"He attacked you. With the Portreeve as his father, I question his innocence in what turned."

"That may be, but he was a piece in the game, nothing more. Krage sent word I must be apprehended. Rognakk is too afraid of him to refuse, and he is right to be. Either the message returned last night with the man Rognakk sent to the farm after our visit to his office, or Krage acted when his spy did not return. Either way, he pulled the strings that made Dillor dance, and I am disappointed the boy needed to pay so dear a price for Krage's manipulation of him and his father."

Synna pursed his lips. "They made a bold move. Krage must have known you would resist."

"That he must. No doubt he hoped we would kill some of Rognakk's men and turn the townsfolk against us. Who knows?

Another sign of his recklessness, like the orders for provisions from Vamma. He fancies himself the leader, my guess, but he lacks Styrrach's shrewd cunning."

Corelle reined in her horse at the entrance to a track that led north. "I will go no further. From here, I will return to the farm and see what turns there. I wish you well. Ride hard, even though you embark on a fool's errand. You must not let Raolos or Wilash come here. They can contribute nothing but their own deaths if things turn awry. Farewell Synna."

"Good luck, Corelle. I fear you will need it before this ends. I know you will not ride with me, but I ask a favour from you none-theless."

"Ask it."

"Do not die." He laughed, nodded his head, and kicked his horse forward.

Corelle watched his back for a moment, then turned her own horse north. "Let us see where this track takes us." The horse shook its head at the sound of her soft words, and she walked it at a comfortable pace up the track.

When she spotted a house ahead, she left the track and picked her way across the countryside. The flat and featureless Eastlands offered little in the way of scenery, and as the day wore on, she followed her shadow as it bobbed east on the ground ahead of her. She imagined she would see the town away to her right at some point, then turn south until she struck the road from the farm to Yerrsun.

It seemed inconceivable Synna could return with Raolos's forces in time to bring Krage and all his men into captivity. They would take too long to arrive. She did not understand why the Guild men had taken such outrageous risks rather than flee south, but she persisted in her belief that some greater motivation than her death lay behind it all.

Corelle guessed she rode to her ruin. If her luck held, she would take Krage and Sisnop with her, but beyond that, she did not care what fates were written for the others. Most of them were nothing more than pieces in the game, as she had been.

As expected, she saw the silhouette of the town to her right as the sun sank low in the sky behind her. She expected to reach the farm after dark, and might even have to stop before then, since it would be dangerous to ride across the land after dark. If her horse stumbled, her mission could be over before it had begun. She must stop at some point, but the thought dragged her to despondency. Sleep beneath the lights of the night sky would be her fate for tonight, at the least, and she knew too well how her back would react to it. It might be a day or more before she saw any opportunity to act, and by then her back may have seized up beyond repair. She laughed to herself at the grim thought Krage might wander over and kill her as she lay incapacitated on the ground at his feet.

Corelle judged she must be close to the farm, but it had grown so dark, she forced herself to stop and sleep for the night. In her pack, she had some fruits and cheese and a small amount of bread, but nothing for her horse. Grass grew all around, and she felt certain the horse would not go hungry. Once she had tethered it to a small tree, she pulled her flimsy blanket around her as she ate some of the bread and cheese. With a smile, she placed the cheese on the bread as Taro had done an eternity ago.

How long ago that seemed to her now. How much she had already been through when she first met him, but how little it seemed in hindsight compared to all that had turned since his death. She had a small flask of water from which she took frugal sips. It felt small in her hand, and she feared it did not hold sufficient for more than a day.

Corelle endured a fitful sleep, unable to find a comfortable spot. Although the day had been warm, the night turned cool, and the blanket proved inadequate to keep her warm. She longed for a warm body beside her and thought of Vamma, so close by in the town. Vamma's vibrant body came alive even more when they made love, and her masterful hands coaxed pleasure from Corelle. Corelle craved such pleasure now, alone beneath the lights of the night sky. She slid a hand into her trousers and pictured herself with Vamma as she took some satisfaction from an otherwise miserable night.

Corelle urged the horse forward as the sun peeped over the horizon, like a child peers out from behind furniture as it avoids its parents. She turned south and hoped she had struck the road before it passed the farm.

Sure enough, after little more than an hour, the familiar copse where she and Synna had hidden their horses loomed ahead, so she left the road and tethered her horse as far into the copse as she could. She studied her surroundings. To move too far from the copse might be a problem if she needed to reach her horse in a hurry. Some tall grass grew at the side of the road, and she crouched down to shuffle forward until she reached it. When she parted the furthest edge of the grass, she had a partial view of the farmhouse. The guards could not be seen, and Corelle could not guess whether that meant they stood elsewhere where she had no clear view. No cover existed closer to the house unless she moved forward to the ditch she and Synna had used. That would take her further from her horse than she felt comfortable with, so she resolved to sneak forward, check what could be seen, then return to the long grass to watch.

When she reached the corner, she inspected the farm. No guards could be seen anywhere. Had they fled already? The fact Synna had killed one of the Portreeve's men and left Yerrsun could not have driven them away. She could understand nothing of what turned. None of it made any sense, and the longer it went on, the more confused she became.

She crawled back to the grass and waited, but nothing moved at the farm as the long day passed. As she had done so many times before, she waited and watched until the sun went down behind the copse, and darkness fell. At last, something changed as lights sprang on inside the house. As Corelle watched, shadows moved across various windows, but she could make out no details. The Guild had not left, at the least. She need only wait for an opportunity to present itself that allowed her to kill thirteen men before they slew her. "An easy task." She spoke aloud and laughed at the jest.

Corelle went back to the horse and ate some fruit. She gave her horse the remains of an apple, which appeared to be well received, took a small sip of her water, then crawled back to her vantage point with her blanket. She lay on her back and stared up at the lights of the night sky as they twinkled above her. Her mind returned to Vamma, and she wrinkled her nose as she recalled Vamma's comment in the square. Had she really lain with both men and women from the town? After all else, she had suggested she would have lain with Synna had Corelle not interrupted them on the first night.

Corelle could not understand why anybody would wish to lie with both men and women. Men held no appeal for her at all, but who was she to judge? She turned her head to gaze at her horse, which nibbled at the grass. "Who am I to judge, horse? Most people do not kill, but I do. What does it matter who Vamma lies with?"

She snorted, embarrassed she had asked the animal such a foolish question. She lay on her side so she could see the farmhouse again. As the lights went out in the house, she pulled the blanket around her, lay on her back, and soon fell asleep.

CHAPTER 34

CORELLE

Rain woke her. The sky attempted to cloak the hour in grey, but morning had come, and a wet one. A pity; it would be unpleasant to lie motionless in the rain, but that might well be her fate today. Nothing had changed at the farmhouse since the previous day. She could see no sign of guards, and no activity in the house. They must believe she had ridden off. Such complacency could not be excused, and she could not comprehend how they were so lax about their security.

The rain stopped toward the midday, and she saw movement at an upstairs window. A face stared out in her direction, but she did not move. If she panicked and moved, she would signal her position to any trained eye. Had they spotted her? It seemed doubtful, but she remained still, as did the face at the window.

Behind her, she heard a faint sound, the whinny of a horse. Somebody rode along the road, she guessed. Anybody who rode east from the town might spot her horse, or it might whinny to the other horse as the rider passed the copse. With a silent curse, she risked a slow turn of her head to look back along the road.

What she saw chilled her heart. Vamma approached on her cart.

What in the Five Cities brought her out here? Had she lost her mind? Corelle had emphasised to her how dangerous these people could be, that Vamma should not come anywhere near the farm. With a sigh, Corelle saw she had no choice but to abandon her post and send Vamma back to Yerrsun. She glanced back at the farm. The face had gone from the window. More complications. Curses.

Corelle crouched and moved as fast as she could back to the copse, hindered by her reluctance to stand upright. Vamma had almost drawn level with her, and Corelle spoke as loud as she dared. "What are you about here?" She did not wish her voice to carry to the farm, but she needed to stop Vamma before she drove the cart to her certain death.

Vamma's head turned to the side, and a look of surprise sprang to her face. She turned her attention to the horse and tugged back on its reins. By the time the cart had stopped, it had all but reached the tall grass where Corelle had hidden to observe the farmhouse.

Corelle again shuffled toward the grass and kept it between herself and the house. "What in the Five Cities are you about?"

"I bring a delivery of food. They ordered it soon after you left town. Why are you here? You told me you rode away."

"There is no time for that now. Why did you come with the food? Have you forgotten all I told you? It is a trap."

Vamma turned her head to glance at the house before she replied. "You do not know that. They believe you have gone."

Corelle pounded a hand on the ground. How could Vamma be so foolish? "Have you lost your mind? I know these people. They do not care that I am gone. If they do not kill you the moment you arrive, they will hold you here. They will wait for me to hear of it and ride to rescue you. They plan to kill us both if they can, but they will kill you either way."

"You do not know that."

"I *do* know that." Corelle struggled not to shout in her anger. "I know it for a fact."

"The Portreeve has not been seen since you killed his son."

Why in the Five Cities had Vamma jumped to tell her Rognakk had disappeared at a time of such peril to herself? "What? That is irrelevant at this point. Your life is in danger. Turn the cart around and return to Yerrsun."

"I could not turn even if I wished. The road is too narrow. I would have to turn in the farm entrance."

Corelle glanced along the road to confirm Vamma's assessment of the situation, and her heart sank still further. Two men rode out of the farm path onto the road. Corelle needed to act fast and could think of only one course of action. "Two men come from the farm. Get down from the cart, fuss at the hooves of your horse. Tell them a shoe is loose."

Corelle crept into the tall grass and crouched at a point that gave her a reasonable view of the road but hid her from casual sight. Vamma hesitated, and Corelle drew a breath to repeat her instructions, but Vamma seemed to shake herself out of whatever lethargy lay upon her and clambered from the cart. She crouched at the rear of the horse on the same side of the road as Corelle.

Corelle slid the dagger from her boot. The men rode toward the cart, unhurried, as though they came out to greet Vamma and no more. Corelle glanced down at her blade, which had acquired two small nicks in its length during its life with her. It had seen more use than she would have liked. She had not wanted to accept it from Wilash, who made it, but he had insisted she needed a weapon despite her long-broken vow to never kill again. That day now seemed a distant memory.

The two men rode up and reined in their horses. Corelle recognised one of them from the Zhanghar Guild, but she did not know the other. The Zhanghar man had a dagger drawn and pressed to the saddle behind his leg. Corelle slowed her breaths and focused on the men, prepared for the worst.

"Hello." The one Corelle did not know had spoken. "What

delays you? We starve at the farm." Both men laughed, and Vamma looked up at them.

She hesitated again, and Corelle tensed the muscles in her legs, ready to spring forward. "My... The horse. It has a loose shoe." Vamma looked pale and concerned, and Corelle shook her head in despair. She gave every sign of a woman who suspected they meant to harm her, and the men would pick up on that and might act sooner because of it.

"Let me help you." The man swung himself from his mount. He disappeared behind his horse for a moment, and when he approached Vamma, he held a dagger pressed to his thigh. Unhurried, he reached down, balled his fist into Vamma's hair, and pulled her head backward to expose her throat. She let out a scream, and all the horses skittered, nervous.

The Zhanghar man's horse took several steps to the left and he fought to control it, hampered by the dagger in his hand. Vamma's horse knocked her, and she fell backward. The man with his hand in her hair stumbled; just a step, but Corelle needed no more.

She leapt from the grass and screamed, and the man glanced toward her at the sound. She landed on the road, and her momentum carried her forward into him. He staggered sideways into Vamma's horse and released his grip on her hair. Vamma sprawled in the road on her back as the man turned and thrust his dagger at Corelle. He had made a hurried stroke, and it grazed her tunic but missed her flesh. Before he could retract it and strike again, Corelle pinned his arm against her side with her left arm and slashed at his throat with her dagger. A familiar sensation shivered along the length of her arm, and instinct told her she had delivered a lethal blow.

His blood pumped from his neck, a long stream that arced through the air, splattered Corelle's face, and landed on Vamma as she struggled to rise from the road. The dead man's horse panicked and raced away in the opposite direction. Vamma's horse moved to the far side of the road and danced, skittish, its eyes wide with fright.

The Zhanghar man had his horse under control and pushed it a step toward Corelle. She did not hesitate. The wide-eyed horse seemed anxious at the noises and movement, and the coppery smell of blood doubtless frightened it even more. Corelle leapt toward it and slapped it hard on the nose. It took a step backward, shook its head, and snorted. Corelle raised both arms into the air and screamed her name at the top of her voice. The horse reared up, and Corelle flinched backward as its front legs flailed a span from her face.

The man let out a screech, lost his seat, and fell over the animal's rump. As the horse's front legs pounded back to the dusty road, it took a step backward, and one of its rear legs kicked the man as he landed on the road. The animal turned and trampled on the man before it raced off along the road away from them. Corelle ran to the man and knelt beside him. He lived, but he had sustained terrible injuries, like Deineike outside Torric. Blood gushed from a wound to his temple, and his right arm lay at an unnatural angle. His breaths sounded ragged and croaky, and his eyes had half-closed. He looked up into Corelle's face. "I am done. Finish it."

She slid her dagger into the side of his neck, and his eyes stared up at the sky as the remnants of his life pumped out onto the road. When she turned to check on Vamma, the stallholder fetched up into the ditch. Corelle ran to her own horse, untied it from the tree, and pulled it onto the road.

Corelle dragged Vamma to her feet and held her chin so she could focus on Corelle. "Get on my horse and ride back to town. Ride like the wind. Now." Vamma stood motionless, her eyes glazed. A trickle of vomit ran down her chin, and Corelle gave her a gentle shake. "Vamma, focus. You must ride back to town. Go home and lock the door. Do not let anybody in until I come there. Do you understand?"

Vamma may have nodded her head, although the movement had been almost imperceptible. Anxious for Vamma to be gone before the rest of the Guild came out of the house, Corelle pushed, pulled, and cajoled until Vamma climbed up onto Corelle's horse, the reins loose in her hands. Corelle took hold of the bridle and turned the horse toward the town, then tapped the horse on its rump. It skittered, then trotted away toward Yerrsun.

Corelle stood and watched as the horse moved down the road. Once it had rounded a corner and vanished from sight, she ran to the long grass and lay down in it. She peered forward at the house. To her surprise, there seemed to be no sign of activity at the farm. There were still no guards, and the barn doors remained closed. They must have seen her kill the two men—why did they not come out to kill her? She thought about the attack on Vamma. She doubted they had tried to kill her because they had lain together. Either they wanted to get to Corelle through Vamma, or they feared Vamma had learned things from Corelle, things that might complicate their plans.

Corelle watched for over an hour, she judged, and still she saw no movement from the house. She had two options—return to town or try to reach the farmhouse. To return to town, she would have to use Vamma's horse, which grazed on the grass at the side of the road close to where the bodies lay. She could either remove it from the traces and abandon Vamma's cart, or she could ride to the farm and turn the cart around so she could take both horse and cart back to town. To sneak forward and try to reach the house held the highest risk, but as time wore on, she wondered if anybody even remained at the farm. If the Guild remained in the farmhouse, the two men must have been watched as they rode out to kill Vamma, but even if nobody observed them, they would be missed by now. It had been well over an hour. It baffled her.

Corelle could not leave the bodies in the open. She did not know how busy the road might be, but somebody must come past at some point, and questions about the bodies would be difficult to answer. Besides, she would rather spare some innocent passer-by from the horror of her work. Anybody who discovered the bodies might call at the house for aid and might also end up dead. Corelle could not allow that to happen, so she left the tall grass and ran to the cart, where she pushed the crates of food around to create a space between them. She dragged the Zhanghar man's body to the cart and lifted him up onto it. Despite his slender frame, he weighed more than she expected, and his body flopped, writhed, and refused to cooperate as she struggled to lift him. She cursed him many times before she got him onto the cart. Rivulets of perspiration ran down her face, the salt sting of sweat in her eyes. Sweat and blood soaked her clothes before she had finished, and she sat down in the road and panted as she sucked air into her fatigued body.

Another body still lay on the ground, but the exertion from the one she had already moved had exhausted her. Regardless, the other must be put into the cart, so she drew in a long breath, then exhaled it with lips pursed as she searched for the energy to start the process on the second body. The horse pricked its ears up and she feared it might bolt. She rubbed the front of its head and spoke calm words to it. Corelle knew precious little about horses other than how to ride them, and she did that with little skill. She could not tether the horse here in the road, so she trusted to luck it would not move off and summoned her reserves of strength to drag the second body to the rear of the cart.

Her fatigue made the task twice as difficult as the first man, and the sun sank low down the western skyline before she had both bodies hidden as much as possible by the crates of food.

Bone weary, Corelle pulled herself up onto the bare wooden bench at the front of the cart and took the reins. Although she did not ride well, she felt confident she could drive the cart. After all else, she had navigated Rukaal's through the streets of Torric long,

long ago. Although she felt sure the house would be empty, it might still be dangerous to turn in the farm entrance. If any did watch from within, they could attack her with ease while she turned the cumbersome cart. With no other choice, she shook the reins, and the horse walked forward. The cart creaked as the wheels turned, and she headed east toward the farm entrance. Her eyes scanned the house, but she saw no sign of movement.

She turned the horse into the path that led to the house and swung it around. The wide farm entrance gave her enough room to turn, and she sighed with relief when at last they headed back toward the town unscathed. As she passed the copse, the pools of blood on the road caught her eye. Anybody who passed by would see them and might wonder what had turned. Unless they enquired at the house, the blood posed little risk to innocents, and in truth she could do nothing about it. She hoped it might rain soon, and the blood would be washed away.

Corelle's jaw ached as she clenched her teeth together to aid her concentration. The large cart meant more effort to keep the horse centred in the road. The light faded as the sun headed for its bed ahead of her, and she needed to dispose of the bodies before darkness fell. Relieved, she saw a large stand of slender trees ahead that reached almost to the road, and she reined the horse to a stop.

It proved easier to move the two men off the cart than to lift them onto it. She dragged each of them to the rear of the cart, then pushed them off with her foot. The bodies landed with an unpleasant thump, but they raised no objections, so she guessed they had sustained no further injury.

Corelle giggled at her own jest, then dragged them into the trees. She took each one in a different direction and pulled them some way in before she snatched up some fallen limbs and dried leaves from the ground to cover the bodies as best she could. She felt sure the local animals would feast on their flesh long before anybody noticed them from the road.

Darkness blanketed her by the time she had finished, and the cart had no lantern. She drove on regardless and peered forward, eyes narrowed in the soft light of the moon as she fought to keep the horse on the road. After an hour or more, the lights of the town twinkled ahead of her, and she exhaled in relief.

At first, she drove the cart into Vamma's street, then reasoned it would attract too much attention outside Vamma's home. She drove out toward Minarko's home and tethered the horse to his tired fence, hopeful the horse would not tear the weary wooden structure apart, walk off, and drag the remnants with it. Minarko would be certain to recognise it in the morning and keep it safe. He seemed to know everything about Yerrsun. The cart would need a thorough clean to remove the blood stains, but beyond that, it had suffered no damage. She pushed the crates together over the blood stains she could see, and set off for Vamma's house, grateful for the darkness that hid her blood-splattered, dusty face and clothes from clear sight.

As she knocked on Vamma's door, she announced herself in a quiet voice. If Vamma did not answer, either because she had fallen asleep or because she had decided Corelle posed a danger to her, she did not know what she would do. To her relief, she heard the bolt slide back inside the house. Light spilled out, and with one last glance around, Corelle stepped inside. Vamma closed the door and slid the bolt into place again, then turned to Corelle. Vamma's eyes were red, shot through with blood, and tear stains tracked through the dust on her face in sad lines. Corelle pulled her close and folded her arms around her. Vamma began to cry again, and Corelle held her tight, one hand on the back of her head, until the tears reduced.

Vamma whispered into Corelle's chest. "Why? Why did they try to kill me?"

"Because they are bad men who do bad things. They will not trouble you again."

"If you had not been there…"

"Nonetheless, I was. Nothing can be gained through speculation on how the dice might have rolled. You are alive, and they are not."

"You killed them. The one with the knife, you killed him."

"I am a killer. You know this."

Vamma looked deep into Corelle's eyes, as if she searched for something. "It is one thing to know something. It is quite a different matter to see it happen. You were"—she shook her head as though it would arrange her thoughts more to her satisfaction—"ruthless. He stood no chance. Yet you are a woman. Durfolk do not kill, and women in particular do not do such vile things."

"That is a myth. There is violence in Dur, and those who tried to kill you tonight initiate much of it."

"Then how is it you can match them? You can best them."

"Because I have been one of them. The Guild, they are called. An organisation of killers that operates in the shadows, unseen. I belonged to the Guild, once."

"How? How did you come to be in this Guild?"

Corelle sighed. So simple a question, but it required such a complex answer, and she could not reveal it all tonight. In truth, she could not reveal everything to Vamma, ever. "That is a tale for another time. I joined the Guild, and they taught me to kill. I say this not in pride, but because it is true. I became skilled at the art, and so many lie dead in my past, I venture none remain alive who are better at it than me."

"I cannot comprehend this." Vamma whispered so soft, Corelle found her difficult to hear, even though she still held her tight against herself.

"Then do not try. What is scribed, must be."

Vamma stayed silent for a time, and Corelle felt thankful she did not pursue the matter. "Where is my cart?"

"I tethered it to Minarko's fence. We will collect it later this morning."

"Is it tomorrow already?"

Corelle laughed, and stroked her hair, amused by the strange question. "That it is. It is tomorrow, and we need sleep, until the sun rises at the least."

Corelle led Vamma up the stairs and they fell onto her bed in their clothes. Corelle's exhaustion carried her off to sleep almost the moment she lay on the bed, and the nightmares came straight away. She dreamt she watched, helpless, as men hacked at Vamma's body on the back of a cart constructed from bones, while a horse lay dead in the traces, its throat opened by Styrrach, who stood beside it, delirious with laughter. Deineike's face formed out of some of the bones of the cart and glowered an accusation at Corelle before she spat, "She did not love you, yet you let her die."

Corelle protested her innocence. "That I did not. I saved her."

One of the men held up Vamma's severed head. "You saved her." He roared with malicious laughter.

"I saved her." Corelle's miserable defence fell on deaf ears.

The men ceased their mutilation of Vamma's corpse and turned to face Corelle. Styrrach joined them, and Vamma's head floated beside them. "I love you."

All the men had said it, but Vamma did not speak the three dreadful words. Instead, her eyes burned into Corelle as she spat out angry words. "I do not love you. You are a monster."

Corelle sat upright in the bed and placed a hand to each ear. Beside her, Vamma stirred. "What is wrong?"

"Nothing. A bad dream, that is all. Go back to sleep. It is still dark." Corelle lay down and closed her eyes. Tears crept from below her eyelids to roll down her cheeks onto the pillow. Sleep took longer to arrive the second time around, but the nightmares still came with it.

CHAPTER 35
CORELLE

Corelle woke in a room darkened by shutters and heard the soft pitter patter of rain. Beside her, Vamma slept on. Corelle welcomed the rain, which would wash away any trace of blood from the road at the farm, but it would make it less pleasant to ride out to the farm again. She must return though. Her vigil must be resumed, and now Vamma had been attacked, her determination to kill Krage had increased tenfold. First, she must clean Vamma's cart and remove all trace of the blood of the two Guild men. Again, the rain would be her ally.

She gazed at Vamma. The events of yesterday must have taken a terrible toll on her, but Corelle remained determined to insist Vamma leave Yerrsun today, and she would no longer be dissuaded by tales of a stall, a home, or a family. Vamma's safety here could not be guaranteed, and she must accept it after all that had turned the previous day.

She shook Vamma awake and whispered her name as Vamma pushed at her arm. "Wake Vamma, there is much to do today."

"Go away, hag. Leave me alone. I am tired." Sleep dripped from Vamma's words.

"That you are, and with good cause. Still, we must rise."

Vamma did not answer, so Corelle decided she could leave her to sleep a little longer while she walked out to Minarko's home to retrieve the cart. She slid from the bed and pulled her filthy clothes on, splashed water on her face to wash away as much of the blood as she could, then went down the stairs. Her pack lay in one corner of the room. Vamma must have brought it into the house from her horse when she got back to Yerrsun last night. Only a remarkable woman would have thought of that small act after all she had witnessed. Corelle pushed her belongings around until she found a clean tunic. No clean trousers remained, but she found a pair with no blood on them and changed her clothes. She thrust the discarded ones into the pack with a vague thought that she must wash them all at some point.

Corelle trudged through the rain to Minarko's home. The cart stood where she had left it, the horse still tethered to the fence. Rain dripped from it, its mane plastered to its neck. She rubbed its face, spoke to it in a soft, calm voice, then untied the reins from the fence.

"Why did you leave Vamma's cart here all night? Is she well?" Corelle sighed, and her head fell forward, her forehead on the horse's neck. This wretched man would be her ruin. His abuse dogged her every time he laid eyes upon her.

She passed the reins up to the front of the cart. "She is well. She sleeps, and I must attend to the cart. My thanks for the loan of your fence."

"Do not leave. I am owed an explanation."

"You are owed nothing, old man. Not by me, at the least."

"I care for Vamma." An awkward silence followed. Corelle stood still, caught between doubt and uncertainty. She did not want him to meddle in the matter, but if he did indeed care for her, she could understand his worry. "She is my granddaughter."

Corelle shot her head around to stare at him. Had he lied?

Vamma had never mentioned it, which seemed strange. Vamma owed Corelle no explanations of her life and affairs, of course, and the old man may well have spoken the truth. Corelle adopted a gentler tone. "She is fine. She lies asleep in her bed. I had need of her cart, but in truth I do not know where she keeps it. I left it here to irritate you, nothing more."

He huffed. "If you had need of it, it should be burned, and the horse with it. They are tainted by your hand. You killed Rognakk's son?"

She sighed again, resigned to his endless interrogation. "That I did."

"You lie, of course, doubtless to protect the one that did. The boy might have become better than his father. A pity he is dead."

"That it is." Corelle climbed up onto the cart.

"If any harm comes to my granddaughter, you will answer to me."

She turned to look at him and nodded. "I will not harm her."

"Will you keep her from harm though, hmm?"

Corelle turned away and gazed down the street in the rain. Puddles had formed, and in places the water flowed like a small stream along the edge of the street. She turned back to Minarko. "That I will, if it is in my power."

"You will answer to me if you do not."

"That I will." She shook the reins. The horse moved forward, and Corelle did not need to turn around to know Minarko watched her with hatred in his eyes.

When she had turned into another street, she stopped and moved the crates to either side of the cart. The rain washed at the dried blood on the boards. It would make her task easier when she came to Vamma's home. She drove on until she came to the house, where she tied the reins to the door handle in the absence of a rail.

When she entered the house, Vamma sat in a chair, and she pointed out the obvious. "You are soaked."

"I brought your cart back from your grandfather's house."

Vamma gave a half-hearted smile. "He told you this?"

"That he did. He told me to keep you safe or answer to him."

Vamma's smile broadened. "He is old, but he is a good man. He cares a great deal about me."

"I see this. I must clean your cart. I used it to tidy the mess I had created. I will attend to it."

"My thanks. Then?"

"Then I return to my task."

Vamma raised her head, slow and purposeful, then lowered it again, the slowest nod Corelle had ever seen. "Is it true? Do you work for the Bailiff?"

"That I do. Raolos. I have known him for some time."

"Do you intend to kill all the men at the farm?"

Corelle considered her answer. She wanted to tell Vamma more, but she did not think it wise. There would be much in her life she doubted Vamma could understand, and she would rather not risk an argument. "That I do not. There are some I wish to see dead. There are others for whom I bear no ill will."

"Do you hate them?"

Corelle shrugged. "That I do not. Hate is a powerful emotion. I prefer not to spend my time on it. I do despise them and the things they have done."

Vamma nodded again, though she seemed distracted. "How can I help?"

Corelle took a short, sharp breath. "Leave here and travel somewhere safe, for now. There are too many for me to deal with if they come for me. I would rather not see you caught up in that."

Vamma stared at her. "What if they kill you?"

Corelle looked down. A large puddle of water lay at her feet, and it spread further as she dripped the rain onto Vamma's floor. "I deserve it. I do not wish you to be harmed, if that is the fate written for me."

Vamma looked perplexed. "Why do you deserve it? To be killed?"

"I have done things I cannot tell you about, things so terrible they would destroy any who heard them."

Silence lay between them for a time. Corelle did not want to hurt Vamma, but if the woman pressed her and forced her to reveal more, the damage to Vamma might be extreme. Corelle recalled Deineike's reaction to the tale of some of the horrors that now lay in her past. When she had heard about Corelle's past and the death of Arella, it had all but devastated both their relationship and Deineike.

Vamma broke the silence. "If I agree to leave, will you come to find me afterward?"

"I am unlikely to survive." Corelle sighed.

Vamma gave a short, bitter laugh. "I suspect you have said those words to others before, yet here you are."

"Here I am, yet they are not." Bitterness swept over Corelle, her guilt reignited by the conversation that had taken her mind back to things she could never erase from her life. "Do not attach yourself to my fate and place yourself in jeopardy."

"What if I wish to attach myself to your fate?"

Corelle did not reply at once. The question had caught her by surprise. She had not expected it, and she did not wish it, in truth, to venture to a place where Vamma might declare her love. That could not be allowed. All who had said those three words to Corelle had died. She looked at Vamma with a desperate sadness. "I have met the Duke."

"Well done you."

Corelle tutted, irritated Vamma had spoken before she had completed her tale. "He asked me more than once if I knew how many times various events had turned. It annoyed me." Her mind had drifted, and she returned to the issue at hand. "Still, no matter. Do you know how many women have told me they love me?"

Vamma shrugged. "Hundreds, my guess."

Corelle laughed sadly. "Three. Do you know how many of them died because they loved me?"

"None, I would venture."

Corelle shook her head in violent denial of Vamma's guess. "All three."

"They did not die because they loved you."

Corelle suspected Vamma had missed her point. "They died because when they loved me, they became embroiled in my fate. Death is my fate. It is my constant companion."

"I have said it before; I will take my chances."

Vamma vexed her, the most stubborn woman Corelle had ever met. Would this be her fate, to meet only women who would not listen to anything she said, would not respond to logic, but would rather press on with their own foolishness and ignore the risks? She sighed. "If I agree to come to you, if I live through this, will you leave for a time?"

Vamma smiled, a smile that indicated more than amusement. "If I say I will leave, will you shut up and take me to bed?"

Corelle drew in a breath to argue about her need to clean the cart and return to the farm. The rain pounded the roof, heavier than at any point in the day thus far. Their eyes met. "That I will."

Vamma held out a hand. "Then I will leave."

An hour after the midday, the rain eased, then stopped. Their passion for one another did not. They pleasured each other without pause as the hours went by, and it seemed they would never stop. Their own exhaustion brought them to a halt. They lay together in the bed, the bedsheets saturated with their sweat and their juices, both still filled with desire they did not have the stamina to satisfy any further.

Corelle stroked Vamma's light brown hair. "You will leave in the morning?"

"That I will, if it will make you happy."

"I am already happy. You did not notice, it seems."

"You scream when you are happy?" Vamma propped herself up on her elbows, and her eyes teased Corelle.

Corelle tolerated the good-natured mockery. "Sometimes."

Vamma paused, but her exhausted smile did not fade from her face. "Where do you suggest I go?"

Corelle parted her legs and glanced downward at her bush. Vamma swatted at her leg, and Corelle smiled. "Very well. If you will not go there, then go to Ort."

"Why Ort?" Vamma wrinkled her nose in distaste.

"I will give you the key to a house in the town where you can stay for a while. You will be both comfortable and safe there."

"Is this house yours?"

"That it is not. It belongs to someone I used to know. She died."

"Deineike?"

Sadness washed over Corelle. She wished she and Deineike had come by a house as fine as Pettra's and had made a life together there, that all the events of the past two years or more could be erased, and she could start anew with Deineike. They could have sailed away together to somewhere safe and lived a life of love and happiness. Instead… "Not Deineike, another. I will give you the address. When you are settled there, go to the Portreeve. His name is Ibie. Tell him you stay nearby, but do not tell him the precise location. Tell him Jorinda sent you, and he will aid you in any way he can, I am sure."

"Who is Jorinda?"

"I am Jorinda. It is a name Ibie knows me by. When I met Deineike, I had fled from the Guild, and I changed my name for a time. After Deineike's death, I abandoned the name and returned to my own."

"Why did you do this?"

Must every conversation with Vamma in which Corelle mentioned any aspect of her past lead to a multitude of additional questions, many of which she did not care to answer? "You ask too many questions."

"You reveal snippets of some new thing I know nothing of every time we speak. How am I to learn if I do not ask questions?"

Her logic could not be argued with. "I could not bear to be called Jorinda anymore. It reminded me of Deineike. I could not stand the pain." The explanation had not been true, but it would suffice.

Vamma fell silent for a time. "Are you hungry? I need food."

"That I am. Not for food, however." Corelle pulled Vamma closer and kissed her.

CHAPTER 36

CORELLE

Next morning, Corelle went out to check on the cart while Vamma packed for the journey. All that remained of the blood after the rain of the previous day was a dull brown stain in the wood. The food in the crates had spoiled, however, and would need to be cast away.

She returned to the house, where Vamma stood next to her pack. Corelle had suggested Vamma ride her own horse to Eastort, stable it there for a time, and take the rowboat across the river. Corelle advised her to pack light, since it would take no more than three days to ride to the river. Vamma had some coin secreted away against her future, so she could afford to spend her nights at inns.

Vamma had left Corelle's horse at the stable where she kept her cart, so they drove there and unhitched Vamma's horse. Vamma had a saddle and tack, since she sometimes rode the horse, and soon they rode west out of Yerrsun. Corelle had decided to ride with Vamma for a time before she turned aside and headed back to the farm. The sun warmed their backs as they rode, but summer waned, and these occasional rainy days warned of the arrival of winter. Vamma asked about Alcmouth, and Corelle talked of the splendour of the Bailiff's Offices and the Ducal Highhome, of the busy docks and the enormous square with its splendid shops. Vamma hung on every word and said she hoped she would see it with her own eyes one day.

They reached the trail where Corelle had parted ways with Synna, and they reined the horses to a stop. "This is where we separate. I will ride back to the farm and await Synna. Be careful. I will see you in Ort."

Vamma looked miserable as she nudged her horse close to Corelle's and leaned over to kiss her. "Do not forget to come to the house." Corelle nodded and turned her horse down the trail. She did not look back as she rode on, and she turned east when she saw the house, as she had done the last time she had ridden along the trail.

As she rode, she considered the previous days. It baffled her how Vamma had ignored everything she had said and had driven out to the farm. Thanks to good fortune, the outcome had been favourable. Krage found himself two men short, which worked in Corelle's favour, but if she had not been there, Vamma would now be dead. The woman must have lost her mind to drive her cart out there. Corelle shook her head, anxious to chase away the dark thoughts of the day and how it would have turned had she not been at the farm.

Corelle had striven to keep Synna's revelations about Arella from her thoughts, and since they had arrived in Yerrsun, there had been little enough time to brood. As the horse plodded across the landscape, however, she could not keep the thoughts from her mind any longer. Had Arella betrayed her, or had Styrrach forced himself on her lover? However it had unfolded, it stung that Arella had chosen to keep the matter from her, not the least the news of the child. The older woman had confided in Wilash without reservation, but not her own lover, and she had chosen to die rather than tell Corelle the truth.

Arella had been right not to tell her. Corelle would have wished to cut Styrrach down then and there, and even with her skills, she could not have survived the attempt. If Arella had told her, however, they might have fled and left for the south, where they may have found a land that viewed their love with a kinder gaze than Dur.

Corelle gave a bitter laugh, and the horse snickered, pricked up its ears at the sound. Her desire to see Styrrach dead could not have been controlled. Even now, if he returned from wherever he had travelled to, she would strike him down again for what he did. Corelle had told Vamma she did not hate anyone, but that had not been true. She hated Styrrach, and she rejoiced she had killed him.

After Styrrach had forced himself on Arella, why had he chosen to shroud Corelle? Had he learned Arella bore his child? Did he hope to take her to wife in the belief she might grow to love him, and they would raise the child as a family? That seemed ridiculous. He had no reason to shroud Corelle. The thought bothered her, and she frowned. Why, then, did he do so? She had been one of his best members, if not the best. Only one conclusion made sense. He must have known about them, despite all the lengths to which they had gone to keep their relationship secret. How had he found out? As soon as she finished her business at the farm, she would head for Alcmouth and question Wilash on the matter.

A promise had been made for her to visit Vamma, however. She did not wish to break another vow, so she must go to Ort, tell Vamma she could return to Yerrsun, then sail to Alcmouth to confront Wilash. He owed her more explanations, and she must know everything. Of course, all these things hinged on her survival once she encountered the Guild.

To her surprise, she realised she had brooded so long on the issue of Arella, she had already ridden far to the east of the town, and she turned her horse south until she struck the road. She gazed around from an abundance of caution as she rode but encountered nobody.

Once she had secured her horse in the copse once more, she crept forward to the corner, where she stared at the house for some time. Nothing had changed. There were no guards and no sign of movement from the house. She lay in the ditch and watched. When she and Synna had lain in the ditch a few days ago, it had been dry, but now water lay in the bottom after the rains. The water soaked through her tunic, and she could not lie there for much longer. She did not mind discomfort, but she did not want to be saturated.

Her only choices were to return to the tall grass or move forward, and she shook her head in consternation. The time had come for action; she had skulked and watched for long enough. The house stood no more than fifty paces away, and she fancied she could cover the ground in a short time. If anybody noticed her, the jig would be up, but she had seen nothing to indicate they watched the road. Nobody stood guard outside, and although they had watched two days ago, nobody had peered out at the road today.

The decision made, she pulled her dagger out of her boot and set off as fast as she could. She changed direction several times. If somebody fired a crossbow at her, she hoped her jagged path might make them miss. No projectile hurtled toward her, however, and nobody appeared from the house. She reached the building and panted from the exertion, flattened against the wall near the door with the house at her back. To let her heart rate slow and her breath recover from the effort of the run, she marked her heartbeats until she lost count, then crouched beneath a window. She rose as far as the sill and risked a surreptitious glance through the window before she ducked down out of sight again. There had been nobody inside the room.

She stood next to the door and listened for any noise from within but heard nothing. Should she enter the house? If they lay in wait within, there could be ten or twelve of them, and she would be cut down. If she stayed near the door, somebody would come out of the house at some point and see her. She could hope they all came out one by one throughout the day, and she could kill each of them before they could warn the others. Such a stupid thought, and she had to place a hand over her mouth to stifle a laugh of derision.

Corelle reached for the door handle and turned it, slow and cautious, while her heart pounded in her breast. The handle did not squeak, and the door moved a small way inward under the pressure of her hand. She drew in a long breath through her nose, exhaled through her mouth to slow her heart rate, then pushed the door open and rushed through. She scanned her surroundings as she stood to one side of the open door.

The door led into the scullery. An unlit fire and cooking station took up one corner, a large table stood in the middle of the floor, with several chairs scattered around the room, and a cupboard had been placed against the far wall. A pump and basin stood beneath the window to one side of her. Unwashed plates and cups were strewn about, and a half-eaten loaf of bread had been left on the table.

Opposite her, a closed door led further into the house, she guessed, and she crossed the scullery in two paces to listen at the door. She heard nothing, so she pulled the door open. A parlour lay beyond, but other than furniture and a blood-stained tunic on the floor, the room held nothing of interest. Slow and methodical, she searched the entire house. She found evidence of recent occupation—discarded clothes, a cask of ale and some tankards, the occasional plate. No Guild members, no Portreeves; not a single person in the entire house but her. They had fled, it seemed, although she could not tell when. The two she had killed might have been left behind to watch for Corelle or to kill or capture Vamma. She had nobody on hand to give her any answers, and she muttered to herself in frustration. The lost time when she might have investigated the house earlier had cost her any chance of vengeance.

Corelle stood at a window and stared out in disappointment at the unkempt yard of the farm, weeds everywhere and piles of rubbish against one wall of the barn. The barn might still hold some information, so she stepped outside, approached it, and reached for the large wooden lever nailed to the outside of one of the doors. She stopped the moment she touched the lever. The unmistakeable smell of death and decay assailed her nose. Its pungent aroma hung heavy in the air, and the buzz of flies sang a discordant harmony to the odour. Someone or something lay dead in the barn, and the stench of decay suggested it had been there for some days.

She pulled the door open, and the smell intensified. A shadowy shape in the rear of the barn caught her eye, and she opened the other door to illuminate the barn further. Despite all she had done and seen in her life, what she now saw horrified her, and she stumbled forward, shocked.

Toward the rear of the barn, a man hung from a beam, suspended upside down. The closer she came to him, the more horrific the scene became. Deep cuts criss-crossed his naked body, and she guessed he had been slashed multiple times with a blade of some kind. As she drew closer, his fingernails had all been pulled out and left bloody fingernail-shaped recesses at the end of each finger. His toes lay on the ground beneath him. He faced the rear of the barn, and when she swung him around, she fetched up. She recognised Velbur, or what remained of him. He must have ignored her advice in the tavern and had returned to the farm. That mistake had cost him his life, and the debate with Synna had been resolved. Guild justice did exist, and small wonder they had all lived in fear of it. Velbur had let Krage down, and now his remains hung for all to see the fate of those who failed the Guild.

His tongue had been cut out and had been dropped on the floor of the barn nearby. His eyes hung down across his forehead, still attached by whatever nerves or sinews held them in place, the eyeballs themselves prised or popped from his head. Far worse indignity had been visited on him, however. His manhood had been cut from him, and as Corelle took her hand from his body and his body turned to face the rear of the barn again, she realised where it had gone once it had been removed. It protruded from his behind.

Corelle fell to her hands and knees and fetched up again. Velbur had died from excessive violence, all for spite because he had failed to carry out orders, and it took her many moments before her stomach settled sufficient for her to stand again. She waved a hand in front of her face to shoo the incessant flies away.

Velbur had rolled the dice on his fate, but Corelle had been right about that fate, and he had not. It brought tears to her eyes. Krage must be as much of a monster as Styrrach had been. She pulled the dagger from her boot, found some long-abandoned crates, pulled one close to Velbur, and climbed up on it to cut the rope that held him to the beam. He fell to the floor with a thump that brought bile to her throat, and she covered her mouth with a hand. She gathered together such hay and straw as remained in the barn and covered him with it.

It seemed Krage had fled after he killed Velbur and left the two guards behind to kill or capture Vamma. Krage would have at least a two day start on her, and the day already turned dark. Corelle trudged back to the copse and untethered her horse. Unhurried, she rode it back to the farm and hitched it to a water pump outside the house. She would not force it to share the barn with the unfortunate Velbur.

The food in the farmhouse had long become unfit to eat, but she washed out a cup and pumped some water to wash the bilious taste of vomit from her mouth. She slumped into a chair, devastated. She had fallen into a life in which so much horror and death had occurred. Had she not gone to Orgel's shop that day, a girl of seventeen years, she might have avoided all she had seen since.

She imagined those who pestered her to see good in herself, Deineike among them, would point out Styrrach and his evil henchmen would still dominate the trade routes of Dur otherwise. They would still kill any who threatened their enterprise had she not become embroiled in their affairs. That would be no consolation to Arella, Deineike, Pettra, Klordia, and now this man, whose end had been so inglorious. It did not atone for all the blood Corelle had spilled in the name of her ambitions and desires. It would not appease the heartache she had inflicted on Raolos, Wilash, Vamma and so many more, too numerous to recall. She had killed so many people, she could no longer count them, and she feared she could not even remember them all. Now she could add an unborn child to that list. She sickened herself, yet she had not finished, and she could not stop now. She must pursue Krage, to her own ruin, if necessary, even though he had an almost unassailable head start, and she had no idea where he headed.

At first light tomorrow, she would set off in pursuit. Krage had doubtless ridden east. What lay to the east beyond Dur, she did not know. He might turn north and head for Dur City, or south to the coast and take a ship to refuge. If anything lay east of Dur, he might travel there. She would pursue him as far as she could and hope she did not roll ones.

Exhausted, she climbed the stairs and lay on a bed, but when she closed her eyes, her mind filled with the sight of Velbur upside down in the barn, his dignity stripped from him by cruel masters. She feared he would enter her nightmares, and she fought against sleep.

The darkness closed in outside, and her eyelids drooped. Although she had no desire to enter a realm where the mutilated corpse of one of her enemies could pile guilt on guilt, sleep would not be denied, and she awoke with a start hours later. The sun had not yet arrived to chase away the darkness, but she had no time to waste. The nightmares had not come. Mayhap her compassion for the fate that had befallen Velbur, and her horror at his treatment, had kept them at bay. Corelle did not know, but now she must ride after Krage. She yearned for vengeance not for Velbur, who had chosen an ill path against her advice, but for Klordia, Pettra, Deineike, and above all, for Arella and her unborn baby.

CHAPTER 37

CORELLE

As the sun rose ahead of her, Corelle's horse walked at a steady pace along the road. She held little hope she could catch Krage; he had far too big a start on her, but she must try, at the least. What had all the death and agony been for if she gave up now?

The sun's position suggested the morning had half gone when she saw a small collection of buildings ahead. As she drew near to the village, she saw no sign of the vast collection of horses Krage's entourage must possess and guessed they had not awaited her here. She smiled when she recalled that Deineike had not known the difference between a village, a town, or even a city until Corelle had educated her.

Corelle meant to ride straight through the village, but she saw a small, wiry woman at work in a garden and decided to ask if she had noticed Krage's men on their way through. "My pardon, I wondered if you had seen a large group of men ride through your village in the last few days."

The woman stopped her work, looked up at Corelle, and made a face that suggested she strove to recall some obscure fact. Corelle stifled a laugh. A group as large as Krage's would not be easy to forget if they had passed through so small a village.

"That they did." The reply had required a great show of thought, as if the woman had cast her mind back over a wondrous life so full of memorable events, a cadre of deadly killers who rode past her gate might barely register in her thoughts.

"When did they pass, if you recall?"

"Three or four days ago. There were around fifty of them."

"Fifty?" Either the woman had lied, she could not count, or she had not even noticed them at all. Her life must have been a whirl of more significant affairs, after all else.

"May have been forty. Lots, in any event. Unpleasant lot, they seemed, to my eye. They did not stop."

It must have been Krage, Corelle decided, though it dismayed her they had, at the least, a three-day lead on her. Of course, the woman's ability to count days could not be relied upon either. "Where does this road lead?"

"Road goes on to Solgarn, then north to Dur City or south to Eastport. Long way to Eastport."

"It does not go east?"

"East of Solgarn? Nothing there of interest to westfolk like you, dear. Nothing there of interest to anybody, in truth. Wasteland for most of your life, then Steinlund, which is worse." She chuckled.

They had passed this way. At the least, Corelle still pursued them, though she did not know how far ahead they were. She would head for Solgarn and seek better intelligence about the direction they took from there. "How far to the nearest inn?"

"Inn, is it? You must have a lot of coin, staying in inns. Next one is half a day's ride from here."

Corelle calculated the distances in her head. Half a day, if the woman even knew how long that represented, would see her arrive long before the sunset. She did not wish to give up part of the day in an inn, while Krage rode on. "Beyond that?"

"There is nothing beyond Esthold but Solgarn."

"Esthold?"

"The next village. Its name is Esthold. The Esthold is the inn there. Small. Nice though, I imagine, to sleep in a bed where somebody else makes it up for you the next morning."

Not the news Corelle had hoped for. Krage would not have stayed at a small inn, his group too large for such a place to house. That must mean he slept beneath the lights of the night sky. If she stopped at Esthold, she would concede even more time to him. Her back had not complained after the night she had spent on the ground while she had watched the farmhouse, but she had no desire to endure a long ride and sleep on the ground every night.

The woman could tell her nothing more, she guessed. "My thanks." Corelle kicked her heels into the flank of her horse. Should she stop at Esthold or press on? She doubted she could make up the start Krage held over her anyway, but she would not abandon the pursuit at the first obstacle she encountered. She would sleep on the ground once darkness fell and ride on to Solgarn tomorrow.

The woman had over-estimated the distance, and not more than two hours later, Corelle passed through Esthold, a small village, and The Esthold, if it had been an inn at all, could not have had more than two or three rooms. She rode past, despondent. The lure of a comfortable bed after a day on the horse tempted her, but she remained determined to do all she could to reel in Krage and his cohorts.

Darkness forced her to a stop, and she tethered her horse to a tree, then removed her saddle and pack. Wrapped in her threadbare blanket, she lay on the ground and tried in vain to find a comfortable spot. Why had she not brought one of Vamma's thicker blankets for the nights? In truth, she had not anticipated repeated nights spent on the hard ground. As she closed her eyes and waited for sleep to take her, she muttered, "Goodnight horse."

Velbur might have spared her the night before, but he did not grant her any mercy tonight. His mutilated corpse swung to and fro before her. His voice could not be understood, for he had no tongue.

"He asks for his manhood." Deineike spoke from behind her, and when Corelle turned, Deineike's eyes hung down her cheeks, held to her head by some bloody sinew.

Corelle turned again to Velbur and cast about in an attempt to locate his manhood. In the shadows, she saw movement, and when she moved closer, she saw Pettra, who thrust Velbur's severed manhood into herself over and over as she cried, "Give me a baby." Pettra held the severed phallus aloft as it pulsed and burst apart into tiny, perfect babies that rained down over her belly.

Pettra cried in ecstasy, and Styrrach's voice echoed from somewhere above Corelle. "I will impregnate you if you wish it."

Corelle whispered in disbelief. "You are dead."

Styrrach's laughter echoed around her. "As are you."

"You lie. I live."

He sniggered. "Do you love yourself?"

"That I do not."

"Then it is you who lies, for you do love yourself, and you are dead."

Pettra, Velbur and Deineike had all turned into enormous statuesque phalluses. Corelle screamed.

Her own scream woke her. The sun would soon rise over the eastern horizon. A shake of her head drove the horror of the nightmare from her, and she pulled herself to her feet. She longed for a goblet of wine, but none could be found out here in the Eastlands wilderness. She saddled the horse and set off for Solgarn, hopeful she would reach it before nightfall. The rented horse walked onward, stalwart, as the sun climbed the sky and passed overhead. The sun brought warmth to the day, and the horse's tail flicked from side to side with a repetitive swoosh as it chased away flies that landed on it in search of food. They pestered Corelle also, and as she shooed them away with her hand, she wondered whether they had pursued her from the barn. She had never encountered so many flies before; they seemed somehow more prolific here, far to the east of Dur.

The day dragged on as she rode. Hunger and thirst troubled her, and, anxious to reach Solgarn, she kicked the horse into a trot. She did not want it to collapse from exhaustion, but the daylight faded, and she saw no sign of the lights of Solgarn. At last, she topped a rise and saw a sizeable settlement ahead of her that could only be Solgarn. Relieved, she slowed the horse to a walk and continued toward the town. She rode around the streets and studied the inns. If Krage's group had spent a night here, they would have needed a larger inn. The Mountain View appeared to be the largest, and she tethered her horse to the rail and stretched to remove the road weariness from her muscles.

The day had become too dark for her to confirm Mount Belram could be seen from the inn, so she entered the tavernroom and gazed about. A few heads turned in her direction, but they soon looked away when she scowled at them. Her clothes were dusty from the road, her hair windblown and untidy. She approached the counter and caught the innkeep's eye. Once she had secured a room for the night, she asked whether any large group of men had passed through the inn in the last sevenday. He confirmed they had stayed there. The inn had only four rooms, and they had booked them all. Several of them had slept on settles in the tavernroom, as he thought they numbered twelve or more. They had left two mornings ago. By tomorrow, she would be three days behind them.

"Did they say where they headed?"

"They did not mention it, and I did not enquire. It is no affair of mine."

Corelle did not want to offend him. "That it is not, but it is of mine. I seek them with an urgent task. A friend of mine rides with them, and I must bring him sad news."

He nodded in sympathy. "They left at the sunrise. They gave the impression of men anxious to reach their destination as soon as possible. One of them drank a little more than the others, and his voice rose. I thought I heard him say they should travel to somewhere, but I confess I did not recognise the name he used."

"Might it have been Vyrrmod?"

He pursed his lips, then shook his head. "I do not recognise that name. I am sorry I cannot be more helpful. Let me show you to your room."

Corelle sat on the bed and reflected on the news. Krage and his men had pressed on without delay, doubtless afraid of pursuit from the authorities. Nonetheless, they could not believe such pursuit would follow as close as Corelle. It would take almost a sevenday for any authority to arrive at the farm, even if it came from Ort, longer from Alcmouth. She must come to a decision and act on it tomorrow.

She weighed three options in her mind. The Guild might ride to Dur City, a city she knew nothing of, where she could not say whether the Portreeve would work to her advantage or theirs. If she had to roll the dice, she would hope he preferred to assist a representative of the Bailiff, but that could not be guaranteed after all else. Still, she might find them there, and with the Portreeve's help she might take them and either kill Krage or have him hanged.

They might ride south to Eastport and thence sail south. If Synna took Raolos's men to Eastport and brought them north, he could not fail to meet them. He would recognise them and would have them captured or killed. Either way, she could not hope to travel fast enough to be involved in that meeting. She rejected following them south. Let Synna exact vengeance if they travelled that way.

The third option—to abandon the pursuit. If they went south, she could do nothing, and they would encounter Synna. If they went north, she would miss an opportunity to pursue them if she gave up now. The puzzle proved too difficult to unravel after a long day on the road, and she decided to go to the tavernroom for a goblet of wine.

Corelle sat at a small table in a corner of the tavernroom. Patrons filled the room, and the tumult of conversation and laughter required her to raise her voice to order the wine. As she sipped at the wine, she watched the patrons play at dice or cards or sit in twos and threes and talk. She could see no more than four women in the tavernroom, all in the company of men.

The innkeep came to her table and asked if she wanted another goblet of wine, and she agreed to another. When he brought it back, he leaned closer to her so he did not need to shout. "One of the men who plays dice, he lives south of the town. Rides his horse in here every night, pretty much. He mentioned the group of men your friend is with. They passed his home when they left here, headed south, it seems."

Corelle thanked him for the information. The place name Krage's man had mentioned and the innkeep had not recognised must be some land to the south few in Dur knew of. Synna would intercept Krage's group on the road, and there seemed little benefit for her to pursue them further. She would turn back toward Yerrsun tomorrow, then travel on to Ort. She would make good on her promise to visit Vamma, then head south to Alcmouth and insist Wilash tell her the full story, as painful as it would be to hear. She drained the goblet and went to bed.

CHAPTER 38
CORELLE

Corelle rose with the sun and set out for Yerrsun early. It had taken an effort of will last night to stop after the second goblet, and she recalled Synna's concern. She thought on the matter during the lonely journey back to Esthold, where she planned to spend the night in the inn before she headed back west toward Yerrsun. Synna had told her more than once she must get her consumption of wine under control. Pettra had warned her it would kill her to continue to drink such large amounts, and Corelle had panted in distress after she had run the fifty paces to the farmhouse. Did they have the right of it? She should make some effort to drink less. Even though she had drunk almost no wine for several days now, she had longed for it on many occasions. She knew such desires to be unhealthy, and her skills may be affected by her weight gain and the wine over time.

Who could blame her that she drank so much, after all else? In a life filled with death and misery, the news that Arella had been with child had been another blow that threatened to crush her. She shook her head. Such moody contemplation would achieve nothing. Synna must kill Krage, and Corelle must live with the disappointment she would not be on hand to see it. She had not guessed he would leave so soon, and that error of judgement had allowed him to make good his escape from the farm. She felt confident he could not reach Eastport before Synna, although it occurred to her she did not know how far south it lay. Synna had left a day or two before Krage had fled the farmhouse. With luck, they would meet up. She could not tolerate another disappointment in a pursuit littered with frustration and setbacks.

Later in the day, she took a room at The Esthold. No other guest slept in the inn, and they had only one other room besides her own, so she walked through the village in the early evening after she had dropped her pack in the room. Within no time at all she had walked past every house. The urge to drink a goblet of wine nagged at her, but she strove to find distraction. Esthold must have been the worst place in Dur to seek entertainment other than the pleasure that might be found at the bottom of a goblet, and she sighed in resignation as she returned to the inn.

When the innkeep brought her the goblet of wine, its poor quality disappointed her. She wondered how the innkeep survived in such a small village through which few people must pass. With no patrons to occupy her attention in the tavernroom, she drank the wine faster than she would have liked. She should head back to her room, but the sun had not yet set, so she ordered another.

As she finished her third goblet, a man entered the tavernroom. He had a red face and a shock of dirty yellow hair on the top of his head. He wore clothes of poor making, repaired by clumsy hands where they had been repaired at all. He did not sit at a table but leaned on the counter as he drank his ale and talked with the innkeep in subdued tones. Corelle wondered if he might be a brother of the innkeep or some such, as with Bushy and Sparse. They both glanced over at her often. The innkeep, Corelle guessed, might have checked whether she wished another goblet of wine. The customer might wonder what had brought her there and might draw the wrong conclusion. She indicated to the innkeep she would take another goblet and to her surprise they both came over.

The newcomer spoke as he stood near her table with his tankard in his hand. "Quiet night."

She glanced around the tavernroom, irked by his company. "That it was."

He seemed to miss the barbed comment. "Do you travel the road?"

The question seemed so ridiculous, Corelle glanced around again and wondered if he had spoken to her or somebody she could not see. Her dusty clothes alone would point to a day on the road. Further, Esthold had been built in the middle of whatever lay in the middle of nowhere. "That I do." No more suitable response came to her.

"Heading to Dur City, I imagine, pretty girl like you. The bright lights."

Even though she had never been to Dur City, she found it hard to believe its lights would be bright. They had not been bright in Alcmouth, Zhanghar, or Torric, all of which must be larger than Dur City, she guessed. "I have not been a girl for a great many years." The man's banal conversation reminded her of Taro. She had not been a girl when she met him either. She had ceased to be a girl that fateful day in Orgel's shop.

The man nodded, although Corelle could not guess at what. "Long ride alone, Dur City."

"I am not going to Dur City. I am going to Ort."

"Oh. So you are Westfolk."

The innkeep placed her goblet before her and loitered nearby as he listened to the conversation. "That I am." Her answers grew terser with every inane thing he said.

"That explains it." The man and the innkeep both laughed.

Corelle's hand moved toward her boot, and she gripped her thigh under the table, shocked at her reaction. She had told Synna they did not execute people for stupidity, but it tempted her now, to her horror, an urge she fought to resist. "Explains what?" She frowned at them.

"Why you travel east when Ort is to the west."

She shook her head and ran the conversation through her mind to find some hint she had given him that might lead him to believe she rode east. Bushy and Sparse sprang to mind again, and she could not understand why so many of these men irritated her so. "Are all eastfolk like you?"

"Eastfolk?" His voice had a tone of confusion to it.

"People from east of the river."

They both laughed again. "We don't call ourselves that, dear."

"We do not execute people for stupidity," she reminded herself. "Then what do you call yourselves?"

"We call ourselves the names our parents gave us." Frenzied laughter consumed them both, and Corelle wondered how far away she could ride before somebody discovered their bodies.

"Yet you refer to us as 'westfolk.'"

"That we do. You are from the west."

She shook her head and abandoned the topic. "I do not ride east. I ride west."

"Oh. Only, Majrie said you rode east. Described you perfect, she did."

"Majrie? Who is Majrie?" Corelle's confusion grew with every word the man spoke.

"Over to the houses. Majrie."

She pinched her thigh and winced at the pain. She had heard that if a person thought they might be in a dream, they could pinch themselves and wake from it. There could be no other logical explanation for the bizarre conversation. "The houses?"

"The houses, the next little village west. In truth, it is not a village, just some houses, so we call it the houses."

Corelle thought back. Did he mean the woman she had spoken

to who had estimated Krage's force at fifty men? "I spoke to her days ago."

"You are westfolk. Imagined you got lost." They both laughed so hard, tears ran from their eyes.

Raolos would understand, would he not? He would see how they had provoked her until she had killed them. He would not hang her; she felt sure of it.

She drained her goblet. "This conversation has fascinated me, but I fear it has also tired me. I must head to my bed." They each gave her a blank stare. "Early start in the morning." She stood, but neither of the men said anything. "Long ride east to Ort." She smiled, and they both laughed. "Good night."

As Corelle headed to her room, she glanced back. They both still laughed, and neither had moved from where she had left them. She had believed Bushy and Sparse strange, but this new man had been more than strange. He required a whole new word for his strangeness. She wished Deineike travelled with her; she would know a suitable word.

She had intended to drink more wine, but the man had driven her to her bed with his bizarre conversation. It had been such an unreal conversation, she could not shake the thought it had been a dream. She lay in the bed and replayed it in her head. As she fell asleep, she gave a snort of laughter. She said out loud, "Imagined you got lost," and sleep took her.

The following morning, she rose early and paid for the room. The innkeep did not mention his unusual friend from the night before, and she saddled her horse and set off toward Yerrsun. A strong, cool, late summer wind blew from the west, so she took her cloak from her pack and wrapped it around her. The wind whipped the dust from the road and threw it into her face, and her horse flicked its head as though irritated as they rode. The clouds threatened rain, but they did not deliver. The wind would not relent, and the effort required to push the horse through it exhausted her. She kicked the horse into a trot as she passed through the houses, afraid she might give into the worst elements of her nature and kill Majrie for the loose tongue that had led the strange man to her.

When she saw the trail to Estway Farm ahead of her in the grey light of early evening, she knew in her heart she could go no further today. Without hesitation, she turned from the road. She and the horse could use some respite from the cold wind and the dust and small stones it battered into their faces. She put the horse in the barn with an apology for the company it must keep, then ran to the house and closed the door behind her with a sense of relief.

A further search of the house turned up no further clues the Guild might have left behind, some indication of why they had remained in Dur for so long. She could not shake the belief something other than revenge drove them, but she found nothing that shed any light on their motivations.

She did find a cask of wine she had overlooked on the previous visit, a dark red wine, with a heavy, almost bitter taste she did not enjoy, but she needed to slake the dust and wind from her and wipe the memory of the strange man in the inn from her mind. She drank on as darkness cloaked the barn through the parlour window, and the room refused to remain still before her eyes. Outside, it sounded as if the wind had given up some of its ferocity at last. When she glanced at the door, she lost her balance, fell from the chair onto the floor, and knocked the table over. The wine oozed from the neck of the cask, and she laughed as she imagined she saw Krage's blood spilled from his neck after she had slit his throat. She hoped Synna would give him a violent death.

Krage would need a Sending, she realised. She tried to struggle to her feet, but had become too inebriated to rise, so she lay on the floor, closed her eyes, and tried to organise her thoughts to compose a suitable Sending for the man who had ordered the death of Klordia. She soon found one. "Good riddance." She fell into an intoxicated sleep.

When she awoke the following day, she still lay on the floor, the nearby cask surrounded by a halo of the dark red wine, dried on the floorboards. Her head pounded as though the small stones the wind had thrown at her yesterday had been replaced by large rocks, and she had fetched up at some point in the night. The bilious reek of her vomit made her fetch up again as soon as she woke. When she tried to raise her head from the floor, dizziness overwhelmed her, and the incessant pain inside her skull increased. The room appeared blurred and indistinct even when she closed one eye. She mumbled, "A good night," and fell asleep again.

The sound of horses as they rode up to the farmhouse woke her, and she sat up in alarm. The headache had not receded, and she cringed at the pain. She reached for her dagger as she wriggled on her behind to a nearby couch. As she peered over the arm of it, voices floated in from outside, then the door of the house opened, and a man's voice shouted. "Who is inside the house?"

Corelle stayed silent. Krage must have returned to the farmhouse. What should she do? She crawled behind the couch, crouched in her hideout, dagger at the ready. Somebody shouted for two men to check the barn and for the others to enter the house with whomever had shouted. She readied herself. Her ruin had come upon her, and she yearned to take Krage with her before she fell to their blades.

Footsteps moved into the house. They made no attempt to be discreet. Why should they, after all else? Then she heard a voice she recognised. Synna. "Let go of me. Corelle?"

Had Krage captured Synna? How could they both be here so soon, and how could Synna have been captured? She did not respond

"Corelle. Are you here?"

A different voice spoke. "Wait, I beseech you."

Synna's reply sounded tense. "If she is not here, we must ride after her."

"It is not safe to enter."

She peered over the back of the couch and saw Synna. He had his back to her as he argued with a man in the red tunic of a Portreeve. She shouted to him. "Synna. What turns?"

He wheeled, but he appeared not to see her straight away, so she stood. "Corelle." He looked and sounded relieved.

"How did you come here so soon? Did you not see Krage's group on the road?"

"They make for Ort?" He wore a mask of bewilderment on his face.

"That they do not. They make for Eastport. I abandoned my pursuit of them in the belief you would intercept them as you rode north with Raolos's men."

He looked downcast. "These are Ibie's men. I went to him because I believed I could be back here sooner. I did not go to Alcmouth, I re-crossed the Alc to Eastort."

She lowered her head, the bitter taste of disappointment in her mouth strong enough to drown the stale aftertaste of the previous night's wine. "Then he has escaped us."

Her voice, though quiet, reached his ears. "A sorry turn, curse it." Misery replaced the bewilderment in Synna's voice. "What has turned since I left? We spent last night in Yerrsun. There is no Portreeve, and no sign of Vamma."

"You did not see her on the road? She rode for Ort."

"That we did not. We did not stay in inns. We rode until dark, then slept beside the road."

"You have contrived to miss her somehow, then." Corelle swallowed her disappointment. Although she had hoped for word Vamma had reached safety, Synna had not met her. Far worse, Krage had evaded them and would doubtless escape and sail south. He had slipped through their fingers. "After we left town, Krage summoned Vamma here to kill her. I killed the two he sent for her, with some help from a horse." Synna raised his eyebrows but did not interrupt. "The Portreeve fled after we killed his son, it turns. Yerrsun has need of another."

A man burst into the house. "Synna. We have found unspeakable horrors in the barn." The man rushed into the room, his tunic splattered with vomit.

"Do not look further. Cover him with the hay again." Corelle spoke in a soft voice. She knew how grisly the discovery must have been for them. She turned to Synna again. "Velbur. He came back here. Guild justice, his reward. It does exist after all else and is not something I ever want to see again."

"That bad?" She heard compassion in his voice

"I fetched up."

He shook his head. "Depravity." Anger replaced the compassion.

Corelle let out a long, exasperated sigh. "There is no more we can do here. Raolos must appoint a new Portreeve. Until then, I suggest you leave two or three of Ibie's men in Yerrsun to reassure the townsfolk. We should return to Ort. We have missed Krage, and now we may never know the full extent of whatever he had planned."

"It concerns me that Portreeves can be bought so cheap."

"Me also, although this one's fate was already bound up with Carshan before these events."

Synna nodded in agreement. "That it was. I cannot spend the night here after all that has turned. Let us ride back to Yerrsun." Something seemed to occur to him. "Where are the bodies of the two you killed?"

"In some trees along the road. I could not leave them here for some innocent to stumble upon."

As they rode back to Yerrsun, Corelle contemplated Krage's outrageous luck, to escape Dur with no retribution for all he had done. She had longed to slit his throat, for Wilash and Klordia, at the least. She recalled how often she had said the words, "This is for Pettra," or "This is for Deineike." She imagined nobody cared about the reason they were killed. Empty words, and emptier results, for it had brought her no joy to say the words or to kill the victims. She still grieved for all those whom her life had touched in such a destructive manner, and her guilt at all the deaths she had inflicted or been responsible for would not be assuaged, no matter what boastful words she used as she executed her victims.

They had left the midday far behind them by the time they reached Yerrsun, and they passed a night in the town. They headed out the next day and left three of Ibie's men behind. Four others rode west with them toward Ort. Corelle felt seven might have been insufficient, in truth.

Synna explained why he had brought so few. "Ibie could spare no more. With you and me, there would have been nine. I had some hope you might have thinned their numbers in my absence, but I did not wish to leave you here to face your ruin alone if I could avoid it. I think we would have triumphed, in truth."

She still felt unsure. Such things never turned awry when one played them out in the mind, and only if Krage had remained could they have known for certain. Nonetheless, she had little appetite to continue the debate. "All we know for certain is we failed here. We have lost Klordia, and remnants of the Guild have survived to flee south. Krage won."

The ride to Eastort passed without event, other than several nightmares. Corelle's unhappiness that Krage had fled could not be eased. It sat heavy on her, a weight she could not shake off. She remained convinced he had some plan greater than her, but she would never find out now. "*What is scribed, must be,*" she thought often, but the thought did nothing to cheer her.

Three days later, they crossed the Alc on the little rowboat. The river threw the boat around without mercy, and all Ibie's men suffered from the malady the water inflicted on many who travelled on it. Two fetched up, and the other two were hard pressed to control their stomachs. Corelle suffered it with no ill consequence, and her thoughts once more turned to the prospect she might become a mariner. She would consider it further once she had spoken to Wilash and found the truth of the story about Arella and Styrrach.

She told Synna she would remain in Ort for a day or two to check on Vamma before she headed to Alcmouth. He wished to leave that day and make a report to Raolos, so they said their good-byes at the docks. Corelle stood on the dockside and gazed at the Alc as it flowed past Ort. The life of a mariner appealed more than the life of a killer. She might not seek out Wilash, after all else. Had she not learned enough dreadful things in her lifetime? Would one more bring her any peace? She doubted it, but it ate at her that Arella had not told her the story. Time enough to decide once she had seen Vamma return across the river to her home. With a resigned sigh, Corelle set off for Pettra's house. Ibie's men trudged in bilious misery along behind her for a time until their paths diverged.

Corelle gazed at the familiar exterior of the house for some time. If Vamma had not stayed, she wondered what she would have done with the key. She might have left it with Ibie, since she did not know he might be reluctant to surrender it to Corelle again.

Speculation resolved nothing. It had been a lesson hard learned, but Corelle had learned it. She strode up to the door and knocked on it three times. The sound of movement drifted from inside the house, and the door opened. Vamma gazed out at her, in a loose dress that flowed not far past her knees. The length would be considered risky in polite circles, but it aroused Corelle.

Vamma showed no surprise when she saw Corelle. "You live, then,"

Corelle had anticipated a warmer welcome and felt dumbstruck for a moment. "That I do." She peered past Vamma to the interior of the house. "You have a wonderful home."

"I have influential friends." A smirk crept onto Vamma's face.

"You must introduce me. My friends are limited to the Duke and his Bailiff."

Vamma smiled, then burst into laughter. "Tell me everything."

Corelle summarised all that had turned since they had parted ways outside Yerrsun. She left out the horrific details of the mutilation of Velbur. The story took a toll on Corelle and again reminded her she had failed to exact any vengeance on Krage but had allowed him to slip away through an error of her own judgement.

When she had finished, Vamma wore a thoughtful expression on her face. Corelle guessed she pondered the story's implications for her, but when Vamma spoke again, her words proved Corelle wrong. "Are you Corelle or Jorinda?"

Once more, the response had not been the one Corelle had expected. "Which do you prefer?"

Vamma's eyes twinkled. "If I tell you, will you shut up and take me to bed?"

Corelle smiled and remembered the line from Yerrsun. "That I will."

Vamma reached forward, balled the front of Corelle's tunic in her hand, drew her forward until their bodies touched. Her lips brushed Corelle's neck like one of the infernal flies between Yerrsun and Solgarn, and she breathed, "In that case, come in, Corelle."

ABOUT THE AUTHOR

HAYLEY PRICE has always been a storyteller. Throughout her life, she has told her story through songs as the principal songwriter in several bands, most recently Adventures With Alice, whose lyrics feature in many of her books.

A New Zealander, Hayley currently lives in Canberra, Australia with her long-time partner and a grumpy, bossy cat called Rosie. She loves baseball and suffers eternal torture as a fan of the San Francisco Giants. Music has been a major part of her life, and outside of her own compositions, she is an enormous fan of Christopher Cross as well as Daryl Hall & John Oates and under-rated 80s UK prog-rock band Voyager, who once named her their #1 fan.

Hayley's first book, The Vermilion Ribbon, received an Honorary Mention in the 2024 The BookFest Award for LGBTQ Fantasy, a 2024 Indie BRAG Medallion, and was a finalist in the ABLE Golden Book Awards 2024. Her second book, The Vermilion Cross, won third place in the BookFest Awards for LGBTQ Fantasy.

ACKNOWLEDGMENTS

"The Way It Must Be"
    Performed by Adventures With Alice
    Written by Debbie Rollason
    © Hand Elephant Records 2008
    Lyrics reprinted by permission

Cover by Adrian DSGNS

Torr Sea map by Lara Mitchell

Dur map by André Barbeto

SPECIAL THANKS

Ailsa. Twenty-eight years and counting.

Jo & Rob, Wendy & Danny, for their unfailing support.

Bec and Bianca, for believing.

Anne, for picking up the mantle of PA and managing my socials so well

The Beta Bunnies: Ailsa and Bec.

Christopher Cross, for his music, which lifts my spirit.

Rosie, who thinks I need more cats in my books.

Everybody who reads my books. I still haven't quite got used to the fact that this is my fourth book, or that people read my words. Thank you.

LINKS

Here are some links I hope you will find useful.

My website: https://hayleyprice.net

More links on the following page

Please leave a review for this book on Amazon Kindle: https:// books2read.com/u/bwkpNP